The
Fortune
Of
David DeRieux

The
Fortune
Of
David DeRieux

A Novel

Jack Huguelet

Cover by Meredith Boos

Published by Jack F Huguelet
www.HagueletPress.com

ISBN 979-8-9913527-0-3

To my wife Linda
My sister Jeannine
My parents Jack and Lois
They are the great fortune of my Life.

Contents

Epigraph

"No man ever steps in the same river twice, for it's not the same river and he's not the same man."

Heraclitus c 535 – 475 BC

Time is nothing in reality but exists only in the human mind's apprehension of reality.

Saint Augustine of Hippo c 354 – 430 AD

"We can easily forgive a child who is afraid of the dark; the real tragedy of life is when men are afraid of the light.

Plato c 428 – 347 BC

Chapter 1

The Interrogation

"**A**re you all right?"

The old man didn't answer, didn't even look up. Sitting at a somewhat scuffed but sturdy wooden table, his attention seemed to be focused on a pool of water growing on the tabletop. Large drops splashed as they fell from the lowered rim of his fedora. Little lakes were forming around the sleeves of his soaked raincoat where his arms rested upon the table. Thunder roared and shook the world outside, but deep within the marble confines of the Federal Building it was hardly noticed. The FBI agent, sitting across the tabletop lakes, wondered if the old man was about to collapse and leaned forward on his elbows to study the eyes hidden under the hat's rim.

"Mister, are you all right? Look up at me here, will you please?"

The old man didn't move. The agent sat back, already uncomfortable in the hard wooden chair; the interrogation room was not designed for comfort. He glanced up at his partner standing behind the old man. The partner raised his eyebrows and shrugged. The agent shifted forward again and spoke slowly.

"Mister. Mister. What is your name? Mister, can you hear me? Are you all right? Look here, Mister, we need to know what's going on. My name is Tom Morgan. I'm a Resident Field Agent of the FBI here in Chattanooga. Can I get you anything? Is there someone you would like me to call for you? Do you have an attorney? Mister, you're probably going to need an attorney. Would you like for me to call an attorney for you? We can arrange to have one appointed for you at no charge if necessary."

The old man's head remained motionless over the beaded water. Tom slowly reached across the table and placed his index finger near the outside edge of a large pool. He paused for a moment, looking for any reaction from the old man. Nothing. He slid his finger through the water, breaking the bead. Little rivers ran across the table draining the pool. Still, no reaction.

"Mister, do you know where you are? Can you tell me what year this is? Do you need a doctor?"

That seemed to get the old man's attention. He looked up and squarely met Tom's eyes. Tom repeated, "Do you need medical attention?"

The old man smiled. He seemed to be coming back to life a little. "Oh one," he said in a calm but tired voice.

"What?"

"You asked what year it is, two thousand and one."

"Okay, okay; that's good. Do you need to see a doctor?"

"Thank you, but no. I'll be all right. It's just been a rather busy day for me."

"I'll buy that," said a voice coming from behind the old man.

The old man turned and watched as the other took off his coat and hung it on a hook next to the closed door.

"Does this mean we are going to be here for a while . . . have a little chat?" the old man observed.

"You bet," Tom said. "This is my partner, Special Agent Szezoponski, Art Szezoponski."

Art extended his hand and the two shook. "Are you Polish?" the old man asked, holding tight onto Art's hand.

"Does it matter?" Art countered.

The old man's grip softened a bit, but his clasp upon Art and his hand remained firm. "Perhaps. Perhaps not. Probably not," the old man quietly responded as he looked deep into Art's eyes. Art talked to a lot of different people every day, people of all sorts, but something here was extraordinary. While the old man's demeanor remained serene, the intensity of his scrutiny was palpable. Art was overwhelmed by its invisible power; he felt captivated. It was as if the old man could literally read faces, expressions, eyes; where others were illiterate by comparison. For the moment, Art's hand was frozen; time was frozen. Art had the odd sensation that the old man was not just looking into his eyes, but was looking through them, like one would look through a window; and in doing so, could see behind his eyes and view the actual ripples of his brain; and from that, completely discern his very core.

"Forgive me," the old man said in a soft but clear voice. "Old habits die hard. I suppose things like that don't matter so much these days." The old man released Art and his hand, and time returned to normal for Art.

"May I take your coat?" Art asked.

"Yes. Thank you, Mr. Szezoponski." The old man stood. Art helped him off with his hat and coat.

The old man settled back into his chair. He seemed somewhat at home, or at least at ease with his surroundings. He looked to Tom and asked, "Would it be too much trouble for me to have some hot tea, please? That is, if we are going to be here for a while."

"Sure." Tom picked up the phone, ordered one hot tea and two black coffees.

"Sugar also, please, if it's not too much trouble," the old man whispered.

"Sugar with the tea," Tom added; then, looking at the gentle man, "try to round us up a few sandwiches too."

The old man smiled. "Thank you, Tom."

Art wiped the table dry with a towel and took the seat next to Tom. "What is your name?"

"Michael, Michael Johnson."

Tom took a pen from his shirt pocket and made a note at the top of a fresh legal pad. "When were you born, Mr. Johnson?" he asked.

"1910."

"That would make you what . . . ninety-one now?"

"Yes. Yes, I suppose it makes me that."

"Where were you born?"

"So many questions."

Tom thumped his pen on the legal pad. "We've asked you several times already. Would you like a lawyer?"

"Goodness no."

"You may be in quite a bit of trouble, Mr. Johnson."

"As you say, I'm ninety-one years old; what could be more troublesome than that? I'm old; I'll be dead before long. An attorney can't stop that."

"You're rather, how shall I say it, exact, aren't you, Mr. Johnson? Are you an attorney?"

"Yes and no."

"What do you mean yes and no? Either you are or you aren't."

"Yes, I am exact. No, I am not an attorney."

The two looked at each other for a moment. Tom continued, "Where were you born, Mr. Johnson?"

"I would have to say Chicago."

"Chicago, Illinois?"

"Yes, the Windy City."

"Tell us about the gun, Mr. Johnson. Where did you get it?"

"Ha," the old man grunted quietly, "the gun."

"Yes, the gun. Where did you get it?"

"It's funny. Whenever there is a gun involved, the first thing people want to know about is the gun." Johnson chuckled to himself. "I haven't thought about that in a long, long time." He shook his head, "The gun is not important."

"The gun is not important; then what is?"

"That's a good question. Indeed, what is important?"

"Why don't you save us both a lot of time and tell me?"

"Trying to explain what is important, to someone who doesn't know, is no way to save time young man."

"And why is that?"

"You don't really want to know what's important; you just want to know what happened."

"What's wrong with that?"

"Okay, you guys gave me the gun. Does that help?"

"We gave you the gun?"

"Well, you didn't. I suppose you could say a fellow agent did."

"One of our agents gave you a gun?"

"Well, I don't think I'd go as far as to call him one of yours. No, I don't think I'd put it quite that way."

"How, exactly, would you put it?"

"Why don't you ask me about the man I killed."

"Are you talking about the man in the parking lot?"

"Yes."

"Did you kill him?"

"Yes."

The two men looked at each other for a few moments in silence. Agent Morgan, breaking eye contact, looked down at his notes and said, "Chickamauga Battlefield is a National Park. That parking lot, it's on Federal property."

Johnson didn't reply. Agent Morgan opened a manila folder, ran his finger down a few pages, stopped, and looked up at the old man. Regaining eye contact with Johnson, Tom said, "The Park Rangers that brought you in have identified the body. Mr. Johnson, do you know who it is that you've killed?"

"Of course I know. Why in the world would I kill someone I didn't know?"

"Okay then, why did you kill him?"

"Why did I kill him? Excellent question, Tom."

"Okay, it's an excellent question. Why did you kill him?"

"I simply couldn't die leaving some things undone."

"Enough with the riddles, Mr. Johnson; please, just tell us what happened."

"I shot him; shot him right in the head. Just walked right up and shot him in the head. Twice, as a matter of fact. Can't say why he didn't expect it. I suppose it's because I dress so nice. People do tend to judge a book by its cover, you know. That and, I suppose, if one gets away with his sins for long enough, he tends to think that they will be tolerated. Come to think of it though, at the last moment, he did look more scared than surprised. Well, maybe that's a little something more to his credit than I would have guessed."

Tom made another note on his pad, then said, "Again, Mr. Johnson, why did you kill him?"

"Does it matter why?"

Tom looked back down at the manila folder and said, "Well, apparently he was an important man. People are going to want to know; the court is going to want to know."

"Tom, you disappoint me. You were doing so well. Okay, yes, yes. I suppose most people would say that he was an important man."

"You don't think so?"

"No. No I don't."

"A lot of people would disagree with you. He was a very wealthy man. A lot of people are going to want to know what happened to him."

"Will any of those people miss him?"

Tom thought for a moment, absentmindedly tapping his finger on top of the manila file folder. "Probably not."

Mr. Johnson nodded his head, "Probably not."

Tom pushed the file folders to the side and said, "Okay, Mr. Johnson, enough. Why did you kill him?"

"Why did I kill him?" Johnson's head drooped down again, focusing on the pools of water that had just been wiped clean and were no longer there for anyone else to see. Tom began to fear that Johnson was about to go back into his trance and started to say something as Johnson continued in a softer voice, "I guess this story begins in 1946."

"1946."

"Yes."

"What happened in 1946?"

"That's when I first met him."

"When you say 'him', who do you mean?"

"Dr. VanZant."

"The man in the parking lot? The man that you say you killed?"

"Yes."

"Where did you meet Dr. VanZant?"

"Oak Ridge."

"Oak Ridge, Tennessee?"

"Yes, but back then it was called the Clinton Engineer Works, part of the Manhattan Project."

A couple of thumps rattled the door to the interrogation room as someone lightly kicked at the bottom to announce their presence. Art opened the door and a young man with his arms filled came in with the drinks: three paper cups, a few packets of sugar, and a couple of plastic stirring straws squeezed together in a wad between his hands. He set the drinks down next to Tom and said he'd be back in a little while with the sandwiches.

Tom slid the cup of tea and the packets of sugar across the table to Mr. Johnson. The old man pried off the plastic lid; his eyes followed the little whiffs of steam that rose from the cup.

The old man reached for a packet of sugar. "I miss sugar cubes."

Tom wasn't sure if the old man was thinking out loud or if the thought was meant for Art and himself.

"What's that you say?" Tom asked.

"You know," the old man mused, "sugar used to come in cubes, served in a nice little bowl, a china bowl, with tongs to pick them out. 'One lump or two?' they used to say. Now it comes all wrapped up in a little paper packet. Tear the packet open and pour the contents out. Sugar's sugar, I suppose. Same stuff, just packaged differently. Cleaner, easier to handle, but not as nice. Yes indeed, a nice little bowl of bright white cubes and silver tongs—seemed more civil. You'd plop your cubes into a nice porcelain cup, sitting on a saucer, a little spoon on the saucer. You'd plop your cubes in and stir for a moment; then, tink-tink-tink, you'd tap the spoon on the cup's rim three times and put the spoon back on the saucer. Gave a person a moment to himself . . . time to reflect."

The room was quiet, quiet enough to hear the paper being torn as the old man opened the packet, poured the sugar into the cup, and began to stir with the little plastic straw.

"Doesn't sound or feel the same," the old man continued. "Wonder how it will taste? Paper and plastic, always paper and plastic. Not the same as china and silver, not the same at all. It's really quite funny. People today make such a fuss over where their coffee beans come from, how they're roasted, how fresh they are . . . and then they dump it all into a paper cup."

Tom took a sip of his coffee and looked over at Art. Art shrugged his shoulders and flexed his fingers.

Tom picked up his pen. "Let's get back to business, shall we, Mr. Johnson?"

"Sure, sure," the old man said as he cradled the warm cup between his hands, raised it to his nose, and breathed in the steam. "You wanted to know where I got the gun."

Still holding the warm cup in his hands, he continued slowly, as if thinking to himself, "If a person is a flame, and his personality the heat from that flame, where does the essence of that person go as the flame burns out and the heat dissipates? Does that heat expand out into the universe and then recuperate itself elsewhere? Or, once that flame is gone, once the visible source of that heat is gone, does that heat just drift away, blend with all the other fragments of heat, making a virtually imperceptible contribution to a general increase in the temperature of the universe? Or does that heat, that remnant of life, merely expand out and dilute into nothingness?"

"Who are you thinking of, Mr. Johnson?"

"I'm thinking of a flame, a flame that has given off a lot of comforting heat, but, these last few years, not a lot of light. Even here, even now, I can feel that heat, but only in my mind's eye can I see that flame."

"Mr. Johnson, who are you thinking of? Not VanZant."

"No, not VanZant."

Chapter 2

David DeRieux

David DeRieux spread the contents of his wallet out on his kitchen counter. It was a mess, a pile of confusion; it was the contents of his long life. For the moment, all was quiet in his house. He automatically pulled a crumpled white handkerchief from his front left pocket and blew his nose while pondering what the next step should be in organizing his wallet. His optimism was always greatest at the initial undertaking of an endeavor—the fleeting moments when the goal was still clear but the actual details of the task were yet to be confronted. That optimism was fading fast. Thwarted by Alzheimer's, his thoughts, their electrical impulses, moved slowly and erratically along the eroding pathways of his mind. A simple plan of action eluded him.

He finished the leisurely ritual of loudly blowing and gently rubbing his nose and returned the handkerchief to his pocket. His balance was bad and his legs were weak, so he leaned against the counter to steady himself. His head, tilting forward, hung over the pile. The muscles of his neck offered little support; his chin rested on his chest. He had tuned out the ceaseless chatter coming from the TV in the next room, but still, through the mental haze, a part of his mind nagged at him: *Something's not right; things seem to be getting away from me. Why is this so hard?* He picked a scrap of notepaper from the top of the pile. It was one of a dozen such notes. Still looking down, he raised it up close enough to read through his glasses. "Wed. April 4, 2001 8:30" was all it said; however, the date was circled and heavily underlined. Obviously, it was an important date. *Wed. April 4, 8:30. What is supposed to happen on April 4th? . . . 8:30 . . . 8:30 . . . That must be a time. Is it 8:30 am or pm . . . ?*

He continued to stare at the fragment of information in his hand. His eyes gradually narrowed into a slight squint. The creases above his eyebrows began to knot as the little muscles beneath tensed, pulling him deeper into thought. *Am I supposed to do something or meet someone? I can't remember . . . Maybe it's a birthday or something like that, maybe an anniversary. Let's see, when is my anniversary? I can't forget to get Lill something. What would she like? . . . I never know what to get.* The knot tightened, *Oh Christ, did I miss it? Oh no, I bet I did. What day is it today?* His eyes rotated up, lifting his head into a level position. He stared out of the window in front of him but didn't see anything as he drew even deeper into himself. *What month is this now . . . ?* He had no point of reference to even venture a guess. His mind groped for a benchmark but there was nothing. He tried to think of something significant, anything, anything to anchor himself to . . . Nothing. *What year is this . . . ?* Nothing. *When was Christmas . . . ?* Nothing. *Surely I can remember Christmas. Let me think now; who was there . . . ?* Nothing. *Where were we; what did we do?*

A Christmas tree started to come into focus within his mind. The muscles of his brow relaxed; he could see his parents. They were sitting across the room from him on the other side of the tree. The image was very clear. They were young; he was young. The two were sitting at the dinner table drinking something. They sat close to each other. It was intoxicating. The family had just finished a big meal; the plates were still on the table. Everyone was full and happy. It was very cold outside, but they were nice and warm inside. He could see his two sisters sitting on the floor next to the tree, working together on something they had just opened. There weren't many packages, but everyone had something; everyone was happy. The radio was playing music in the background, Christmas music. David was sitting in an overstuffed chair next to a window. Over the howl of a fierce wind, David could hear the nighttime sounds of a big city street one floor below. Chicago. He loved Christmas in Chicago. He turned to look out the window but could see only his own reflection in the glass. He didn't bother to lean forward to see outside; what lay beyond was clear in his mind. A loose pane standing against the wind rattled lightly in its frame. The caulking that held the glass in place was old, dry, and brittle. There were seeps. The pane still held out most of the wind, rain, and cold, but David knew the forces of nature would grow stronger as winter progressed, and in terms of years, those forces were relentless. He could feel both a slight chill from behind the frigid glass and a bold heat from the radiator beneath it. For now, the combination was delightful. He sank deeper into the worn cushions of his chair. Beneath the soft glow of a lamp on the table next to his chair was a wad of neatly crumpled wrapping paper. In his lap was a new book, a nice thick book with a hard leather binding. David could feel the raised lettering on the cover. He raised it to his nose, smelled it, and smiled.

He looked down at his book, but it was gone. In his hand was the annoying note that he had grappled with just moments ago. "Wed. April 4, 2001 8:30," *Eight thirty . . . eight thirty . . . eight thirty . . . ? What time is it now?* He looked at his watch. He had several nice ones, old ones, gold ones; but today, as most days, he wore his black, plastic, digital one. He liked it, and for some reason it always seemed to be the easiest one to find. He wasn't quite sure where the others were. Something about them being broken, out for repair—he wasn't sure. He'd have to look into it.

"34:57", the digital watch indicated. Randomly pressing buttons earlier had switched it to the stopwatch mode. *What does that mean? What kind of time is that? I need to write that down.* He set the note scrap down on an uncluttered part of the counter. His shirt pocket bulged with pens and notepaper. He selected one of the felt tipped pens, rechecked his watch, and wrote "35:" below the "April 4, 2001 8:30" notation, rechecked his watch, and finishing the number, wrote "12". He loved writing notes. It took all of his concentration, but the process gave him a sense of purpose, a brief reprieve from uselessness. For the moment, he was back at work, his old self, doing something important, something that needed to be done. Lives depended on his decisions; all the muscles in his body firmed with resolution. Pen in hand, he read, "Wed. April 4, 2001 8:30 35:12." The elation began to dissipate. *What in the world does "35:12" mean?* He decided to underline the new notation, then circled it. It was still unclear. He tried underlining the entire note, then drew a box around it. Now it really looked important. *I better set this one aside for later,* he thought, finally giving up on it. He set it far to the side in a special new pile all by itself and picked another scrap from the clutter.

"4,728.23" was the only thing written on the next scrap. *What does that mean . . . 4,728.23 . . . ?* He read it over and over to himself. *Maybe it's an amount, maybe my checking account balance. That's it, my account balance . . . although, it could be something I owe? . . . What else could it be? . . . Oh my God, did I forget to pay someone? I'm so embarrassed. I hope I haven't put someone in a bind. What's the date on this? What day is it today?*

David was overwhelmed. He needed someone to talk to; he needed help now! Confusion, frustration, and insecurity swept over him. Depression leading into rebellious anger might soon follow. Anger. Door kicking anger. Door kicking let-me-in kind of anger. Anger at himself; anger against himself. Anger against himself but directed outward at others, whoever was nearest. Anger against his sense of incompetence, anger against his insecurity, his vulnerability. The anger wasn't David's; it belonged solely to the Alzheimer's, but it was difficult to separate the two. At his core, David was a gentle man. He didn't want to be a burden to his family, but that very thought drove him to despair.

Desperate for some sense of worth and control, he reached for his cash. It was there, bulging within the fold of his wallet. It looked like a lot; he felt better. Cash was a security blanket, a reassuring and indisputable means of control, a symbol of value and worth. There was much that David had forgotten, but he was still very aware of how helpful and polite people were to a man with ample cash. If necessary, money could be exchanged for help, problems could be solved, difficult or embarrassing situations could be smoothed over. Cash was a tangible reminder that he still had some dominion over his circumstances, that he wasn't a burden, that he still had value, that he was still useful, that he was still needed. He could open his wallet and take comfort in its sight. He could run his thumb over the top of the bills and feel their thickness.

And it meant even more. To David, cash was sacred; at least his was. Cash was sacred because, to David, a man's word, his promise, was sacred; and what is the exchange of cash if not the exchange of a promise. Cash, the marker of the promise that one man receives from another, even a stranger, in return for his efforts. A promise that at some point in the future, that promise can be exchanged in good faith for the efforts of another man, and so on. David felt good about his money because he had no reason to feel bad about it; he had acquired it by helping others. He could no longer identify why, but when David looked at the money in his wallet, he felt the same as if he were looking at a pile of thank-you notes. The notes were from friends and strangers alike, but they all said the same thing to him: "Thanks, David. You once helped us; now we'll help you." David had enough money, and his value to his family was immeasurable, but neither was in his wallet. The stack of bills was mainly ones with just a few larger bills mixed in for effect. His wife, Lillian, and granddaughter, Susan, were careful to maintain the illusion.

David pulled the thick stack out and began to count. The bills seemed out of order; some were upside down; he lost count. The third try was interrupted by a sound from outside. He glanced to his right through the breakfast nook window. It was Susan. He smiled and his shoulders straightened at the familiar sight and sound of her car stopping at the end of the driveway. Life seemed to pour back into his body. No longer a priority, he left his money on the counter.

"Hey, Granddad," Susan said with a big smile, coming through the kitchen door. "How are you doing today?"

"Bonjour, Madam. I'm so glad you stopped by just now. I was just thinking of you." David looked somewhat perplexed at her large midsection.

Susan lightly rubbed her stomach; this would be her first child. "Any day now you're going to be a great-grandpa," she reminded him. David and Lillian had two children and five grandchildren, but this would be their first great-grandchild. Except for Susan and her husband, Jeff, all the kids and grandkids lived out of town, but their photos covered the refrigerator. David cherished them all but preferred to see them one or two at a time. Too many, too loud, made him nervous, and in large groups he was less certain as to who they were. Exact relations were blurred. Susan resembled her mother, David's daughter, Kay. It used to confuse David, but not so much anymore. Now, whenever he saw her, David *knew* that Susan was his daughter. She had given up correcting him on such matters, and often, particularly when she was tired, simply called him Dad just to keep the questions less repetitive.

Still smiling, she leaned forward and gave him a gentle peck on the cheek. He couldn't have been happier. "What are you up to here?" she asked, walking over to the counter.

David followed. "High finance," he chuckled. "Help me get this back together, will ya?" David's problems usually seemed manageable whenever Susan was around. He pointed to the scattered bills on top of the clutter. "I've been trying to get a count on these all morning. See what you come up with, will ya?"

Susan hated the little white lies and distortions that she found increasingly necessary in dealing with her grandfather. She knew that the stack was mainly ones; she had put them there. But anything less than two-hundred dollars would be unsettling to David, compelling him to insist that he be taken to the bank to cash a check and verify his balance. There would be no getting around it. The way he inadvertently flashed his wallet around in public made Susan nervous that it would attract attention from the wrong sorts and bring harm to them.

Susan tried to keep David's wallet in a state that reassured him while at the same time contained little that couldn't easily be replaced. Unless someone told him, David had no way of knowing the driver's license and all but one credit card in his wallet were expired. David never went out alone, and either Susan or Lillian made sure that he always used the "best" card.

"Looks like you've got quite a wad here," she said, trying to reassure David while avoiding an actual count. "All this, plus your credit cards, should be plenty. Let me help you get this stuff back together."

Quickly putting the bills back into their slot, out of sight and hopefully out of mind, she continued the distraction. "Take a look at this," she said, handing a white plastic card from the pile to David, knowing that it was one of his favorites. David's name was printed under an impressive looking seal along with other official looking print. "Know what that is?"

"Sure," he said uncertainly, holding the card up for closer examination.

Not leaving time for an awkward moment of David stumbling for an answer, Susan injected, as if they both knew, "It's your FBI Association card, isn't it?"

"Oh yeah . . . oh yeah." David looked fondly at the card. He was proud of his days with the Bureau and loved any reference to them. "You know, I joined the FBI in December, a year to the day before Pearl Harbor." David said that exact phrase almost every time the subject came up.

Susan just about had the wallet back together, minus all but a couple of the meaningless notes. She took the FBI card back from David and handed him two bar association cards, one for the State of Tennessee and the other for Illinois. He was proud of being a lawyer, so Susan made a point of reminding him whenever the opportunity arose. David held a card in each hand, looking back and forth between the two as if comparing them for differences.

Finishing up, she handed the wallet back to her grandfather, hiding a twinge of sadness. In many ways, the wallet reminded her of her grandfather. Stuffed beyond its capacity, it was now merely a familiar shell containing only a shadowy filler of its original contents. The mass was still there, but much of the substance was gone. The various association cards were testaments to great achievements and assumed abilities, but the cards were inanimate and by themselves could accomplish nothing. The erosion had been gradual, almost imperceptible at first, but the inevitable prospect of continued deterioration was horrifying.

Susan found herself looking at shoe scuff marks on the base of the door leading from the kitchen to the laundry room. It occurred to her that not all storms originate from outside the house. The door had held, but exactly how much was it originally designed to suffer? It would open and shut, but it was loose in its frame. It would still keep much of the machine noise and laundry clutter isolated out of sight in the back room, but it would not stand against many more assaults. The family had resisted as long as they could, but eventually the reluctance to artificially manipulate David's personality, the very essence of his nature, became meaningless. It had been long since David's personality had been entirely his own. His pudding was not just pudding; it was loaded with powerful medicine, just as was now his brain. The medication appeared to have somewhat restored David's personality to his old self; but now, it was a personality that was significantly manipulated by others.

"How 'bout I take you gals out to lunch today?" David said as he struggled to slide the wallet into his back pocket. It was designed to make it difficult for pickpockets. The outer cover was made of a material that stuck to cloth so that it wouldn't slide easily. David was sure he'd know if someone tried to sneak it away from him.

Chapter 3

Lillian

While David stood at the kitchen counter trying in vain to organize his wallet, his wife, Lillian, sat in her rocking chair at the other end of their house, struggling in earnest to organize her thoughts.

The pink room, the bedroom that had been their daughter Kay's room while growing up, had become Lillian's sanctuary. In the relative quiet, behind a closed door which helped to mute the relentless clatter from their TV in the nearby family room, Lillian spent hours: hours reading, praying, studying, thinking. The last few days she had mainly been thinking—thinking about her appointment today with the eye people. Lillian was all but certain that a simple change in her eyeglass prescription would alleviate many, if not all, of the quirky tricks that her mind had been playing on her—for how long, she couldn't be certain; a year perhaps, maybe two.

Lillian studied the large face on her wristwatch for over a minute, making certain that she was seeing the numbers in their correct order. Interpreting the relationship between the numbers, which remained constant, never moving; and the hands, which were in constant motion—some sweeping across the face at an alarming pace, some imperceptibly slow—of late had become somewhat of a challenge. *Yes,* she thought, satisfied that she was in fact interpreting what she saw correctly. *Yes, my granddaughter will be here any minute now to drive us to my appointment.*

She closed the large book that rested on her lap and settled back in her cushioned, heirloom rocking-chair for a quiet moment of peace, a peace that she longed to find within the covers of her books, a peace that would withstand all assaults—an elusive peace that continued to remain just beyond her horizon. If only she could satisfy herself that her thoughts were in order, that she was correct in her view, that her understanding of the universe and her place in it was unimpeachably correct. If she could achieve such perfection of thought, if all misgivings could be removed, if through sheer conviction she could remove every last speck of doubt, then she would be free from all and every form of evil and corruption. If she could achieve such purity and confidence in her thought, in her belief, then all would be well; she would be well; she would be healed; she would be at peace. That was her goal; that was her Holy Grail.

But of late she felt that she had regressed, that she had slipped a bit, that the ground upon which she stood had shifted. At first, just a little tremble, but that little tremble revealed a small crack in her foundation. She didn't want to examine the crack; doing so would only give sanction to the fault. But the fault was beyond her ability to ignore or justify, and the more she looked, the more cracks she saw. Once, once she had been so close, but now . . . now she was plagued by doubts. Those fearful doubts that she shared with no one, those nagging doubts that she was loathed to admit even to herself; but nevertheless, doubts she simply could not shake or dismiss. Those doubts from which, despite all her might, she simply could not free herself, had, like a demon, risen up to form a seemingly impervious barrier, a barrier thwarting her peace. Not that long ago, before her doubts had taken power, the gap between what she believed and what she experienced had seemed manageable, almost inconsequential. But as that distance grew, so did the power of that malignant force. She had to get a handle on it before that gap, that barrier, became insurmountable.

The soft cushions and slight recline of the chair invited her to relax, but she remained resolute with one foot on the floor and the other resting on a small matching footstool pushed slightly to the side. Her left thumb twitched back and forth against a smooth spot worn on the side of her first finger. Short, irregular jabs from her ankle and calf muscles rocked the chair back and forth a few inches in each direction; the back of her head pressed deep into a large feather pillow taken from a bed. She didn't feel like shutting her eyes so she gazed at the ceiling and a primordial thought popped into her mind: *If the ceiling wasn't there, could I see heaven? That's silly; heaven isn't in any particular direction.* Yet she continued to stare at the ceiling.

If she turned her head, the view was entirely different. The view through the bedroom window onto the backyard was lovely—nothing but grass, trees, and sky. David and Lillian had built their dream home forty-one years earlier atop Signal Mountain, a small but growing bedroom township a mere twenty minutes from downtown Chattanooga. The house sat on a corner lot, an irregularly shaped acre resting slightly above the two roads that defined the front, one side, and part of the back of their lot. Neighborhood houses were close, but not too close. Much of the community's charm came from its irregularities, the gentle grades giving way to steepening ravines sloping down to idyllic mountain creeks in which children built dams and captured crawdads, shielded by the woods from the watchful eyes of their parents. The irregular topography predestined windy roads, some cut into the curve of a gorge, some following the path of least resistance over a gentle hilltop.

The road from the valley to the mountain top, however, was less than gentle and had different effects on different people. For the most part, that road was steep and curvy, and towards the top, it clung to a rising stone cliff on one side and, on the other, dropped off into nothingness but a clear view, anchored at the bottom by a large flowing river. Some found the drive relaxing, some stimulating, some merely a pleasant distraction from the everyday. Others viewed the drive as a nuisance, some as an unwelcome challenge to their propensity for motion sickness. And then there were those, the truly timid, who found the drive disturbing, even frightening. Few of those made their home on the mountain top. But like the journey to most destinations, the unfamiliarity of the first passage made the trip seem longer, and for those who went on and established a familiarity with the route, the trip became what it was: a daily routine of moderate length.

From Lillian's window, the road that defined part of the backyard's border was hidden below a simple, mountain-stone, retention wall about four-feet tall. From inside her sanctuary, that road was invisible. Occasionally, the sound of a passing car would cause one to look up; however, only the top portion of the car could be seen as it passed, giving the only clue that a road was in fact there.

But, for the moment, no sound diverted Lillian's attention to that window. She continued to gaze at the ceiling, desperate to see what could never be seen, to know without doubts what could never be proven—at least not from her side of the window.

*   *   *   *   *

Their house had been well built from the start and then fortified over the years with additional features. The carpets were bleakly worn, but the roof was new. The addition of storm doors and windows a decade or two earlier made the house practically airtight. There were three bathrooms spaced throughout the house, with an exhaust fan and louvers in the ceiling of each. When the house was all buttoned up, pulling open any of the exterior doors tugged enough air from the attic through those vents to jostle the fans, making a distinct boop-boop-boop sound, not loud, but enough to apprise anyone in the house—that knew for what to listen—of an entry or exit.

Right on time, Susan pulled open the back door, and the bathroom fan-sentries announced to Lillian an arrival. Lillian quieted her thumb twitch and rocking motion to listen. Fortunately, the TV volume was much lower than usual. She could hear Susan and David. Their voices traveled from the kitchen, across a moderate-size family room and down a short hallway to Lillian's closed door. She could identify the voices and the tone but couldn't quite make out the content.

In any event, Dave was sure to keep Susan busy for a bit. Lill's mind wandered to another topic: *What will we do when the baby comes? Why do precious gifts so often come with difficult price tags? When the great-grandbaby comes, who will drive us; who will get us out of the house; who will bring us groceries; who will help with the meals? When the baby comes, Susan will need some time to recoup. Susan's mom will be coming in from Nashville in a few days to be here for the birth and to help Susan establish her new routine; but, when the baby comes, when the baby comes . . . When the baby comes there will be a new baby in our family. Our daughter's daughter is having a baby, a little boy I'm told. Boy or girl, what could be more precious?* At the thought, the tenseness in Lillian's body dissipated. Without conscious effort, her eyes slid closed as a clear image came into focus within her mind of Susan sitting up in bed, the new baby nestled close into the folds of her arms—total tranquility.

Time lost all meaning as Lill rested with her eyes closed, watching Susan and the new baby. She could feel the heat radiating from the two snuggled together. Creaking footsteps coming down the hall refocused Lill's awareness, but much of the tranquility remained . . . A few light taps on the door, then David's joy-filled voice, "Lill, we have a visitor." David tapped a few more times on the door, then cracked it opened. "Bonjour Madam," David cheered, poking his head through the crack. Susan, from behind, nudged David forward and followed him into the room. "Look who's here," David continued. "Feel like going out for a little lunch?"

"Sure," Lillian said softly, reaching over to give Susan's hand a gentle squeeze. "How are you, Honey?"

"Fine," Susan smiled. "Are you ready to go?"

Chapter 4

The Exam

"Where shall we dine today, ladies?" David asked as Susan backed the DeRieux's car out of the garage. Excursions out of the house were a delight for David and an essential break from the unnatural monotony for Lillian.

"Wherever you like, Dad. Don't forget we have an eye exam first."

"Oh, that's right, that's right."

"How about Cracker Barrel?" suggested Lillian from the back seat.

"That sounds mag-nif-eek." David leaned forward and rubbed his hand across the top of the dash. "This is a nice car. When did you get it?"

"This is your car, Pops. It's an Oldsmobile. You've had it for a couple of years now."

"Oh yeah, oh yeah," David said, not completely sure that it was. After a moment's contemplation, he pressed on with his thoughts, "I don't think I have the keys to it though, do I? What if I need to go somewhere?"

"Check your pockets. I'm sure your keys are there."

David leaned over in his seat to get his hand into his pocket and pulled out his key ring. "Are these mine?"

Susan glanced over. "Yep, the big one is your house key, and the two smaller ones are your car keys."

While the house key and trunk key worked fine, Susan's husband had filed a tooth off of the car's ignition key. So far, David hadn't tried to take off on his own, but a sudden wave of confusion or belligerence could change that in a heartbeat. Too many keys had already vanished from his ring; three was as low as they could go for now.

"Aren't there some others that I should have here? Seems like I'm missing a few," he pursued.

Lillian leaned forward and gently patted her husband on the shoulder. "Let's just be quiet for a while and enjoy the ride, okay, Dave?"

Susan wondered how her grandmother held up so well to the constant, repetitive questions. For Lillian, her days were like the drip-drip-drip of a Chinese water torture. Anybody could handle it for short periods, but long exposures were dreadful.

"Okay, okay, how about I take you gals out to lunch someplace? Where would you like to go?"

* * * * *

Susan brought the car to a stop in the mega-mall's parking lot. She liked to park far enough down the row where no one was likely to park next to them, giving themselves plenty of room to get in and out of the car; plus, they all enjoyed a little walk. "Gets the blood flowing," David would say.

At the end of the row was the Vision Center. The moment Susan hit the unlock button, both Dave and Lill popped out of the car. She felt guilty about not getting them out more often, but the latter stages of pregnancy had really slowed her down, while her "list of things to do before the baby comes" seemed to have grown larger rather than smaller. She took a deep breath and let out a quiet little burp, hoping to alleviate her building heartburn. Pushing against the steering wheel, she swung her legs out of the car and onto the ground. David had made his way around to Susan's side of the car and offered her his hand. "Here, Honey, let me help you here."

Susan wanted to let him help but was afraid that she would pull him down. "Thanks anyway, Pops, but I've got a system here."

Grabbing the doorframe with both hands, she pulled herself up onto her feet. David shut the door behind her, and Susan began her side-to-side waddle towards the mall's entrance.

There was a little traffic on the row, so they walked in single file. Susan chuckled to herself; she felt like a mother duck with all her babies in tow. "All you little ducklings back there?" she said over her shoulder. First, David, then Lillian, started quacking and flapping their elbows. For the moment, they didn't have a care in the world. Susan laughed out loud. *My god*, she thought. *This is the same man who used to go toe to toe with vicious criminals: bank robbers, murderers, kidnappers . . . even spies and saboteurs during the war. Wonder what those people would think if they could see Granddad now? I can't imagine any of those people acting silly, carefree. Well, maybe some, but not the truly evil ones. What do evil people do for fun? I can picture them doing something mean and laughing, and I can picture them at a party or a nightclub; but when they're at a party, are they really having fun, really enjoying themselves; or are they just mimicking what they think fun is supposed to be, hoping that by copying an appearance they can duplicate the happiness they sometimes see in others? I can't see it. I can't imagine them acting silly. How unfortunate for them.*

*   *   *   *   *

After settling David and Lillian into a corner of the waiting room, Susan signed in at the receptionist desk and waited for the young girl behind the counter to get off the phone. After a few moments, the girl covered the phone with her hand. "We'll call you when we're ready, okay?"

"Uh, I've got my grandparents here. They both have appointments scheduled for today. When I called, I was told that we could all three go together through the exams. Also, I need to have a minute with the doctor, alone, before he sees us."

The girl frowned and said into the phone, "Call ya back, okay?" and hung up. Then, looking down at the sign-in sheet, she asked—even though the "No" boxes had been checked—"Has their address or insurance changed since their last visit?"

"No, but my grandfather has Alzheimer's. It really would be a lot easier for everyone if we could just all stay together for this. And, like I said, I need to speak with the doctor for a minute or two, alone, before he sees them."

"Okay, let me just check something." The girl disappeared for a few minutes and then returned. "Okay, here's what you might wanna do. First, a tech will run them through the basic tests before the doctor comes in. What ya might then wanna do is after that, wait outside in the hall and catch him before he goes in. That okay?"

"That's fine, thanks."

The wait wasn't too long. For David and Lill, the waiting room was much more entertaining than TV. Lill enjoyed the activity of being out in the world. Too much time sequestered in her sanctuary made her feel somewhat like a prisoner, a prisoner being punished for an unknown crime. David liked watching the activity without the annoyance of having to remember a plot. A little boy in his terrible twos was getting cranky. His mother had run out of new toys, so the boy, always in search of something fresh, kept trying to wander off. David hoped the little fellow would get down his way so that he could tease him a bit.

"David and Lillian," called a young girl in a short, white, lab coat from the doorway to the examination rooms. Susan followed her grandparents, who followed the technician, into one of the rooms. When the door was closed, the girl looked down at her clipboard and asked, "Now, who has Alzheimer's?"

Susan cringed and wondered how much of such comments were understood by her grandfather and what effect they had on him. "We're all fine," she said coldly. "Let's just get on with this."

The girl shrugged her shoulders and pointed to the examination chair. "Who wants to go first?"

Always the gentleman, David said, "Why don't you go first, Lill."

Lillian settled into the chair. The technician set Lillian's glasses on the counter, dimmed the lights, and flipped a switch which resulted in a projection of letters on the wall. "Mrs. DeRieux, please read the lowest line that you can make out."

David, desperate to be helpful, chimed in, "I see an E, and then a D, and a Z—"

Susan, laughing quietly, gently grabbed her grandfather's arm and whispered in his ear, "Be quiet, Dad. Mom's supposed to take this test."

"Oh, I see; I see," David whispered back, not sounding completely convinced, although he did keep quiet for a bit.

After two minutes, the girl with the lab coat had no idea what Mrs. DeRieux could or could not see. She decided to move on to the next part of the test. A circle filled with colored dots was projected onto the wall. "Mrs. DeRieux, do you see a number in that circle?"

David had resisted helping as long as he could and pointed to the wall. "I see a circle of dots bordered by white, the dots in the—"

"Dad!" Susan laughed. "Mom's supposed to be doing this."

"Okay, okay."

David's turn went much faster. He loved talking to people, and making conversation didn't get any easier than taking an eye test. No memory was involved, no complicated chain of reasoning or current events to keep up with. The technician asked simple questions; David answered. It took just enough concentration on his part to keep it interesting for him, and, better still, he was helping her do something that seemed important to her. The girl made a few final notes on their charts and told the DeRieuxs the doctor would be with them in a few minutes. Susan told her grandparents she would be right back and followed the girl out.

Out in the hall, Susan stood waiting for the doctor. She had been on her feet throughout the two tests, and after a minute of standing alone in the hall the desire to sit was gaining urgency. She spotted a secretary's chair down the hall, rolled underneath a small desk and supply station. Problem solved, she sat outside her grandparents' door waiting for the doctor.

When he came, Susan explained quietly, "Listen, I'm here with my grandparents," she nodded towards the door, "but I would like to speak with you for a minute before you see them. Um, can we go down the hall here a little so we won't be overheard?"

"Sure," he said, taking their clipboard file from the door hanger.

Susan pushed the rolling chair, using it like a walker, back to its desk. The doctor lagged slightly behind, scanning the file as he walked.

"Please, sit back down," the doctor said. "I hope you know that we don't deliver babies here," he joked. "When are you due?"

"Not for a week or so, they tell me," Susan said as she plopped back down on the chair. "But from the size of me, you'd think it should have been last week."

"How can I help you?"

"Well . . ." Susan didn't quite know how to begin. "We have a little bit of an unusual situation here with my grandparents. We know what's going on with my grandfather; he's been diagnosed with Alzheimer's. But . . . we don't really know for certain what's going on with our grandmother. We're thinking that she might have had a few small strokes—mini-strokes or something like that—maybe in her sleep. Um, about a year or so ago, she just woke up one morning having trouble with her speech. She wasn't slurring words or anything like that, but it was odd. She seemed to have a lot of trouble with pronouns for instance, mixing them up, using the wrong ones, that type of thing. Also, she had trouble, a little bit, saying words in the wrong order; things like that. After a few days, her speech did get much better, but not quite back to normal. Now, over the last few months, it seems to be getting worse again. She seems to speak slower now than she used to, and she seems to need to pause and think a little bit before she begins to talk, like she needs to get her thoughts in order before she begins. If she's rushed or a little excited, her speech can sometimes be a little, uh, garbled. She's really become very self-conscious, understandably though, about talking to people. Also, we've come to notice, or at least we think, that she might sometimes be seeing things in an odd sort of way, or maybe her mind isn't processing what she sees correctly. Sort of like dyslexia or something. For instance, it's very difficult for her to dial a phone. I think when she reads off a series of numbers they get out of order—maybe reversed or something—in her mind. She'll look at a number in her book and then press a different number on the phone. In the eye test she just took, I think she could really see a lot of the letters she was getting wrong. I think she just might have been saying them wrong, or in a different order, or something like that. I think her mind just isn't processing correctly what she sees. Anyway, she's convinced it's her vision and thinks if she had stronger glasses, she wouldn't be having these problems. But what makes me wonder about that is the other day we were in a parking lot, and she was looking right at her own car, but didn't seem to see it. It took me a moment to figure out what was going on with her. I mean, her memory is really pretty good, and I know she knows what her car looks like. But the other day, like I said, she was looking right at it, but didn't seem to recognize it. I'm not sure what is going on with her or what the real problem is, but I know her sight isn't so bad that she can't see something as big as a car. Anyway, it was really odd and surprised me."

"What does her doctor say?"

"Well, this is the awkward part. Are you, or uh, do you know anything about Christian Science, the religion?"

"Uh, just that they don't believe in doctors, or don't go to them, or something like that. I know where their church is here in town, but that's about it."

He paused for a quick moment as the focus of his thoughts changed. "Are you one?" the doctor asked, trying to hide his concern.

Susan didn't miss the doctor's quick glance down at her pregnant stomach. "No, no," Susan assured him. "But my grandparents are, particularly my grandmother. She's completely devoted to it, most of her adult life, I think; and, you know, I've got to respect her wishes and beliefs on this. But anyway, Christian Scientists will go to dentists, and get eyeglass prescriptions, and things like that; but they, well she, won't go to a regular doctor, at least not yet. Anyway, that's why I don't know for sure what's going on with her speech and vision and other things. Like I say, we're just guessing that she might have had a mini-stroke or something like that. I just thought you needed to know what was going on before you saw them. Anything you can guess at or tell me would be helpful."

"Well, if your grandparents don't go to doctors, who diagnosed your granddad?"

"Um, yeah well, that was a pretty big thing. There's really no way to know for certain, but from what I gather, he might not have been as devoted to the religion all along as she has been, at least going back a few years. Now, well, I don't think it enters his mind much one way or another, other than I know it bothers him sometimes that she spends so much time with her Christian Science books. Anyway, when he first began to develop significant symptoms, his children—my mom and her brother—coaxed him to go see a doctor, hoping it might be something fixable. But he shushed it, afraid the very idea would upset her—my grandmother that is. Eventually, we hit a point where something had to be done; even she could see it. As time went on, my grandfather would, from time to time, get more and more agitated, really frustrated at things. It just kept getting worse. I didn't realize it before, but I don't think people who haven't dealt with it know how much Alzheimer's can affect a person's personality, their mood, or temperament. Anyway, it sometimes got to the point that we really began to worry. I mean, no one could believe that Granddad would ever hurt anyone, but at times, well, he was really more and more losing control. I mean, he would kick at doors, slam things around, you know, things like that. Sometimes he would even swear, pretty bad. I don't think he ever used to do that. Things seemed to be heading in a really bad direction. I think for my grandmother, it was kind of like having to come to grips with a really bad toothache. She knew something had to be done, so, eventually, she agreed to let us take him to see a doctor. Doctor Harch—do you know him? He seems really good. Anyway, he diagnosed Granddad with Alzheimer's and got him on some medication. We had to tweak it a little bit at first, getting the dosage right and all. But now, it seems to have evened him out a bit, keeps him from erupting anyway.

"But again, if you have any ideas about my grandmother, I would appreciate hearing them. And also, we don't let Granddad drive anymore. I think deep down he knows it, but sometimes he gets pretty upset; ah, you could say he even becomes angry and belligerent with us for telling him he can't drive. Not door kicking angry, at least not anymore, but sometimes he gets really insistent about it. He hasn't made too big a deal about it when I'm around, but from what my grandmother says, it can be a little bit frightening when he gets wound up. Mostly that was before we got him on the medication. Anyway, it might be helpful and take some of the pressure off of us if you, as a doctor, mentioned to him that you didn't think it wise for him to drive. Just if you feel comfortable about it, but after you see him, I'm sure you'll agree. I mean, he won't remember you saying it, but at least we can then say to him in all honesty that his eye doctor told him not to drive. Anyway, that's it."

David was still in the examination chair when Susan and the doctor came in. "How are you folks doing today?" the doctor asked.

"Just great," said David, eager for the testing to continue.

The doctor dimmed the lights, shined a penlight into David's eye, and asked him to look straight ahead at the center of the wall. At the conclusion of the exam, the doctor emphatically suggested to David that he not drive. David, being in an agreeable frame of mind, agreed wholeheartedly, explaining to the doctor at length how he had given up driving some time ago. To Lillian's great disappointment, no change in her prescription was suggested. The doctor, offhandedly, mentioned that a general physician might be able to help her. Lillian remained quiet after that. She would need quite a bit of time in her sanctuary to sort out the day's events.

Chapter 5

Joey

The Cracker Barrel was just across the interstate from the mall. The DeRieuxs loved the food—David the breakfast items, Lillian the vegetable plate—but today, the rocking chairs looked particularly inviting to Susan as they walked past them on their way to the front door.

David whispered to Susan, "I need to duck into the restroom for just a minute. Where are they?"

"Let's all go," Susan said as she led the way.

Susan waited just outside the bathroom doors. Dave went in one side, Lill the other. Someone had to be there to intercept David when he came out. Susan worried how they would handle public bathrooms in the near future. David's bad days gave hints of what might soon be typical. Sometimes it was worrisome how long it would take him to come back out. Sometimes he would get into conversations with himself in the mirror, not realizing that he was speaking to his own reflection. When they went out in the evenings or on the weekends, her husband, Jeff, would go in with him to help. He was heartwarmingly patient with her grandfather, and she loved him for it, but they were going to need more help soon.

A young man, looking to be in his late teens or early twenties, came out of the men's room shaking his head with a strange smile on his face. Susan wished she could go in and check. Instead, she cracked the door and called in, "You okay, Dad?"

"Be right out," he answered.

Both grandparents came out at about the same time. David had dribbled quite a bit on his khaki pants. Susan didn't think he was aware of it and hoped that it would dry quickly.

Lill and David waited as Susan took a quick turn, and then they made their way to the rocking chairs out front. The hostess had told them it would be about a ten-minute wait. Susan and Lillian sat down next to each other on one of the double rockers. David stood next to Lillian with his hand on the back of the rocker, eager to strike up a conversation with anyone. Susan had mixed feelings about their public outings. She knew how much her grandfather enjoyed them but worried about the impression he sometimes made. David was well known and well respected by those near his generation and almost always ran into someone who knew him well enough to call him by name and say hello. However, Susan was constantly amazed at the lack of comprehension or understanding by younger adults of the presence of Alzheimer's. She hoped David's peer group at least understood; she was pretty sure most did.

Susan was both tired and restless; rocking back and forth felt good to her. It was a nice day to be sitting outside. April, early spring in East Tennessee—the weather was perfect. Nice and pleasantly warm in the sun, not yet the sweat-inducing humidity of July.

Lillian put her hand on Susan's and asked, "Tired, Honey?"

"A little. It just feels good to get off my feet for a while. How have you guys been doing?"

"We're fine. Your grandfather gets a little restless sometimes. How are you and Jeff doing?"

"Good, I'm looking forward to being able to see my feet again. Jeff's been spending a lot of time at the plant; you know, trying to get a little ahead, if that's possible, so he can take off some when the baby comes."

Susan flinched and stopped rocking. "You okay?" Lillian asked.

Letting out her breath, Susan started rocking again slowly while rubbing her stomach. "Just a little twinge. At least it's a change from heartburn."

"Maybe we should go on home," Lillian offered.

"No, really, I'm okay. There's nothing I would be doing at home that I'm not doing here. Besides, at home I'd have to fix my own lunch. Let's just eat here. I'll probably take a little nap later this afternoon."

David had struck up a conversation with an old acquaintance. The man stepped closer and introduced himself to Lillian. "Hello, Mrs. DeRieux. I'm Joey Franks," he said with a pained smile that expressed his unsaid sympathies. "David and I were just hashing over old times. I used to be a reporter for *The Chattanooga Times* back when your husband was with the FBI."

"Nice to meet you. Please, call me Lill."

"Sure wish your husband had been this talkative back when I was covering him; though I know back then he couldn't really— "

The smile left Joey's face. Lillian followed his gaze over to Susan. She was holding her breath and her eyes were bulging a little. Finally, she let out her breath. "Mom, I think I'll be having lunch later today at the hospital. I think this is it."

Lillian patted Susan's hand. "Can . . . Can you drive, or, or, should we get an ambulance you?"

"Can I help?" Joey offered. "I'd be happy to take you."

Susan tensed for a moment and then let out a strange nasal sound. "That would be great. Let's go."

Joey pulled his car around; everyone helped Susan into the back seat. She was glad older folks liked big, four-door sedans.

Lillian went around and got in the other side next to Susan. Joey shut Susan's door. David stood, wondering what to do. Joey opened the front passenger door. "Why don't you sit up here, David?"

Number 01 on Susan's cellphone speed-dial was her husband's work number. "This is Jeff Gates. I'm in the office today but either in a meeting or away from my desk. Please leave a message at the beep, or dial 0 if you need immediate assistance."

Susan pressed 0. "Hi, Adel, it's Susan. I'm on my way to the hospital. I think it's baby time. Is Jeff there?"

"He's on the other line. I'll get him."

"That's okay; ah listen, just tell him what's up and that I'm on my way to the hospital. Friend of Granddad's is giving us a ride; should be there in about ten minutes. So he doesn't kill himself getting there, tell him it'll probably be a while yet till the main event. Thanks."

David remained quiet while sitting sideways in his seat, looking back at Lillian. Joey glanced back. "Everyone okay back there?" he asked cheerfully. "This your first one?"

"Yeah," Susan answered.

"You'll do fine. I remember our first child. Seems like a million years ago. You'll do fine."

Joey kept the conversation light. When they were a few blocks out, Susan began taking loud, rapid, short breaths. Joey wondered if she had been through one of those Lamaze classes, or whatever was popular now, or if she was just doing what she had seen in the movies and found that it worked for her . . . or maybe that's just what women naturally do. Probably taken a course or read some book, he decided.

Joey followed the hospital's signs to the emergency entrance and pulled up under the covered entryway. David hadn't said a word since leaving the Cracker Barrel, but he was watching and listening to everything. He knew something serious was going on and was doing his best to get a handle on it. Susan's breath was back, close to normal. Joey got out and came around to Susan's door just as she swung it open. No one had come out of the building, so Joey said to Susan, "Why don't you wait here, and I'll go in and get some help."

There was a wheelchair just inside the door. Joey rolled it out. David and Lill were standing around Susan's opened door but stepped aside to let Joey help Susan up and into the chair. Since it was early afternoon in the middle of the week, there were only a few people in the waiting room and no one ahead at the check-in counter. Joey rolled Susan up to a lowered section of the counter designed for people in wheelchairs. Susan gave her name and her doctor's name to a perky young nurse who punched up Susan's file on her computer. It was all there. Susan was expected; most of her admission paperwork was pre-filled and already on file. Just a few more routine things to sign in case things didn't go routinely. If it was determined that Susan was really in labor, her OBGYN or his partner on call would be paged.

David remained quiet, watching over Susan's shoulder as she signed the last few documents. He hated waivers. He hated lawyers who sued for any excuse. He hated to hate. At one end of the waiting room, big double doors to a long hallway were propped opened. A doctor, with an official-looking ID card clipped to his lab coat, a stethoscope slung around his neck, and a small paper cup in his hand, came through the doorway and crossed the room. David tried unsuccessfully to see what was in the cup as the doctor passed within a couple of feet from him before going out through a closed, swinging double-door, at the opposite end of the room, marked in big red letters: "Authorized Entry Only".

Something about the waiting room and the doctor made David uneasy. He couldn't put his finger on it. The doctor's passage had gone by in a flash, but a feeling of familiarity lingered. It was not a good feeling; it was growing worse. The doctor had been tall, lanky, and in his early to mid-thirties. Something in his walk, or maybe it was his manner in general—a wake of supreme arrogance as he passed through the room—left David with a feeling he knew that guy.

An image of the doctor began to recreate itself in David's mind. The shape of his head—yes, that was it. David would never forget the shape of that head. It was a long, skinny, rectangular head. And then there were those ears . . . those little bitty ears. Not big, red, goofy, country-boy ears that would vent heat out into a summer's day; but little, big-city Yankee ears. Pale, bloodless little ears that were better suited for the cold. Small, smart-ass-New-York-City-Yankee-ears . . . on a long, skinny head. The face began to come out of the shadows and into the light within David's mind, like an old World War II movie—black and white; black and white and shades of gray. Slowly the grayscale became clearer. At first, the distant image appeared to have the benign beauty of an ordinary human face, but as the details came into focus the beauty dissipated, replaced by harsh angles and hardened features. The eyes—the eyes were clear, cold, and penetrating; the pupils were too small. There was purpose in those eyes, a focused and driven purpose; but there was no comfort or kindness in them.

A shiver ran through David's body. *I know that guy. Who is he? He's dangerous as hell; I know that. Who is he? Did I arrest that guy once? What's going on here?*

Still looking at the closed swinging door through which the doctor had left, David automatically gave an inconspicuous tap with his right hand on his left side, slightly below his armpit. It was an old habit, one he hadn't done in decades, to tap his gun before dangerous confrontations to verify that it was secure in his shoulder holster. A quick shot of nervous adrenalin popped him; his gun wasn't there. He looked down. To his surprise, he wasn't even wearing a suit coat, the uniform which, in his past, had hidden his gun.

Joey observed David's nervous fixation on the doctor and now the closed door. He placed his hand lightly on David's back and leaned closer. "You okay, Buddy? You've been awfully quiet. Everything's okay you know; women have babies all the time."

David turned his head to Joey, then to an approaching orderly.

"Excuse me," the orderly said, pointing to the back of Susan's wheelchair. "I'll take her."

David was blocking the orderly's way, but didn't move, desperately trying to hide his bewilderment.

"Come on, David," Joey repeated as he gave a gentle tug on David's arm. "Let's get out of their way and have a seat over here while they check her out."

David held firm.

Susan, finished with the paperwork, turned her wheelchair around to face David and Joey. Lillian was to her side. David looked down at Susan. She didn't know what to make of his deadpan expression; she wasn't sure what to say.

"Listen, Pop, they're gonna take a quick look at me to see if I'm ready. I'm pretty sure they're gonna check me in; I think this baby is coming."

David didn't budge. He gave the waiting room another overall look. To him, it was packed with happily chattering pregnant women, most wearing sun dresses. He, alone, could feel the thick humidity of July in the air and the slight movement of air from the large, slow-moving, ceiling fans. He returned his attention back to Susan and said, "This isn't good. Come on, Edna; I'm getting you out of here."

"Dad . . . who's Edna?"

Lill said, "Dave, that was a long time ago. Edna's not here. She's gone. That's all over with."

"Wooow," Susan gasped. "Gotta go. Mom, you guys gonna be all right? Jeff should be here any minute."

"You go, Honey."

"I can wait till Jeff gets here," Joey offered.

The orderly worked his way around David and backed Susan's chair away. She was holding her breath again. "Thanks," she eeked with a short blast of compressed air.

David watched as Susan was rolled away. Joey's attention was on David. His hand was again on David's shoulder; he could feel the tension in David's back and in the air.

When the doors closed behind Susan, David whispered to himself through clenched teeth, "God damn plutonium."

Chapter 6

The Clinic

Vanderbilt University Hospital Prenatal Clinic
Nashville, TN
July 1946

"Hi, Edna. Have you been feeling any better since your last visit?" the doctor asked as he skimmed through the pages of her chart.

"I guess," she attempted unconvincingly from her perch on the examination table. Edna hadn't seen this doctor before, but it didn't matter. Everyone knew how good Vanderbilt's doctors were, and since the clinic's fees were based on what a person could afford to pay, and she wasn't paying much, she felt an extra obligation to please the doctor. Her feet, not quite reaching the floor, knocked back and forth slowly against each other. Nashville's July humidity didn't seem to bother the doctor or his nurse as much as it did her. She was glad the window was cracked open, but there was no ceiling fan like there had been in the waiting room to move the muggy air. She heard a car stop outside and wondered if it was her brother.

"Let's see," the doctor continued, still looking at the chart. "It looks like you've got about three months to go yet before you're due. I sure would like to see you gain a little more weight before then."

"Me too, Doc. It just seems that some days it's hard to keep anything down."

"That so?" he said as he scribbled something on her chart and showed it to the nurse. "Well, we're going to give you something that I think will make you feel a little better."

"Another liver shot?" she asked, squirming to see what the nurse was doing at the counter.

"No," he chuckled, observing her directly for the first time, "nothing like that."

"Is it something else for my thyroid?"

"No, no," he said as the nurse handed Edna a small paper cup with something fizzy in it. "Those are vitamins and nutrients. Now drink up."

"Vitamins and nutrients?"

"Yes, it's just a little cocktail to make you feel better. Come on now, be a good girl."

Edna swirled the liquid in the cup a few times. "A cocktail? I don't usually have a cocktail in the middle of the day." She took a trial sip. "Tastes sweet, kind of like cherry coke." She gave the cup one last swirl and drank the rest.

Another car pulled up outside. Edna's head turned towards the open window. "I hope that's my brother. He's supposed to meet me here and take me to lunch. He has his own car you know," she boasted, and then immediately began to worry that her pride might cost her extra when it came time for the clinic to figure out what she could afford to pay.

"Really?" The doctor seemed interested in this new piece of information. All the women using the prenatal clinic were white—Segregation was strictly enforced—but most were from families with modest incomes at best. "What does your brother do?"

"He's an FBI agent."

"An FBI agent," the doctor's head jerked towards the empty cup in Edna's hand. "Isn't that nice."

"He didn't buy it," Edna managed a little giggle. The fizzy drink did seem to be settling her stomach a bit; plus, she liked talking to the doctor. "Our dad and his brothers have a parking garage in Chicago. Before the war, you know, the Depression, lots of folks couldn't pay their bills, so they just gave the garage their cars for payment. Nobody to sell them to, so, my brother and some of our cousins got cars. Thinking about it, though, the one he's driving today is probably a Bureau car."

"Nashville is a long way from Chicago; what brought the two of you down here?"

"Well, he came down first . . ." she looked at her hand, counting fingers ". . . about three years ago, 1943. I remember because it was on my twenty-third birthday. The FBI transferred him from Albany, New York, to Chattanooga. The next year, he told me about a big plant that was hiring, so I came down. You know, the T-12 plant at Oak Ridge."

The doctor flipped to the first page of Edna's chart. "Says here you live in Murfreesboro?"

"Well yeah, now. I met my husband while I was working in the T-12 plant. We got married there, then moved here after I got pregnant. T-12's no place for a family. My husband's folks have a farm outside Murfreesboro. We're staying with them for a while. Next year Hank, that's my husband, he's going to build us our own house across the creek from his folks. After growing up in Chicago, I really like having all that space, and if I start missing a big city, well, we're still pretty close to Nashville."

"What's your brother's name?"

"You mean David? His name is David DeRieux. He lives in Chattanooga."

"What's he doing here in Nashville?" the doctor asked as he jotted David's name down on the back of his prescription pad.

"He has business here all the time. Think he looks up records here a lot. You know—birth certificates, marriage certificates, things like that. I think it's for security on the hirings at Oak Ridge. They still do that, you know. Think he interviews past employers sometimes too. You know, things like that. Checks addresses of people they're not sure of, really everyone, I guess. I used to not have any idea of what he did, but now that the war's over, things seem a little looser. Not a lot though, but I think that's some of what he does. That and bank robbers . . . things like that."

Edna's neck craned forward, and her head pivoted from one side to the other, looking carefully at both sides of the room; she was about to tell a secret. "You know what though," she said in a much-lowered voice. "He doesn't really talk much about it, but I think he spends a lot of time following people. You know, communists, things like that. I don't mind telling you because, well, you're a doctor and everything; just don't say you heard it from me. I mean, I wouldn't have even told you except the war's over, and, like I said, you're a doctor and everything."

"What's he say about them, the people he follows?" the doctor asked.

"Well, not much really. Mainly just funny stuff, I guess. Like the other day, he told us about this guy he was following—a Russian spy, I think. David says sometimes they shop, just like us. He says they have families, just like us, and sometimes try to send stuff back home. David says they don't really have much over there in Russia; sounds pretty bad. Anyhow, David said he was following this Russian guy, trying to keep out of sight and everything, and the guy goes into a department store. Think they were in downtown Knoxville. Anyway, this guy, you know, the Russian spy guy, goes into this department store. So, David gives him a little time and then follows him in. The guy goes to the toy department, so David goes over and pretends to look at toys. That's not so bad because David's got two kids, a boy and a girl, so he pretends he's looking for stuff for them. The guy picks out a stuffed bear and buys it. Guess he's got a kid too. Anyway, here's where it gets funny. The guy goes over to the lady's intimate department—you know, underwear, nighties, stuff like that—and starts looking through all that. Well, I tell you, I'd of died to have seen David because you know he had to follow the guy over there and pretend to look at that stuff too. Knowing David, I bet his face turned as red as a radish. Anyway, David likes a good laugh, even when it's on him, so he told us about that. Don't know if the guy ever knew David was following him or not, but David says some of them are just regular people, pretty much like us. Says sometimes plain ole good people just get caught up in things that, all in all, they'd rather not have anything to do with if they had any choice about it. Anyway, that's what my brother says. Guess he knows."

"So, you said your brother is here to pick you up for lunch?"

"Yep." Edna stretched and straightened with a great deal of importance. "Called me last night, long distance you know. He lives in Chattanooga, like I said. Called me and said he was going through Murfreesboro on his way to Nashville, and did I want him to stop by on his way up or back. Told him I was going to be here around noon for my appointment—so he's taking me out for lunch."

"So, he's here to pick you up?"

"Yep, that and lunch."

*　*　*　*　*

The waiting room was packed. David had never seen so many pregnant women gathered together in one place before, but he was not surprised. Everywhere you went it seemed like half the women were pregnant. People, David thought, are all so different, yet they share so much in common. The war had put so many lives on hold that when it was finally over and the boys returned home, everyone had pretty much the same idea: marriage, jobs, families, new homes.

Most of the women were bunched together in the middle of the room near the receptionist, chattering away merrily, comparing notes as if they had known each other their entire lives. The chatter let off when David came in, like it does when a woman walks into a barber shop. David scanned the room but didn't see Edna. It was a few minutes before noon, so he checked with the receptionist and was told Edna was in an examination room. He found a quiet, inconspicuous spot against the street-side wall, and soon he was forgotten as the chatter returned to its gal's-only level.

At exactly noon, a man dressed in a well-tailored suit and carrying an expensive-looking briefcase entered the clinic from the street. The chatter again waned for the few moments it took for him to cross the room. He was a thin, lanky man, of above average height, who didn't pause to take notice of the people or the layout when he entered, but moved quickly and with purpose across the room and through the door from which the ladies were being called one by one for their appointments.

David caught just a glimpse of the side of the man's face as he entered and his back profile as he crossed the room, but that was enough. David had seen him somewhere before—the Clinton Engineer Works—but what was his name; what exactly did he do there? Clinton was a huge place, much bigger than most rural cities. It nagged at David, something about the ears; what was it? They were conspicuously small. *Oh yeah,* David laughed to himself; *VanZant, that was his name. Dr. VanZant, a medical doctor, not a PhD like many of the brainiacs there.* David and another agent, Bert Ashton, had spoken with him briefly at Clinton four or five months ago—a chance, purely unofficial conversation in one of the Personnel Records buildings. VanZant had said he was there for just a few days, was based out of Washington, had something to do with the medical facilities, traveled a lot.

From David's perspective it was a short, innocuous, and unplanned conversation; but for some reason, VanZant had immediately annoyed Bert on a visceral level. Bert was like a friendly dog that suddenly snarls at someone to whom nobody else has given a second thought. As soon as they were alone, Bert went off on a passionate riff about VanZant being a smart-ass Yankee with smart-ass-little-Yankee ears. There was a lot more; but at the time, David was laughing so hard at the "little ears" commentary that he didn't hear or remember much of the rest.

Bert Ashton was a self-made man; born, bred, and educated in Alabama. David enjoyed working with Bert more than any other agent with whom he had been paired. They had both joined the FBI at about the same time. Bert had been transferred to Chattanooga from the Atlanta bureau in late 1942; David from Albany, New York, in early 1943. Bert Ashton was a deceptively simple and unassuming man. He was huge, at least six-foot-four, and built like a plow mule; but he had a laid-back, easy-going personality that was completely disarming. David was constantly amazed at the things strangers would confide to him. But the guy was smart, smarter than one would gather from a casual conversation. He had put himself through college and law school by buying truckloads of chickens cheap in the South, driving them overnight, and selling them in the big cities of the North for a handsome profit. He hadn't had time to work on his school's law review or participate in any other scholastic extracurricular activities, for that matter, but Bert's education extended well beyond the walls of his classrooms. He knew the North; he knew the South; and he knew most of what lay in between. Bert knew people and knew what buttons to push to get what he wanted from them. "Thank God you're one of the good guys," David often kidded Bert, "otherwise, I'd probably have to report you to somebody."

David and Bert hit it off from the start. Their extremities were opposites, but their cores were identical. David was from the North; Bert from the South. David had joined the FBI despite the dangers—it was the Depression, and he needed a job. For Bert, the hazards were part of the attraction. David preferred to get his thrills vicariously through books, movies, and interesting conversations. Bert had made it clear that school was out, and he didn't have to read any more books. David liked to fish; Bert liked to hunt.

But despite their differences, or more so because of them, their personalities locked together like a jigsaw puzzle, and, over time, the two came to realize that in many ways, it was the differences that kept their friendship interesting. After all, if two people are too much the same, then being together isn't all that different from being alone; and it was the enjoyment of each other's company that made the dull periods, such as long surveillances and other tedious fact-finding missions, pass easier. But some of the people under their scrutiny were the most violent, ruthless, and unstable criminals on the planet; and there had been a handful of episodes in which hours of drawn-out tedium had quickly turned into flashes of terror. It was in those telling moments—those moments in which nature's creations cannot help but to largely reveal themselves—that David and Bert learned volumes about each other. At their cores, they were both rock solid. By the summer of 1946, they had known each other for a little over three years; their trust in each other was absolute.

*   *   *   *   *

David remained staring at the closed door through which VanZant had just passed without hesitation or invitation. He couldn't help but wonder what VanZant's connection with the Vanderbilt Clinic might be. If VanZant had stopped at the receptionist's station, David might have let it go, passing it off as a medical administrator inspecting or gathering information from one of many medical institutions. But he hadn't stopped; he'd gone straight through the door as if he owned the place. This wasn't VanZant's first time here; he knew exactly where he was going. The fact that Bert had reacted so vehemently to VanZant a few months earlier, with no apparent provocation, made David all the more curious.

David replayed that conversation over again in his mind. It was just some quick chit-chat, and VanZant really hadn't said that much. Looking back on it, David wished he had encouraged a longer conversation. Maybe if he had more pieces, this puzzle would make sense.

But at the time, back then, David had no reason for misgivings, and Bert had seemed more annoyed than suspicious. Besides, VanZant wasn't on any of their lists, and the mere fact that he was inside the gates of Clinton Engineer Works, a secured facility, substantially vouched for his credentials. In hindsight, David wished he had ginned-up the conversation a little—that he had asked VanZant why, as an MD, he carried a briefcase rather than a little black doctor's bag. Obviously, VanZant was more administrative than medical practice. If only he could go back in time. Often, it was the little offhand, innocent sort of questions—keeping everything casual—that yielded the most surprising information.

Well, thought David, *Bert's already picked up a scent on VanZant. I'll run this all by him later.*

*   *   *   *   *

VanZant gave two quick knocks on Dr. Mallard's office door and entered without waiting for an invitation. Mallard wasn't there. VanZant knew he'd be there soon; they had a noon appointment. *Just as well*, thought VanZant, *I could use a minute alone.* He slid into the chair behind Mallard's desk, but before setting his briefcase on the desktop, he paused to scan the papers there to see if any were of interest to him. *Shit, this is just ordinary pregnancy stuff.* He pushed the piles off to the side, clearing a space for his briefcase. Just as he clicked it opened, Dr. Mallard entered. VanZant was surprised that Dr. Mallard hadn't knocked but then remembered it was Mallard's office.

Mallard plopped down in one of the two visitor's chairs across the desk from VanZant and said, "See anyone interesting, anyone in particular that you might know . . . in the waiting room?"

Chapter 7

Edna

Chattanooga, TN
April 2001

David was on the edge; Joey didn't want to bump him over. He moved his hand from David's shoulder down to his upper arm and gave an encouraging tug. "Come on, Buddy. Really, it's okay. Come on; let's have a seat over here and wait. Susan is going to be fine; you'll see."

"VanZant's here," David said crisply. "That bastard was supposed to stay in D.C. That was the deal."

Who the hell is VanZant, Joey wondered. *For that matter, who the hell is Edna, and why in the world is David so worked up about plutonium?* Joey was dying to know. It had been four years since Joey had gone from semi-retirement to full retirement, but his reporter's curiosity had never waned. It was who he was. Now, however, was not the time to start fishing.

Lill took David by the hand and, in her quiet voice, said, "Come on, Dave. Let's just sit down for a minute."

David, with some reluctance, allowed Lill to lead him to an isolated corner of the waiting room. Off to themselves, the two sat down. Joey, still standing near the check-in counter, thought for a moment, then reached into his pocket and pulled out a little notepad and pen. Old habits die hard; Joey would sooner leave his apartment naked than leave without his notepad. He turned to a fresh page and jotted down three words in a column: Edna, VanZant, and Plutonium; put a question mark after each, and tucked the notepad back into his pocket.

Not certain as to what his next step should be, Joey glanced back over towards the DeRieuxs. He didn't want to intrude on David and Lill—he couldn't help but like them—but he didn't want to abandon them either; and naturally, he was more than a little curious as to what was going on within David's mind. Standing still, looking at the DeRieuxs, Lill made the decision for him by inviting him over with a smile and a welcoming wiggle of her fingers.

As he approached, Joey could see David's lingering distress diminish, as does one who spots an ally while in the midst of hooligans. David, obviously glad to see him, stood, extended his hand to shake, and greeted Joey with, "Well hello, it's good to see you. I'm sorry; I know you well, but I'm drawing a blank on your name."

Joey, a little hesitant, shook David's hand and introduced himself. It was an exact replay of their initial meeting at the Cracker Barrel.

David's response was enthusiastic. "That's right, that's right. It's been some years, but I always enjoyed working with the press. It's good to see you. How have you been?"

Joey didn't quite know what to say.

Lill reached up from her seat, patted Joey on his arm, and said, "Thanks for helping us today. We'll be okay now, if there's somewhere you need to be."

"Oh no, no. I've got plenty of time. What's the use of being retired if you can't spend a little time with your friends? I'll at least stay until Susan's husband gets here; unless, that is, you would rather be alone."

Lill smiled. "Thanks so much. Why don't you two sit down for a minute." Lill patted the chair next to her. David sat down.

Joey took the seat on the other side of David, sitting sideways on the forward edge so that he could see and include Lill in their conversation.

"Do you two have any other family here in town?" he asked.

David said, "No, no. I don't think so," then turning to Lill, "do we, Lill?"

Lill collected her thoughts and spoke slowly. "We have Susan, our granddaughter here, and her husband Jeff—he should be here soon." Lill paused, putting together her next string of thoughts. "We have a son and a daughter. Kay, our daughter, lives in Nashville, with her husband Mike. They visit often. Kay is Susan's mother."

"That's nice. And where does your son live?"

"Tim, Tim is his name. Tim and his wife, Elizabeth. They live in Evanston, just outside Chicago, on the north side. They have three children, but we don't see them as often. It's a long ways time, you know, and everyone's so busy."

The automatic door opened, and a young man hurried in. "There, there . . . look Jeff," Lill said waving her hand to get his attention.

Jeff spotted them and rushed over. "Hi Gram; hi Pop." Jeff extended his hand to Joey. "You must be the friend who gave them a ride; thanks."

"Name's Joey Franks. Glad I could help. Susan just went back. They're checking her out now. We haven't heard anything yet."

"Thanks," Jeff said, turning his attention back to David and Lill. "If you're okay here, I'm just going to check on her."

They were all nodding as Jeff hurried off to get directions from the receptionist.

*   *   *   *   *

Susan's door was open. She was sitting up in the bed, alone in the room. The contractions had stopped for the moment. Jeff slowed down as he approached her door and peeked in to make sure it was her room.

"Hey, Honey", he said as he entered. She seemed relaxed; he glanced around the room. Susan wasn't sure if he was looking for a chair or a baby tucked away somewhere. She guessed he was looking for a baby because he ignored the empty chairs and walked over to her bedside. "How you doing, Honey?"

"Fine. Our little guy is giving me a break right now, but I'm sure he'll wind back up in a minute or two. So far, it's pretty much like we expected."

"I kind of expected a small crowd . . . or at least a doctor and a nurse. Where is everybody?" Jeff asked. "You know, I think I've got the cigar smoking part of it down, but I'm gonna need some help with the technical stuff."

"A doctor was here just a minute ago. He said everything looked fine, but it would probably be a little while yet before delivery. He said someone would be here in just a bit to move me to the Maternity Unit. Did you see Grandma and Dad when you came in?"

"Yeah, met Joey too. Seems nice enough. Do you know him?"

"No, but I think Granddad used to know him. Kind of hard to tell how well though. Granddad thinks he knows pretty much everybody he meets these days."

A nurse tapped on the door and came in followed by the orderly who had helped earlier. "How's everybody doing? Pretty exciting, isn't it? I see this is your first one."

"Hi," Susan said. "What's the plan?"

"Well, we're going to move you up to the Maternity Unit on the third floor. Dan here will take you." The nurse nodded to Jeff, "You the father?"

"Yep, I'm the husband."

"Good, you can go on up with your wife then."

"Oh boy," Jeff said. "Hey, um, do you have any idea how long it will be; or, what I mean is, well, how fast is this all gonna happen now?"

"Can't really say for sure, but my guess is that it's probably going to be at least a couple of hours yet. If it goes much longer, they'll probably induce. Don't go far though, contractions will start coming more frequently the closer we get, and I'm sure your wife is going to want to share them with you."

Susan laughed, took Jeff's hand, gave it a tight squeeze, and said, "Yeah, Hun, I'm gonna wanna share this with you." Then to the nurse, "Listen, my grandparents are in the waiting room out there. Is there a waiting room on that floor, near where we'll be?"

"Sure," the nurse said. "They can go up with you if you like."

"That would be great."

Jeff said, "Look, I'll get them and meet you up there. That okay?"

*   *   *   *   *

David, Lill, and Joey were just where Jeff had left them. David had bounced back and was having a great time chatting away with Joey. Lill looked happy just to be doing something normal.

"Everything's fine," Jeff explained. "Looks like this is it. They're moving her up to the Maternity Unit on the third floor. It sounds like it could be a little while yet until the delivery, but there is another waiting room up there in Maternity that we can move to."

Jeff turned to Joey and extended his hand to shake. "Listen, we really appreciate your help today. Hope we can return the favor sometime."

"Glad to help, really. I haven't talked to David in years. I've got some time though. I can stay for a while if it would help, or I can give David and Lill a ride home if that would help. Really, it's no trouble."

"Well, I hate to impose more than we already have." Jeff thought for a moment. "I'll tell you what; if you don't mind, could you come up with us for a minute and let me check with Susan about what she wants to do?"

Jeff led the way. David and Lill walked arm in arm with Joey slightly behind and to David's side. The elevator was ahead, just past the intersection of two hallways in the middle of the building. They passed several rooms on their way. A few had their doors open and Joey could see the people inside—some alone, some with visitors, some with family camped out for the duration. The room Susan had been in was empty. A few doors past Susan's room, on the other side of the hall, was an X-Ray room with the door closed. Outside the door was a large plaque with a radiation warning symbol in red, on a white background. David stopped to look at the sign and the closed door, then looked back at Joey. Their eyes meet. David gave a discrete nod to Joey, then a pointed nod at the warning sign, then returned his eyes to Joey. Lill, still arm in arm with David, was used to prodding him along. "Let's keep moving, Dave," she said with a little tug.

David started back up. Joey paused, wondering what David was trying to convey, then, realizing he was being left behind, caught back up in a few quick steps.

*   *   *   *   *

The third floor waiting room was much smaller but far more comfortable than the one they had just left—nice, soft, overstuffed chairs, carpet on the floor, TV, a small kitchenette area with a coffee maker and microwave. Joey and the DeRieuxs settled in while Jeff went to consult with Susan. She was on her phone when he entered the room. "Okay, Mom, I'll see you and Dad in a few hours then, thanks."

Susan set her phone on the rolling table that partially hung over her bed. "That was Mom. She and Dad should be here in a few hours. Sounds like they already had their bags packed and had it set up to get off work any time they needed. Good thing. I don't think Mom is as surprised as I am that this is happening a few days ahead of schedule. I guess I just got so used to seeing that due date on the calendar that I just assumed that that would be the day. Anyway, I told them to call your mobile number when they get here since I might be a little busy."

Jeff sat on the side of the bed. "Sure would be nice if they got here before the delivery, but then again, I'm sure you don't want this to drag on too long. How ya feeling?"

"Pretty good. The ride up was kind of funny. I had a pretty good contraction in the elevator, and there were two high-school-aged girls in there with me who looked pretty uncomfortable. They relaxed a little once the orderly explained to them that I was just having some labor pains, but I think they've probably got something new to think about at their next prom."

"Do they still think you're a few hours away?"

"They haven't said anything new either way. How are the folks doing? We didn't have lunch; I bet they're getting pretty hungry by now."

"How about you? Are you hungry?"

"Well, yes and no. I don't think they'll let me eat anything now anyway. Probably best. I'm okay."

Jeff nodded in agreement. "Joey has offered to take your grandparents home. What do you think?"

"Yeah, that might be best. Otherwise, they'll be stuck here for who knows how long. They could get something to eat here, but I hate to keep Joey waiting. He had just finished eating and was on his way out when we met him at Cracker Barrel."

"I'll ask him to take them home then. How about if they stop at a drive-thru on the way home to get something? They're really pretty much past cooking anything for themselves now, aren't they?"

"Yeah, except for cereal. Even microwaving Stouffers is pressing it. I think more and more they're just eating ice cream. Listen though . . ." Susan thought for a moment. "I want to talk to Gramma-Lill for a minute, without David. He never turns down a trip to the bathroom. Could you take him, and send Lill down here while you're doing that?"

"A little girl talk, huh." Jeff patted Susan's thigh as he stood up. "I'll send her down. Us bow-wees will be in the waiting room smoking stogies if you need us. Take your time. Ya know, I'm feeling better about this already."

"You light one up and they'll throw you out."

"There's an idea. Okay." Jeff leaned over and gave Susan a loud peck on the lips. "See you in a little bit."

*   *   *   *   *

Joey was happy to help and didn't seem to mind waiting a little longer while David and Jeff went to the restroom and Lill went to see Susan. The restrooms were right next to the waiting room. Susan's room was several doors past on the same side. Lill assured Jeff that she could find room 312 on her own. David entered the restroom while Jeff paused in the hall as Lill made her way towards Susan's room. Jeff watched as Lillian slowed almost to a stop at each door to read the numbers as she passed. Lill was passing the second door when Jeff heard David say something. Jeff entered the restroom and found David standing in front of the sink with his hand extended towards the mirror as if to shake hands.

David said, apparently for the second time to the image in the mirror, "I say, don't we know each other from somewhere? I can't help but think you look familiar to me. I'm David DeRieux."

Jeff hesitated, then walked over to David. Jeff cleared his throat to get David's attention and said, "Uh, Pops, I think that's just the mirror."

"Oh, oh. Oh yeah. The light's tricky in here, isn't it?"

"Yes. Yes, it is." Jeff pointed, "Toilet is right over there if you need to go."

"Oh great, I could stand to go a little bit," David said in a stage whisper.

Jeff made himself busy washing his hands and then waited by the door. He wondered if David had already forgotten his conversation with the mirror. He hoped so.

*   *   *   *   *

Lill was pretty sure she had found Susan's door. For the second time, just to make sure, she rechecked the number. From left to right she moved her finger below each digit as she whispered, "three-one-two," then tapped lightly on the partially closed door.

It swung open as she tapped, and she could see Susan sitting up in the bed.

"Come on in, Mama-Lill," Susan said.

Lill was beaming as she walked over to Susan's bedside and gently cradled Susan's hand between her two. "How are you doing, Honey?"

"Oh, I'm okay, I guess. You know; you've been through this yourself. I'm excited . . . but a little scared at the same time. I guess I'll just be glad to get this part over with. Once I've got this little guy in my arms, none of this will matter. Listen though, there's something I wanted to ask you about, if it's alright?"

"Sure, Hun. What is it?"

Susan patted the bed. "Sit down here, Mama-Lill."

Lill wiggled her way up onto the side of the bed.

Susan continued, "Mama-Lill . . . what was Granddad talking about downstairs when they rolled me off? He seemed to be really bothered about something. We've all seen him confused and agitated before, but this seemed different. He called me Edna. What was he talking about?"

Lill turned her head slightly and looked down at the floor; her head bobbed very slightly up and down as she thought.

"Is this something you mind talking about?" Susan asked.

"No, no, Hun. It's okay," Lill said, returning her attention to Susan. "It's a little bit of a long story. I think parts I still don't know; probably never would even if Dave didn't have memory. Anyway, let's not talk about with Dave. We haven't talked about in years, but would just upset him. Besides, all past now."

Susan hesitated. She knew when Lill was flustered, her speech sometimes got a little garbled, but Susan really wanted to know and thought this might be as good a time as any for this type of conversation, so she proceeded, asking, "Well, what happened; who is Edna?"

"Edna was Dave's sister. She died a long time ago, long before you were born. Your mother, Kay, was just a child at the time . . . maybe a teenager. I guess she was about 15 when Edna died. A few years after, Edna's son died. I think he was only about . . . eleven."

Lill paused. Her head began the bobbing motion again. "Poor little guy . . . he didn't have much of a life. Her husband, Hank, really took it hard—his folks too. I wish we had kept in touch better; they were good people. We did for a while, but we just had different lives, different towns. After the boy died, we just lost touch. David used to stop in on them sometimes when he was in their area. They were farmers, had a small farm near Murfreesboro. But, you know, after a while, I think his visits just made everyone sad. Edna was really only thing they had in common. I think she and her boy were all they thought about when Dave visited, even when they talked about something else. I think Hank's folks are gone now; not really sure what became of Hank."

"What happened to Edna? Why did Granddad call me her?"

"Well, Honey . . . couple of things, I guess. In some ways, you look a lot like Edna. You have some of her features. A lot of the DeRieuxs do—your mom too. I think that's why Dave confuses you so easily with your mother. That and your voice. You two sound a lot alike sometimes."

"Well, what else? Why was Granddad so worried? Something was really bothering him. It scared me a little."

Lill tried to smile, but it looked more like a grimace. "Honey, I don't know that this is a good time to talk about this. You know how Dave gets. He's okay. Let's talk about this later. I promise."

"Come on, Mama. I'd really like to know—unless I'm being too noisy. Oht! Oh . . . Give me a minute . . . Contractions."

Lill was happy to wait. This was perfectly normal, and Susan was doing great. The contractions lasted only a few moments; however, the span of a particular moment can vary dramatically among the various participants.

When the contractions were over, Susan continued, "Wow, they're getting a little rougher. Maybe I'm closer than they think."

Lill patted Susan's hand. "You're doing fine, Honey."

"Mom, tell me about Edna. What happened to her?"

Lill thought for a moment. Susan was about to say something when Lill started— "Edna had a miscarriage. She had a bad hemorrhage and died. There were a lot of other things wrong though. Hadn't been the miscarriage, something else would have got her. It was her second miscarriage, after her son was born. The first time—miscarriage—it was bad too. But they got her in time. He had to give her transfusions—blood. The second time, by the time they got to hospital—they lived far out on a farm— she was gone."

Susan waited before speaking. She hoped that Lill would continue, but she didn't. Susan said, "So, is it because I'm in labor and kind of look like Edna that's stirred all this up with Granddad?"

"I guess so, Honey."

"I've never heard any of this before. You said something else was wrong with Edna; tell me about her. What was wrong?"

"Well, I don't know what the material claim was. Dave might, or used to. I just know that a few months after her son was born, everything just seemed to go wrong for her."

"Like what?"

"Well, a few months after she got home from the hospital, her face swelled up on one side. Big water blisters—her eyes turned black. Then her hair fell out. It grew back, but ever after that, she was always tired. She and Hank tried to have other children. But like I told you, she had miscarriages. Second one killed her."

"What happened to her son; what was his name?"

"They called him Little Hank."

"Well, what happened to Little Hank? What caused him to die so young?"

"He was a slow boy. I think he was smart enough, but like his mom, was always tired. Take naps instead of play."

Again, Susan waited for Lill to continue. "Mom," she prodded.

"Must have had cancer, poor little guy."

"Is that what they said?"

"I'm not sure. I know you don't know Christian Science, since your mom left the church when she was young—before she got married and had you. But we don't like to give a label to disease. If you have to call it something, I'm pretty sure it was some sort of cancer. Lymph nodes under arms would swell up. Had tumor, above knee, I think. Poor little guy. Lost leg . . . but didn't help. I think less than year after that he died."

"How did that happen to both of them? Did they get into something, some sort of carcinogen, something on the farm, their water; fertilizers or pesticides, or something like that, that caused all of that?"

As Lillian took in a long, slow, deep breath, her head rose up a bit and her eyes met Susan's. Sadness and exhaustion had crept deeply and unmistakably into Lillian's eyes. Susan's eyes were filled with an odd blend of compassion and eager curiosity. As the air went slowly back out of Lillian, her shoulders curved inward; her head lowered. Her eyes, momentarily disconnected from her mind, pointed towards her lap. In a low but clearly audible voice she said, "It was the clinic. Edna went to a pregnant . . . pregnancy clinic . . . run by Vanderbilt doctors— Nashville. I know it was. Had her drink radioactive something. Some experiment they were running about good nutrition. Never told the girls what they were doing. Said the drink was something good for them. Nobody, except for Dave, seemed to care at the time . . . and even he didn't know how bad until too late. Didn't seem to try to cover it up either, though. Vanderbilt made a news deal about it in the papers after it had all been done. Dave was furious when he read the story. Nobody cared. I guess lots of girls who went there stayed okay—I don't know. Edna wasn't only one. I remember him saying, 'these people know better.' He talked to a lot back then—at Oak Ridge—when he was an agent. Didn't say much specific to me, couldn't, but I know he thought a lot was wrong. Enough to go around, I think. Enough to make him leave the FBI. It was a difficult time. He loved the bureau, the people in his office, the work that they did; but something went wrong. Something made him leave. He told everyone it was just time to do something less dangerous, better hours."

Lill stopped. She looked up at Susan with a funny, embarrassed sort of expression, like she had been caught daydreaming and talking to herself.

Lill said, "Sorry, Honey. I'm rambling on. These are precious times; should be happy times. Let's just keep this to ourselves."

"Okay, Grandma-Lill. I'd like to hear more sometime though, if it's okay."

"Yes. Yes . . . Okay. I should get back to Granddad. He gets restless fast."

"Grandma, how do you do it? Are you two okay?"

"We're fine, Honey. Thanks. We'll see you tomorrow. Kay and Mike will be here. They'll bring us. Everything is going to be fine. You'll See"

Chapter 8

VanZant and Mallard

Vanderbilt University Hospital Prenatal Clinic
Nashville, TN
July 1946

VanZant reflected on Mallard's question: Had he seen someone in the waiting room that he might know, someone who would be of interest? What the hell was Mallard talking about? Making himself comfortable, VanZant rocked back in the soft-leather swivel chair and glared across the desk at Mallard, who was sitting in one of the two visitor's chairs facing the desk. VanZant rested his right elbow on the chair's padded arm and cradled the side of his face between his thumb and index finger. Mallard, squirming in his own visitor's chair, was not so comfortable. VanZant thought Mallard looked like a scared little dope—probably like one of Mallard's scared, nervous patients—scared of what they had just learned, scared of the unknown yet to come, looking for guidance, looking for someone who spoke with confidence, someone with answers that would, hope upon hope, allay their fears and reassure them that everything would be all right.

VanZant, to Mallard's relief, finally broke the silence. "What the hell are you talking about, Mallard? How would I know anyone in your waiting room? It's a collection of the biggest nobodies on the planet."

"David DeRieux! That ring a bell?" Mallard blurted, raising his eyebrows, tilting his head slightly to one side, and jutting his face forward at the end of his question, as if punching the air with his face would add emphasis to his concerns.

VanZant remained unmoved in his chair. "No. The name means nothing to me. Should it?"

"You tell me; he's an FBI agent."

Looking more impatient than worried, VanZant said, "Well, I don't know him. I don't know everyone in the FBI. Who is he; what's he doing here? Get to the point, Mallard."

"The point is, I've got a patient here," Mallard looked down at his chart, "Edna Miller. Mrs. Miller tells me her big brother, David DeRieux, is an FBI agent, and that he was here, probably sitting in the waiting room, waiting to take our little Miss Edna out to lunch. For all I know, you might have walked right past him."

"So, what if I did? Is that it?"

"What do you mean, 'Is that it?' You're here; he's here; that's a lot. It's not like we're just handing out cotton candy here; we're giving these gals some pretty serious shit."

"Look, Mallard, don't get all wiggy on me. It's probably just what you said; the guy's just here with his sister, and then they're going to lunch. No big deal. Don't get your bowels in an uproar. So what if we're all here; we've all got good reason to be here. You've got permission to use my isotopes; I've got permission to make them available to you. Look, it's not like we're feeding them straight plutonium, it's just iron-59 for Christ's sake. And, on top of that, we've got the Rockefeller Foundation's blessings on all this. Nobody's going to look twice at this."

The two stared at each other for a moment. VanZant rocked forward in his chair, shifting his arms into a teepee shape with his elbows on the chair's arms, his fingertips making the pointed top. "You given this Edna gal some of your special drink?"

"Of course, you know we have."

"Well, maybe cut back on hers a little. Maybe best not to give her anymore."

"Wasn't planning on giving her anymore. She just took the last of what we had planned for her. She's had plenty."

"So, what's the problem? You've given that junk to lots of gals. They're lab rats; they're never going to know. Nobody's going to know. And if they find out, if something goes wrong, nobody important is going to care; you'll see. Look Mallard, we need these studies to build up our bona fides—our credentials. We're building a pyramid here, and, for now, this is part of our base. We need these kinds of programs; they're what we're building on. Without these programs, the money stops flowing."

Mallard fidgeted in his chair. "I hope you're right. This stuff, this stuff we're giving these gals—it isn't Kool-Aid you know. Like I said, she's had plenty; she's had a lot. Those batches we got at first from the MIT cyclotron, those were iron-59. That was our plan, you know; even though I still think giving these gals 59 is pressing our luck. But this last batch from the Oak Ridge pile, well, it's looking like there's a lot of iron-55 mixed in with it. My god, we've gone from giving them an isotope with a half-life of forty-seven days, to one with a half-life of five years . . . FIVE YEARS!"

Mallard and VanZant, once again, sat in silence staring at each other. Mallard had wound himself up, but slowly the air seeped out of him, and in a quiet, deflated voice, Mallard said, "Look, sometimes I worry that we might be getting a little ahead of ourselves here. Maybe we should just slow this all down a little."

VanZant, his impatience turning into disappointment, rapidly approaching disgust, shook his head and said, "Look Mallard, you might be too nervous a guy for Washington. Maybe you should just stay here in Nashville; stay here in Nashville and go back to your regular practice."

"Now hold on," Mallard recoiled, suddenly worried that the rug was about to be pulled out from under him. "You've made promises to me; I've made plans. I've about got my house sold. You can't back out on me now."

"Okay, okay," VanZant said in a quasi-soothing voice. "You're still going to Washington; you'll be getting some of the big money soon. Just keep your cool. If you're going to fit in with my group there, with what all we're doing, you're going to have to learn to keep your cool. This . . . this here . . . this is no big deal."

"I know, I know," answered Mallard, somewhat mollified. "But still, would you drink any of this stuff? Would you let your wife or daughter drink any of this stuff? Or better yet, would you want little Miss Miller's big brother to find out what we're doing here? I know that we've got our butts covered ten ways to Sunday with all sorts of permission slips, but really, if push comes to shove, well, it's hard to justify the risks that we're putting these gals through with what little we're probably going to get out of it."

The two stared at each other for a long moment. Mallard caved, "Okay, okay; sorry. Forget it. You're right. It's probably nothing. Forget what I just said—shouldn't have even brought it up."

"Look, Mallard, we've talked about this before. If you're going to Washington, you're going to have to change your whole way of thinking. We don't need good results; we need good projects. And by good projects, I mean projects that cost a lot of money. Hell, how do you think we make money? We're not some corporation struggling to make a profit; we're government, and the last thing we need to be worried about is our results. Our results, they're as good or as bad as we tell people they are, and, for that matter, we don't say much. And if we do get pressed on something—it's pretty rare—but, if we do, we tell them, whoever, how important our work is and what great progress we're making. Hell, everything we do here bumps up against secrecy—the war effort, beating the communists, the public good. First sign of trouble, all we have to do is reach over and pull that blanket over us."

VanZant rocked all the way back in his chair, taking in a deep breath. His head, following the rocking motion of his body, tilted back; his face looked up at the ceiling. Still leaning back in his chair, he exhaled loudly as he lowered his head back down to where his chin was resting on his chest. Facing Mallard, VanZant said, in a voice typically used to explain something simple to a second grader, "Look, Mallard, you're missing the point. Of course, if you spot something or someone who might be trouble for us, of course say something. Just don't get all wiggy about things that aren't, or probably aren't, problems."

Mallard held up his hands. "Okay, okay. I said I'm sorry. Let's just forget it."

VanZant rocked forward, plopping his forearms on Mallard's desk. As the weight of his body shifted over the desk and onto his arms, his shoulders raised up to his ears, his head sunk into his body, and the top of his back hunched into a slight curve. It was time to put this silliness of Mallard's to bed; it was time to lay down the law. Sternly, VanZant said, "Alright, Mallard, just remember, Washington is full of important people. They're there because that's where the real power is; that's where the serious money is; that's where the serious decisions are made. Hell, it's amazing how much money flows through that place. Think of it, all that federal money. All that money is filtered through Washington first, before it goes anywhere else. The people there are the ones who decide where it goes, how much goes, how much stays. Lots and lots of it stays, gets stuck there, never leaves, gets skimmed right off the top—you know, kind of a service fee that nobody even gives a second thought to. I remember my first few days there. To think about it from a distance is one thing, but to see it up close, to be right there where it's happening, right there in the private rooms where the real decisions are made; well, it gives you a whole different perspective. All that money . . . flowing through Washington . . . that big wide river of money . . . hell, all you have to do is reach down and scoop out a little as it flows past. It's so easy. But first; but first, you've got to get yourself a toehold; you've got to get yourself established—entrenched. That's what we're doing now. Once we're established, once we've been there a while, we become entrenched. We become part of an unquestioned system. If we're seen there long enough, eventually, no one will give us a second thought. Anyway, that's what we're doing now, and we've got a good start. We're almost there, but not quite. We've got to keep this money flowing through our little niche in the system, get the system used to seeing it flowing in our direction. We can't let anything or anyone stop that. Soon, we'll be just another part of the status quo, part of what has become expected. Once you've been in Washington for a while, you'll understand. It's much easier to start something new than to end something old. And to start something new, hell, all it takes is a little guts."

Feeling proud of himself, VanZant gave a smug little chuckle and continued, "Hell, it's easy; it's so easy. It'd be hard if you were pulling money directly out of someone's pocket. They wouldn't let you do that; they'd call that stealing. But, by the time it gets to Washington, it's really nobody's money. It's nobody's and everybody's; it's public money, but the public doesn't control it; Washington does. And no one in Washington really cares if a little is scooped out here and there, as long as it doesn't interfere with their own gambit. It's so easy. In the first few days you'll be amazed. After a month or two, well, you'll never be able to go back. Playing small-ball for a living? Hell no. After a year in Washington, you'd feel too much like a chump to do something as stupid as that. Yep, with public money, you're either on the inside or on the outside. Lot more people on the outside—chumps and suckers. Yep, chumps and suckers. Lots of powerless people out there, and after a month in Washington, you sure as hell won't want to be one of them. Hell, even an assistant to a nobody in D.C. can have amazing power and influence. Yep, after a year in D.C., you'll never look back.

"So, think about it, Mallard. Think long and hard before you go doing or saying anything stupid. There's huge money to be had, but not if you're stupid, not if you're a chump. And one more thing—that river of money that we're dipping into, it's even better than most of the other rivers that flow through D.C., because ours is a secret river. That's right. Think about all that money that goes through Washington; then think of the massive amount spent on secret shit—top secret shit, shit that hardly anyone is watching.

"That's right; the people who are writing our checks—the Senators and Congressmen—most of those dumb-asses don't really know what they're buying. And really, they don't care; they've got their own scams going. As far as our part goes, they don't care. They're just told it's important—so important that even they can't be told what it's for. A few on some of the special oversight committees think they know, but they don't. It's too funny. Those dumb-asses think they know what's going on; they think that they are in control. It's too funny—all of those programs, all those huge budgets, this huge amount of cash that hardly anyone is watching and virtually no one is allowed to talk about openly.

"It's beautiful, really beautiful, for us anyway. Think of it—a system that collects money from people in the name of keeping them safe, and then tells them it's too secret to tell them how it's spent. A system that no one questions, and, if they do, we have a deck full of aces that we can play—national security, it's a safety issue, oh, and best of all, it's to keep our children safe. We're talking about a system that forces people to pay into it, tells them it's for their own good, tells them it's too secret to talk about, but assures them that responsible people have oversight, and then pays a guy like you to feed poison to a young, wide-eyed, pregnant woman; don't tell her what it's really for, but tell her that it's for her own good, and then have her thank you for it. What do you think the chances are of a system like that catching us?

"Yep, go to Washington, Mallard. Keep your cool; don't get wiggy on me. Really, all you have to do is to act confident; act like you're really important. Before long, that's what everyone will think—that you're important. The more important you act, the more important everyone will think you are. Hell, before long, you'll start believing it yourself.

"So, that's it. Do your job and we'll get rich. Forget about the little Miss Ednas of the world, and forget about their big brothers. Hell, if this DeRieux fellow does become a problem, well, you never know. Maybe we'll just get him to come to work for us. Probably wouldn't take as much as you might think.

"Anyway, like I said, forget about them. Leave them in the trenches where they belong. It's enough for them; they're happy there. We, we know better; don't we?"

Chapter 9

Mihail

Nashville, TN
July 1946

Mihail Nikolayevich Grigory was a Russian spy. He sat quietly on a bench, at a bus stop, across the street from the Vanderbilt Clinic, pretending to read a newspaper.

Other than being a spy from a different country, and a hostile country at that, he was much like anyone else. That is to say, he certainly looked like anyone else—anyone else who might sit at a bus stop, on a busy street in Nashville, Tennessee.

A man so visibly average, so common, so expected in his environment, that he was completely unremarkable, and thus, rendered virtually imperceptible to the common observer. Had he been sitting empty-handed and naked on the bench, he would be loudly visible to all; yet, by merely covering himself in a common cloth and a common ritual, he became temporarily invisible to the world.

That was what he needed people to see—an innocuous man simply reading his paper, catching up on the happenings in his community and throughout the world. It was all there before him, printed clearly on the pages of the newspaper held upright in his hands. Anyone taught to read could construe, through that medium, the world in its entirety: news, sports, business, politics, gossip, religion, astrology, editorial, comedy. From birth announcements to obituaries, it was all there—all the elements of life and death, clearly presented in black and white. Black and white—how clear, how simple, how pure; how deceptive, how incomplete.

As expected, no one brushing past Mihail saw the red, the Soviet Red, the infiltrator. Dressed as he was, even if he had been the devil himself, no one walking by, or even sharing the bench with him, would have recognized him as such. How readily we accept the apparent as truth; how rarely we question that to which we are accustomed; how often we believe that all we see is all there is and all that matters. But in terms of reality, black and white, at most, presents only a shadowy clue on the wall of a cave. Reality was not the image that passersby saw—a man reading a paper—nor was reality printed on the pages Mihail held in his hands. Reality, at best, can only be glimpsed beyond the top of those pages; and then, only after a process, a progression through a series of filters and diversions. Sensations, memories, imagination, fear, desire, time—all conspire in the creation of our realities.

The reality for Mihail was that time was running out. Each day, the fiction that he presented to the world became harder to sustain. For him, each day, as truth clashed with deception, the world grew more dangerous. He watched over the top of his paper as a car pulled up and parked in front of the clinic. David DeRieux got out of the car and entered the clinic. Hidden beneath Mihail's suitcoat, a wave of relief cascaded throughout his body. Until that moment, he had worried that, for any number of reasons, David might not have shown up there that day. Mihail's breathing became easier, longer, deeper, slower. The muscles in his chest, arms, and legs relaxed. The rigidity in his face tempered, but not so that anyone would notice, as he remained well hidden behind his newspaper. And even if someone did happen to glance at his face, chances are, the miniscule changes would leave no impression, as most are not attuned to such subtleties.

Mihail felt it deep within his bones; it wouldn't be long now. If the information that he had painstakingly gathered over the last several months was correct, soon, David would be leaving the clinic with his sister Edna, and the two would go somewhere for lunch. He assumed that Edna was already inside the clinic. He had watched several women as they entered, but he had no idea what Edna looked like. That wasn't important; she would be with David when they came out, and he would know her by him.

But then something unexpected happened; VanZant entered the Clinic. Like the Devil himself, he seemed to have come out of nowhere. After David entered the building, Mihail had narrowed his scope of focus from the entire block—looking for arrivals coming from any direction—to just looking for departures coming from a singular doorway, a careless and highly unusual lapse for Mihail. When VanZant unexpectedly appeared in Mihail's self-limited frame, his reflex was to take in a quick, short breath and hold it for a moment as he began to process the unexpected.

This is bad, he thought, *very bad.*

Well, maybe not. Maybe it's just a coincidence that they're both here at the same time; surely that's it. But if this is planned, if David is here to meet with VanZant, if they're colluding . . . No! That can't be it. It's got to be a coincidence. David can't be a part of this; they're here for different things. David's here just to meet his sister for lunch; VanZant's not here for that. But wait, what if Edna is David's cover, his excuse for being here to meet with VanZant, off the record? No, that can't be. If David is in cahoots with VanZant, if David knows what's going on here, then surely he wouldn't let his sister come here . . . unless . . . unless . . . if he is a part of this, it would be easy to arrange for his sister to come here, get the benefits, the prenatal care, yet keep her safe from the radiation. Would he do that? Would David do something like that? It doesn't fit; no, it just doesn't fit with what I've seen. He'd have no part of this. I've watched him. I've watched him. I've watched him and his wife, his friends, people he's friendly with. I've listened to his conversations. I've watched him; I've watched what he does when he thinks no one is looking . . . he's a good man. There's no way he and VanZant are working together . . . But if they are; if they are . . . then I'm in trouble. If they are, it changes everything.

Mihail's brain went round and round. As one part reviewed all that he knew, all that he had learned about David, another part thought to occasionally turn a page of the newspaper that he was not reading. Everything he had learned, everything that he knew about David, no matter how he put the various pieces together, arranging them in all the possible ways, each permutation painted the same picture—David had to be a good man, a decent man.

The part of Mihail's brain that was mechanically turning the pages saw David in the doorway, coming out of the clinic. It was like an alarm clock going off, bringing the bulk of his brain back to the here and now.

That girl with David . . . yes, that has to be Edna . . . kind of even looks like him, a little bit anyway. Wonder where they'll go for lunch; hope they walk. It'll be a lot easier if they just go somewhere close; lot easier not to have to follow them in a car. Good, he's walked past his car.

Mihail stood up, looking like a man at ease, folded his newspaper under his arm, and proceeded down the sidewalk, keeping some distance and people between himself and David. After two blocks, in the middle of the third block, David and Edna entered a Woolworth's. *Ah,* Mihail said to himself, *that's it, good; they're eating at the lunch counter.* Mihail slowed a little, putting a bit more space and time between him and David, now that he knew where they were going.

Woolworth's was perfect for what Mihail had in mind. It was a huge, open-air, five and dime store that ran the depth of the block, with storefront doors and checkout registers accessing both of the parallel streets. Most of the display shelves and clothes racks were low enough so that any standing adult could be seen from one end of the store to the other; yet, to disappear for a moment, all one needed to do was stoop down for a look at something on a lower shelf. The side walls, from a hardwood floor to the high ceiling, were a red, well-finished brick and mortar. Both store fronts, from waist height to ceiling, were glass from side to side. The large windows, combined with all the florescent lights hanging high up on the ceiling, gave the store a bright, clean, open appeal.

As David and Edna entered the store, the luncheonette section was nestled against the side wall to the left. A couple of booths ran along the storefront window. Beginning where the booth section ended, the grill and countertop area paralleled the side wall. Stainless steel refrigerators, coffee pots, deep fryers, and gas grills lined the red-brick wall. Customers, sitting on padded swivel-stools bolted in place to the floor, ate at the long countertop as they watched the backs of the two short-order cooks, with their white paper hats, hustling to keep up with the lunchtime rush. It was a show of constant motion as the cooks worked their way through a line of order-tickets dangling from a stainless-steel bracket mounted above the grills while waitresses busied themselves between the customers and the cooks. As customers finished their meals, a busboy helped clear the dishes and worked the dishwasher and sink area under and behind the front counter. A small cloud of steam would rise whenever the busboy opened one of the dishwashing machines at the end of its cycle. Hot, damp, but clean, he would then place the renewed dishware back into rotation.

By the time Mihail entered the store, David and Edna were just sliding into the back-corner booth against the window, with David, his back against the wall, facing outward towards the middle of the store. Mihail turned to the right and headed for the opposite wall. He didn't think David had seen him and was certainly not going to expose himself by looking back until he had some cover. Against the wall ahead of him and a little to his left was the book and magazine section—perfect. The magazine racks were slightly higher than most of the other display shelves in the store, affording Mihail the opportunity to shield the bulk of his body behind one. He squatted a little, pretending to scan the selection of magazines, as he peeked over the top of the rack towards David. No, David had not seen him. David's attention was divided between chatting with his sister and selecting something from the menu.

Good, Mihail had some time. He had played variations of this encounter out in his head a thousand times; but still, he needed a moment to compose himself. Seeing VanZant had rattled him more than he would have expected. Anyway, he would wait, at least until after David and Edna had ordered their food.

He scanned the magazine selection again, this time actually reading the covers. America! It was amazing; they had magazines about everything. He picked up a thick one that featured new home designs and building tips. He flipped through the pages; it was an assortment of floorplan designs and photographs of the finished products, inside and out. He stopped on a half-page, glossy, color photo of a family sitting around a dinner table. The photo had captured a familiar moment, the start of a meal. It was a setting that Mihail had seen portrayed often in advertisements, and, for a time, he had wondered if it was indeed typical or merely some form of propaganda or wishful thinking. The wife in the photo, still wearing her apron, pearls, and heels, had apparently just set a perfectly browned turkey before her husband, seated at the head of the table. A freckled young boy and a girl with a long, blond ponytail looked on with eager anticipation at their father, carving knife and fork in hand, poised to make the first slice. The table was covered with plates, bowls filled with steaming vegetables, fresh bread, and glasses of cool milk. In the middle of the table stood a large, fresh-flower centerpiece. The luxury of it all was almost beyond Mihail's comprehension. Everything, down to the last detail, was perfect. And to top it off, reflected from a mirror hung on the wall, a fireplace could be seen in the background of an adjacent room. Yes, he thought, these pictures are true. He had walked through the well-stocked grocery stores and ridden through the sprawling neighborhoods. Turkeys were affordable, and houses were springing up everywhere.

Mihail's thoughts returned, as they often did, to his family in Moscow. He pictured them in their apartment—his wife and young son, sitting around the small, plain, metal table in their cold, cramped kitchen. They didn't drink cool milk; they drank cups of hot tea—hot, weak tea in mismatched cups. A bowl of potato soup or some sort of potage, and a chunk of hard, black bread was before each. Sometimes, if they were lucky, a little butter, sausage, cheese, or jam. *Funny*, he thought, *I rarely picture myself with them. I'm so rarely at home, and . . . I almost always picture them as being cold. It's the middle of summer, and in my mind, they're cold—cold; cold and grey. There is no color to our life . . . except perhaps the red. Yes, there is too much red.*

Well, he reconciled to himself, *they are better off than most. At least they are in Moscow. Yes, at least they have a small apartment in Moscow. Small, yes; small and modest.* Modesty was the key to staying alive in Stalin's Russia. Too small, too poor; and you would starve, freeze, and die. Too big, too successful, too much ambition; then envy or fear would raise its ugly head. Envy from those who had less. Fear from those who had more. The wretches' struggle for life; the affluents' fright that those below might usurp power—how many prominent people had disappeared in the purges? How many of the meek and meager had died in the famines? There was no way to know for sure. Everyone knew that the Soviet Newspapers were not to be trusted; even though, in a backwards sort of way, elements of truth can be gleaned from a known lie. But the American Papers, they were trickier. Most of what they printed was accepted as being true; however, there was just enough that was false, just enough skullduggery mixed in, to prevent them from being taken as gospel. But sometimes, it was the intentional omissions that were the most misleading.

The American reporter, Walter Duranty, popped into Mihail's mind. Mihail closed the magazine that he had been holding, placed it back on the rack, and turned around to look at the large selection of newspapers on the opposite side of the aisle. There it was, *The New York Times*. In the early 1930s, Duranty, as *The*

New York Times' Moscow correspondent, had written several articles denying the hardships and famines that were occurring within the Soviet Union. Millions had died, yet Duranty had faithfully reported to his readers that reports of such privations were 'exaggeration or malignant propaganda.' *Malignant propaganda,* Mihail repeated to himself. Stalin had no greater minion than Duranty. And why shouldn't Duranty be believed, after all, he had won the coveted Pulitzer Prize for his portrayals. Even President Roosevelt had been influenced by what he read in the papers.

The United States and The Soviet Union, Mihail reflected, were two different worlds, isolated from one another by a contrived barrier with heavily guarded portals. The individuals occupying those separate worlds, their experiences, their realities, did not readily pass through those portals unaltered. No, the Americans could hardly understand the lives of the Russians any more than the Russians could understand the Americans. It is hard to fully understand what has never been experienced.

Mihail was one of the few who had experienced both worlds. He thought again about the life of a Russian. It was commonplace for people to disappear. First, their bodies would be taken; then, their official records, their history—all would vanish. If memory of them could be successfully obliterated, then, eventually, they would cease to exist as a person. The State had that power. One day, a person would be in a picture. The next day, there would simply be an empty, blurred out space in the photo where they had once been. A person would become a non-person. Stalin's world was a zero-sum game. Ambition, knowledge, influence— whether real or imagined—could take you to great heights, but it could also kill you faster and more brutally than starvation.

Yes, thought Mihail, *best not to be noticed. It is a balancing act—an act that no one should be forced to perform. A balancing act between life and death. An act, a performance in which many in the audience, if they cannot be the one to rule, then want to see the notables killed or tormented. Why, why? What created this kind of world? What power is needed to break this spiral? Cruelty breeding cruelty. Depravity doesn't breed compassion; would compassion ever breed depravity? Starvation doesn't nourish the soul. What force is it that attracted the Romans to the horrors of the Coliseum? Did that desire originate from within or from without?*

Activity at David's table interrupted Mihail's rambling thoughts. He watched as a waitress unloaded an armful of plates onto David and Edna's table. He decided to give David a few more minutes, time to eat a few bites of his lunch before being interrupted. *A few bites to take the edge off his appetite before being pulled away—would that be better or worse?*

Okay, it's time. Mihail left the newspapers and magazines behind and began his walk across the store towards David. Now, Mihail was in the open. He didn't want to surprise or startle David, so he walked slowly and looked directly at David, trying his best to maintain a pleasant smile. To his surprise, the smile came more naturally than he had anticipated.

David noticed Mihail when Mihail was a little more than midway across the store. Mihail could see that David had just taken a bite from his hamburger. David, upon seeing Mihail, set the hamburger back on its plate and finished chewing the bite taken, never lowering his gaze from Mihail once he had spotted him. Of course, David knew at once that something was up. Both knew that Russian spies did not routinely walk up to FBI agents; that's not how the game was played.

Edna noticed that David had stopped eating and turned to see what had captured his attention. David stood as Mihail approached the table. Mihail thought a handshake might be a little too bold, so he said, in as calm and pleasant a voice as he could muster, "Hello, Mr. DeRieux. How are you?"

"I'm fine," David replied in a non-committal voice.

"Forgive me for interrupting your lunch," Mihail said, looking down at Edna. "I'm Michael, Michael Johnson. Your brother and I know each other from work."

"Are you an FBI agent too?" asked Edna.

"Heavens no," Mihail answered with a slight chuckle, trying to keep the meeting as light as possible. Then to David, "Mr. DeRieux, David, would it be possible for me to talk with you for a moment . . . in private, if you please?"

"Of course," David replied, extending his arm and open hand outward in a low graceful sweep, like an usher showing a patron to his seat, or a jailer introducing a prisoner to his cell.

"Thank you." Mihail knew that David would not turn his back to him, so he nodded his head to Edna in a polite gesture, turned, and began a slow walk back towards the middle of the store.

David, keeping his eye on Michael, raised his index finger to Edna as if to say, "Give me a minute," and followed Michael. Mihail, sensing David behind him, turned his head slightly and said over his shoulder, "Perhaps we could just step over here for a moment—over here to the magazine rack. There is something that I would very much like to show you."

David followed in silence. When they got to the rack, Mihail found the magazine that he had previously viewed and began to flip through the pages.

"Please, allow me a minute," he said. "I was just a moment ago looking at something that I would like to share with you."

David, silent, with no expression but that of patience, watched Michael's face as he searched the pages.

"Ah-ha, here it is; yes, yes, this is it," said Mihail as he turned the magazine for David to see. It was the picture of the family about to eat their turkey dinner. David glanced at the photo, keeping his peripheral vision alert for any movement from Michael.

After taking in the photo, David responded, "Yes, it's a nice picture."

Mihail, with a degree of enthusiasm, said, "Yes, nice, nice; very nice."

David, looking directly at Michael, again in his non-committal voice, asked, "What can I do for you, Mr. Johnson—Mr. Michael Johnson, is it?"

Mihail turned the magazine page back towards himself, and the photo seemed to absorb him. His smile, his veneer, morphed into solemnity.

In a voice, not so much sad as serious, Mihail said, "I have good family . . . but not this. I will never have this. My wife, my son—they will never have this. Not in Soviet Union. I believe there is great truth in this photo." He raised his head from the magazine and then looked back and forth at the array of magazines on display. "Yes, I look at these racks, these racks of magazines. These are America. Yes, I believe this is truth of America. Of course, of course, I know this is not all . . . but this is her soul. This is what America wants to be. I want this for my family.

Mihail gently closed the magazine, set it back in its place, raised his head, looked eye to eye with David, and said, "Mr. DeRieux, sir . . . with your help, I would very much like to defect."

Chapter 10

David and Michael Talk

Nashville, TN
July 1946

David and Mihail, each taking close measure of the other, stood looking eye to eye in thoughtful silence. David maintained a poker face; Mihail showed a slight smile.

David studied the smile. *What is going on here*, he wondered. All the obvious questions were in play. David thought through the possibilities. *So, he says he wants to defect. Is this guy just looking for a better life? Is it as simple as that, or is this some part of a bigger play? Could we flip this guy, use him as a double . . . or is he trying to play us?*

Relief, David thought; *yes, that is what I'm seeing in this man's face—this man who calls himself Michael, Michael Johnson. His smile . . . it's just a slight smile, but with a trace of apprehension. Yes, it's a smile of relief. Relief—not victory, but hope of victory. Yes, hope of a good outcome, a good chance of success. Like a student turning in an important exam paper or a hopeful buyer turning in his first mortgage application. Yes,* thought David, *this is a student who has studied hard; this is a buyer who has good credit; this is a person who has good reason for hope, but knows that fate may not be through with him yet. This is a smile of resignation, knowing that much of what can be done has been done, but also keenly aware that the next play is largely beyond his control.* David continued to study Michael's eyes. *No,* he thought, *I don't think this is deceit, not entirely anyway. Still, there are many cards yet to be turned over. We'll see.*

David spoke, "So, Mr. Johnson, you say that you would like to defect. What exactly does that mean; what exactly would you be defecting from?"

"I will tell you what you already know. I am, as you would say, a spy—a Soviet spy. Please, let me ask you something, David. I call you David, not out of disrespect, quite the opposite. I call you David because it is my hope that we are friends—that we become friends. Anyway, David, do you know the difference between truth and propaganda?"

"Please, Michael, tell me."

"It is quite simple. If you believe it, it is truth; if you don't believe it, it is propaganda. I believe that America is largely as it appears. America is this magazine rack. Americans see what they are, what they can become. They chose their own path, set their own goals. There is great happiness in that. The Soviet Union, Russia—that is something different. Our leaders, like all leaders, have vision; but what that vision truly is, only they can know. But visions, most visions, are heavily influenced by the visions and actions of those who came before. Of course, there are twists and turns, but each build upon its past. We all begin in a world that we, ourselves, did not create, and in our youths, our minds are blank slates on which others write the first few chapters. Our histories—your American, my Russian; The East, The West— they are very different. To some extent, we choose what we read, but we can only choose from what is available. And so, The East, The West—we have different publishing houses; we read from very different books.

"Churchill described us Russians well. From your prospective, we are indeed 'a riddle, wrapped in a mystery, inside an enigma.' He said that of us because much of what we do makes no sense to those whose lessons have come from a different book. But there is a simple clue that unwraps at least a part of this riddle: Our border—our heavily guarded border. That is the clue; that is our undeniable truth. Our leaders, the ones who strive to control our vision, they tell us the guards, the border, are there for our good, to protect us from The West. But that is not so; that is not true. This barrier that they have created is not there to keep The West out; it is there to keep us in, to keep us from escaping, to keep us from escaping their vision of how we must live our lives. It is there to keep us ignorant of much that is good so that we will accept as necessary much that is evil. No, this barrier was not built to protect the Russian people from Western invaders. This barrier was built to protect the political elite from Western ideas.

"Yes, our leaders have vision. They have five-year plan. They have vision to modernize Russia. We have far to go, so, we have plan. Is plan good? Is our pain necessary? Who knows? Millions have starved; millions have died. A surgeon cuts off a person's arm—is it good; is it bad? A diseased arm, gangrenous—yes, cut it off. But what if the arm is cut off because the surgeon believes the patient might strangle him if the arm is allowed to grow strong?

"In Russia, who knows what is truth, what is propaganda? Those who live in the city know that people, many people, disappear. Cars and trucks arrive in the dead of the night. Storming footsteps up the stairs, in the hallways. Sometimes shouts and screams, sometimes begs and pleas for mercy, sometimes they go quiet. Sometimes the silence is the more frightful. The next morning, neighbors are gone. Even Party officials disappear. No one acknowledges they are gone; no one acknowledges they were ever there. No one dares to ask. But we know. We know many are tortured, killed, sent to the brutal Gulag camps of Siberia; not only for their failures, but often for their success. In the country, peasants are taken—taken off their farms and gathered into what they call collectives. They are told to grow food, but the food is not theirs. The food belongs to everyone; the food belongs to no one. The food belongs to the vision of our elite.

Yes, some, a very few, live well in Russia—their dachas, their health clubs, their private markets. But it is not spoken of, not openly. It is guarded. But wealth, wealth in your county is celebrated in the open, in the magazine racks, on billboards. In my county, it is carefully hidden behind closed doors, guards, walls. And still, there is one certainty, one tangible reality. There is a border between The East and The West. And at this border, there are guns and barbed wire. But the guns, the guns on our side of the wall . . . they are pointed inward."

Mihail paused and looked a bit sheepish. "I say too much, forgive me. My whole life, I dare not say what I think. And now, and now too much comes. But yes, yes; I would like to defect, to come to your side. Can you help me, David? Will you help me, David?"

David reached his hand out; the two shook. David, in a friendly but still guarded voice said, "Yes, Michael. I will see what I can do. But this is not up to me. I will have to pass this on to others. Really, a whole different agency will take this up, if they want. Is there anything else you wish for me to pass on, any specific type of offer that you would like for them to consider?"

"An offer, an offer? Yes, of course. There is always a price to be paid, is there not? A price to pay to get through the gate. How do you say? Someone must pay for the lunch, the dance, the piper. I will pay what I can. I hope it is sufficient. There is no one in my government I wish to protect; I will tell what I know. Of most value, you have many leaks. There are many, many players. I know only a few by name, but I know to some degree, roughly, where many are scattered. Your President, Roosevelt . . . yes, he is now dead, but he had, many times, very much the heart of a communist. His "New Deal", yes, very much the communist. A communist with a kind heart, perhaps, but his administration, yes, whether they meant to or not, they opened wide the door to communists. His government, your government, the bureaucracies . . . there are many communists now entrenched. People forget, even though the war has not been long over; people forget, we were allies. We, and the French, we were allies. Many in the French Resistance were communists, many with Roosevelt were communist.

"So yes, I pay price, gladly. But here is what I must buy: my freedom, and that of my wife and of my son. I have way to get them out—across the border and into Germany. From there I need your help. But there are many bad people in this world. There are many bad people on my side of the border, as there are many bad on your side as well. Our systems are different; but people, people are all made from the same stock. If you don't mind my asking, who will you report this to; who will judge; who will be the one that decides my fate?"

David, with a very slight shake of his head, said, "You're fishing. You know I can't tell you that."

Mihail hastily replied, "Of course, of course; you are quite correct, quite right . . . This game, this game we play, this dance of trust that we must do; it is very difficult, very dangerous. The first to say, to talk . . . the first to tip hand, show cards, is loser. The first, as you say, to stick neck out. But I go first; I make good-faith payment. This payment, it is for you alone; it is important. Dr. VanZant, he is not your friend."

Mihail watched closely for David's reaction. David was thinking, the wheels within his mind were turning. *Yes,* Mihail thought, *David knows VanZant—but how?* Mihail couldn't tell, but—*Yes, David knows VanZant.*

Mihail had to press for more, he continued, "You know him, this VanZant?"

David replied, "I'm not here to give you information, Mr. Johnson."

Mihail thought for a moment, weighing his options, then said, "You, you and VanZant . . . you were both in the Clinic today. Same time, yes?"

David answered in a deadpan manner, his suspicions rising. "If you say so."

Mihail took a deep, quiet breath; then, speaking softly said, "Neither of us should trust this VanZant. I know this, but I think that you, perhaps, do not. I do not believe that the two of you, how do you say, run in the same circles; yet today, yes today, you were both at the clinic. That made me uncomfortable, nervous you would say. I'm thinking you also have good reason to be nervous."

"What is it that you're trying to say?"

"I am saying, Mr. DeRieux, that if you are associated with VanZant, then you are not the man I am counting on you to be. If you are associate with VanZant, then I have made terrible mistake exposing myself to you."

David responded, "You say VanZant should make me nervous; why do you say that?"

Mihail paused, then said, "Many reasons." He paused again, gathering his thoughts; then, watching David's face closely, said, "Most immediate, in Clinic, they run experiments. They feed the young pregnant girls radiation, in a drink. It is dangerous; they pretend it is not. But still, they do not tell these girls what they do; they do not ask permission. Your Edna, very nice girl, very pretty girl. Have they told her? Has she told you? This is the world that men like VanZant create. They pretend to help others; they help only themselves."

David stared at Michael, trying to grasp what had just been said. It was such a blind-side comment that he wasn't sure just how to process it.

David wanted to blurt out, "Are you crazy?" Instead, he managed to say in a calm voice, "That sounds crazy."

Mihail said, as if stating the obvious, "Crazy, yes . . . world is crazy. And yet, we must do our best to live in this crazy world. What choice do we have?"

A wave of relief washed over Mihail. No, David and VanZant were not comrades. The alarm in David's face was obvious.

Mihail continued, "I must go. We talk here too long already. Not safe. I leave you with this. I will defect, yes. I will tell, and help, all that I can, but from the outside. My price—my price is that you help me, my wife, my son. You help us hide; you help us live. I know you must work under direction of superiors, but I have one condition, and it is important. You, only you, remain my contact, my liaison; at least until I, and my family, get settled. Take great care with whom you speak. As we say, both sides have good, both sides have bad. I have studied you; I believe that you are good man. I am putting my trust, and the life of my family, in you. There are men that we sometime, against our desire, must stand next to. But we—you and I—we must work to insulate each other from these men."

David looked in silence at Michael, then said, "Speaking in riddles isn't all that helpful. If you want me to understand something, speak clearly."

"Yes, yes; you are an honest man, Mr. DeRieux, and honest men speak clearly. VanZant is the center of a circle, a very dangerous circle, a circle with edges that cannot be seen. Be careful. I must go now."

David said, "How can I contact you?"

Mihail replied, "In a week, maybe two, I'll catch your eye. If good, if you are alone, scratch your ear and follow me. If not convenient, scratch your chin, and I will come back another day. But if you find that I am in danger, if I should run, if I should disappear, blow your nose into handkerchief."

David nodded in agreement and said, "Okay."

David remained at the magazine rack; his eyes followed Michael as he left the store. Then, still visible through the storefront window, David watched Michael walk down the street until he vanished from sight.

David turned his attention back to Edna. *What the hell? Surely the Clinic isn't exposing these women to radiation, running experiments without telling them. That's crazy! That's too hard to believe. But why would Michael lie? Why would he do that? He knows that I'll look into this. Why would he lie? If he really wants to defect, telling an obvious lie would ruin everything for him; why would he do that? But, oh my God, what if he's right?*

David started to make his way back to Edna. He had a few questions for her.

Chapter 11

Dorothy

Chattanooga, TN
April 2001

Joey dabbed the corner of a piece of generously buttered toast into the over-easy yoke of his egg, took a bite—being especially careful not to drip yoke onto the front of his shirt—and chewed leisurely as he returned his attention to the obituary page of his morning's newspaper.

Most of his mornings were becoming largely indistinguishable from one another, each unwinding with the sameness of a clockwork routine. Joey would wake, without an alarm, at roughly the same time, 7:30am, turn on the cable news channel, pee, brush his teeth, shave, shower, put on deodorant, comb his hair, and dress. The second-to-last step in getting dressed, putting on his socks, was without doubt the hardest part. Joey had a small barstool with a slick wooden top that was the exact best height for this process, which was becoming increasingly difficult as the months and years accelerated by. The stool was a little higher than a normal chair—about the limit onto which he could comfortably lift his foot. With his bare foot on top of the barstool, it required only a slight bend of his back and stretch of his arms to maneuver a sock over the tips of his toes and halfway up his foot. Then, the slickness of the smooth, wooden top allowed his semi-socked foot to easily slide up and back again as he pulled the sock over the rest of his foot and up tight over his sparsely haired calves. With the aid of his barstool, donning socks was doable; but for how long, he wondered? The rest was easy. His shoes were at their ready on the floor of his closet by the front door. With the assist of a long-handled shoe horn, he would slide his freshly socked feet into a pair of loosely laced, highly padded tennis shoes, pick his morning newspaper from a small rack installed on the wall outside his door in the hallway, walk down the hall, ride down the elevator, and then just a short easy stroll to the dining hall of his assisted living complex for a reasonable breakfast.

Enjoying his eggs, toast, orange juice, and coffee; Joey was pleased to see that the obituary section that morning had fewer listings than usual. He looked at the photo above the first one and then read the tribute:

> Charles A. Barnes, 82, of Chattanooga, went home to be with his Lord and Savior Jesus Christ on Saturday, April 14, 2001. He passed away peacefully at his home, with his wife and loving family at his side.

Lucky bastard, Joey muttered silently to himself. *He died with a trifecta: at home, family by his side, and he believed in an afterlife. Yeah, all three of his horses came in, and me, I'm not even holding a ticket. And this afterlife business—I don't know. Maybe there's still time for me, time 'to see the light', as they say. I don't know; I just don't know. Maybe I just think about it too much. But what's going to change; I'm never going to know, not for certain. I don't know; maybe at my age what you believe is more important than what is true. Sure would be nice to be one of those who believed. Sure wish that I could just believe—just believe, and let it go at that.*

He looked around the dining hall as he took a sip of coffee. There were about twenty-five or thirty of his fellow residents having an unhurried breakfast. It was getting close to 9:00; residents trickled in and out. It was rare for anyone to be in a hurry, but on those rare occasions when someone appeared to be rushing, it was immediately a topic of great interest and discussion. Joey's mind wandered, *how many here will die alone, be found in their room by a paid attendant? That wouldn't be too bad, if it was quick, or in their sleep. Better that than dying in some hospital, alone for days on end, only then to be ushered into the great beyond by nurses rushing into the room to silence that flat tone which announces the cessation of life as we know it.*

Why am I dwelling on this? This isn't like me. Maybe it's because I spent so much time in the hospital yesterday with the DeRieuxs?

Walking the halls of a hospital always hit Joey harder than he liked to admit, especially when he saw an elderly person left alone to navigate, without assistance, their last days. Alone—alone and probably confused. Alone, with no one there to hold their hand. No one there to say goodbye. No one there to say that everything will be all right. No one there to reassure them, to show them that they are loved. Some days, Joey worried that he would die too soon; other days, he worried that he might live too long.

A chill went through his body. He shook his head, took another sip of coffee, and forced his mind onto a happier topic—how good the coffee tasted, a dark, bold-roast; straight with no cream or sugar to dilute the flavor. The caffeine was kicking in; *life can be good,* he thought. He loved to people-watch and continued to gaze around the room. It was interesting to Joey to note patterns. In the dining hall, people generally ate their meals about the same time each day, favored the same tables and places at the tables, and generally clung together in small, well-defined cliques.

It wasn't like a cruise ship here, he thought to himself, *meeting and mingling with strangers, not having enough time to establish a routine, not enough time to wear a well-defined groove that, as it deepens, becomes easy to fall into and comfortable to stay within as the days, in an instant, become years. But the destination—maybe in that sense the living center is somewhat like a cruise ship—a ship taking its passengers to some destination. After all, the next destination for everyone here, like it or not, is the same place. Yes, that's it: a cruise ship in which most of the passengers feel confident as to where our little ship is ultimately docking. But some aren't so sure. I'm not so sure. And then there are others, a few, amazingly enough, who don't appear to care enough to give it any thought one way or the other, even though it is painfully clear that our voyage is nearing its end. But for those that think they know, there sure appears to be great comfort in that—knowing the destination, knowing that the stern but gracious captain will see them safely home.*

But what if there is no captain, no engine, no rudder? What if the man adorned in uniform, whether sitting pensively at the head of the Captain's serene dinner table, or confidently barking commands from the chaotic bridge of a ship in distress—what if he is only a figurehead? What if he exists only in our imagination? What if life is just a tub in the water? Just a rudderless tub, bobbing around in a turbulent sea with random currents? "Rub a dub dub, three men in a tub, a butcher, a baker, a candlestick maker."

Having had enough breakfast, Joey scooted his plate to the side; a younger person would pick it up. He took another sip of coffee, rested his mug back down on the table where his plate had been, and, keeping his hand on the handle, scanned the room.

Yes, it is nice here—nice and comfortable.

But as he watched the people, their various levels of activity, his mind again returned to the morose, again wondering how many here would die alone. His thoughts drifted to his father, and his father's father. His father was the son of immigrants. It was a large family. For them, having time alone wasn't a problem; it was a rare pleasure.

Joey thought of all the events, the family milestones that he had attended over the course of his life. Christenings, birthday parties, school plays, graduations, weddings, wakes, funerals—lots of funerals.

But maybe we make too much of death? Maybe death is no more of an event than getting onto a bus—just going from one place to another. You don't need someone to be with you for that; do you? You don't throw a party every time you step off a curb and onto a bus. And how many buses have I taken; how many more will I take? But what if, what if . . .

Snap out of it Joey. You make too much of everything. Things are what they are. You've finished your breakfast; get on with your life. Do something interesting.

His thoughts turned to the events of yesterday, his afternoon spent with the DeRieuxs.

Now that was interesting! What was pinging around in David's mind? Sure, the guy's got dementia, but he was spooked. Something spooked him, something bad, something that's really stuck in his brain. That didn't just spring from nothing; something happened.

Joey let go of the coffee mug's handle and thumped his thumb on the tabletop a few times.

I need to make a phone call.

His breakfast ritual completed, Joey left the dining hall with a mug-full of coffee in one hand, his folded newspaper in the other, and made his way back to his apartment. Upon entering his unit, he made a beeline to its nerve center, his rolltop desk. Without giving it any conscious thought, he set his coffee down in its usual place and pulled his well-worn office chair out from under the desk. The chair's leather was old and cracked in many places yet polished smooth and soft from a lifetime of use. Joey melded into the chair, which floated easily atop a plastic carpet-protector, and glided into position at the helm of the large desk. The rolltop had many pigeonholes filled with various papers and knickknacks, but the desktop itself was largely uncluttered. A large paper-calendar blotter took up much of the center of the desktop. The number on each day past had a line stricken through it, ostensibly to keep track of one's place in time, but also as if to say that there was no going back. Within easy reach just off the right side of the blotter, his coffee rested upon a coaster made from what appeared to be some sort of a woven-spiraled, cord-like material. Not far above the coaster was a cylinder-shaped pen and pencil holder, and pushed near the upper corner of the desk rested an old-style black phone.

A nice morning light was coming in through a window to his side. Joey pulled his notepad from his pocket, opened it to his last entry, and set it down on the middle of his desk blotter. Staring at the notepad, he read the three words that had been pinging around in his mind, off and on, since the moment that he had written them. The actual note was not so much a memory aid as it was something to occupy his hands and eyes as he reviewed the words in his mind—a focal point outside of his mind, something tangible to help pull out his thoughts and organize them, allowing him to visually connect the dots.

Over and over his eyes reviewed the written words: Edna, VanZant, Plutonium. He took a sip of coffee, plucked a yellow, number-two pencil from the cylinder and, leaning forward in his chair, thumped the eraser end of the pencil on the blotter next to his note. Of course, the word "plutonium" had a common meaning; but "Edna" and "VanZant", those were just words, nouns, proper nouns. Without a specific memory or knowledge of those individuals, they were just words without meaning—words that had no life or meaning until something or someone gave them meaning. He picked up the phone and dialed; it was a number he knew by heart.

A pleasant but hurried voice answered the phone, "Chattanooga Times, Research Department, Megan speaking. How may I help you?"

"Is Dorothy there please?"

"May I say who is calling?"

"Yes. Joey, Joey Franks."

"Just a minute please."

Joey waited on hold for about a minute, and then, "Hey, Joey. Been a while; how's retirement?"

"Can't complain. You not answering your own phone these days? Must be coming up in the world."

"Well, no, just busy. Got a summer intern, a newbie journalism major. Wants to change the world. Tried to tell her that we don't make the news; we report the news. But I don't think that's what they're teaching 'em these days. Okay, old man, I know you didn't call me for a dinner date; what's up?"

"I need a little information on someone. I'm guessing from pretty far back, probably a little before you started—say mid-forties, fifties, maybe sixties."

"Joey, we're really pretty busy here, and—I'm just throwing this out in case you forgot—but ... you don't work here anymore!"

"Ha, ha; still a funny girl, aren't you. Listen, this shouldn't take you long. I just need a little background information, something to give a little context to something I've stumbled onto. Could be nothing, but I've got a funny kind of feeling about this one, and I'd just like to put a few pieces together, see where it points."

"Joe-eeee".

"Come on, Dorothy. Look, here it is. I just need something on a man named VanZant—don't have a first name on him. I'm looking to see if he had something to do with David DeRieux; remember him? He was an FBI agent here in town several decades ago, sometime in the late forties, I think. If I remember right, he left the FBI when he was still fairly young, surprised everyone a little with that, and then practiced law with a small firm until he retired—in the late seventies I think it was. A couple of times people tried to get him to run for a local office—and we'd run a story about it—but he never did. Anyway, I'm curious about this VanZant fellow. See if you can find anything on him and if there is any connection between him and DeRieux. Might have something to do with atomic energy, radiation, plutonium—anything like that. Also, see if the name Edna pops up anywhere in the search."

"Anything else we can do for you?" Dorothy asked a bit facetiously as she made some notes on her pad."

Joey, ignoring Dorothy's tone, said slowly, as an additional recollection from David's comments unfolded, "Yeah, if nothing of substance comes up on VanZant, check the Washington, D.C. paper's archives. Better yet, check the D.C. archives either way."

"All right, all right. Enough already. I'll see what I can find, mainly because I can't hang up on you, and I know that you won't hang up till I say yes. But if you find something interesting, you'll feed it back to us, right?"

"Right as always. Thanks, Dorothy."

Dorothy hung up the phone, looked at her watch, sighed to herself, and called out to the intern, "Hey Megan. Come over here for a minute. I've got something for you."

Chapter 12

A Question for Edna

Nashville, TN
July 1946

Edna picked at the last few french fries on her plate as David slipped back into the booth. David's thoughts were not on eating, but he took a bite from his burger to give himself a little more time to gather his thoughts.

Edna knew her brother well. "What's wrong?" she asked.

"Not a thing," David replied.

Edna smiled a little; it wasn't like David to talk with food in his mouth.

David finished chewing and said, "Why do you ask?"

"Well, you seem kind of quiet, kind of staring at me like something's on your mind. What is it?"

"Sorry, it's nothing." David smiled and tried to look relaxed. He glanced down at his hamburger, picked it up in a seemingly casual sort of way and said, "So, tell me, how was your appointment today?" and then took a big bite from the burger.

Edna gave a shrug of her shoulders, rocked her head loosely from side to side with a smile, and said, "Ah, you know; it was okay. Didn't have to get a shot or anything, so that was good. Just drank some vitamins."

"So, what did they say? Everything look good? You said before that you had a lot of nausea. Has that gone away?"

"Well, I don't know. I do feel crummy a lot, and I'm not really gaining the weight that I'm supposed to. But they don't seem to be too worried." Edna arched her back and stretched her arms out in front of her and said, "Today's lunch was good. I'm stuffed; I don't usually eat this much."

David, still trying to keep it casual, continued, "Somebody was telling me the other day about some sort of new radiation treatment that they're giving these days to pregnant women. Hear anything about that?"

"Nope. All I've had is a few shots for my thyroid and some vitamins."

"What kind of vitamins are they giving you? Did they say?"

"Nope, didn't say. Just regular old vitamins, I guess. Anyway, I'd rather drink a boat load of vitamins than get another one of those dadgum thyroid shots. I hate those things."

"Wonder what's in those? Did they say?"

"You mean the shots? They didn't say, and I didn't ask. Like I say, I hate those things."

"But nothing about radiation, huh?"

Edna, being a little sarcastic, replied "Pretty sure I would have remembered that. Why you so interested in that?"

"Oh, I don't know. Like I said, someone was just telling me the other day about this new treatment. Sounded kind of dangerous to me. You used to work at Oak Ridge; you know how closely they monitored anyone working anywhere near that stuff for exposure. It's no secret that it's dangerous. Anyway, I was just curious."

David thought it time to change the subject. "So, how's Hank doing? He started a new job recently, didn't he?"

"Yep, at a small machine shop in Murfreesboro. They stay pretty busy though. Been giving Hank lots of overtime. He likes that for now."

"He still going to all those political meetings?"

"Come on, Dave. I know you don't like his political views, but he's a good guy. He's going to make a great father. Anyway, he wants to save as much as he can before our baby comes. We've about got enough to start our house. Been great staying with his parents; really better than I thought it was going to be. Wouldn't have been able to get our own house as fast if we were having to pay rent. It'll be nice to have his mother there when the baby comes, but, like I said, I'll be glad to have our own place before long. We'll still be close enough to Hank's parents after we move."

David took a sip of his Coke, barely enough to wet his lips. "I'm glad you guys are getting your own house, really I am; but I gotta say . . . Hank, going to all those meetings, flirting with those communists—it's a dangerous game."

Edna started to speak but David put his hands up, palms pumping towards Edna like he was signaling a truck to slow down, and said, "I know, I know. He's a good guy and all, and I know he says they're just union meetings. But that's not all there is to it. Really, there's a lot of overlap, and, well, it's something about which he needs to be careful. I like him; I really do. But this business with communists, it's serious stuff, and it worries me that you guys just don't seem to see it, to really understand what all those guys are up to. Most of those people, the ones who are running the show, they're really not what you and Hank think they are."

"Come on, David. They're not all that bad. They're like Hank; they just want what's fair for regular ole working people."

Chapter 13

David Returns from Nashville

Chattanooga, TN
July 1946

David awoke in his bed. He was back at home from his Nashville trip. The alarm clock had not yet gone off, but with the daylight just beginning to break, he knew it wouldn't be long. Lill was curled up on her side, facing outward from the bed. From her gentle breathing, he could tell that she was still fast asleep—*sleeping the sleep of the just,* he thought. In the quiet of the early morning, he could hear the tick-tick-tick of the large, wind-up alarm clock on the nightstand next to him. He twisted his neck and body to see—*yep, 5:45am.* He still had a good half hour before he had to get up. A half-hour of quiet before the alarm went off and the household became a beehive of activity.

David felt well-rested. Given how much was on his mind, he was surprised how well he had slept. Even though he had gotten home late, he still went to bed around his regular time, and, by then, he was so mentally and physically exhausted that sleep came easily. The time he had spent with Edna for lunch had caused his day in Nashville to run late, and after his chat with Michael Johnson, David had been tempted to cancel the rest of his afternoon appointments to concentrate on the looming consequences of that unexpected encounter. But he couldn't. His other tasks, though minor distractions in comparison, still had to be attended to. And then, when he was finally able to call it a day and break free from Nashville, the drive back to Chattanooga added a few more hours to his already long workday.

For the most part, the drive between Nashville and Chattanooga was an interesting one. The road leaving Nashville was relatively flat, not by Chicago or Midwestern standards, but compared to what was ahead, as he drove south and east, it was flat. Gentle-rolling hills, lush fields of corn, tobacco, soya; grassy hills with grazing cattle, and barn-tops painted with "See Rock City" signs bordered the two-lane state highway, broken every so often by a little community, a town square, a stop light or two. Some of the towns were anchored in the center by a red-brick county courthouse with manicured lawns and park benches shaded by the sprawling canopies of ancient oaks. Some towns sported a random honky-tonk at their outskirts—beer joints with large gravel parking lots, many with live bands, potbelly stoves, and sawdust on the floor. Over the years, David had been inside more than a few, on Federal matters. Most did a trickle of business during the week, exploded with life late Friday and Saturday nights, and then went dead quiet on Sunday morning. Outside the city limits there was, what David called, the farm traffic. Every so often, around a curve or just over a hill, a tractor would appear traveling slowly down the highway with complex, jerry-rigged implements hanging off the back, or a large trailer in tow with bales of hay stacked high. When the soil was damp, their tires would leave large, solid chunks of rich, dark mud on the highway. Traffic would slow, build up, and wait for the tractor to pull off or for a long enough straightaway where at least a few cars and pickups could pass. The danger was to drive too fast over a hilltop or around a curve and run up on one from behind, or to meet head-on someone coming from the other way trying to pass when there really wasn't enough room to get around safely.

Getting closer to Chattanooga, leaving the rolling hills of Middle Tennessee behind and approaching the bottom of the Appalachian Mountain range that formed much of East Tennessee, the first mountain that stood between Nashville and Chattanooga, Monteagle, loomed ahead. Entering the base of the mountain, the road paralleled a stream that had long ago cut a notch into the massive stone, providing an entry point for the ascent. The streams gave life to the local trout, crawdads, frogs, and whiskey. As the road steepened, it broke away from the stream, leaving behind the cultivated fields of the flat lands as it cut its own path up through the thickly wooded forest and rock-faced cliffs that formed the side of the mountain. Once on top, the road flattened again for a bit. The temperature was noticeably cooler, less humid; the soil rocky, not as deep and rich as the bottomlands. Here, the native trees outnumbered the plowed fields and cultivated crops. Another little community passed by David's window—a little store, a gas station, a few small houses. Lazy dogs snoozed on front porches while fearless chickens strutted around the yard plucking plump little worms from the ground and swallowing them up into oblivion. Ponds with ducks, trailer homes, kids playing with dogs, sticks, and tires—another thick forest, a smattering of grass fields, goats, horses, more chickens, more forest; and then the road descended into the valley on the Chattanooga side of the mountain. Once it reached the bottom, the road clung to the valley, meandering its way back to Chattanooga—Chattanooga, comfortably surrounded by three mountains and a ridge. Crossing the Tennessee River meant that Chattanooga was near—then, bright lights and tall buildings. David's subdivision, Brainerd, was just beyond the ridge on the far side of the city. To get there, he had to go through town and through a tunnel bored beneath the ridge, but it was after nine o'clock so there was little traffic. Then, finally, David was home.

Usually, it was a drive that David enjoyed; but that evening, the drive was more useful than enjoyable. After his meeting with Michael Johnson, David needed some time to sort things out. The defection, Edna, the clinic, radiation, VanZant—a few hours alone in the car was just the ticket. But nevertheless, a long drive at the end of a busy day, towards the end of the drive, became exhausting. A shorter drive would have been better; but then, without the exhaustion, he probably would not have fallen asleep so quickly and gotten the rest that he needed.

The alarm went off. David, still awake, rolled over, grabbed the clock, and pushed the lever that stopped the little arm from striking the two large bells on top. With the clock still in hand, he swung his feet out of bed and into his slippers on the floor, gave the crank on the back of the clock a few turns, and returned it to its place on the nightstand. Lill rolled over into the center of the bed and stretched her arms like a cat waking up from a nice nap. David had a good incentive to get moving. Their nice little three-bedroom, one-bath house, which had seemed like a mansion when they first moved there from their one-bedroom apartment, no longer seemed so spacious now that they had two young children. Still, the morning routine worked well enough for everyone. David got in and out of the bathroom first, and his rustling around was like a snooze alarm for the rest of the household. When he was finished with the bathroom, it was time for the rest of the house to get up.

Breakfast on weekdays was generally kept simple: cereal, milk, and orange juice for the kids; toast and coffee for David and Lillian. The house had one phone, a wall phone in the kitchen, near the doorway to the hall. A long cord allowed it to reach over to the breakfast table or into the hall, if privacy or relative quiet was desired.

David dialed the phone and leaned against the doorframe, watching the breakfast activity unfold as he waited for Bert or Bert's wife to answer. Everyone but David was still in their pajamas. His son, almost three; and daughter, five, sat eating their cereal while Lill buttered some toast that had just popped up out of the toaster.

"Hey, Bert, it's David . . . Listen, I got back late last night from my Nashville trip—brought the company car home. How about I swing by, save you some bus fare this morning? . . . Okay, see you in a bit. I'll be leaving here in about ten, fifteen minutes . . . Okay, see ya."

David sat at his place at the table. Lill had already poured some coffee for him. She set a small plate of toast before him and nudged a jar of marmalade closer to him. "Sounds like you're going in a little early today?"

"Yep, picking up Bert on the way in. Lots to do today."

Bert's house was just far enough out of the way that Bert knew "save you some bus fare" was code for "we need to talk before we get to our fishbowl of an office." The FBI office was on the second floor of the Federal Building—a large, marble, paperweight of a building in downtown Chattanooga. Though the FBI, as an organization, housed many secrets, the office layout gave the impression of openness. There was no buffer from the pubic hallway. The door opened directly into a mid-sized room that had six metal desks. Four of the desks were paired together into groups of two, pressed together and facing each other, with the side of one pair pressed against the window side of the room and the other pair pressed against the opposite wall, allowing for an adequate isle down the middle of the room. The remaining two desks formed the back, second row. Several file cabinets of varying height lined the front wall, and a table with a well-used coffee brewer was placed against the back wall between two doors. One of the doors led to a small storage room, the other to a small conference room. The humming florescent lights, grey metal furniture, beige speckled floor tiles, and off-white paint gave the room a bright, sterile, institutional feeling. Other than a storage closet and the conference room, there was no place for a private conversation, and two people going together, unscheduled, into either of those rooms for any length of time was the equivalent of announcing over a loudspeaker that secrets were being exchanged.

David stopped the bureau car in front of Bert's house and gave two quick taps on the horn. Two minutes later, Bert slid onto the bench seat.

"What's up, Pal? Bert said. "You burning the candle at both ends yesterday? What time did you get back?"

"Not too late—a little before ten. I had an unexpected meeting yesterday afternoon."

Bert's house was only about a ten-minute drive to the office. At the end of Bert's block, David turned in the opposite direction.

Bert said, "I see we're taking the long way in today. Must have been some meeting."

David got right to the point. "You remember Teddy Bear?"

"Yeah, sure. The Russian guy you followed into a department store a few months ago—bought a teddy bear. What about him?"

"He says his name is Michael Johnson; says he wants to defect."

"No kidding? Wow, what happened? He just walk up and tell you that?"

"Pretty much. Came with a little speech about wanting a better life for his family. Gotta tell you though, he was, well . . . he was pretty convincing."

"How'd he approach you; where were you?"

"In Nashville, sitting in a booth at Woolworth's, having lunch with Edna. The guy just walked up, introduced himself, and then he and I went over to the other side of the store, off to ourselves, and talked."

"Holy shit."

"He dangled some bait—some things you'd expect. Said we had lots of leaks, lots of communists in our ranks. That's his deal. Sounds like he has a plan to get his family across the border, out of the Soviet Bloc. From there, it's our show to get his family here to the States safely. Then, he spills the beans on his commie friends. If he's for real, this could be a pretty big deal. Once we start pulling layers off of this onion and get a peek inside, there's no telling who we might see or what we might find. One way or another, there's going to be some really unhappy people. But, listen, Bert. There's something else—a twist, a couple of twists that I'm not sure how to handle."

"Okay."

"You remember a guy we ran into at Oak Ridge about a year ago, a medical doctor, Dr. VanZant?"

Bert lightly bit the lower side of his bottom lip; his head made shallow bobs, as he tried to put a memory to a familiar name.

"Yeah, I know that name."

David, refreshing Bert's memory, said, "He was hanging around in the Personnel Department at the same time that we were there. We were getting a list of some stenos that they wanted to hire, some gals from Knoxville that we had to clear. Chatted with him for a minute. I don't think he ever said what he was doing there. I remember though, right off, you didn't like him. Said he had little Yankee ears."

Bert laughed, "Yeah, yeah. I remember him now. What about him?"

"Well, it's squirrelly. You know I was meeting Edna for lunch in Nashville. She's been going to this prenatal clinic at Vanderbilt. I was going to meet her there after her appointment, so, I was just sitting there in the waiting room, waiting for her to come out . . . and in from the street walks VanZant. Walked straight through the lobby and out through the door to the treatment rooms, without a pause, like he owned the place. I was sitting out of the way, against the back wall; he didn't see me. In and of itself, it wasn't that out of place. I mean, he is a doctor, and, after all, the clinic is a medical facility, but something about it seemed a little odd—something not quite right, just a feeling. Then, sitting there, I got to thinking about how much VanZant got your dander up when we met him at Oak Ridge. Didn't make any sense to me back then that he should get you so wound up. But now?"

David paused. They were still heading in a direction away from the office.

Bert coaxed, "But now . . . what? What else happened?"

"A couple of things. Teddy Bear, or Johnson—at least that's what he was calling himself—gave a pretty elegant speech about how much better life is in America. Like I said, he was pretty convincing. If I'm being played, he's pretty good. But there are two or three things—pretty big things. One, he knows a lot more about me than we know about him. He, or someone, has to have been watching me for a good while. That, in itself, is pretty disturbing; but that aside, he says he trusts me and will only work with me."

Bert looked over at David and said, "That's gonna be interesting. The powers-that-be don't like outsiders trying to run their show. And, lickety-split, they're gonna want this show moved to Washington; pronto. They're gonna want this circus under their own tent with their own ring masters holding the whip and running the program. Wonder what our local chief will say? Not that it matters much; it's Washington that gives the orders."

"Yeah, there's no doubt that's where this is going. But I'm wondering how this will play out with Teddy Bear. Like I said, this guy's got trust issues; made that real clear. Not that I blame him, but here's the thing. He specifically called out VanZant. He must have seen him go into the clinic—flat out said he was a threat to both of us. By 'both of us', he meant himself and me."

"What the hell?"

"I know; I know. But here's the thing. That meeting didn't happen by accident. He didn't just happen to run into me there, and I don't think he followed me all the way from Chattanooga to that Woolworth's in Nashville. Somehow, he knew that I was going to be at that clinic yesterday, and he picked me up there. He said some wild stuff about the clinic—stuff I don't think he was just making up on the fly. He knew I was going to be there. But I don't think he was expecting to see VanZant there. He sure seems to know all about that clinic though, and he seems to know a lot about VanZant; but, for some reason, I think he was surprised to see VanZant there. Actually, I think he was a little shaken to see VanZant there. He was probably watching from outside—lots of places he could have been—probably watched me go in. Then VanZant, probably out of the blue, wanders into the picture. Then, when Edna and I came out of the clinic, Teddy Bear follows us to Woolworth's. It's only a couple of blocks away; we walked. Would have been easy for him to follow us.

"But," David continued, "here's the kicker—two things really. Johnson told me, in a left-handed sort of way, that VanZant was someone that I needed to be worried about. He was really spooked about VanZant—described VanZant as being in the center of some sort of ill-defined circle. But then he said something about the clinic; something that, I've got to tell you, has me a little bit rattled. He said the clinic is doing experiments on the pregnant gals there—giving them radiation, but not asking or telling them about it."

"What the hell?"

"I asked Edna about it, in a roundabout sort of way. Told her I had heard of some sort of new radiation treatment for pregnant women—asked her if she's heard anything about it."

"What'd she say?"

"Nothing. Hadn't heard anything about it. I tell you, Bert, something's really wrong here. On the one hand, I just can't believe that they're experimenting on pregnant girls, exposing them to radiation . . . especially without telling them. But it doesn't make sense that this 'Michael Johnson' guy would lie to me about something like that. If he's trying to play us, or if he really wants to defect, escape from the Soviet Union; either way, why would he tell a lie like that? He knows it's something I've got to look into now. If he's lying, he knows I'll find out."

"Ya know, Dave, there's something else here."

"What?"

"You said he was spooked about VanZant being at the clinic. If this guy really wants to defect, if he thinks VanZant might be a problem, then it makes sense to warn you about him. But it doesn't make sense to tell you about the clinic; that just stirs shit up. It stirs shit up just when he needs things nice and quiet. He's got to know that he's started you on a mission to check up on the clinic. You go in asking a lot of questions, especially if it's about something they don't want to talk about; well then, you've just put yourself smack dab on VanZant's radar screen. Doesn't make sense that Teddy Bear would want that, not if he thinks VanZant is someone who could cause trouble."

David turned the car towards the office. The two rode in silence for a minute or two. Bert broke the silence.

"So, what's the plan? When you file your report on this Johnson meeting, are you going to include information about VanZant or the clinic? You gonna tell the chief that we've talked? He's not going to like that."

"Yeah, I know. Talking to you out-of-school, well, that's on me. I know the protocol is that I tell him first and he decides who else to bring in, but with this . . ." David paused, "I'm not doing this alone. Sorry, Pal, but you're the only one I trust watching my back on something like this."

"Okay. How you gonna handle it? You gonna mention anything about VanZant or the clinic?"

"You know, I wish we could check some of this stuff out quietly, by ourselves, before we get too many people involved. But, well, things are going to start moving fast. There's just too much here that could come back to haunt us if we're not careful. I'm thinking I have to lay it all out, right off the bat. But that's why I wanted to brainstorm all this with you before I went in. What do you think?"

"Yeah. I think you're right. I mean, I trust Rogers—think he's a straight shooter, a good Senior Agent. I like working for him and everything. But like you said, this is all gonna move fast; this is going up the pipeline in a hurry. We don't really know the guys in Washington, and we really don't know the guys in the other agencies. Gonna be hard to shuffle Johnson's family out of Europe without any of them noticing something going on. If there are lots of leaks, like Teddy Bear says, and if this VanZant guy is someone we really need to be worried about—then, yeah, the less those guys know the better. At least until we're clear of all of this. But if Teddy Bear is playing us, then, well, screw him. We'd need to get all of this out, the sooner the better. Yeah, I think the best way for us not to get bit is to just lay it all out—VanZant, the clinic, everything. The powers-that-be will do what they're going to do. And we, well, we . . . we're just going to have to keep our eyes open."

Chapter 14

David's Dinner in the Diner

Leaving Washington, D.C.
July 1946

With his dinner knife, David pushed the last piece of trout and a sliver of almond, sautéed in butter, white wine, and delicate herbs, onto his fork. *Delicious,* he thought, as he dabbed his lips with a white, cloth napkin and returned it to his lap. Fresh trout almondine, wild rice, asparagus, buttered rolls—traveling by train was one of his favorite things. The dining car, with the wood paneling, white tablecloth, and uniformed stewards, was old-world civility and elegance at its best. He rotated the tall, cool glass of iced tea back and forth between his thumb and fingertips as it rested upon the table, noting how the linen tablecloth absorbed the droplets of sweat running down the side. Visible through the clear glass, a crisp slice of lemon and a sprig of mint leaf gave the tea a nice touch.

It was approaching eight-thirty in the evening; the train was about two hours out of the Washington, D.C. station. David wasn't exactly sure what time the train would arrive at the Chattanooga terminal—the precise time wasn't important. Well past the dinner peak, the dining car was beginning to thin out.

David had made this commute to Washington and back several times now, and, from the first trip, he had established a routine that suited him perfectly. After work hours but before dinnertime, he would board the train. Being in no particular hurry, he would find a comfortable spot to read the evening paper while waiting for the train to depart and for the latter half of the second dinner seating to be well underway. After a leisurely dinner, he would stretch his legs, get the blood flowing a bit, by canvassing the train, strolling where he could, hopping from car to car. Once he had scouted as far as he could in both directions, he would again settle into a comfortable spot for a last round of reading—typically from a novel, collection of short stories, essays, or memoirs. Although he was the embodiment of orthodoxy in his daily life, in literature, he migrated towards the bohemians. After an hour, sometimes an hour and a half, he would tire and grudgingly give in to the inevitable necessity to let go of the day, secure in the knowledge that when he woke, the train would be still, safely at rest, nestled against the platform in its predetermined slot at the terminal. Unlike a ship at sea, which could be steered to any port or shoreline by the deliberate manipulations of its rudder, the train could do nothing more than to follow its tracks. Stretched out in his bunk, the sheet tucked tightly under his chin, the rhythmic sounds and motions of the train would quickly lull David into a gentle slumber. When he woke, he would shave and freshen up on the train, return to the dining car for a hearty breakfast, and then, stepping from the train, walk the few blocks to his office at the Federal Building.

But for now, much of the evening was still ahead of him. Since the dinner traffic was winding down and no one was waiting for his table, David decided to linger a bit longer while he finished his tea. Raising the cool glass to his lips, he took a leisurely sip and turned his gaze out through the window while reflecting on his day at Headquarters. What a day it had been—for that matter, what a week—and it was only Wednesday night. It seemed impossible that the week was little more than half over. It seemed impossible that it had only been two days since Nashville—two days since his innocuous lunch at Woolworth's, with his sister Edna, had diverged into his meeting with Michael Johnson; one day since his meeting with his boss, Senior Agent Rogers, in the Chattanooga office, followed by a hurriedly arranged evening train trip to D.C.; and then today. He had spent today at FBIHQ, aka, FBI Headquarters. Some called it SOG, short for Seat of Government. Names and acronyms aside, the Justice Department Building in D.C. was a place of lightly constrained power. The Director of the FBI and the Attorney General of the United States, though they were on opposite sides of the building, had their offices on the same floor, just down the hall from each other. Deputies and other acolytes of their elite inner sanctum surrounded them and filled the other floors, clustering outward in descending order of rank.

Today's visit had been vastly different from all of his previous trips to D.C. The others had been solely for routine training and bureaucratic matters. In fact, most of David's time at HQ was spent at their quarters in Quantico, Virginia, a suburb of D.C., in which the FBI shared training facilities with the Marines. David had spent a little time within the actual Seat of Government—D.C. Proper—but most of that time was during his off hours as a tourist taking in the various sights, sounds, and attractions of the Capitol.

But today, David was not just some tourist-come-to-the-big-city. Today, David had been the main attraction. He had spent most of the day with an Associate Director, a little time interacting with a handful of the Associate Director's aides, and lastly, a few minutes with the Director himself. David was not impressed. Familiarity does indeed breed contempt.

David took another sip of tea as his mind continued to wander—yes, only two days since the trajectory of his life had so quickly swerved onto an unanticipated path.

Free of the city's congestion, the train was beginning to pick up speed. Soon it would be dark; soon the train would be entering the curved terrain of the mountainous region. Darkness would not slow the train since the curves were manageable and the track need not be seen to be followed. The integrity of the rails would keep the train safely on its course; and David, without giving it much thought, in general, had confidence in those who designed the tracks, bridges, and crossings, and in those whose duty it was to maintain and operate the system. David found that managing inanimate objects was easier, and typically, more predictable than managing people. Whether or not that was a source of comfort, David couldn't say because the tracks, though inanimate in and of themselves, were, after all, ultimately managed by people—people with egos, quirks, and wills all of their own. Nevertheless, once those tracks were laid, the train had no choice but to follow them. From the moment the train left the station, the destination was pretty much set. Maybe under certain conditions an engineer could change the path, call ahead for a switch to be thrown, but not a passenger. No, the passenger was just along for the ride. The passenger was going wherever the train was going. He could choose to get off sooner if he wanted, but when the train stopped at the end of the line, everyone still onboard had to get off.

As the daylight outside faded with the setting sun, while the light within the dining car remained constant, the glass window through which David gazed began its measured transformation from a portal through which to view the outside world, into a mirror that could only reflect the lighted interior within. It struck David as odd that it was possible to look from the dark side of the glass into the lighted side but not possible to look from the light into the dark. *At night, if you stand outside in a yard or on a street, and if the curtains are not drawn, you can easily see into a lighted house. But if you are in that house, if the room is lit, the windows might as well be mirrors. The same with a cave,* he thought. *If you are standing among the shadows, in the darkness within the mouth of a cave, you can glimpse the world outside; that is, if you are facing in the right direction. But if you are standing in the light, outside of the cave, trying to look in, it is not possible to see beyond the light into the darkness beyond the opening.* At first, it seemed backwards to him. *Surely, one standing in the light should be able to perceive more than one standing in the dark—that seems rational. But that is not how the universe works. The reality of the universe is that the important thing is not where one is standing; the important thing is the illumination. We see that which is illuminated. Without illumination, there is no perception. But what is illumination; what is its source; what does the word even mean? What determines, what mechanism or entity chooses what is illuminated and what is not? If something is never illuminated, does it ever exist? Is illumination a form of creation? If something ceases to be illuminated, does it eventually cease to have meaning, cease to exist? Can something, really anything, exist if it is not perceived? But the mind, by itself, is capable of perception—isn't it? With one's eyes shut, there is no light, but within the mind there is still perception—isn't there? Yes, certainly, without a doubt—illumination, perception need not be limited or constrained by the physical.*

Yet, light—or its equivalent—is critical. Even a small amount can make a huge difference. Even the smallest amount, a mere flicker, is all that it takes to illuminate. Yes, just a flicker is sufficient to ruin the sovereign of the darkest of places. But conversely, darkness wins by default when illumination is absent.

A waiter interrupted his thoughts, asking to take his plate, if he was finished with his meal.

"Yes, yes. Thank you," David replied as he got up to leave the dining car. *Time to read for a bit,* he thought. *Perhaps I'll find a flicker of illumination within my book.*

Chapter 15

Mallard Calls VanZant

July 1946

The intercom box on VanZant's desk buzzed. He leaned forward and pressed a lever down. "What is it, Miss Wallace?"

"A Dr. Mallard in Nashville wants to speak with you, sir; says it's urgent."

"Okay, fine. Put him through," VanZant ordered with no hidden amount of exasperation.

"Good lord, what now," he muttered to himself as he put the phone to his ear. Pushing another button, VanZant blurted, "What is it, Mallard?"

Mallard was too rattled to even notice VanZant's impatient tone and, relieved to have reached VanZant in person, hurriedly replied, "Thank goodness I got ahold of you—weren't sure where you'd be. How'd you get back to Washington so fast? I was afraid I was going to have to just leave a message for you to call me. Wasn't sure how long it would take to get a message to you and then for you to call me back. I was afraid that it would take too long."

VanZant rocked back in his chair and shifted the phone to his other ear. "Okay, Mallard, settle down. I flew back to DC from Nashville yesterday after our meeting. Tell me what's going on."

"It's the FBI; they're asking questions."

"What are you talking about? Who's asking questions? Is it that guy you were talking about yesterday, that FBI agent; what was his name? David, David something, wasn't it? I thought you said he was just there in the waiting area, just there to pick up someone, just his sister or someone."

"That's right. I told you—I told you that you probably walked right past him in the waiting room. But you convinced me that it was no big deal, just a coincidence. But this afternoon—this afternoon another agent was here. Bert, Bert Ashton is his name, an FBI agent from Chattanooga. That's where David is from. David DeRieux is his name—the name of the other agent. No appointment, no call, no nothing. This guy, this Bert Ashton agent—he just shows up with no warning or anything, wanting to talk to me. I mean, what could I do? He knew I was here; I had to see him."

"Well, so what. You're not doing anything wrong. You've got paperwork—documentation on everything you're doing there. You've got cover for everything. Hell, you haven't even moved to Washington yet . . . So, what did he want? What did he want to know; how did he leave things?"

"Well, that's what's got me worried. He started off asking about the radiation; it didn't take him long at all to get to that. I showed him the press release we had done on that back in December—showed him that we were just a part of a larger study on women's diet and nutrition, and its effect on their pregnancy and delivery, and condition of their baby. Even showed him material about the funding that we're getting from the Rockefeller Foundation. He was surprised that so few people, in the public that is, knew what we were doing—that we were giving these women radiation to drink, that it didn't appear that any, or many, of them knew, and that we weren't telling them about it. I explained to him that it wasn't like we decided not to tell them; we just felt that it wasn't necessary."

"So, was that it? Was he just there—just there mad at us for not being more open about the radiation?"

"No! That's the thing. I mean clearly he was angry about the radiation. But what's got me worried, well, it's about you. I mean, at first, when he was just asking about the radiation, I kept wondering why he was here, why he was here instead of Edna's brother, David. I mean, that would have made more sense. But then he started asking about you. Out of the blue, he started asking about you. I mean, I didn't mention anything about you to him. None of the documents or press releases that I showed him had anything at all about you. It had to be because you were here yesterday. I mean, in all the paperwork out on this project, you're a footnote here and there at the most. There's no reason why they should be focused on you. It had to be because you were here yesterday and DeRieux saw you. But even that doesn't make sense; like I said, at most you're a footnote. I can understand why he might be mad, but the list of people he would reasonably be mad at—on that list—you're a long way down, a long way down even if at all. And I mean, he was really, really interested in you. For some reason he kept circling back to you even though everything he asked about you was pretty much a straightforward dead end. I told him that you are just the contact who coordinates us getting our shipments of isotopes from other facilities, but that didn't seem to satisfy him. In a way, he was trying to play down his interest in you, but it didn't make sense; it really stood out as odd. I mean, if he had asked about a lot of other people—other people who are more obviously involved in this project—even if he only asked about a few of the others, well, that would have made a little more sense. But he didn't. When all was said and done, I can't help but think the main reason he was here was to find out about you.

VanZant rocked forward in his chair. Mallard was right; this might be a problem, but he certainly didn't want Mallard to fret over it. Mallard was clearly not a cool player—never was going to be. VanZant needed to keep Mallard composed. If there was something going on, if they were getting close, then a frazzled Mallard would only add to any suspicions.

VanZant composed his thoughts and said to Mallard, "Okay, listen. This isn't great, but I don't think this is going to be a problem, certainly not for you anyway. What you showed the agent was real; we've got permissions and blessings from all sorts on that project. What can they do? Really, at the most, they can make us stop, make us tell the gals what we're doing, make us do another press release. Big deal. Even if we have to stop giving doses to new patients, we've already got plenty started to complete the study. Even if we didn't give any more doses out, it would be stupid to make us stop with the follow-up tests, and that's all we really need from here on out if it comes to that. For that matter, if we need to, we could just make up some excuse, drop the whole thing and walk away. Really, in the scheme of things, this is just a sideshow. No, we're okay on this one. You're right though. It doesn't make sense for them to be so curious about me. I'm going to check with my sources and find out what's going on with that. In the meantime, don't worry. I'm sure it's nothing. I'll find out about this. I'll get back to you when I know more. Like I say, in the meantime, don't get yourself all worked up about this. Okay?"

"Okay," Mallard answered. He wasn't completely at ease, but he was surprised at how much better he felt after talking it over with VanZant. Mallard felt like he had taken the weight that had been dumped on him and had handed it over to VanZant.

"Okay," Mallard repeated. "So, you'll call me when you find out about this?"

"Yeah, I'll call. For now, just go on as always. Nothing changes. We'll talk later."

VanZant could hear in Mallard's voice that his little speech had worked; Mallard was indeed calming down. VanZant, keeping the phone to his ear, pressed the cradle with his finger to hang up. When he got a dial tone, he dialed a local number.

"Hey," he said, "it's me."

"What do you need?" the voice on the other end replied.

"Two guys I need information on. Both, FBI agents. Pretty sure they're both operating out of the Chattanooga, Tennessee office. You still have that contact at the Bureau, your guy that's pissed off with Hoover?"

"You bet. What are their names; what kind of stuff are you looking for?"

"First guy's name is David DeRieux. Second guy's name is Bert Ashton."

"What kind of stuff are you looking for?"

"Just trying to get a general handle on them for now. Nothing specific. Just see what all you can find out about them in general, anything unusual. Would be great if you could tell me what they're working on right now."

"Okay, give me a day. I'll get back to you tomorrow; might be late tomorrow."

"Okay, thanks."

Chapter 16

David Back from Washington

Chattanooga, TN
July 1946

A soft-boiled egg held upright in its porcelain cup, narrow strips of buttered toast without the crust, freshly squeezed orange juice, and strong black coffee. David had slept well on the train back from Washington, and now he sat, finishing the last few bites of his breakfast, people-watching through the window of the dining car as travelers, senders, greeters, conductors, and porters buzzed along the platform of the Chattanooga terminal. One last sip of coffee and he would step off the train and make the short walk to his office.

Yesterday, towards the end of his day at HQ in Washington, he had sent a telex to Special Agent in Charge, Rogers, confirming that he would be on that evening's train back to Chattanooga and would be ready to meet with him and Bert first thing in the morning.

David was the first to arrive at the office. He unlocked the door, flipped on the lights, and dropped his briefcase on his desk as he passed it on his way to the closet at the back of the room where he stored his suitcase.

Wonder what's in that manila folder on the top of my in-box, David wondered as he set his bag on the floor in the closet, pushed it in a little further with his foot, shut the door, and turned back towards his desk. He had a pretty good idea as to what was in the folder; but then again, you never really know until you've opened it, especially the unmarked ones. When he had left the day before for Washington, he had left his in-box empty.

As he approached his desk, his attention, as it so often was, was drawn to the window. Particularly when alone in the office, he liked to stand at the window and look out. He glanced at the clock on the wall; it might still be a few minutes until anyone else arrived. Moving closer to the window, he looked at the people walking down the sidewalks. The elevation from the second-floor window was perfect—high enough to get a clearer, less obstructed view than from street level, yet, not so high as to see only the tops of people's heads, nor so far away as to be unable to distinguish significant details. Approaching the top of an hour, the foot traffic was at a peak as the starting time for many businesses was nearing, and few could afford to be late.

All those people, all those stories, David thought, as the pace appeared to quicken as the top-of-the-hour drew nearer. *All those people, all those stories—how similar they all are, how different they all are.*

Again, David looked at the clock on the wall. *Better get started with the day,* he thought, and, after stalling for just a moment longer, he walked to the back of the room and got a pot of coffee going, for that was one of the many unwritten rules: First one in, starts a pot of coffee.

With the smell of coffee brewing, he sat down at his desk, picked up the unlabeled manila file folder, and opened it . . . yes! It was Bert's raw notes from his investigation of Dr. Mallard, the Clinic, and VanZant. David had really wanted to be in on that interview with Mallard, but the meetings in Washington were the priority, and besides, David's burning desire to confront Mallard was, in itself, an overwhelming reason for David not to attend. David hated it, but he knew that emotions of such strength were counterproductive in the long run to the results that he wanted. Bert would do a great job; he wouldn't miss anything; and now, here before him, were those notes.

David was about halfway through the file when Bert walked through the door, looked at David's long face, and said to David, "Incredible, isn't it?"

David, shaking his head, could only say, "What the hell, can this be right?"

Their boss, Senior Agent Rogers, came through the door. He seemed to be in a fairly chipper mood.

"Morning boys," he said to the room, then sniffed the air. "Ummm, smell that coffee," he said as he passed David and Bert on his way to his desk at the back of the room. After setting his briefcase down on top of his desk, he walked over to the nearby coffee maker and, while pouring himself a cup, said, "Grab a cup, get your files, and let's get started in the conference room."

Rogers sat at the head of the conference table furthest from the door. David and Bert sat across from each other at the end near him.

Rogers began, "Well, we all had a busy day yesterday." Rogers had a small stack of manila folders directly in front of him and a yellow legal pad offset to his right. He opened the cover of the file on top and looked down at the official-looking document. "Got your coded telex late yesterday from HQ. Looks like we're in the spy-defection business; you must have had quite a day yesterday, David. Tell us about it."

David began, "Well, like you say, they're wanting us to play along for now. As you know, my first meeting in the morning was with the Deputy Director of Counterintelligence, Wayne Wagner. Spent about an hour and a half in his office; went over everything I know about Johnson. That's the name we're still using for him, for now. We went over my conversation with Johnson a couple of times—fielded lots of questions about that.

Then, the Deputy told me to get myself a cup of coffee and wait outside his office while he checked up on a few things. I'm sure he made some calls. A handful of people, three, came and went from his office; none stayed very long. One of them, the guy who came in first, he stayed the longest of the three. He glanced at me and nodded as he went by. The other two, as they came and went, it just jumped out at me as being somewhat odd. The way they walked by—it wasn't like they just didn't notice me; it was as if they went out of their way to not notice me. They had, I don't know, kind of a really stiff manner about them. Not sure what that was all about. I mean, it's not like it hurt my feelings or anything; it was just weird. I'm not sure why it made such a big impression on me, but it did. I guess it's just that their behavior seemed so unnatural, so forced, the way that they carried themselves; it just stood out. You know, sometimes not glancing at someone draws more attention, more suspicion, than just looking right at them. Even saying hello or hi, as they passed by, would have been more inconspicuous, if that is what they were trying to be.

"Maybe I'm making a bigger deal of this than I should. It's just that they struck me as being, well, creepy. I guess it's just one of those instances in which you just have to be there to know what I mean—you know, when the actual experience, when put into words, just doesn't have the same impact, the same intensity. Nevertheless, those two were creepy, and, to me, it's a little unsettling having creepy guys like those two, and at that level, walking around HQ. Never did get the names of either of them. I started to ask, but, somehow, I felt the question would be unwelcomed.

"Anyway, that's just between us, off the record. The first guy, the guy who nodded when he went by—turns out that he's going to be my main contact for this operation. His name is Charlie, Charlie Parker. He came back for the afternoon meeting that I had with the Deputy. Maybe a little overly formal, but he seemed okay. I asked him if he was the one who they named the checkpoint after—you know, Checkpoint Charlie. He was pretty deadpan; not sure if he knew that I was kidding; probably shouldn't have done that. Just hoping to break the ice a little. But, overall, he seemed like someone we'll be okay working with. The other two, the two creepy guys from the morning—I didn't see either of them again.

"Moving on, a little before eleven, after my first meeting with the Deputy—he has me waiting in his outer office area—he comes out and says, 'Go get yourself a nice lunch. Have a walk around, if you like. Be back here by twelve thirty.' Suggests a few places I might try.

"So, I have lunch, walk around a bit, get back well before twelve thirty. His secretary buzzes the Deputy and sends me right in. Mr. Checkpoint Charlie's already there. He introduces me to another agent, his partner, Gus Harris. The Deputy tells me that they have decided to go ahead with this operation—Johnson's defection. Agents Charlie Parker and Gus Harris are the agents in DC that we'll be working with. Charlie is the senior of the two. Like I said, Charlie seems okay. The other guy, Gus, he seems alright. Didn't make much of an impression one way or the other, but I think he's going to be okay. I'm to keep them posted; they're to provide direction and any assistance that we may need from HQ. And if this thing goes off, Parker and Harris are the ones who will handle the rendezvous with Johnson's wife and son at the border—we're guessing probably Berlin—and then transporting them back here to the States. They're suggesting that we fly them to our Army Base in Tullahoma—Camp Forrest. I have to agree with them about that. When you think about it, it would be the perfect place. Reasonably close to here but remote enough, secure enough, that it will be easy for us to keep a handle on things in a, more or less, controlled environment. It will be interesting to see how Johnson reacts—can't imagine why he wouldn't approve. If Johnson's legit, then everything is, so far, pretty much falling right into place for him.

"Anyway, we went over a lot of the details—things that might or might not come up at my next meeting with Johnson. So much depends on that. At this point, we're assuming that Johnson is authentic and that he plans on going through with what he said to me. We're taking him at his word for now, but, at the same time, keeping our eyes open for flags, inconsistencies, any hint that something else may be going on here. As you know, what Johnson said was pretty straightforward: his wife and son get themselves across the border, we connect with them and bring them to the States, he tells us what he knows, and they live happily ever after in anonymity, under the quasi-protection of our umbrella. But that still leaves a boatload of details still unknown and unaddressed. We talked for around two hours about all those blanks that need to be filled in: operational details, possible variations that he might throw at us, things we can and can't do, things that would be a deal-breaker, what to do if he does start hedging, what to do if I, or we, start to think that he is just trying to play us. We have to be really careful—particularly at this stage in the game while he's still somewhat of a loose cannon—about the questions that we ask him. If we're sloppy, many of the questions that we're tempted to ask could very well tell him, or them, volumes about us. If we're not careful, we could end up inadvertently telling him more about us, with our questions, than he tells us about them, with his answers. It's certainly a possibility that that is the game he's playing. So, if that turns out to be the case, and if we start to believe that he is playing us, do we keep up the façade, bring him in, feed him disinformation? Also, Wagner pointed out that, right now, there are a handful of known Russian agents that we would like to pick up, but can't; because, if we did, it would blow the cover on some of our other sources. But if we brought Johnson in, then maybe we could nab some of those people, and the Russians would assume that Johnson was the source on them. There's really a lot of variables to consider.

"Anyway, we covered a huge amount of territory in those two hours. Main thing is to keep alert and flexible. As I said, the thinking is that he is legit; still, you never know. We've got to be prepared for anything.

"Let me go over my notes, organize them a little, and we'll go over this all again in a more detailed, organized manner."

"Is that it then?" Rogers asked.

David said, "Well . . . that was it for the formal groundwork part of it. Agents Parker and Harris gathered their notes and left. Said they would be pulling together all they can find on 'Johnson'. Not really sure what other sources they'll be tapping—where all they would be 'pulling' from. It appears to me that most of the information that they have on him has come from us. Whether they realize it or not, so far, they've just been feeding back to us information that we've sent to them. Sure, we've tracked him around a lot lately, got a pretty thick file on him. But nothing we have on him tells us much about him, personally. We know a lot about where he's been and what he's seen, but that doesn't really tell us much about what he's thinking. We don't really know anything for certain about what may be driving him. Of course, we know what all he said to me in the Woolworth's—about getting his family out, starting a new life, all of that. Like I said, I thought that he was pretty convincing, pretty sincere, but I can't deny that it's possible that it was all just an act."

Rogers interrupted, "Remind me again. What was it that first put us onto Johnson?"

Bert answered, "It wasn't Washington; it wasn't HQ. It was the local boys at Oak Ridge. The Sheriff there saw Johnson snooping around outside the plant, and when he asked him what he was doing, the Sheriff didn't buy the answer. Apparently, Johnson was watching the gates and some of the main roads, trying to figure out what all was going in and out of the plant. Some of the locals picked up on it and told the Sheriff. The Sheriff there is a pretty sharp fellow and a cool cucumber. After he talked to Johnson, he had a pretty good idea of what was going on, so, he called us."

David, finishing for Bert, said, "And that's when we started keeping tabs on Johnson. We didn't bring him in. The thinking was that we could probably learn more from watching him than we would learn from interrogating him, arresting him, or deporting him. If we took him out of the game, they'd just put someone else in, and then, who knows how long the newbie would run before we figured out who he was, if ever. 'Better the devil that you know,' as they say, as long as he's not doing too much damage."

Rogers drummed his fingertips on the tabletop and said, "What it all boils down to is what we can get Johnson to tell us."

"That's right; that's right," David agreed. "If he's willing to talk, like he's offered to, then, well yeah, we all agree that he could be a pretty valuable source. But, like I reported, when Johnson talked to me, his emphasis was on information that he has about moles that they have in our agencies. If he comes through and hasn't exaggerated about what he knows, then, well, no telling what we might find out about ourselves. HQ acted like they want that information, but they seemed much more anxious about getting intel from Johnson on stuff going on within the Russian agencies—intel on the status of the Soviet's technology, military; bios on their key players, and so on. If Johnson has that sort of information, then great. But in my brief conversation with Johnson, he was trying to sell what he knows about us. By that, I mean what he knows about the people who are working for us, who maybe shouldn't be. What he knows or is willing to share about the Soviet's internal affairs—information about their internal workings—well, he said nothing about any of that in my encounter with him. That doesn't necessarily mean that it's a dead end; maybe Johnson will tell us plenty about that. It's just that it's still a question that needs to be addressed. HQ never said that that was a deal-breaker, but they sure avoided saying how hard they were willing to push Johnson on it. They were really squishy about it; I was surprised. But again, they did make it clear, really clear, that it was very important to them.

"But, back to what we currently know about Johnson. When you add it all up, it's precious little. For now, I'm giving HQ the benefit of the doubt that they haven't been holding back on us. Even so, I did question them about that."

Rogers jerked his head towards David in surprise and said, "You're kidding! You asked the Deputy Director—you asked him straight out if they had been holding back on us?"

Bert laughed and said, "Good for you, Pal. What did he say?"

David raised his hands, palms out, and pumped them, like he was signaling to put on the brakes. "Hold on, hold on," he said. It wasn't that bad. I simply mentioned to him that we had requested information on Johnson in the past but hadn't really gotten much. I asked if they had come across anything when looking at their files that day, about Johnson, that I could take back with me—that it would be helpful in my preparation for my next meeting with Johnson. They said no, but something seemed a little squirrelly. I had the impression that they might have been doing a little tap dancing; not sure why.

"Then it occurred to me, maybe they're not holding back on us. Maybe they seem squirrelly simply because they've got nothing, and they just hate to admit it. But now, since part of this operation will be taking place outside the States, in Europe, I asked if they would be coordinating with other agencies to get additional information or intelligence that those agencies may have. I hope that they come back with something, but I'm not holding my breath on it. Reading between the lines, I don't think the lines of communication between those guys, those agencies, are all that great. All those turf wars, especially between Hoover and Wild Bill Donovan, certainly haven't helped. Lots of grudges. I think Hoover and Donovan have beat on each other quite a bit these last few years; but neither won the war, since Truman ended up not giving foreign jurisdiction to us—the FBI—or to Donovan. Who knows, maybe Hoover will turn it around and end up getting foreign jurisdiction for us, at some point; but for now, I think a large part of the problem is that no one really knows who's running what, when it comes to international affairs."

Rogers said, "My understanding is that since the beginning of this year, non-domestic intelligence and operations are under the CIG, Central Intelligence Group, under Admiral Souers. That's still the case, isn't it? Or are they saying something different now?"

David nodded, "Well, yeah, technically that's right. But it's really a hodgepodge of bureaucracy over there. The CIG is the operational end of it, but they're monitored by the NIA. When they shut down Donovan's SSU and started the CIG, they split what was left of the SSU into three divisions, and those three divisions were split between the Department of State and the Department of War. Apparently, it's not working out all that great, so, there is already talk about consolidating and moving everything into a new group. There's talk that they're planning on calling it the Central Intelligence Agency, the CIA.

"Whatever those people decide to call themselves, it would be nice if they turned up something useful for us on Johnson, but who knows. Like I said, I'm not holding my breath. I mentioned to Deputy Wagner that it is possible that during the war, the OSS got some information on Johnson, but even if they did, who knows if they ever passed that information on to SSU when they took over."

Bert asked, "What did he say about that?"

"Not much really. Like most of the conversation, when we were talking about working with other agencies, about who might have what, and who was going to do what, Wagner seemed to hem-and-haw a lot. On that topic, about the only thing that he went out of his way to make clear was that this was solely an FBI operation and that other agencies would, at most, play a minor, supporting role. Just from the little that I can see," David glanced at his boss, "and this is totally off the record . . ."

"Go on," Rogers nudged.

"Well, it occurred to me that maybe, just maybe, the reason HQ gets squirrelly about some of this is because the information that they seem most interested in—the internal goings-on within Russia—are technically out of their jurisdiction. I mean, technically, we're supposed to limit ourselves to domestic affairs and let CIG handle international stuff. I know that doesn't sit well with Hoover, but that's the way it's been laid out."

David raised his hands, in a lifeless fashion, a few inches above the tabletop and then let them fall on the wooden surface with a small thump. He concluded, "It's ridiculous. So much of this is just petty, self-inflicted wounds. Sometimes, really way too often, it's like we're not at all on the same side. But, at this level, at this point, well, it looks to me like if there is any communication or coordination going on between us and the different agencies, well, it's certainly not going on through any official or organized channels—not smoothly anyway. With all these turf wars going on, those files, if they even exist, could be anywhere, with anyone."

Rogers shrugged his shoulders in a noncommittal sort of way and said, "Okay then, anything else? Was that it?"

David gave an uncharacteristically large grin and said, "That's it, as far as the operational planning goes."

Bert saw the grin and perked up. "What! What happened then?"

David replied, "After Agents Parker and Harris left, the Deputy Directory said, 'Grab your things, we're going up to the fifth floor, there's someone there who wants to meet you.'"

Bert slapped the table and said, "Holy cow! You met Hoover?"

David, still smiling, said, "Yep. When we got to his office suite, Miss Gandy buzzed him—told him we were there. He and Tolson come out of their inner sanctum; we shake hands. Hoover's smiling at me; Tolson's looking me over, a bit more serious. Hoover says, 'I understand that you are originally from Chicago; you'll be interested in seeing this.' He leads me over to his Dillinger display, the one in his outer office that everyone talks about, and there it was, all under a glass case: Dillinger's death mask, the straw hat that he was wearing when he was shot, and the .380 colt pistol that he pulled when Purvis yelled at him to 'Stick 'em up.' It's all there, bigger than life. Then Hoover starts talking about teamwork—how it's teamwork that got Dillinger and what a great team all of us make when we work together. He goes on, saying things about how important we all are but to always remember that everything we do reflects directly upon the Bureau. That the integrity and the reputation of the Bureau are paramount and must never be compromised."

Bert was curious. "So, what was your impression of him, Hoover?"

"Well," David said in a drawn out hedging sort of way as he looked over towards his boss. "That's a loaded question, a dangerous question."

David's boss was also curious and piled on, "Come on, Dave, tell us. Off the record, how'd he strike you? I've seen him a couple of times, in person, but nothing like the meeting you just had with him. I shook his hand once but have never really had a one-on-one exchange with him like you did. Come on, what's your take on him?"

"Well, okay. I guess initially, my first thought was that he was quite a bit shorter than what I had expected." David looked at his boss for confirmation. "You probably noticed that too when you met him." Rogers nodded. David continued, "Seems like a lot of famous people—people that you see on television, or in newsreel clips at the movies, or photos in the paper; even some people that you've just read about and have never even seen a picture of them—when you actually meet them in person, they're often shorter than what you'd expect. In the abstract, these 'big-deal' people seem larger than life, as they say. But when you meet them, when you talk to them, well, it's amazing how often the mental image that you've concocted just doesn't match up to the reality. But anyway, he did have a lot of energy—just really radiated energy. Talked fast, moved fast—in an anxious sort of way. Like he was anxious to get from one moment to the next. Lots of energy—not at all what you would call an easygoing sort of man. Like I said, a little shorter than what I was expecting— and stockier. In a nutshell, a fireplug of a man with a huge amount of energy. When you meet him, talk to him, you can see why he's in charge—why he's the director. I mean, the man is driven. For good or bad, the man is driven."

Rogers prodded, "What do you mean, 'for good or bad'?"

"Nothing really, just a figure of speech. I mean, some people are really driven, some aren't. Some people crave to be the chief; others are happy to be Indians. Then there's the entire spectrum of dispositions in between. Most everyone, probably at some time or another, thinks they would be happier if they were more driven or less driven—more of this, less of that. Typically, at some point everyone dreams of what it would be like to be what they are not—or some slightly different version of what they consider themselves to be. They wonder how things would be different had they, at some point, taken a different path. But ultimately, people are what they want to be. Not to make a decision is itself making a decision, exercising a choice. Ultimately, people are what they have chosen to be."

Bert sat quietly, nodding his head ever so slightly in silent agreement.

Rogers leaned back in his chair. "Jesus, Dave, maybe you should start browsing through magazines instead of reading books on your train rides."

David laughed, "Okay, okay. I get it. You asked me what time it is, and I drone on about the different kinds of clocks. Anyway, that was the gist of it. The meeting with Hoover wasn't very long. I think, mainly, he knew I was there; knew what was going on. He just wanted to be able to put a face with the name—sum me up with a first impression. I imagine that if I had rubbed him the wrong way, he would have pulled the plug on my involvement in this. Not really sure where that would have left them; but anyway, we're on for now. The next step for them is to pull together anything else they can on Johnson. The next step for us is to wait for my next meeting with Johnson, and, for now, when that happens is more up to him than to us. I don't think I'm likely to spot him until he's ready to meet."

Rogers asked, "Anything new on VanZant come up in your meetings?"

"Nope. I don't know if that's good or bad. Like I said the other day, I hated like the devil to broadcast what Johnson said about VanZant, but there was really no way around it. When Johnson spoke about VanZant, I had the clear impression that he was giving me a private warning. And that bit about a dangerous circle with edges that can't be seen—I just don't know; I just don't know. Really, at this point, there's just no way to know. Maybe it was a warning that I will regret not keeping to myself, or maybe it's part of some deceitful game that he is playing, a way to muddy up the waters. Anyway, it's not like I had much of a choice, so I certainly didn't omit anything in my report to HQ. However, I didn't go out of my way to emphasize it or elaborate on it any more than I had to. I have to say though, I was surprised how few questions they had about that part of my report. It's not like they skipped over it, but if it had been me, if it had been me asking questions about the VanZant warning, well, that part would have put a hook in me. I would have wanted to understand all that I could about what is going on there. Unless, of course, it was something I already knew about and didn't want to draw any more attention to it than necessary. That's kind of interesting in itself—what if I and HQ are both minimizing the VanZant issue to each other, but for different reasons? I don't know. It gets complicated fast. Anyway, we'll know soon enough, I guess. For our part, we've got all of our cards on the table; just hope HQ isn't holding anything out on us."

David looked over at Bert. "I scanned through your notes from yesterday. Didn't see much new, but what you did find was pretty amazing."

Bert nodded, "Yeah, Teddy Bear was right, about the Clinic anyway. They're definitely giving those gals some sort of a vitamin elixir that's chockfull of radioactive isotopes. But like you say, it's amazing. They aren't telling those gals what they're doing—that they're part of an experiment. But then again, they're not exactly keeping it secret. They actually issued a press release a while back on what they're doing—pretty proud of it actually. The amazing thing is that it looks like no one really cares about this. It's like there are two groups of people here: the people who have read or have heard about the press release and have then put it out of their mind and moved on to the next story or thing in their life since it doesn't involve them. And then there are the people who have gone, or are currently going to the clinic—none of whom have apparently seen or heard anything about the press release or the experiment—and, unbeknownst to them, are being slipped this radioactive drink. The medical people brag to the one group about their study but then act as if it isn't important enough to even mention it to the actual participants—the clinic's patients—to let them in on what they are doing to them. How did Dr. Mallard put it, 'We never decided not to tell them; we just felt that it was unnecessary.' It's incredible, really beyond belief. They give these gals, these pregnant women, a potion to drink; tell them that it's good for them, and neglect to inform them that it's chockfull of radioactive material. I'd bet anything that those doctors would want to know if they were given that very same potion. They'd have a fit if someone did that to them—slipped them or someone in their family a radioactive cocktail. Bottom line, they're hiding in plain sight. But technically speaking, as incredible as it seems, at this point it doesn't look like they're breaking any laws."

Bert leaned way back in his chair, raised his hands up in front of his face, motioned his fingers as if he was directing a car to pull forward, and gave a smile that David had seen a thousand times before.

David said, "Okay, Bert, what's not in your field notes."

"I thought you'd never ask," Bert said, rocking forward in his chair. "They're dirty, man! Dirty as the day is long. I can tell. That Dr. Mallard, I don't know what kind of doctor he is, but I'm telling you, he's a lousy liar. That Mallard, he was trying to play it cool, had all the right answers, but that guy was nervous as hell. Every time I brought up VanZant, I thought the little feller was gonna pee himself."

Bert nodded sideways towards Rogers and said, "Boss man and I talked this over late yesterday. I've got a few more things on my plate that I want to follow up on, but we're thinking once I get this report in order, we'll turn it all over to Sanders at Justice and see what their take on it is."

David looked down at the table, withdrawing into himself. His head shook ever-so-slightly back and forth as he thought about his sister. Speaking just loud enough for Bert and Rogers to be able to eavesdrop on his solemn thoughts, he whispered, "It's like they're lab rats. They're treating my little sister, Edna, and those other women too, like lab rats."

David looked up from the table and saw that Rogers and Bert were looking at him. David repeated, in a clear voice, "They're treating these women like lab rats. No one tells a lab rat that they are being experimented on; what would be the point? No one asks a lab rat for permission. And the sad thing is, these women, these poor naïve women, they really don't help themselves much. I'm not making excuses for what these doctors are doing, quite the opposite, but, damn it, these women sure make it easy for them. They don't read the papers; they don't question anything. They just assume that those in charge—those who exercise so much control over their lives—are benevolent; that they have their best interests at heart. It's terrible, unconscionable, the way that they're treated. But, damn it, they play the role of a lab rat, so, eventually, they get treated like lab rats. Think about it. Lab rats don't question their destiny. If a lab rat dies, so what. There're millions of them, an endless supply. When one dies, you just pull another from the cage. And in their cage, right up until that hand reaches down and grabs one at random, they're happy. As long as they're fed, they're happy, they're content. For them, life is good in that life is easy. It takes so little to keep them satisfied, so little to dull their ambition. As long as they're getting food and water, they breed, they run around on their little wheel, going nowhere, protected from the elements. When someone speaks to them, they're not really speaking; they're just making sounds, cooing sounds, sounds whose only purpose is to quiet the animals, not to communicate an idea, certainly not to send a warning.

"And those ivory-tower elites, those bastards. Those elite bastards—whether they're some politician, some bureaucrat, some executive, or, in this case, some group of doctors who have, simply because there is no immediate check to their authority, taken it upon themselves to exceed their province, to exceed the authority given to them by man or nature—they take it upon themselves to play God. Maybe for some, at first, it may well be a desire to do good. But that initial virtue, that impulse to do good, how quickly it becomes self-aggrandizing when rooted upon no foundation external to oneself. It's such a small, easy, seamless step—moving from wanting to help others to believing that the object of their benevolence is their inferior. How quickly it becomes second nature for those elite bastards to disconnect from and totally discount the common man—to be totally oblivious to the concept that no person or entity has bestowed upon them superior rights and privileges over the lives of others.

"No, for society at large, it's always going to be a fight against a vicious downward spiral. The elite spiral up in their estimations of themselves while, at the same time, too many ordinary people get themselves into a downward spiral. They get fat and happy, content in the relative easiness of their lives. They allow themselves to become not much more than lab rats—lab rats happy in their environment—until it's too late. They accept their lot without question because, in a short passage of time of easy living, they cease to consider any alternative. Their lives become limited because their thoughts are limited. As long as they have easy access to food and shelter, as long as they live in relative comfort, they have little drive. They rarely look beyond their next picnic or weekend. They have little interest, little curiosity of events of the world beyond their own limited horizon. Those press releases that you mentioned, Bert, they don't read those kind of reports or news stories. None of them read about the very experiments that are being conducted upon them. Such is not their interest. At most, they use the pages of a press release to line the bottom of a bird cage. Hell, they're the ones who are in the cages, and, for all practical purposes, they rarely look beyond their own confine. They don't see beyond the narrow world that contains them. But those poor, trusting people. Those poor, trusting people who go to the clinics. They're not rats; they're people. And their greatest sin, the sin for which they pay a price greater than most will ever fathom, is that so few of them ever take the time or effort to look beyond their immediate horizon—a vista that is limited only by a lack of will to simply open their eyes a bit wider and look beyond."

David, the course of his thoughts concluded, looked to Bert and then Rogers, and said, "Sorry guys. I guess I wandered off topic a bit there. Sorry."

Bert kicked David's foot under the table and said, "Jeez professor, what do you say we don't put any of that into your report?"

Rogers tapped the table with the bottom of his fist, as if gaveling the meeting to adjournment. "Alright guys. David, finish up anything that can't wait until tomorrow and then go home. You've been on the road a lot these last few days. Go home, take a shower, get a good meal and some sleep. We'll see you tomorrow. Bert, drive him home when he's ready. Tomorrow and the next few days, while we're waiting for Johnson to make his move, you two get that report together on what all you've found on this Clinic's business. Look it over and let me know if there's anything else about them that we should follow up on. Then, if we're still of the same mind, we'll turn it over to Justice."

Chapter 17

David and Bert Have Lunch

Chattanooga, TN
July 1946

Half an hour past the time that they usually broke for lunch, Bert's stomach began to grumble. David, still busy at his desk, could hear it from across the aisle. A few grumbles later, Bert shoved back from his desk and rolled over in his chair, closer to David, and said, "How's it looking, Pal? 'Bout time I either take you home or go to lunch."

"I've got fifteen, maybe twenty minutes of paperwork left here. I hate to have to come back from lunch for just that little bit. Just give me a couple more minutes to finish up and then we can grab lunch on the way home?"

"Alright, twenty minutes, max," Bert said, punching his index finger towards the clock on the wall as if starting a timer. "This ole country boy is getting hungry."

Forty minutes later they were sitting in a corner booth at Bethea's Restaurant—a nice, pleasant little family restaurant, a meat and three, one of their favorite places. The menu was printed on two mimeographed sheets of paper, inserted into the inner pockets of a red plastic booklet with rounded metal flanges to protect the corners. At the top of the inside left page was a plastic clip, in which a smaller sheet with the daily specials hung in front of the regular offerings. David glanced over the Daily Specials, then, looking up at the waitress, ordered a pork chop, green beans, baked cinnamon apples, side salad with blue cheese dressing, and unsweet tea, and handed his menu back to the waitress. The waitress, smacking her gum without interruption, tucked the menu under her arm and looked down at Bert, nudging him along by simply raising her eyebrows. Bert ordered the fried chicken livers, mashed potatoes and gravy, mac and cheese, fried okra, and sweet tea.

"Be right up," she said, finishing her scribbles as she started towards the kitchen.

With his index finger, Bert hooked the plastic, wicker-like basket of biscuits and cornbread sitting in the middle of the table, pulled it next to his bread plate, pulled back the red and white checkered cloth that nestled the contents, selected a big, hot, fluffy biscuit, and pushed the bread basket back to the middle of the table. Next to the basket was a small, chilled, white, ceramic bowl filled with chips of ice and pats of butter sandwiched between a piece of slick, white, cardboard stock on the bottom and a piece of stiff, semi-clear, waxy paper on top.

David sipped his tea and watched, for what seemed like the millionth time, as Bert pulled opened the flakey biscuit like an oyster shell and inserted two pats of butter. He raised the biscuit to his mouth, paused before taking a generous bite, and said, "Okay, Davy-boy, tell me what you didn't say at our meeting this morning."

David pinched the lemon wedge resting on the top of the ice in his glass, squeezing a few drops into the tea, and took another sip, barely wetting his lips. If it had been anyone other than Bert or Lill, he would have said, "What do you mean?" But this was Bert asking, and they both knew that despite all the things that David had said, there were still unsaid things lingering in his mind.

David began slowly, "You know, there's a lot of stuff that's great about working for the FBI. There are a lot of really good people, smart people, kind people—people with a lot of integrity. But, you know, outside of the world of ideas, nothing is entirely pure. There's always some degree of impurity, some degree of devilment that's seemingly impossible to shake. I don't know. Sometimes I chalk it up, saying to myself, 'that's just life; there's no getting around it.' Other times I have to wonder if it's really more of a matter as to how much crap a person is willing to put up with. It's almost as if we are continually being tested. I don't know. Maybe it's beyond the individual; maybe it's a matter of how much, collectively, we are willing to accept."

David swirled his glass of tea, tilted it slightly and wiped the cool sweat dripping from the bottom corner onto the coaster beneath. He continued, "A lot of the time, I think we just tell ourselves that it's easier to just let things go, to not let yourself get bogged down with all the minutia, all the debris and impurities that seem to creep into almost every aspect of our lives. But sometimes, well, there's just no escape. It's not like you're actively looking for problems, but crap, sometimes it's just like the saying goes; sometimes familiarity does breed contempt. So many things, so many people, from a distance—you just don't see the flaws. You see a façade, but you don't really see what's within. You see what they want you to see; you see what you want to see. Some things just bear scrutiny better than others. And, for the most part, I suppose that's not a big deal. So many things seem trivial, and we tell ourselves that it's not worth the bother. We tell ourselves that we can ignore them with relative impunity. We avoid the prospect that, over time, all these little things, well, they can add up. But some things, some things are just too big to avoid without a conscious effort. Some things are just plopped in the middle of our path, and, like it or not, we are forced to make a judgment."

David paused and wet his lips again. Bert, not wanting to rush David's thoughts, slowly chewed his biscuit. David, organizing on the fly some of the many divergent ideas that had been pinging around in the back of his mind since leaving D.C., continued, "A person's character is like a mosaic. For that matter, so is an organization's, or even an entire society's. It takes time for it to develop, to mature; but, over time, thousands of different pieces accumulate and meld together. As time passes, as events etch out their marks, a pattern forms. Bit by bit the picture fills in and the essence, for lack of a better word, of a thing gains clarity. For good or bad, the natural character of a person or an organization can't help but to reveal itself as its image gains clarity. No, clarity isn't quite the right word. Maybe consistency or familiarity is a better word; I don't know. Most days, it seems like there is some consistency, some overall direction or guiding force at play. It's great when most of the pictures are pretty, pleasant ones. Then, it's easy for people to believe that an all-powerful God is in heaven, keeping the devil at bay, and all is right with the world. But what are we to think when a lot of the pictures are not so pretty? And then, what about the days, days in which it feels like there is no pattern, no direction, no guiding force; days in which the randomness of it all becomes the predominate feature. Like someone or something has reached down with their thumb and smudged the picture or placed a random, unexpected tile in the mosaic and the consistency of the picture gets a bit distorted. What are we to think when randomness appears to overtake the deliberate, when randomness surpasses the intentional, when a growing segment of an image appears as nothing more than an indiscriminate blur of colors? I suppose that even randomness, true randomness, can also be evidence to . . . well, I'm not sure what. Maybe the ancients were right; maybe it's just the gods trying to stir up a bit of entertainment to alleviate their boredom?"

Bert, having finished with his first biscuit, rubbed his lips with the side of his index finger and observed, "You don't trust the Ring Leaders at HQ, do you?"

David leaned forward in his chair, closing the distance between them so that they could speak in a softer, more private voice. Resting his elbows on the table with his hands together, forming the top of an upside-down V, he felt a rough spot on his thumb's cuticle and looked down at it as he picked on it for a moment. Then, looking up eye to eye with Bert, David gave a slight nod of his head and said, "You know, Bert, 'Ring Leaders' is probably the exact right word. It's a circus up there, an act, a huge deception. They're a bunch of clowns—with paint-on faces—telling us a story. But all too often, it's a made-up story, a fiction. And what's worse, some days we're part of the show; we're up on that stage with them. Other days, we're part of the audience. It's like a magician's show, when the magician gets someone from the audience to come up on stage for a while to be part of the act. The volunteer has no real idea what's going on, has no idea how the tricks are pulled. And then, even if the hapless stooge does happen to figure out what's going on—what's he going to do? He's not going to say anything; he's not going to do anything. He's not going to be the one who ruins the act. No one wants to be booed. That volunteer from the crowd—he plays a vital part; he gives credibility to the stunt. But in the eyes of the magician, that volunteer on stage has no more value than a puppet at the end of a string. He's just another prop."

Bert remained quiet. David continued, "You know, Hoover talks a big game about teamwork and integrity and all, but, looking at that Dillinger display, the irony was, really, almost too much. When a person looks at that death mask, you would think that they would think about Dillinger—how bad he was, what happened to him, all the great teamwork that went into getting him. But it was strange. When I looked down through the glass into that display case—when I looked at that mask, really looked at it—my mind shifted. I started to think about what happened to Purvis, the agent who got the bulk of the credit for finally getting Dillinger. I remembered how the papers really talked him up, made a hero out of him, and justifiably so. But Hoover couldn't stand that. He couldn't stand for anyone to outshine him for even a moment. So, we all know what happened to Purvis. Sure, technically, Hoover left Purvis in charge of the Chicago field office, but he kept him out of the limelight, away from reporters, by sending Purvis on a never-ending series of 'inspection tours' to one podunk town after another. And on top of that, Hoover made it quite clear to everyone that it was Purvis who was to blame for those people getting killed at Little Bohemia. Well, maybe so. But the point is, Hoover couldn't stand for anyone else getting some of the spotlight, not even for a minute. Hoover knew he couldn't fire Purvis outright; the backlash would have been untenable. So, he does the next best thing; he makes Purvis's life so miserable that he finally quits.

"But, beyond all that, the thing that is even more troubling to me about this Dillinger business is what happened to Anna Sage. Hoover reneged on his deal with her. Hoover reneged on his deal to work with the Labor Department to cancel her deportation, and then he gives her only half of the reward that was promised for turning in Dillinger. We can dance around the facts all we want, but when it's all said and done, Hoover didn't keep his end of the bargain. I know Miss Sage isn't exactly a model citizen or a pillar of the community; she was a madam for a whorehouse. But does that excuse Hoover for breaking his word to her? Is our integrity—whether or not we keep our word to someone— dependent upon how we view their level of virtue or righteousness? I know, I know; you can make a case that justifies lying in extreme instances, say, to a Hitler or someone who is really bad in order to stop them from doing tremendous harm, but that's not what we're talking about here. Take that police officer for example. That police officer who introduced Miss Sage to Purvis . . . what was his name? He was a policeman from Indiana."

"Sergeant Zarkovich," Bert said in a simple, quiet, matter-of-fact manner.

"Yes, that's it. Sergeant Zarkovich, Martin Zarkovich was his name," David acknowledged, nodding his head. "From what I understand, Zarkovich was a customer of the good Madam. I mean, I'm not trying to build a case against him or in defense of Miss Sage. All I'm asking is, was she so bad that it is justifiable to lie to her, to throw her to the wolves because she is deemed to be an inferior person? Yeah, she was a madam; she was a seller of human flesh, but Zarkaovich was a buyer. Zarkaovich was no saint; he was in on the deal. And from what I've heard, nothing happened to him. He's still an officer of the law with all of its rights and privileges. Hell, when you group Sage, Zarkovich, and Hoover together, knowing what we both know about all of Hoover's skullduggery, one could argue that Hoover would easily take the crown in a moral turpitude contest. That is, I mean, if you're going to go by the Marquis of Queensberry rules."

Bert responded with a simple, "Okay, I grant you all that . . . so what's your point. Does any of that change anything for us? What are you suggesting that we do?"

David gave a slight shrug of his shoulders and said, "I don't know, Bert. Nothing, I guess. All I'm saying, all I'm thinking is that sometimes it's easier to pretend the world is what we would like for it to be, rather than having to deal with it as we know it really is. Sometimes you can get away with doing that, but, then again, sometimes ignoring reality can really bite you in the ass. All I'm saying is that there are some really bad people out there, and some of them might be inconvenienced by what we're about to do—and that goes for both sides. The Russians, well, it's no secret that there are some horrifically devious and dangerous players on their side. And we both know that those guys play for keeps. But, hell, even on our side, if even a fraction of what Johnson says about infiltrations into our organizations is true, then, well, those guys have a lot to lose—everything to lose, if we expose them. Some of those guys could potentially get the death penalty; look at what happened to the Rosenbergs.

"All I'm saying is that we, the two of us, have gone into some pretty dark, deserted buildings, looking to bring out some pretty desperate people. But the two of us have some history together; we know each other; we know that we can trust each other; we've got each other's back. But this new business, well, everything seems to have a tinge of murkiness about it. I'm talking about this business with VanZant. Johnson has warned us about him, but we're so accustomed to viewing Americans as the good guys and the Russians as the bad guys that it's real easy to pooh-pooh

Johnson's warnings. After all, VanZant is an American. He's an American with government clearance. He can waltz in and out of the Oak Ridge labs as he pleases. He's supposed to be on our side. Then we find out about the Vanderbilt clinic, the shenanigans that they're pulling, and look who we find in the middle of all that—VanZant. And then, to put the cherry on top of the cake, we put an awful lot of faith in Hoover and his acolytes while knowing full well that Hoover will lie if it suits his purpose. But then, we tell ourselves that he's on our side; he's doing it for the good guys. But that's not always the case. This Dillinger-Sage business isn't the only example. Hoover, he talks a big game about teamwork and integrity, but, if we're going to be honest with ourselves, we have to admit that, to Hoover, the reputation of integrity—the perception of having integrity—supersedes the importance of actually acting with integrity. We're pretty quick to overlook a lot here just to keep our lives simple and not stir anything up. I don't know; are we being a bit naïve here, or am I just letting a lot of little things get to me too much? Life would sure be a lot simpler if the good guys wore white hats and the bad guys wore black—God, with his white robes and a halo; the devil in red with his pitchfork. Yeah, it would be a lot simpler if everyone wore a uniform."

Bert gave a slight, outward-turning motion of his hands towards David, the equivalent of an uncertain shrug. David said, "Okay, okay. Maybe I've gone off the rails here a bit, but, come on, that mask—it's just creepy to keep a death mask on display in your office. I mean, what kind of a person does a thing like that? It's ghoulish. No, maybe I'm being a bit of a Boy Scout here, but decent people don't parade around with scalps hanging from their belts. Hell, Johnson has trust issues with his people—and for good reason with all the purges and quirks of Stalin and everything else going on over there. But you have to admit, there's more than a little irony at play here. The Russians are more openly brutal with their secret police, closed borders, and purges; but then, we're the ones displaying death masks and other trophies in our lobby."

The waitress arrived with their food. David and Bert watched in silence as she set their lunch before them on the table, marveling that she was able to deliver it all in one load, balanced on one tray.

When she left, David picked up his fork and concluded, "All I'm saying is that, standing in the Justice Building, in front of Hoover and Tolson, looking at that dead face, that mask; all I could think about was integrity. It just feels to me like we're about to walk into a really dark building with Mr. Deathmask watching our back."

Chapter 18

VanZant's Associate

Washington, D.C.
July 1946

Daytime work hours were almost over. VanZant was catching up on some routine reports and tedious housekeeping matters that had piled up on his desk, but all day he had had a hard time keeping his mind on the mundane. His eyes kept wandering over to the intercom at the top of his desk. Why hadn't he called yet? Was this business with David DeRieux and Bert Ashton going to be a problem for him, or was this all going to blow over soon, just another flash in the pan?

He picked up a red pencil to circle a few items that needed to be revisited, when the intercom on his desk buzzed, followed by the voice of his secretary, "Mr. Trimble from The Book Store is on line one for you."

"Okay, I'll take it." VanZant picked up his phone, punched a button, and said, "I'd about given up on you for today."

"I told you it might be late in the day."

"Okay, okay. Anything interesting turn up on those names I gave you yesterday?"

"Yeah, beyond interesting. I'm not sure what all you've got going on right now, but just asking about those guys is getting me closer to the fire than I normally like to get."

"Tell me."

"Let's get a soda."

"Okay, twenty minutes."

"See you in twenty."

VanZant hung up the phone. He thought for a brief moment, then pulled a key from his front pocket, unlocked his desk drawer, selected three thin file folders, and locked them in his briefcase. After relocking and testing his desk, he stood, put the key back in his pocket, grabbed the handle of his briefcase, and headed for the door. Without slowing as he passed his secretary's desk, he turned his head slightly in her direction, gave two quick taps on her desktop with his fingertips, and said, "I'm gone for the day."

The soda fountain area of the neighborhood drugstore was a narrow, secluded sliver in the back right corner of the building. As far as soda fountains go, the best feature of this one was that when it wasn't crowded, it was fairly private; and, even at lunchtime, it was rarely all that busy. There were no booths, just an L-shaped counter with a row of big, red-cushioned, high-back barstools. A wall, running just behind the stools, allowed for a narrow but adequate aisleway and added a great deal of privacy for the patrons in that no one could sneak up or listen from behind. At the far end of the aisleway, against the back wall of the building, was a large, wooden phone booth. When it wasn't in use, the door was left open, making it easy to see if any eavesdroppers were lurking around there.

When VanZant entered the fountain area, the man he was looking for was already there, sitting alone at the far end of the counter, on the last bar stool which was only a step or two away from the open phone booth. He was sipping on a freshly made fountain Coca-Cola. Other than the young soda jerk, who was cleaning up around the twin, shiny, long-neck, chrome soda faucets that were positioned midway down the counter, no one else was there. VanZant let his hand glide across the smooth tops of the high-back stools as he walked the length of the counter and took the seat next to the man.

As VanZant passed by, the soda jerk set his cleaning towel down and followed VanZant to his seat, set a square napkin on the counter in front of VanZant, and asked, "What can I get for you?"

VanZant pointed to his associate's drink. "The same."

"Cherry Coke, coming up," replied the clerk.

The two men sat in silence and watched as the clerk pulled a frosted glass from a freezer cabinet, pumped a few squirts of syrup from one spout, then a single squirt from another spout, held the glass under the big chrome faucet with one hand and, pulling the long handle with his other hand, filled the glass halfway full with the fizzy, pressurized water. A scoop of small ice cubes brought the fluid level up close to the top of the glass, and a plump red cherry with a long stem, plopped on top, finished off the process.

The clerk walked the drink down the counter to VanZant, set the drink on the napkin in front of VanZant, and placed a straw to the side. "Anything else I can get for you two gentlemen?" the clerk asked.

"No, thank you." VanZant replied. As the clerk wiped his way back towards the middle of the counter, VanZant picked up his straw, removed the paper cover, jabbed the cherry resting on top of the ice to the bottom of the glass, stirred slowly, and when the clerk was a suitable distance away, said, "Okay, tell me."

All that remained of the associate's cherry was the stem sitting on the napkin next to his glass. He picked up the stem and twirled it between his thumb and forefinger. Turning his head and body slightly towards VanZant, he asked, "Where'd those names come from?"

"Let's just say they've been heckling a friend of mine. What's the story on them?"

"Well, the story on them is that DeRieux spent the day here yesterday, here in D.C., at the Bureau's Headquarters. Even spent some time on the fifth floor."

"Do you happen to know why?"

"Seems a Russian spy has decided to defect. For some reason this spy, named Johnson, at least for now, has singled out DeRieux as the guy who he wants to do business with. Appears this Johnson fellow has some serious trust issues and, for now anyway, David is the guy he trusts, the guy he wants to be his conduit. Nothing, out of the ordinary, came up on Bert Ashton."

"So, they're staging a defection. Anything else?"

The associate tossed the cherry stem back down on his napkin, turned his head, and looking directly at VanZant said, "DeRieux asked them about you."

VanZant's poker face slipped a bit. His eyebrows went up a tad as his eyes widened. "What the hell? Why'd he ask about me?"

"You tell me. You asked about these guys; you must have had some reason for asking. This ain't a coincidence."

"Well, what was the context? What were they saying about me?"

"I don't know. All I could gather for now was that somehow your name came up. For some reason, DeRieux brought your name into the conversation. Why, I don't know."

VanZant sat in silence, thinking.

The associate continued, "I thought your interests were purely . . . domestic?"

VanZant, quietly introspective, said, "They are; they are. This doesn't make sense. I did cross paths with DeRieux recently, but it was slight, insignificant—seemed like a coincidence at most. I didn't even know that he was there, that he had seen me, until a colleague mentioned it to me after the fact. I think I might know what's going on here, but it seems largely out of proportion. It seems out of context that he should be asking about me at HQ, especially in the middle of a defection planning session."

"Well, like I said, I don't know the exact context. I don't know if it was just a casual reference or inquiry, or something more. But in any case, your name was mentioned, and that in itself—in the context of such a meeting—is, well, notable."

VanZant appeared to have recomposed himself. "Okay, well, see what more you can find out. This defection business, what did you say that Russian's name is?"

"Johnson."

"Yeah, right; Johnson. Find out everything you can on this defection business—all the details, all the players, timetables, places . . . really everything. I need to know everything that's going on here. Our whole operation depends upon not ever being surprised by anyone. As long as no one is interested in us, we're golden. Whatever has put us on this DeRieux guy's radar screen, well, we've got to get ahead of this. Sidetrack it if that's enough, but I'm not willing to take a chance with anything or anyone who might draw us into a spotlight. You gonna have any problem getting me this information?"

The associate looked down at the cherry stem, placed his hand next to it and started to rock it back and forth on the napkin with the tip of his index finger. Without looking up, he said, "I'll keep my ears open. My people know I'm interested. It may take a little longer than usual; I don't want to poke too hard on this. I don't like to poke a nest when I don't know what's in it. And this nest, well, I'm thinking there's something lurking in it that could sting me."

VanZant swiveled slowly on his stool towards his associate, moved his hand near his associate's hand, and made a soundless snapping motion with his thumb.

The associate turned his head to VanZant. VanZant's cold eyes looked directly into the associate's. In a slow, deadpan voice, VanZant said, "You'll get me that information, and I mean fast."

Chapter 19

Preparing for Defection

Chattanooga, TN
July 1946

David was late to work. It was a week to the day since his return from his trip to DC. When he walked through the door, Bert, seated at his desk, pointed to the clock on the wall and then rubbed his right finger over his pointing left finger, like a school-aged boy taunting a chum who had gotten into trouble. David replied with a silent chuckle and smile, then pointed to the conference room, indicating that they needed to talk.

Rogers, as Senior Agent in Charge, supervised the office from his desk in the back corner of the room. As David approached, Rogers looked up and quipped, "Running a little late today, David? I was getting a little worried, about to call your wife."

"Had to make a stop at the library on the way in."

"Jesus, David . . . enough with the books already."

"Johnson's turned up. Conference room?" David suggested, raising his eyebrows and pointing to the door at the back of the office.

Rogers nodded. "Let me grab my file."

When Rogers entered the conference room, David and Bert were just settling into their usual seats across from each other at the far end of the table. Rogers closed the door, walked the length of the room, and took his place at the head of the table—Bert to his left, David to his right. "Okay," he began while setting a short stack of files to his left and a fresh legal pad and pen in front of himself on the table. Then, looking at David, he gave a slight wave with his open hand and said, "Tell us."

David cleared his throat and began, "Well, it's happening. And, one way or another, it's going to happen much faster than we had anticipated. Like it or not, Johnson's started the clock. In fact, we need to make this meeting quick so that I can get on the horn to HQ. When I got to my bus stop this morning, a young man, late teens – early twenties, someone I don't recall ever having seen before, was standing at my bus stop. When the bus came into sight, he handed me an unaddressed, sealed envelope. A note within said, 'Public Library — Go Inside — Go Now', and was signed 'MJ'. No doubt, Michael Johnson."

David paused. Neither Bert nor Rogers made a sound or a gesture. David continued, "The young man told me that someone he didn't know, a middle-aged man, had given him five dollars to go to that bus stop, wait, and give me the note. The young man said that he was instructed to wait until the bus was in sight before giving me the envelope, to make sure that I read the note inside the envelope right away, to not get on the bus with me, but to walk away as soon as I had read the note. Conveniently, of course, the library's stop is on my bus's route in."

Bert raised his finger and asked, "How did the man know that you were the right person to give the note to?"

David answered, "I had wondered the same thing. There wasn't time to ask. The bus was there and I had to decide, on the spot, whether to follow the instructions to the letter and get on the bus without the young man, or potentially jeopardize the meeting by deviating from the instructions. Clearly, Johnson didn't want me spending much time with the young man. Whether it was just Johnson being nice and not wanting to get some random person caught up in this, or if he had some other reason as to why he didn't want us to question the young man—who knows. I hate to venture a guess, but my gut feeling is that Johnson simply doesn't want any more people than necessary dragged into his affairs. However, there's always the possibility that there is more to all of this than Johnson has led us to believe. For instance, what if we got to questioning the young man, and the description of the person who gave the young man the five dollars did not match our description of Johnson. What would that mean? Anyway, Bert, to answer your question, I have no idea how the young man could know for certain to whom he should give the note. Johnson wouldn't have just said, 'give this to the man at the bus stop.' That could be anyone. Even giving the young man a good description of me would still be chancing it. I wouldn't be at all surprised if Johnson has a picture of me and showed it to the young man. That would really be the only way to be certain, unless that young man is more involved in this than we suspect; and that, I think, would really be a long shot. In any case, one thing we have learned about Johnson is that the man does do his homework and covers his bases the best that he can.

"Moving on, when I entered the library, Johnson wasn't in the lobby entry area, so I went into the reference reading section; you know, the big room with all the periodicals and the tables in the center. He was there. He caught my eye from across the room. I scratched my ear, the signal that Johnson had said to use if everything was okay. He turned, and I followed him back into the archive stacks. He asked if I'd be missed for the next hour. I told him that I had some time; that it would be okay. He handed me this map." David unfolded a sheet of paper—a rough, hand-drawn map, in pencil, and set it between Rogers and Bert where they could both see. Pointing to parts on the map as he spoke, David continued, "This square is the Public Library, and this area is the University of Chattanooga's campus just behind the library. Over here, on the other side of the campus, is that old graveyard that borders the University on the north side. Here, in the middle of the cemetery, he's marked a spot for us to meet. There are two entrances to that cemetery: one, here, that's on the border with the University's grounds. The other is over here, on the opposite side of the cemetery. The cemetery is about a block wide and borders up against Third Street on that far side. Other than the two entrances and a gated service entrance, it's walled and fenced all around. Anyway, as you can see, Johnson has outlined a route that takes me through the entrance at the farthest side of the cemetery, the one off Third Street there. The path that he's drawn for me to follow takes me up and around the far west end of the rectangle. He asks if I mind taking that long route. Says he will be going a different route and will meet me there. Obviously, he takes the much shorter route, entering the closer side, and gets there well before me. By getting there first, from that high ground in the cemetery, he could easily see if either of us was being followed. He told me that, as I approach that spot, if I don't see him, to just keep walking and we'll try another time.

"Of course, I agree. I leave first and all goes as planned. We meet at his spot in the cemetery. I walk at a normal pace, and it takes me about eight, maybe ten minutes to get there. He's anxious, a little worried. I'm a little surprised at that. I had him pegged as a really cool cucumber. I still think he is. I don't know. No telling what he's got going on at his end. No doubt, he has good reason to be worried; after all, the lives of his wife and son are at stake, not to mention his own. He asks me if everything is okay. He asks me if we'll help him get his family out. I tell him we will, but that Headquarters wanted the answers to a few questions first. He asks, 'what kind of questions?' I tell him they want more specifics about the type of information that we can expect from him. He cuts me short; says there isn't time. He tells me that he's worried that things might be coming undone at his end. Says it's too dangerous for his wife and child to wait. He's afraid that they could be picked up at any time. Between our people now knowing of his plan to defect, and the few people in Russia who are helping with his wife's travel and crossing—even though he trusts those people in Russia, still, he says, just too many people know. He's afraid, and really, I don't blame him. He tells me that they, his wife and son, have already left their apartment in Moscow and are en route to the border as we speak. He says he's reasonably confident that they'll be successful in crossing the border, but he is concerned about what happens to them once they get across. Says once they cross the border, they're largely on their own. Said they have an address that they'll go to, in a town near where they'll be crossing, but, at best, it's a tenuous safe-house, and they can wait there for only a short time. He said that if all goes well, his wife and son should cross the border two days from now. He said he needed to know now if we would help, if we would meet them. He said they would be crossing the border the day after tomorrow and asked if that was enough time for us to arrange to take them in. I told him I thought so but would have to check with HQ—that they were really wanting some more answers before they committed. He said, 'The cards have been delt. The game has started. What do we do?' I asked where along the border they were crossing. He clearly didn't want to tell me without a commitment and assurances from me, but even he could see that, particularly given the short time allowed, we couldn't commit to a rendezvous without knowing exactly where it was going to be. I told him that and reminded him that not all of the Western side of the Soviet Bloc border was in the American control zone. He said he understood that. He said his wife and son would be traveling through Czechoslovakia, and that the crossing place they had planned was in Bavaria, which is definitely in the United States Control Zone. Said his wife and son would make their way to a town not far from the border and, hopefully, rendezvous with our contacts there. Then, he told me the name of the town: it's Passau. For now, he's holding out on the specific address that they're going to. It's a good-sized town in Lower Bavaria. Really should be no problem for us to arrange a pickup there. That is, if our people are willing to go along with this expedited timetable. I hope so. I mean, at this point, I don't really see a downside. Once we have Johnson's wife and son in our custody, a lot of the pressure goes away. Once Johnson knows they've made it safely across and are in our custody, he should be able to settle down. After that, it'll take a little time to get them back here to the United States, and then, a little more time to get them to Tullahoma. By the way, I mentioned to Johnson that that is where we think the reunification with his family should be. It only took him a second or two of thought—he is fine with Tullahoma. He's obviously familiar with our Army Base there. I wouldn't be surprised if he knows more about it than the three of us do. Anyway, once we have his family in custody, we can slow the clock down again if we need to. Even after he's reunified with his family, if something doesn't seem right, if the wheels start to come off this wagon, well, at that point we've got him; we've got his family; we've got all the cards.

"In any case, Johnson has started the clock; he has put his plan in motion. But time is short, and his plan just gets his family to Passau. Once they're there, in Passau, what he's telling us is that from there, it's up to us. Sure, it's possible that he's intentionally rushing us so that we make some sort of mistake, overlook something in our hurry to help him, but I don't think so. It's up to us, or . . . I don't know if he has a plan B."

"All right," Rogers said, making a note on his pad. "I guess you need to advise HQ, pronto. Send them a coded telex."

"First thing on my list."

"One quick thing before you get started. How have you set up your next communication with Johnson?"

"We're meeting tomorrow, late morning, eleven o'clock at the Brainerd Mission Cemetery. You know, it's that really old one that's about a mile past my neighborhood—down Brainerd Road."

Rogers cringed a little and gasped, "Jesus, David. What's with this guy and cemeteries?"

"I don't know. These old cemeteries, though, aren't really a bad place to meet. There's good cover to hide, and it doesn't look all that odd for two people to be standing, talking for a few minutes in one place. Plus, this one should be pretty quiet; not many people go there. I think the people buried there are mainly missionaries from the early 1800s. Like I say, not a lot of visitors and you can see from a pretty good distance if someone unexpected shows up. Anyhow, he picked the place. I think it's fine."

David continued, "Could be, though, maybe it's as simple as subconsciously his mind just takes him to places of death. I hope that's not it, but it's obvious he's worried. Now that his wife has fled her apartment, he's got to be more worried about the people on his end than on ours. He's got to know that if we're going to betray him, there's not a lot he can do to protect himself, other than to bolt and disappear. He's got to know, at this point, there's no good reason to be coy with us about setting up meetings. That would just slow everything down, and, for all practical purposes, he can't afford for any of us to waste any time. No, he's worried about the guys on his side. No telling how closely he's watched and checked on by his people. Yeah, all in all, it's not a bad place to meet. If he's seen in one of these cemeteries, there's lots of cover stories he can use. He could say he's scoping out dead drop spots; he could say a lot of things.

"Anyway, if he isn't convinced at tomorrow's meeting that we're all on track, I'm not sure what he'll do. I mean, well, his family is en route; there's no going back on that now. Really, about the only card he still holds is the address in Passau that his family is going to. If we give him reason to think that we might not be committed to meeting them on time, well, I don't know what, or if, he has a plan B. I wouldn't think that he could get a message to his wife now, even if he wanted to. I get the feeling that if we stall, well, I'm thinking he might bolt. Like I say, regardless of whatever happens at our end, his family is en route, and they'll be somewhere in Passau, Germany in about two days. If he doesn't think that we'll come through for him, I don't know what he has planned, but I'll bet we'll have seen the last of him if we get too cutesy with him. I don't think anyone wants that— hopefully not HQ."

Rogers, still writing and looking down at his pad, asked, "One more thing, Dave. Did you get the name of that young man who gave you the note at your bus stop?"

"Yeah. It's in my notes. You don't need that now, do you? I mean, unless the wheels really come off this wagon, I don't anticipate the need to investigate that guy. At least not for now. If he's just a random person, then we'd be wasting our time investigating him. If he's part of a scheme, then investigating him may tip our hand to who knows who, especially given the limited amount of time that we have."

Rogers looked up at David. "Yeah, okay. Get your telex off to HQ. Keep us posted. Keep us current as best as you can."

David, consolidating all his material into one stack, replied, "I'm on it," then stood and headed out the door.

Bert started to get up. Rogers pointed his finger towards Bert and said, "Bert."

"Yeah, Boss?"

"Watch his back."

"Count on it."

Chapter 20

Camp Forrest

Middle Tennessee
July 1946

"Today is going to be an interesting day," David said in a low voice to himself.

David and Bert had been riding well over an hour in their Bureau car as they emerged from the mountains of East Tennessee, crossing the indeterminate border onto the somewhat flatter topography of Middle Tennessee, heading north and west from Chattanooga towards Camp Forrest, an army base near Tullahoma. Bert was driving. David, leaning on the passenger door's armrest, looked out the window to his right. The warm morning breeze felt good on his face as he watched the countryside's open fields, barns, silos, ponds, and forests pass by; occasionally interrupted by a house with a large, covered front porch and a yard full of chickens, children, and dogs at play; a woman with a mouthful of wooden pins hanging laundry, a farmer bouncing on the seat of his tractor. Bert heard David, but between the softness of David's voice and the rushing hot summer air from the open window, Bert couldn't make out what David had said.

"Speak up, boy," Bert bellowed in a voice loud enough to overcome the noise. "Can't hear ya."

David turned from the window, swiveling his torso left on the large bench seat to direct his voice towards Bert. Seeking to overcome the ambient sights and sounds, David stretched his left arm out across the top of the middle portion of the large bench seat and leaned his head and upper body slightly towards Bert. "I just said, 'Knee-high by the fourth of July.'"

Bert replied, "You say that every time we pass a corn field."

"I know, I know. When I was young, my mom and dad used to take my two sisters and me on a road-trip vacation every summer. Back then, once you left the city, once you left Chicago, it was all pretty much gravel roads—tar and gravel I guess—until you came to the next town. One year, we went all the way to California, all the way to the coastline, the water's edge. My father said he had always wanted to put his hand into the Pacific Ocean—and then he did. I can still see it now, so clear, like it just happened moments ago. I don't even need to close my eyes to see it. It's funny how some memories remain so clear no matter how many years have passed. I can't image those type of memories ever fading. Anyway, that trip, we stopped at lots of the National Parks and camp sites along the way. We had a big tent. At least back then it seemed big to me. At night, we would just pull over somewhere and set up camp. Nobody seemed to mind, you know, as long as you didn't camp right in someone's front yard or somehow make a nuisance of yourself. In the morning, my mom would mix up a gallon jug of lemonade and we'd drink on that all day. That trip, we stopped and camped in Yellowstone National Park—saw Old Faithful. I was probably ten or twelve that year. Yeah, back then, you could camp almost anywhere. Not all that many people in the Parks either. Not many restrictions; not many rules and regulations. We camped—pitched our tent—within sight of Old Faithful itself. Anyway, whenever we passed a corn field my mom would always call out, 'Knee-high by the fourth of

July,' and then she'd laugh. She'd say that was what the farmers always said and prayed for. That if it was knee high by then, everything was alright. If it wasn't, then they were in trouble."

"That's a great story, David, but it's been miles since we've passed any corn, and what corn we've passed is high enough. What were you really mumbling about over there?"

"Alright . . . I was just thinking to myself that this was going to be an interesting day."

Bert nodded his head. David leaned forward and, with his right hand, adjusted the little triangle window on the front side of the door to direct more air onto himself. They had gotten an early start, but it was late July and already the day was promising to be a hot one. Dave settled back again on the seat.

Bert asked, in a monotone voice, "You worried?"

"Yeah, maybe a little."

"What's on your mind?"

"Well, all in all, this should be a good day—Johnson getting back together with his wife and son. The end of a chapter and the beginning of a new one for them, hopefully a better one. Really, for them, it's like being reborn into a new life, for all of them, a better life; at least a decent chance at one."

They traveled a quarter of a mile as Bert waited for the rest of David's thoughts. Bert prodded, "Okay, Dave, still not hearing the part about why you're worried."

"It's nothing, really. I was just thinking about what different worlds we live in compared to Johnson and his family. In our little world, since the end of the war anyway, things have been going pretty well. This business with Johnson, of course, has jazzed things up; but all in all, everything has gone reasonably smoothly; everything seems to be falling into place. We sit in a conference room, and we make our plans. I meet a spy in a park, a cemetery, a dime store; but this is America, modern-day America, and on the whole, in the great scheme of things, we're not the ones in danger. People like us, since we're in law enforcement, we live with more danger than most Americans, most law-abiding Americans. But even so, at the end of the day, we lay our heads down on our pillows, our families safe and sound down the hall, we are dry and warm, our bellies are full, and we get a good night's sleep. In our world, the likes of a Hitler, Stalin, or Robespierre are not likely to come and snatch us from our bliss.

"But Johnson's world is so different; it's hard to imagine. Really, I don't think it's something we can imagine. We're just fooling ourselves if we think we can. When Johnson lays his head down, what goes through his mind; how does sleep come? In Johnson's world, he can be snatched up at any time. The slightest misstep for him has the gravest consequence. Hell, in his world, it doesn't even have to be a misstep. It might just be a whim of someone's—someone with a lot, or even a little power—thinking that it would be better for them if he were dead. And think about how often we catch a criminal just because of some stupid coincidence or happenstance. Same applies to Johnson, and he has to know it. One stupid thing, one wicked thought—one inadvertent thought accidentally verbalized at the wrong time or place and bam, it's over for him. And if it's over for him, it's over for his family, and vice versa. Right now, his family is on the move. It's not like here, where we go where we want, when we want, and nobody thinks a thing of it. For them, they have to have a reason; they have to have permission, and they have to have documents. Or maybe they're being smuggled by someone who has a legitimate or plausible reason to be traveling. There's a thousand ways they could be scheming this, but they're all dangerous as hell; they all require that a handful of people keep their secrets. And if they get caught, Johnson probably wouldn't even know about it until someone started to beat on him in some interrogation room. That's how he'd find out if his plans went bad."

Bert replied, "Well, that hasn't happened. We know Johnson's wife and son made it over the border; we know our people have them. We know that they're on a plane right now and that they'll be landing at Camp Forrest in a couple of hours. And, by now, Johnson knows it too. No doubt he's seen your ad in this morning's paper, and he's on his way. By the way, what did it say?"

"It was in the lost-and-found section. Said a German Shepard had been found on Lookout Mountain and to call a Mr. Forrest Gates after 11:00 a.m."

"Okay then, Johnson knows. He knows we've got them; he knows to be at the Main Gate at Camp Forrest at eleven."

"Yeah, yeah, I know. I need to shake this. I guess Johnson has just rubbed off on me a little. He's always so worried, always so cautious. But that's the world he lives in, can't really blame him. Like I said, hopefully this is the end of a bad chapter in his life and the beginning of a really good one. I'm happy for him, but I'll sure be glad to get today behind us. All this cloak-and-dagger business wears on you. His world starts to become too much our world."

Bert said, "So the plan's still that I'm meeting the family at the plane and taking them to one of the guest houses that they've set up for us?"

"Yep. And I'll meet Johnson at the gate. I'm betting he'll be there right at eleven, right on time. We agreed that I'd be where he can see me from a distance. There's a little guard shack building at the entrance. I'm to position myself at the front right corner—front right as you're approaching the building from outside the camp. Anyway, he won't approach until I give a signal to indicate that his family is safely here and everything is okay. When he shows, I'll bring him to the guest house. This should be something to see. You know, I don't think I ever asked him how long it has been since he's seen his wife and child. I get the impression that it's been a good while. Obviously, communication is strictly limited, but I think he's been able to send things to her from time to time. That teddy bear I saw him buy—that, and a bunch of other stuff. It was like he was putting together a care package of sorts for his family. Someone must have been going back, someone he could send a package along with. I imagine that teddy bear had to be for his son."

A few more miles went by, Bert said, "Let's have a snack. You hungry? I'm hungry. Grab those bags in the back seat there, will ya, Dave."

Dave stretched over the back of the seat and retrieved two brown paper bags that Bert's wife had packed for them.

"What do we have here, Bert?" David said as he opened the first bag.

"Sausage biscuits and sweet tea. Jenny said she made us up two biscuits apiece. In the other bag should be some iced tea."

David pulled a handful of paper napkins from the top of the bag, then a sausage biscuit wrapped in wax paper. "What do you want first," David asked, "a biscuit or the tea?"

"Hand me a biscuit."

David handed Bert a big picnic napkin, and once Bert had it all spread out, he handed him a wrapped biscuit. As Bert pulled the wax paper back from one side of his biscuit, holding the wheel steady with his knee, David opened the bag with the drinks. Inside were two mason jars filled with sweet tea, a slice of lemon, a slice of orange, and partially melted ice cubes. The jars were insulated from each other by a couple of layers of paper napkins, damp from the sweat of the cool drinks.

David pushed the button on the glove compartment and a large door swung down, making a little level shelf. After unscrewing the lids, he set the jars into the slight indentions on the little tabletop of the glove compartment door, made just for that. Eyeing the precarious nature of the jars, David said to Bert, "don't do anything crazy or this will be all over me. Let me know when you want some tea."

David reached into the bag and pulled out a biscuit for himself, pulled the wax paper back, and took a bite. "That Jenny's okay," David said with a mouthful of biscuit.

*   *   *   *   *

When the front gate of Camp Forrest came into sight, there was nothing left of their snack but a bit of ice and some citrus fruit peels in the bottom of their mason jars. They each threw what was left from their jars out the windows. David rewrapped the empty jars so they wouldn't rattle and put them back in one bag, gathered up the used napkins and wax paper, and put them in the other, then threw them both into the back seat as they pulled up to the guard station at the main gate.

Both held their badges up as a guard standing at the side of the little building bent down to look into their car. Through the open doorway on the side of the guard building, Bert and David could see another soldier sitting at a desk within the building. Bert announced to the guard at their window, "FBI Special Agents Bert Ashton and David DeRieux."

"Yeah-yeah. Come on through," the guard said, barely looking at their badges and waving them forward with a casual, easy-going gesture of his hand.

There was no barrier or gate, just the small guard building with extended curbs and an overhanging roof, forming an island median between the entry and exit lanes. On top of the little building was a large sign that simply said "Camp Forrest".

Bert let his foot off the brake and the car rolled slowly forward as he looked around for a place to park. "Pretty easy going around here, isn't it?"

"No kidding," David replied. "I guess once a base goes on 'inactive status' it's a whole different ball game. But then again, that's what makes it perfect for what we're doing—a little security, but not enough to interfere or call undue attention to us."

Just off to their right, adjacent to the guard shack, a hard-packed dirt and gravel area extended seamlessly off from the side of the road, forming a small parking area. A scattering of mature, well-groomed hardwood trees, with lower limbs trimmed off so that cars and people could use and enjoy the shade beneath, air could circulate, and visibility not being unduly restricted, gave the area a clean, open, peaceful appeal.

A car and a short, bus-type vehicle were parked next to each other just off the road, making the beginnings of a short perpendicular row. A little further in, off by itself, was another parked car. David pointed to it. "I'll bet that's the car they left for us. Hope it is, anyway. Let's park next to it and then check in with the guard at the desk."

A Corporal looked up from his desk as David and Bert walked into the little building. "Can I help you gentlemen?" he asked.

David gave his name, flashed his badge, and said, "There's supposed to be a car waiting here for me to use."

The Corporal, without hesitation, said, "Yes, sir; yes, sir. I believe there is." He shuffled through a short stack of folders. Finding the one he wanted, he opened it, removed some stapled-together pages, flipped through a few pages, then folding back a page, set the paperwork on the edge of his desk, and said, "Sign here please."

David bent over, scanned the page, and signed next to where the Corporal had placed his finger. Rising from his chair, the Corporal said, "The keys should be in the car."

David followed as the Corporal walked the few feet to the open side door. Pointing to the car next to David's Bureau car, the Corporal said, "It's that one, third one in over there. Like I said, keys should be in it."

"Thanks, any messages for me?" asked David.

The Corporal returned to his desk, rechecked his clipboard and a stack of folders overflowing his inbox, and said, "No, sir, I don't believe so."

"Okay, thanks," David said, looking around the small office, noting a large clock on the wall, and checking its time against his own watch. Looking back at the Corporal, David said, "I'm going to be hanging around here for maybe an hour or so." Pointing at the phone on the Corporal's desk, he asked, "Mind if I use that from time to time?"

"No problem, long as the conversations aren't too long. If you need a phone for something like that, I can direct you to another building nearby."

"No, that's fine." David pulled some paper from his pocket with a phone number written on it and showed it to the guard. "Is this the number for that phone?"

The guard glanced at the note. "Yes, sir."

"Great, okay, thanks. I'll be right outside if anyone calls for me."

"Yes, sir."

David thought for a moment, then said, "If someone calls and you don't see me right off, check around outside for me. It's important."

"Yes, sir."

David and Bert stepped outside and walked over to the car. The Corporal was correct; the keys were in the ignition. David slid behind the wheel. Not bothering to close the door, he started the car. "Good," he said out loud to Bert and himself. "Seems to be fine."

David turned the car off, removed the keys, and put them in his pocket as he got back out of the car. Checking his watch again, not so much to check the time but to organize his thoughts, he said to Bert, "Our plane should be landing pretty soon, probably within the next forty-five minutes or so—give or take. Let's just keep to the plan unless we hear something different."

They both pulled a few letter-size pages of notes, folded longways, from their inside suitcoat pockets. For many, it was a little warm to be wearing a suitcoat, but the benefits outweighed the costs. The pockets were useful and the jackets hid, from casual view, their pistols, resting in their shoulder holsters under their left arms. But, most importantly, a suit projected rank and authority. It was undeniable that people treated a man in a suit with more deference and respect than that same man dressed in a casual or sloppy manner.

Unfolding their paperwork, they both scanned through the pages. Then, turning to the last page, David said, "Okay, here's the map of the base." He moved to the back of the car and placed the map down on the trunk lid so that they could both view the layout. Reviewing their plan for the umpteenth time, David continued, "There's Northern Field, where Johnson's family will be landing, and there's the hanger that their plane is supposed to be directed to. That's where you'll meet them as they come off the plane." David moved his finger to a little square on the map indicating a building about a half mile from the airfield. "There's the house that you'll take them to." David glanced at the back window of their Bureau car. "Probably need to clean those paper bags out of the back seat." Then, looking back to the map, "When you get to the hanger, call the tower to verify their flight is on schedule and to verify that they know to direct that plane to our hanger. Call me here at the gate once you've spoken with the tower so I'll know everything is on track. Call me again once you've met and have Mrs. Johnson and their boy in your custody. Johnson was adamant that I don't signal him to come in until I am certain that his family is safe in my custody—yours and mine, that is. I think, really, the two of us are the only people he's comfortable with over here, so far at least. For everyone's sake, I hope he makes some new friends fast over the next few days."

David, focusing deeper on their plan, placed his hands on the trunk, framing the map between his hands as he leaned over it. A hint of a breeze caused David to place his thumbs over each edge of the paper to keep it from moving. Thinking out loud to himself, David murmured, "All our plans are but scraps of paper, and the slightest vagary of breath from God or Nature can change everything."

Bert, hearing David's concern, said, "Don't worry so much about this Dave; we've been over it a thousand times."

"Okay," David said, standing up straight and giving a single clap of his hands as if to break the spell and change his mood. David refolded his papers and put them securely back into his jacket pocket as the two walked to the driver's-side door of their Bureau car. Bert had absentmindedly rolled his notes into a tube while they were reviewing David's map, so it took him a moment longer to get them unrolled, refolded, and back into his pocket. David opened the door and gave Bert a solid double pat on his shoulder as Bert slid behind the wheel. "Call me as soon as you've talked to the tower," David reminded, as he shut Bert's door. "As soon as Johnson shows up, we'll drive over and meet you all at the guest house for their happy reunion."

David watched as Bert drove off, then walked back to the guard shack, pausing just outside the side door, watching the incoming and outgoing traffic. The guard who had earlier glanced through his car's window and waived him onto the base was now talking to a man driving an old pickup truck. Behind that truck, a large, flatbed truck waited, then a car, and then another pickup truck. The traffic appeared to come in waves. Nothing, then a handful, then nothing again for a while.

There were two empty chairs inside the guard shack in addition to the one occupied by the Corporal seated at the desk, but after the morning's car ride from Chattanooga, it felt good to stand, stretch, and walk around a bit. David felt a little antsy, sensing that Johnson was already in place, hidden somewhere within sight, waiting for the signal from David that his family had arrived. David had felt it overcautious, but Johnson had insisted that he would not come in until David verified that they were safely in his custody. Since David couldn't be in two places at once, Johnson was willing to allow Bert into the small, but hopefully growing, circle of those he trusted. The understanding was that Bert would meet the plane, and David would wait at the front gate for word of their arrival. When David received confirmation from Bert that Johnson's wife and son were with him, he would signal Johnson by holding, conspicuously, his handkerchief in his hand, where it could be seen from a reasonable distance. Johnson would then openly approach David at the gate. From there, David would take him to the guesthouse where Johnson would be reunited with his family to spend a comfortable, yet brief, reorientation period before moving on for some lengthy debriefing sessions elsewhere.

David, following their plan to the letter, walked over and leaned against the outside front corner of the building on the approaching traffic side. Trying not to be too obvious, he scanned the area along the sides of the road, wondering from where Johnson would appear. There weren't really that many good hiding places.

After a few minutes, his mind began to wander. Having recently reviewed the particulars of the base in preparation for the day's events, he began to reflect on its history. The base was located on the outskirts of Tullahoma, Tennessee. Originally called Camp Peay and built as a National Guard Camp in 1926, Camp Forrest and the adjoining airfield, William Northern Field, grew into one of the Army's largest bases during World War II, covering 85,000 acres.

Towards the beginning of the war, in 1942, Camp Forrest became the nation's first civilian internment camp. Around 800 so-called alien civilians—Japanese, German, and Italian Americans—were arrested and interned, many without legal process, under the "Alien Enemy Control" program. In 1943, those internees were transferred to other internment camps as Camp Forrest transitioned into a POW camp for Italians and Germans who were captured on the battlefields of Europe. By the end of the war, over 24,000 members of the Wehrmacht were under guard there.

Camp Forrest was also a huge induction and training center for the army. Twenty-five thousand young men had their initial physical exams there. The infantry, artillery, engineers, and even cooks trained there. Rangers, medical units, supply units, signal organizations, and Air Corps personnel trained there. B-24 bomber crews trained there. Village mock-ups were built for house-to-house combat training. General Patton drilled his 2nd Armored tank Division there, and the Second Ranger Battalion— the men who scaled the cliffs of Pointe du Hoc on D-Day— trained there.

There were service clubs and guesthouses. There was a hospital, library, Post Exchange, post office, and chapel. For recreation, there was swimming, archery, tennis, a sports arena, and even a nine-hole golf course. The place was huge. At its peak, there were thirteen hundred buildings, fifty-five miles of roads, and five miles of railroad track.

Over 20,000 people were employed in the construction of the camp, and up to 12,000 civilians worked there. In 1940, the population of Tullahoma was 4,500. By the end of the war, many who had moved to the town to construct and operate the base stayed, and by the end of the war the population of Tullahoma had grown to 75,000.

In 1945, as the War came to an end, things began to wind down and the government implemented what they called an "Intellectual Diversion Program" to educate German POWs on the American way of life. Using educational and recreational media, they were largely successful in changing the views of POWs to view America more favorably before sending them back home.

By 1946, the war was over. Its purpose no longer needed, the Camp was declared "Surplus" and given "Inactive" status. The War Assets Corporation auctioned off everything. The buildings, sold for their lumber, were torn down and hauled off. Equipment, right down to the kitchen utensils, was sold. Even the water, sewage, and electrical systems were sold as salvage.

The traffic now coming in and out of the base was largely the scavengers hauling off their bounty. That which was essential in times of war was superfluous in times of peace. The State was keeping the land, but soon, all that would remain would be the roads, brick chimneys, and concrete foundations.

But the land would not remain fallow for long. David had no way of knowing, but in the blink of an eye, the base would have a new name and a new purpose. The Air Force would give new birth to the grounds. Soon it would become known as the Arnold Engineering Development Center, and then, only the remnants of a few overgrown concrete foundations—like obscure, weather-worn markers in a cemetery—would remain of Camp Forrest.

*   *   *   *   *

David's thoughts were interrupted by the sound of the phone ringing; he turned his head toward the side door. The Corporal manning the desk got up and walked to the threshold of the door. Not leaving the building, he leaned his head and upper body out past the plane of the doorway, as if it didn't matter where his head went as long as his feet were firmly planted safely within. Turning his head, he saw David and called, "Mr. DeRieux, there's a phone call for you, sir."

David waved in acknowledgement and answered, "Thanks."

David walked into the guard shack. The Corporal pointed to the phone receiver laying at the edge of his desk near David. David picked up the phone. "David DeRieux speaking."

As expected, it was Bert. "Hi Dave, everything's looking good. I'm at the hanger. Just spoke to the tower; the plane is about twenty minutes out. The tower confirmed that they will call me here when the plane is on final approach."

"Great. Keep me posted." David looked at his watch. "Looks like we're pretty much on schedule, maybe even a bit early. Call me when you get word from the tower that they're on final."

"Will do."

David hung up the phone and said to the Corporal, "I should be getting another call within the next twenty minutes or so. I'll be just outside or nearby. Make sure you find me."

David returned to his post, leaning against the front corner of the building. The trickle of vehicles in and out of the Camp helped David pass the time. He never tired of people-watching, but after about ten minutes it occurred to him that he had been on his feet since arriving, and the thought of sitting down was starting to have its appeal. However, as time drew near, he needed to remain visible to Johnson. He still couldn't spot him, but he was sure that Johnson was out there. Yes, time was drawing near—Johnson was out there, somewhere, watching. The more his feet grew tired, the more time began to drag. He shifted from leaning against the building to standing up straight and then back again to leaning. *Walking is easier than standing,* he thought. He looked at his watch; only another five minutes had passed, a total of fifteen since he had last talked to Bert. *Yes,* he thought, *it's much easier to walk for fifteen minutes than it is to stand in one place for the same amount of time.*

The phone rang. So far, since David had been there, every time the phone had rung it had been for him, so he started for the door. The Corporal was just getting to his feet as David came through the door. Seeing David, he sat back down and pointed to the phone. "It's for you again, sir."

David picked up the phone; it was Bert. "They're on short final. I can see their plane. The direction that they're coming in from, they won't have far to taxi once they land. Should be here in a few minutes, I'd think—five, ten at the most."

"Great. Call me once you have them."

Hanging up the phone, the adrenalin began to flow. David, nodding towards the front of the building, said to the Corporal, "I'll be just outside at the corner there. There'll be another call for me shortly. It's important."

"Yes, sir."

David returned to his post outside. Scanning the roadway leading up to the camp and all the possible spots along the way in which Johnson could conceal himself took his full attention. The history of the base or the condition of his feet no longer had a place in his consciousness. *Where could he be?* David wondered, trying to penetrate the depths beyond the road's shoulders. The trees weren't thick, and there was little if any underbrush, like in a natural forest, but there were enough trees to obstruct a clear view. *He's got to be in there somewhere.*

The phone rang. Even though he was expecting it, it startled him a little. The moment he heard the ring, he started for the door. He entered the building and was through the door before the Corporal even had the chance to set the phone down. Seeing David, the Corporal simply handed him the phone.

"That you, Bert?" David said.

"Yep, they're here. I've got them. They seem fine. Looks like they brought a surprise package with them. Go ahead and signal Johnson. We'll meet you at the guesthouse."

"What's the surprise package?"

"You'll see when you get here. It would take too long to explain right now; things are a little bit in flux here. Everyone's a little bit anxious; I need to get back to them. Everything's okay. See you at the guesthouse."

"All right. I haven't been able to spot Johnson, but I bet he'll appear pretty quick once I give the signal. See you in a few minutes. I'll call you at the guesthouse if there's any delay at this end, but I'd be surprised if there were."

"Yeah, okay. See ya."

David pulled his handkerchief from his pocket as he walked quickly back to his front corner post. Wanting to send a clear signal but not wanting to look silly by waiving his white handkerchief up high, as if he were surrendering the base, he briefly shook his handkerchief out before himself in an exaggerated movement as if shaking dust or something from it, and then held it to his side, a little to his front where it could be clearly seen. He watched the roadway and shoulders for any movement. He was anticipating that Johnson would pop out from behind a tree or something, immediately upon seeing the signal, but as the moments passed, he didn't see anything . . . then a truck at a distance. *I wouldn't think that's him, but maybe so,* David thought. As the truck drew nearer, David watched, not yet able to make out the driver. As it got closer it started to look like there were two people in the front. He squinted his eyes, trying to get a clearer view.

"David," —a quiet voice from behind. He turned; it was Johnson.

"Where'd you come from?" David asked, a little bit startled.

"I've been watching from inside the camp."

The two shook hands—a long, firm handshake, each happy to see the other. David smiled, a growing sense of relief washing over him. Johnson's smile seemed a little forced to David, as if Johnson wanted to overcome his sense of apprehension but just wasn't quite there yet.

Still firmly grasping Johnson's right hand, David patted Johnson on the outside of his shoulder with his other hand and said, "They're here, Michael. Your family is here. They're safe; they're with Bert. They landed just a few minutes ago, and Bert has taken them to a guesthouse. Car's right over there," David said, pointing to the car. "Shall we go?"

David led the way with Johnson trailing to his side, barely a quarter step behind. The car was facing inward to the base so the driver's side, David's side, was closer. David gave two pats on the roof of the car above the door as Johnson walked around behind the car. As Johnson neared the passenger's door, David opened his and slid behind the wheel, not yet closing his door. Through the passenger's window, David could see Johnson's torso but not his head or face. Johnson appeared to be just standing there looking over the top of the car back towards the guard building. David turned back to his left and watched as a uniformed man approached their car. Johnson remained standing. As the man got closer, looking directly at David and Johnson, it became obvious that the soldier, wearing Sargent stripes, was wanting to speak to them. David slid back out of the car and stood as the approaching man covered the last few feet.

"Special Agent DeRieux."

"Yes."

"There is a phone call for you, sir, at the guard's desk," the Sargent said pointing to the little building.

"Who is it?" asked David.

"I don't know, sir."

David looked at the name stenciled on the front of the sergeant's shirt. "Sergeant Cooper, is it? I haven't seen you around here the last hour or so; where did you come from?"

"Just got on duty, sir."

David looked over the roof of the car and said to Johnson, "I better take it; might be Bert. Just wait here in the car. I'll be right back."

Johnson didn't look happy, but as his natural inclination was to conceal himself in times of uncertainty, without saying a word, he got into the car and closed the door.

David followed Sergeant Cooper back to the guard building. David entered the building; the Sergeant stayed outside. The phone handle wasn't in its usual position on the edge of the desk;

it was in its cradle. David said to the Corporal at the desk, "I was told there was a phone call for me?"

The Corporal handed David a small piece of note paper. "There's a number here for you to call."

The Corporal slid the base of the phone over to the edge of the desk. David stood at the side of the desk and dialed the number. A man whose voice was unknown to David answered the phone, "Private Murphy."

"Private Murphy, this is Special Agent David DeRieux. I was told to call this number."

"Oh, yes, sir. There is someone here who needs to speak with you. Please hold while I get him."

Before David could ask who, the phone went silent while David was placed on hold.

David looked out the door towards his car and Johnson, but a small truck blocked his view as the driver asked directions. David grew impatient, but being on hold, there wasn't a lot he could do to hurry the call.

Unbeknownst to David, as soon as David had entered the building, the sergeant turned back towards the car, making a semicircular path inward towards the camp, keeping himself out of David's line of sight for as long as possible as he made his way back to the car.

Johnson, with great apprehension, watched the path of the sergeant as he approached. Straightaway, the sergeant opened the driver's door and sat down behind the wheel. Before Johnson could speak, Sergeant Cooper said, as he turned the key to start the car, "Sir, I have orders to take you to a guesthouse."

Johnson turned away to open his door. Cooper's left hand, hidden low to his side, came up and across his lap. With his right hand, the soldier grabbed the shoulder of Johnson's suitcoat and held firm.

Johnson turned back and looked into the eyes of the soldier. For a few heartbeats, neither spoke, then Johnson looked down and saw the gun, steady in the soldier's left hand, pointed at Johnson.

The soldier spoke, "Sir, I have orders. We are going to the guesthouse."

Johnson eased back into his seat, saying nothing. The soldier let go of Johnson's sleeve and put the car in gear. Moving forward, the soldier said, "That's better. Just take it easy. We'll be there in a jiffy."

Johnson turned and watched as the guard building receded into the distance, then said, "FBI Agent DeRieux is supposed to accompany me."

The soldier didn't respond. Johnson continued, "You say you have orders; who gave you those orders?"

The soldier remained silent as he drove—halfway watching the road, halfway watching Johnson, his left hand resting in his lap with the gun still pointed at Johnson. Johnson studied the driver; he knew the type. Sort of nice looking, good enough anyway to make a somewhat favorable first impression; but that initial impression, upon slight scrutiny, gave way to an underlying dimwittedness. Johnson had seen the type a thousand times—craving power and respect, coming so close so often, but never quite making the grade. It was a life of frustration—frustration and resentment, resentment giving way to a craving to demonstrate superiority by employing the only means left: physical dominance. But while that sort of behavior, in the thug's own mind, reinforced his superiority, to others it only served to prove that he was a man worthy of only limited, well-defined responsibilities. Giving such a man a gun made his imbalance worse.

Johnson decided the best way to get the thug to talk, so as to quickly get some inkling of what was going on, was to bait him. Johnson, with as much arrogance and condensation as he could muster, blurted out, "Look, ass-face; I don't think you know what you're doing here."

The driver glanced over at Johnson and made a guttural sound that was more of a grunt than a smirk. Johnson poked again at the man's latent inferiority, "That's right, ass-face; I'm talking to you."

The driver looked again, obviously agitated at Johnson, then slowed the car as he turned onto a street that led past an assortment of buildings, the purpose of which Johnson was uncertain, then turned again onto another street that shortly led to an area with a cluster of small, homelike structures. Johnson hammered out again, "Come on, ass-face; tell me whose orders you're following, or don't you know? How pathetic, you don't even know who's running this show do you? Too stupid to be told—I can tell by looking."

The driver broke, "Shut up you commie bastard. You're not running this show; we are. Now just shut up and sit quiet. We're here now, anyway." Off the end of the guesthouse was a parking area. Another car, Bert's Bureau car, was already there.

The car stopped, the engine off, the two glared at each other. "What now, ass-face?" Johnson asked, wanting to keep the thug rattled.

"Now we get out and go inside. Your family's inside. Isn't that why we're here?"

Johnson was unsettled. Yes, this was why he was here, but this was all wrong. They both got out of the car. A narrow sidewalk led from the corner of the building to a door midway down the front of the house. The Sargent pointed to the walkway with one hand and said, "Let's go." His other hand was to his side. Johnson couldn't tell if he still held a gun but was betting that he did.

Johnson came around the back of the car, then hesitated, stopping as he placed his hand on the trunk.

"Come on; let's go," the thug barked out again, waiving his hand towards the sidewalk, indicating for Johnson to go first.

Johnson straightened up tall and with great formality marched past the thug.

Chapter 21

The Guesthouse

Camp Forrest, TN
July 1946

Bert hung up the phone and looked out over the airfield. He agreed with David; once the signal was given, he didn't imagine it would take long for Johnson to appear. So far, so good. It seemed their plan was unfolding without any glitches.

He turned to Johnson's wife. Natasha was her name, but she wanted to be called Mary now that she was in America. Her English was very rudimentary, but by speaking slowly and using exaggerated hand gestures, they could communicate. Bert conveyed to her—calling her Mary at every opportunity, which seemed to give her much pleasure—that he had just spoken to the man who would soon be bringing her husband to meet them at a nice house, to which they would now be going.

Little more than an arm's length away, two little boys happily played, each with a small plastic model airplane that they had been given somewhere in route. The two looked to be of about the same age, three years old, give or take, and were remarkably similar. One was Johnson's son. The other was the son of the courier who managed to get Natasha safely from Moscow to the border. The courier, upping his price at the last minute, demanded that Natasha adopt his son as one of her own, take him with her to America, and include him in her family in her new and better life in America. The price increase was non-negotiable. If his son was not going to America, Natasha was not going to America. That was the "surprise package" that Bert had mentioned to David without further explanation.

At present, the most notable thing that distinguished one boy from the other was that one of the boys was beginning to have trouble with his digestive system. Bert guessed that it was nothing more than a sensitivity in adapting to the rich food with, maybe, a little airsickness thrown in. In any event, one of the boys was having to take frequent bathroom breaks.

Bert estimated that the drive time to the guesthouse was no more than five minutes, and that the last bathroom visit was recent enough for them to head on over. The thrill of riding in a car, especially an American car, was still fresh with Mary and the boys. The Bureau car was, by American standards, ordinary; but by Soviet standards, it was luxurious. Mary and the boys sat in the back chauffeured by Bert in the front. Mary felt like a high-level Politburo's wife being escorted to somewhere special, perhaps one of the special department stores which were only for elite officials, their families, or foreigners with hard currency. Stores that had no lines. Stores that always had their shelves stocked not only with items of necessity but also actual items of desire. The two boys watched with quiet awe, their heads bobbling back and forth as they watched the novel scenery pass by.

To Mary, the guesthouse was a palace. The front door entered into a modest living room, huge by her standards. Straight across the room, a back door led outside to a patio area, a charcoal grill, and a small yard. To the left was a hallway that led to two bedrooms and a bathroom in between. To the right was a doorway to a kitchen and small dinette, a laundry area, another bathroom, and then one last bedroom at that far end of the house which also doubled as an office space with a twin bed, desk, and phone.

Bert held the front door open for Mary as she entered. The boys, happy but not yet secure enough with their new surroundings to let go of Mary's skirt, clung to her sides as she inspected the living room. By the time she got to the kitchen they had let go but still remained close. Bert opened the refrigerator and was relieved to see that it had, as promised, been stocked. He pulled a bottle of Coca-Cola from the fridge, looked at Mary, and nodded to the boys. Mary smiled and nodded her consent. Bert opened two cabinets before he found where the glasses were stored but found the bottle opener in the first drawer that he tried. He set the glasses on the table and, going back and forth between the two glasses several times to get the levels exactly even, poured half the bottle into each glass. Looking at the boys, who were fixated on the glasses of soda-pop, Bert pulled out two chairs, and the boys eagerly took their seats. As they reached for their glasses, Mary, in Russian, gave a gentle sounding command. Bert couldn't understand the words but, watching the boys react, knew that he had seen that exact exchange countless times before between moms and their kids: "Use both hands."

As the boys enjoyed their sodas, Mary and Bert gave the kitchen a quick look-over, checking through the fridge and pantry, Bert making sure she knew how to use the stove. The bedroom-office off the kitchen was not for Mary's use, so next on the tour were the bedrooms and bath at the other end of the house. They exceeded Mary's expectations. Fleeing Moscow, she was able to take only a small travel bag with a few things for herself and her son. With that in mind, a few items of clothing and basic toiletries had been put in place for them at the guest house. Wanting to freshen up before Michaels's arrival, she excused herself. Bert and the boys made themselves comfortable in the living room. The boys, quickly becoming at home with their new surroundings, played with their model airplanes while Bert relaxed on an overstuffed chair with a footstool.

The boy with digestive trouble came over to Bert, holding his stomach. Bert knew from recent experience, and from kids in general, that that was the universal signal indicating that a bathroom trip would be prudent. Since Mary was still in her bathroom, Bert led the boy by the hand to the bathroom off the kitchen side of the house. He had just made it back to the overstuffed chair in the living room when he heard the phone in the back bedroom-office ring. The sounds coming from the bathroom as he passed it on the way to the phone were not pretty. Diarrhea was playing havoc with the poor little guy.

Bert picked up the phone expecting to hear David's voice. Instead, an unfamiliar man's voice asked, "Special Agent Ashton?"

"Yes," Bert replied.

"I have a call for you from Special Agent DeRieux. Hold for just a minute please."

After a long minute, Bert became a little impatient. "Hello, hello?"

The voice came back on the line. "Sorry for the delay, Mr. Ashton. Special Agent DeRieux will be with you in just a minute."

"Who is this," asked Bert.

"Agent DeRieux will be with you in just a moment," the voice on the phone repeated. "There's been a few changes that he needs to go over with you."

Bert, on hold, waiting for David, was too far from the opposite end of the house to hear the car with Johnson and the Sargent arrive. Outside, at Mary's end of the house, Johnson, having just gotten out of the car, paused, evaluating his options. In one sense, it appeared that he had been delivered to where he had planned and wanted to be—at the guesthouse where he was to be reunited with his wife and son. But the particulars were all wrong. Where was David? Where had he gone? Who was this Sargent fellow, and why was he brought here by force to the very place that he was eager to go and would have gone willingly. Was his wife even here? Looking at the Sargent, Johnson summed it all up in a moment. There was only one way to find out. Gathering up all of his strength, he stood straight and marched past the thug with the most formidable manor that he could muster. With the Sargent in close escort behind him, Johnson passed the corner of the house and began down the walkway. Before he came to the first bedroom window, the front door opened and a woman holding a small boy stepped out onto the front stoop. Her movements were very slow and stiff, as if she had been frozen and was now only partially thawed. Seeing Johnson, she turned slowly towards him. Immediately, they recognized each other, but neither said a word. Seeing panic in her eyes, Johnson stopped for the briefest moment to assess the situation. Something was very wrong, but for the life of him he couldn't figure out what purpose was being served. A gun shot rang out from inside the house. Natasha crumpled to the ground, releasing the boy as she fell forward. The boy hit the ground on his feet, but the forward momentum was too great, so he flopped forward hard onto his stomach and outstretched hands. Disorientated, he picked himself up, slowly turning back towards the loud bang that had come from the front door. Raising his arms to look at his skinned hands, he started to cry when two more carefully timed shots rang out, the first hitting the boy in the chest, the second in the face just below his nose. The boy fell on his back, the top of his head towards the street, shoulders level with the ground, his face pointing upward towards the sky. There was an eerie silence. The world was still. Michael Johnson stood frozen.

The boy, life passing from his little body, moved. His head, his disfigured face, slowly rolled on its side towards Michael. The boy's eyes, untouched, were open and looked directly at Michael, but there was no life in them.

Mechanically, Michael started forward, but he was stopped cold by the thug's hand coming down hard, grabbing Michael by the outside of his shoulder. Michael could feel the muzzle of the gun pressed hard on the small of his back. From a block away, the sound of a vehicle turning onto their street caused the thug to twist a little to see what was approaching. Johnson felt the movement in the thug's hand, still tense on his shoulder, and took the opportunity. As the thug turned, Johnson also began a slow turn of his head, natural enough to see the approaching vehicle. In an instant, Johnson's turn accelerated into a blurred, spinning motion, ending with Johnson behind the thug. The thug, surprised at being relieved of his gun, now found it pressed into the small of his back and a chokehold across his throat.

*　*　*　*　*

Bert heard the gunshot coming from the living room. His head snapped away from the phone and towards the doorway just in time to see a man in a mask step into the doorway while pointing a pistol directly at him. "Freeze," the man ordered. The sound of two more quick gunshots came from the same direction. The man in the mask motioned with the gun and said, "Now, slowly, put your hands up, turn around, and face the wall."

Bert said, "What's this all about?"

The man waived the gun in an impatient gesture and said, "Hurry it up if you want to stay alive; I'm not fooling."

Bert hesitated for a moment. The man cocked the revolver with his thumb. Bert said, "Okay, okay," and turned to face the wall.

The man said, "Okay, stay there. Don't move an inch."

Bert stood facing the wall for all of fifteen seconds before he slowly turned his head. The man at the door was nowhere in sight. Bert drew his gun and, with caution, made his way down the hall. The bathroom door was cracked open; no sounds came from within. With the muzzle of his gun, he pushed the door the rest of the way open. He didn't see anyone in there. *Where was the kid?* he wondered. Picking up speed, he made his way through the kitchen and into the living room. As he approached the front door, he could see a body lying on the ground just outside the doorway. It was a woman—it was Natasha. Using the front-door frame as partial cover, Bert slowly peeked around the corner.

*　*　*　*　*

Johnson's attention was drawn to movement at the front doorway. First, a drawn gun . . . then, Bert became visible as he stepped sideways into the doorway, his back against the frame, his gun pointed squarely at Michael and the thug.

Nothing made any sense.

Bert kept most of his attention towards Johnson and the thug, but with slight, quick, turns of his head, Bert kept glancing back into the living room and then back again at the two bodies. The woman's, Mary's, was only a foot or two from Bert beyond the doorway. The little boy's was a little farther away, but it was obvious that both were dead.

Johnson, pulling the thug along with him like a reluctant dance partner, backed up against the side of the house to protect his rear—holding the thug at an angle, partially towards Bert at the front door, and partially towards the street out front. A small pickup truck, which had provided the needed distraction for Johnson, approached the front of the guesthouse. At first, it looked like it would speed on past the house, but when the driver noticed the woman and small boy laying on the ground in the short distance between the road and the house's front door, he braked suddenly to a stop, hopped out, and ran towards them yelling, "What's wrong, what's wrong!" wondering why the three nearby men stood motionless.

Then, the Good Samaritan noticed the blood pooling around the bodies before him, the gun in the hand of the man partially hidden in the doorway, and the choke hold on the man at the corner of the house.

"Oh my, oh my," the man said barely loud enough for the three to hear, as he slowly began to backpedal, raising his hands to shoulder level in a surrendering gesture.

"Hold it!" shouted Michael from behind the thug. The Samaritan continued to back up slowly. Michael glanced back at the car in which he and the Sargent had just arrived. With a quick motion, Michael fired a round into the front grill of the car, quickly returning the gun to the small of the thug's back. At the sound of the shot, the thug flinched and the Samaritan froze. Bert backed slightly more into the house, maximizing his cover while keeping Michael and the thug in sight.

The Samaritan, in his haste to help, had left his truck running. Michael could hear the smooth sputter of the engine and see a trace of smoke coming from the exhaust pipe. He glanced back at the car he had just crippled. The radiator had been pierced; engine coolant was pouring out.

Michael, nodding his head towards the house, said to the Samaritan, "You, go over next to the house there and lay down. Stretch your arms out in front of you."

The Samaritan walked slowly towards the house. "Hurry it up!" Michael yelled.

The Samaritan quickened his pace towards the house and laid down in the yard on his stomach. Michael said in a low voice to the thug, "Come on," as he pushed him forward. As they moved towards the truck, Michael rotated the thug, using him as a shield between himself and Bert. "Do nothing stupid," Michael whispered to the thug. "It would be real easy for you to be dead."

Michael and the thug made their way around to the far side of the truck. Michael felt a little better once he had the truck between him and Bert. Bert remained crouched in the doorway with his pistol pointed at the truck. The driver's door had been left open; Michael looked inside. It was a plain bench seat with a tree shift on the steering-wheel column, so there was nothing in the way to keep the thug from easily sliding over.

Michael kept pressure on the thug as he pushed him into the truck, saying, "Slide all the way over."

Now their roles were reversed. The thug sat in the passenger's seat, Michael in the driver's seat with a gun in his lap pointed at the thug. Bert watched over his gun's sights as the truck drove away.

*   *   *   *   *

Across the street, behind a bedroom window, there was an ever so slight motion of a crack in a curtain being closed. No one, except the man sitting in the chair behind the window, saw it. After pulling the curtain tight, the dimly lit room became even darker, now illuminated only by the little light that bled in from the hallway. The man leaned over and picked up the phone sitting on the floor and placed it on his lap. He dialed a number. After two rings, the phone picked up, but there was no voice. The man said, "It's done. Everything turned out just as planned," and hung up the phone. The man stood up, walked over to a night stand next to a bed, and placed the phone back from where it had come. He then moved the chair, which he had left in front of the window, back to its usual place nestled against the wall. Standing in the doorway, he turned, giving the room one final look to verify that everything had been returned to the way in which he had found it. Satisfied that nothing was amiss, he slipped out the back door and was quickly hidden amongst the everyday.

Chapter 22

Circles and Lines

Chattanooga, TN
April 2001

Circles and lines, circles and lines, Joey thought as he walked across the old, but beautifully restored, Walnut Street Bridge. Now a pedestrian-only walkway, the upward bowing archway spanning the Tennessee River connected the trendy, revitalized shops and houses of the North Chattanooga district on one side of the water with the riverfront edge of Downtown Chattanooga on the other side. *I walk in circles, but I search for lines*, the thought repeated in his mind. Halfway across the expanse, with the deepest part of the river below and the riveted construct of the metal suspension soaring above, he stopped and took a seat on one of the public benches to enjoy the view and consolidate his thoughts.

I walk in circles, but I search for lines. It was no mystery as to why that notion, that phrase, cycled within his mind at that moment. From early on, Joey had formed the habit of categorizing most of his activities into one of two categories: a circle or a line. A "circle" activity was simply a housekeeping sort of chore—like eating a meal, taking a shower, mowing the lawn, or taking a walk. Something that had to be done to maintain himself, but also something that didn't advance himself. At the end of a "circle" task, he was essentially back to the same point from which he had started, and, eventually, that same activity would have to be repeated time and time again. A "line" activity, on the other hand, was something that changed the status quo, hopefully in a positive direction, but not always. Learning a skill, reading a book, having an epiphany, making a new friend, building something novel, for instance, were examples of "line" activities. Once a "line" activity was started, things were different from then on. Whereas a circle always ends up back at its beginning, movement down a line takes the traveler farther and farther from the point of origin. Unless, of course, one backtracks on that line. But is that even possible? *Perhaps there's a third category that's entirely different,* Joey speculated.

Joey dreaded the prospect of his life devolving into nothing more than a series of circles while letting line activities grow fewer and fewer and farther between. He had seen that happen to all too many of his friends and associates as they grew older and retired. The only thing sadder was to see someone in their youth let that happen to themself, as if there was nothing better to do than to simply run out the clock. He vowed that he would not allow that to happen to himself.

Since the beginning of his retirement, a large part of Joey's routine was to take frequent walks. He enjoyed the activity, the scenery, the people he passed, the physical exercise that it provided; and, most importantly, the time to think, the time to give free range to his mind, allowing it to wander a bit. Typically, he managed to get in a good walk, which he defined as a walk of a fair but somewhat less than brisk pace, of a duration of at least thirty minutes, but typically closer to an hour, about four to five times a week. When the weather was cold or rainy, there were several indoor spots that he frequented: the large shopping malls or other enclosed public places such as the long hallways at the downtown Convention Center. But he preferred nice weather and walks in the outdoors, and his favorite course was to drive to

North Chattanooga, find a free parking spot on one of the residential side streets, and make a large circuit, crossing over on one of the three nearby pedestrian-friendly bridges into downtown Chattanooga, wander a varied route through and around downtown, and then cross back into North Chattanooga, usually via a different bridge, but not always. The Walnut Street Bridge was, by far, his favorite, so it was put into the mix more often than the other two.

On occasion, maybe a few times a year, Joey would explore one of the many nature trails in the area. They were nice, many would say spectacular, and Joey could appreciate how some would prefer the wonders of nature over the constructs of man. But Joey was, at heart, a city guy, and long walks by himself in the woods usually left him with a sense of isolation. He was cognizant enough to realize that, in general, he preferred the things that man had built with, perhaps, the assistance of God, over the things that God had built without the assistance of man; and sometimes, he wondered if thinking so was a sin, for lack of a better word. After letting his mind wander down that path one day, he concluded that perhaps nature and nurture were equal, which then immediately begged the question as to whether giving equal ranking was hubris? Walks always provided plenty of fodder for thought. On days in which there was more time than things to do, he would often stop and sit on a bench to extend and enrich the time of his venture.

But the one thing that all his walks had in common was that they ended at the same place that they began. In that sense, these walks were the very definition of a circle activity. Even so, during the course of those circles, a variety of thoughts would present themselves; and often, a new thought was the starting point for a new line; or sometimes, a boost along an established line in which the pace had slowed or stalled. After all, sometimes just a thought by itself was movement along a line, in that some thoughts were life changing.

Yes, for Joey, thinking seemed to be easier, more effortless, more fluid, on these walks. Just as some people had trouble falling asleep when it was too quiet, Joey found that a little background noise and activity gave his brain a slight jolt, a little nudge, if you will, which seemed to enhance the range and depth of his thoughts.

Sitting on the bench, Joey allowed his mind to continue its wander. *In less than an hour, in time measured in minutes, I'll be back at my car. Another circle will be completed. In a matter of days, I'll most likely be back on this bridge. For variety, I'll probably sit on a different bench, but eventually, at some point, I'll almost certainly return to this very bench. Another circle, albeit a bigger one. A circle measured in days and months rather than minutes and hours, but a circle nevertheless. But, in the course of that larger circle, in a few days, I have a doctor's appointment. Is that another circle, a small circle within a larger one . . . or is it a line?*

When I was young, I always thought of doctors' appointments as circles, something I did to maintain my body. Each year I would return, and each year it would be the same: "You're fine. See you next year." But then one year, I was slightly less than fine. Nothing alarming, but, although I didn't recognize it on that day, that circle had changed into a line. The goal, the end point, was no longer to simply monitor my health. The goal was now to extend my life, a life which I had taken much for granted. The goal was no longer to simply complete another circle but to extend the length of a line. A line that starts at birth and ends at death—the line from mortality to immortality. A line upon which I have already traveled far. A line that has an end point and a beginning, or does it? I can see neither from my vantage point. Where am I on that line? Why do I so often feel like a toy soldier—a windup toy soldier? The spring is wound, the toy is set on the table. It's let go. It has no choice but to march straight ahead, across the table until either the spring winds out or the toy simply walks off the edge of the table, like a ship in a vast and ancient ocean was thought to sail off the edge of the earth if it ventured too far from the shore. The line from start to finish, from mortality—ending where? The toy soldier doesn't know when the spring will stop or what's beyond the edge of the table. At some point, we all go over that edge; we all take that fall. But what lies at the bottom? Map makers didn't know what lay beyond the edge of the oceans, but that didn't stop them from drawing dragons. But, in geometry, there are lines and there are line segments. Line segments have a defined beginning and end, but ideal lines are infinite in both directions; there is no beginning; there is no end. Is my life a journey along a line, a line segment, or is this just another circle? If a circle is small, it is easy to identify it as a circle. But as it becomes large, cosmically large, from a limited vantage point it's hard to distinguish a large circle from a line, just as it is difficult to see that the earth is a ball when you are standing on it. A large circle and a line may look the same up close, or over short periods of time, but that is not the reality. In reality, they couldn't be more different.

His mind drifted to a time in his past. He remembered a math teacher from his high school days, a geometry class. They were working on proofs, a type of thought exercise. The teacher illustrated a format to begin the process, a generic template to write down on a worksheet to initiate a momentum to help coax an idea out from the ether. The format provided structure, order, and a place to grasp a concept that lived solely in the universe of ideas, and, for a time, capture it within symbols written on a piece of paper. Joey discovered early on that having those initial formalities down on paper made it easier to formulate the proof, compared to staring at a totally blank page. Throughout his life, Joey found that method to be helpful in a variety of applications; indeed, a blank page could be a formidable obstacle. Ideas did not readily spring from nothingness.

From where do new thoughts come? Joey wondered as he leaned back on the bench and tilted his head up to gaze at the sky-blue painted iron superstructure above him. Calliope music crept into his awareness. He closed his eyes for a moment to enjoy the festive sounds coming from the riverboat below as it approached the bridge from downstream. As it passed under the bridge, Joey looked down and watched as the tourist on the upper deck of the boat waved cheerfully at the walkers on the bridge who had stopped at the railing to exchange greetings with those passing below.

As Joey watched the riverboat push its way against the current, the thought occurred to him: *This river, it's a mix. It's both a line and a circle. The water flows along a line, from top to bottom, from beginning to end. Yet, the boats on top and the fish beneath, for the most part, they just travel in a circle. All day long they go back and forth, back and forth and round and round, all within the same line. Yet the river upon which they travel is in a state of continual change, as is the shoreline that they pass. And even when the river empties itself into the ocean, it's not the end; it's the start of another beginning. That water, now resting in the ocean, evaporates back up into the sky, clouds form and carry that very same water back over the land, and the rain dumps droplets back onto the land at the headwaters. Those droplets come together in the streams, and the process begins all over again.*

I wonder; if the river is a timeline, does it go against nature to fight the current and travel upstream? Fish do it. History is what we remember it to be, but what is the future? The future, what we imagine to come, sometimes seems to unfold within our minds with more clarity than our remembrance of the past. Who is to say which is more accurate?

Joey continued to watch the riverboat plow its way up the river. It passed under the next bridge and shortly thereafter came even with the massive red brick complex set a short couple of blocks inland from the river's shore—"The Baroness d'Erlanger's Hospital", named after its generous French benefactor and his beautiful Southern wife, Marguerite Mathilde Slidell. Joey knew its history hwell; he was born there. As a lifelong resident of Chattanooga, he had visited that hospital many times—sometimes as a visitor, sometimes as a patient. Baron Frederic Emile d'Erlanger, who had done well with the railroads in the region, made his substantial donation in 1889. In

1891, the cornerstone was laid. In 1899, the hospital opened with 72 beds. Now, it had grown to be a city within itself.

How many people have been born there, Joey wondered. *How much water has flowed past those banks since that first birth? How many have died there? Will I? Another circle?*

Joey's attention was drawn to the rows of tiny black squares against the red brick structure. *Maybe Susan is behind one of those windows? Her family is probably there with her. Maybe David is there.*

Joey gave his head a slight shake, bringing himself back to the here and now. *I need to call Dorothy. She's had half a day; maybe she's got something by now on this VanZant business.* Joey leaned back, straightened his leg, and pulled a flip phone from his front pocket. Dialing from memory, he waited. Dorothy picked up on the fourth ring.

"Chattanooga Times, Free Press. Dorothy speaking."

"Hey, Dorothy, Joey here. Got anything for me yet on VanZant?"

"Yeah, wait a minute; let me move over to my desk." Joey heard the phone go on hold. A moment later, Dorothy picked back up. "Joey, you still there?"

"Yep, whatcha got?"

"Well, I'm not sure what you're looking for. I gave it to Megan, the intern. She didn't find anything local on him, but he did pop up here and there when she checked the Washington Papers' archives. Let's see; wait, give me a second here. Yeah, here it is. The first thing we found on him was an event that he was at in 1948. Looks like some sort of hoity-toity fund raiser for something. Anyway, doesn't really say what he was doing there. Picture shows him rubbing elbows with some of the rich and famous but doesn't say anything about him. The photo's not posed, probably didn't even know it was being taken at the time 'til the flash went off. Then, again, he shows up two years later at some other ritzy event. Let's see, between 1948 and, um, 1980, Megan found eight hits on him. But none of them really tell us anything about him other than apparently over the years he's been on a pretty exclusive guest list, at least from time to time. It's kind of strange; it's like he's there, but just on the edge of being there. I mean, he shows up on the periphery of a handful of events, events that typically include the movers and shakers, but, from what Megan turned up, he's always just an 'also there' part of the story. We didn't find anything in which he was in any meaningful way involved in the story. But again, to even be at those events, even though it's just sporadic, well, he turns up at enough of them that he's got to be somebody. It might be that we just haven't dug deep enough, but, like I said, and you yourself know, it's odd to see someone at the edge on a semi-regular basis, but never in the limelight." Dorothy gave a little laugh, "Maybe he's a spook? Like a ghost, he's there but he isn't there."

"Okay, thanks, Dorothy. I really appreciate it."

"Well . . .," Dorothy said, stringing out the word. "There is one more thing."

"Okay, what is it?"

"Well . . ., I wish she hadn't done it, but Megan got a little overzealous in her work and did something that I should probably tell you."

"Okay, what?"

"Since she didn't find anything definitive on VanZant in the archives, she decided to give him a call."

"What, you're kidding."

"Wish I was, but, nope. She called him. It's really become a little bit of a problem around here. Some of these new kids are so anxious—don't have enough experience to understand the business, don't understand any of the boundaries, just want to hit the ground running. Sometimes it works out well, but sometimes it really bites us in the butt. Anyway, she apparently doesn't quite grasp the fact that she is an intern research assistant and not a cub reporter calling people for interviews."

"Well, did she find out anything?"

"No . . . well, she did find out his current address, but other than that, I'm afraid she gave more information than she got."

"What do you mean?"

"Well, she looked him up in the phone book. Wasn't there. And since there was no obit on him, Megan thought he probably just had an unlisted number. So, she calls a friend of hers, a classmate interning at a Washington paper, and asks if VanZant is a subscriber of theirs. Pretty clever really. Turns out he is, and Megan, through her friend and their subscription department, got his contact info, address, and phone number. Turns out he lives in a really expensive neighborhood."

"So, did she call him, talk to him?"

"Yep."

"So, what did he say?"

"Nothing. But Megan said plenty."

"What do you mean?"

"Well, Megan had my notepad with the things that you asked me to look for. Apparently, he didn't want to talk, but he didn't hang up either. I had Megan repeat the whole conversation back to me. Going down my list of items, Megan asked him what he had to do with plutonium, and what was his relationship to David DeRieux."

"Wow," was all that Joey could say. Then he asked, "Did this Megan gal identify herself as being from the paper?"

"Yep, afraid so." After a pause, Dorothy continued, "Well, if he didn't know someone was looking at him, he knows now. Hope we haven't created a problem, but I thought I should tell you what happened here."

"Yeah, don't worry about it. Thanks for telling me though. Probably won't amount to anything, but, like you said, I wish she hadn't done that. Anyway, I'm still flying blind on this one, so . . . I don't know if we've stepped in anything or not."

"Okay, well, sorry about that, Joey. Stop in and say hi to us sometime."

"Okay, thanks, Dorothy." Joey snapped his flip phone closed with considerably more gusto than normal. *Okay*, he thought. *Is this a circle or a line? As far as learning anything new about VanZant, I'm pretty much back to where I started. But Megan— damn her. I wonder if she's started us down a line, a line that*

*could very well take us over an edge and into the mouth of a
dragon.*

Chapter 23

We Have to Kill Him

Chattanooga, TN
April 2001

Crap, crap, crap, Joey said over and over again to himself as he sat on the bench with the closed flip-phone still in his hand. *I can't believe that dumb-ass Megan called VanZant.*

The bench was starting to feel a little hard. Joey's stomach told him it was getting close to lunchtime. He flipped his wrist over and looked at his watch: 10:55am. *The DeRieuxs missed their Cracker Barrel lunch yesterday. I wonder what they're doing today? Probably be at the hospital for at least a little while, not the whole day though. Hell, Susan might even be going home today. Wonder how long they keep women these days, if everything goes well, no complications. Yeah, I bet she's going home today—tomorrow at the latest.*

A woman pushing a baby carriage was coming up the arch of the bridge towards where Joey was sitting. *I bet she knows how long they keep women,* thought Joey, *but I can't ask her. Odd how we isolate ourselves from one another. Can't really be helped, given the way people are; but odd, kind of a shame, really a shame that it has to be that way.*

Back to lunch. I could do Cracker Barrel again today, and I bet the DeRieuxs could too, if they're not doing something with their family. Surely they are though, especially since their kids are here; what are their names? He pulled his notepad from his pocket and flipped through a few pages, stopping on the one where he had listed all the names that he could remember, where they lived, and how they were related. *Okay, here it is: Mike and Kay are Susan's parents, Mike and Kay from Nashville. Kay is David and Lill's daughter; Mike is the son-in-law. They probably have David and Lillian with them today, but then you never know. They might be busy with Susan, getting her home and settled from the hospital. If so, maybe David and Lillian are on their own; maybe they would like to go out for lunch? Really would like to see them; figure out what's going on with David, if that's possible. Yeah, lunch at Cracker Barrel with Dave and Lill, good enough excuse as any to call. That, and to check up on Susan.*

Joey flipped open his phone, looked to his notepad for the number, and dialed the DeRieux's home phone.

No one answered. A recording came on, but Joey hung up without leaving a message. Looking upstream from his perch atop the bridge, Joey again took in the huge, red-brick hospital complex; and again, he marveled at how large it had become. Even a century ago, it was considered to be a large building, but nothing compared to what it had grown into. The complex's footprint now encompassed well over a large city block. Just the parking garage alone would dwarf the original building.

The flashing light from the hospital's helicopter pad caught his attention. If you saw or heard the whirlybird coming in or going out, you could be pretty sure that something bad had just happened. A bluish-purple bird—the "Purple Vulture", he had heard it called. A bad joke: "The Purple Vulture", because it swooped down and picked dead things up off the street. Yes, a bad joke, but every time he saw it overhead he couldn't help but to think of that moniker and feel bad for whomever was onboard.

Joey returned his attention to the dots of windows and thought, *Chances are, Susan is in one of those rooms, behind one of those windows. I bet all the DeRieuxs are there. If I had a telescope, I might even be able to see them.*

Joey stood up and slid his phone back into his pocket. *Hospitals are pretty open and informal these days. I'll just pop in over there and say hello.*

*   *   *   *   *

Susan sat upright in her hospital bed, nursing her new baby boy. Lill, perched nearby on the very edge of the bed, looked on. Kay stood next to her mother, with her hand on her mother's shoulder.

This is his very first day of life, thought Lillian, her contentment growing into euphoria as she gazed upon the first of the newest generation of DeRieuxs. Life, new life, in all its purity and innocence. The newborn's innate love for its mother, the mother's joy in giving nourishment to her child, the invisible yet rock-solid bond extending down from the great-grandmother, through the generations, and into the baby, only hours old. At that moment, for those women and the suckling baby, the magnitude and power of that bond was beyond measure in terms of matter, time, or space. Lill had experienced this very moment countless times within her own mind. Typically, the mere thought of a hospital dampened Lill's spirits, but now, she was so absorbed in the happiness and serenity around her that being in a hospital was in no way a part of her current consciousness.

Since both of Susan's parents were there, Jeff, after spending the morning with his wife and new little boy, had taken the opportunity to duck back to his office for a few hours but had promised to be back later that afternoon. David sat in a rocking chair in a corner of the room. To his right, light shined in from a nice-sized window. Over the top of some buildings and trees, the Tennessee River could be clearly seen along with a couple of the bridges that connected downtown Chattanooga with the North Shore. Along the wall to his left was David's son-in-law, Mike, sitting in a state of bliss, on a plastic institutional chair, watching his wife, daughter, and now grandson. Mike was clearly soaking in the joyful aura that filled the room to the exclusion of all else, except, that is, for the lurking anxiety within David's mind.

The baby was now, for the moment, full and content. Susan rocked him back to look at his face; mother's milk bubbled around his lips. She gently rubbed his chubby cheeks with the back of her index finger as she cooed at him, wiped his lips with a soft towel, held him to her shoulder, and gently patted his back. She could count on one hand the number of times she had burped a baby, but already it looked so natural, as if she had done it countless times before.

Mike was smiling. He turned to David and said, "I can't believe I'm a grandfather." Then leaning forward in his chair, he patted David on the leg. "How's it feel to be a great-grandfather?"

"I don't know," David replied a little uneasily. For David, this was a strange place, and even though the faces and voices that filled the room, taken as individuals, were familiar; still, taken as a group, they were not. For David, there was too much going on, and to him it was confusing, and thus, unsettling. For David, the institutional sterility of the room had an innate coldness that was disturbing. His level of stress was building, teetering on the edge at which it could begin to spiral. Mike could sense the tension in David's overly quiet demeanor.

Kay watched as Susan gently patted her newborn and thought how in some ways it seemed like just yesterday she was burping Susan for the first time; but, in other ways, with all the days, events, years, and milestones that had passed, it seemed like something from another life. Kay glanced at her mother, now a great-grandmother, whose full attention was also on watching the burping, and wondered if the same thoughts were going through her mother's mind that were going through hers. It occurred to Kay that in a flash, she would be sitting where Lill was sitting. She wondered if that passage of time would again change her perspective. How could it not?

Kay decided that her mom would be more comfortable if she were scooted a little further onto the bed. Putting her hand under her mom's arm she said, "Let's scoot you a little more onto the bed; you're right on the edge." Lill wiggled a little, trying to help. Kay quickly saw that symmetrical help would be better, so she called to Mike, and the two of them, one on each arm, gently lifted and slid Lill to a more stable perch on the bed.

As Mike turned to go back to his seat, he saw a man standing in the open doorway with his hand up, about to knock on the door frame. "May I help you?" Mike asked.

Susan leaned forward to see around her mother and, seeing Joey, called out, "Hello, Mr. Franks, Joey, please come in."

Joey took a step into the room, nodding his head to the group at the bed, and then gave a little wave with his hand towards David to his right, saying, "Hello, hello."

Susan said to her parents, both standing next to the bed and now facing Joey at the door, "Mom, Dad, this is Joey Franks, the gentleman who gave me a ride yesterday from the Cracker Barrel. Mr. Franks, this is my mom and dad, Kay and Mike."

"Please, call me Joey," he said as he shook Kay's extended hand and then Mike's.

"It's a pleasure to meet you, Joey," Mike said with a smile as the two shook hands. "We've heard a lot about you; you were quite the hero yesterday."

"Oh, I was glad to help. It was fun to have a little unexpected excitement." Turning towards Susan, Joey continued, "I see that everything went well."

Susan was about to answer, when a nurse came in. David saw the nurse as she came through the door. Everyone else was facing Susan but turned at the sound of the nurse's voice as she announced in a cheerful yet authoritative voice, "It's getting a little crowded in here. The doctor is making his rounds and should be here in a few minutes. Most of you are going to have to go back to the waiting room for a little while, if you don't mind."

Mike had been aware for some time that David was growing increasingly anxious. He knew his father-in-law well and was sympathetic to David's current state of mind. Adding more people into the room—Joey, and now the nurse—didn't help.

Mike, looking at his wife but speaking to all of the women, said, "How about we men go out to the lobby for a while?"

Kay agreed, "That sounds like a good plan," and watched as Mike made his way over to where her father was sitting.

Mike said to David, while reaching out his hand to help him up, "What do you say we go stretch our legs?"

David liked the idea. "That sounds good," he said, grasping Mike's outstretched hand. Mike pulled slightly with one hand and steadied David as he rose with his other by grasping David's arm just above his elbow.

"Stiffened up a little sitting there," David said as he began to straighten up after a few steps. Joey was waiting just outside the door as the two came through. David reached out his hand in greeting. "How are you?" he said to Joey, shaking his hand. "You look familiar to me, but I'm having trouble placing your name."

Mike said to David, "This is Joey Franks," and seeing that David appeared at ease with Joey, turned to Joey and said, "Please join us for a few minutes if you have the time."

"I'd like that," Joey responded as the three walked down the hall towards the waiting area.

Mike said to Joey, "I understand you spent a little time here yesterday. It was really a big help; thanks so much."

"Oh, really, it was my pleasure," Joey replied.

Mike continued, "The baby, coming a few days early, kind of caught us off guard. Kay and I, of course, planned on being here; just thought we had a little more time than we did. But anyway, glad you were here, thanks again."

Joey replied, "Lillian said that you and your wife Kay live in Nashville. Is that right?"

"Yeah, we love Chattanooga though. Kay would really like to live up on Signal near her parents; but, Nashville, for us, is where the jobs are."

"What do you do?"

"Kay and I have a little PR firm. We handle some of Nashville's celebrities."

"That sounds interesting. Do all your clients live in Nashville?"

"Well, no. Most have some sort of roots in Nashville, but a handful have moved away, and then, over the years, we've picked up others here and there. I guess you could say that most are Nashville-based, and most of the others are in L.A., a few in New York. The thing is, from a business point of view, our clients like to think of us as being close by—in Nashville that is—even though we don't see them in person as often as you might think. Plus, Chattanooga just doesn't have many direct flights to other cities. We don't have to travel all that often, but it's enough of an inconvenience that it's a factor in keeping us in Nashville, at least for now. And, like it or not, there is some cachet in living in a 'hip' town like Nashville. Kay and I have talked about it, and for now, we feel that if we changed our base to Chattanooga, in the eyes of some of our clients, whether they would admit it or not, even to themselves, our stock would go down, at least a little. It's funny. For a lot of celebrities and big-deal people, it's cool to be in a really big city or, sometimes, in a really small town. But that space in between, for some reason is, I don't know, mocked, snubbed, at least a little in some circles. Anyway, if we did move to Chattanooga, it certainly wouldn't help our business, and it would probably do at least a little damage. In our business, where you live is part of your packaging, and it's your customers who decide if it's good or if it's bad."

Joey nodded in agreement and said, "Yeah, you're probably right about that. Anyway, I bet by hanging around with the 'big-deal' people, as you say, you've got to have some great stories."

"Yeah," Mike said with a laugh, "but then I guess you could say that a good part of my job is in keeping those stories from being stories."

Joey laughed, "I'm sure you're right. I guess you could say that we work the opposite sides of the street."

Mike said, "That's right; Susan told us you are a retired newspaper man, a reporter. That that's how you know David."

The three entered a small waiting area across from a nurses' station where three hallways came to an intersection. Mike pointed to a corner that looked to be about as far out of the main flow of activity as they could get for now. "How about right over there?" he suggested.

Joey sat against one wall. A small table with a few magazines and an empty, paper coffee cup filled the corner space. Mike and David sat against the other wall with David in the middle, next to the table. Upon sitting down, Mike immediately realized that he might have made a mistake. David's seat was facing the nurse's station, and David appeared to be somewhat disturbed by the activity going on there. Usually, if David was far enough removed from an unfamiliar activity, far enough away so as not to be concerned that he might be called upon to participate or involuntarily sucked into the activity, he enjoyed watching the show—provided, of course, that the activity itself was benign. But "disturbing" is a subjective term, and if an observed activity is disturbing, then perception will trump distance, and even great distances or large amounts of time can be rendered inconsequential if the degree of sensation is substantial; and anyone, at any time, can be drawn across such a span. Mike looked back and forth between the concerned looked on David's face and the limited activity going on at the nurses' station. It looked, to Mike, like all that was going on at the nurses' station was simply a nurse portioning out medicine and loading the doses onto a cart.

Mike wondered if it was the activity that was fueling David's anxiety or if it was remnants of the anxiety that Mike had observed growing within David from the activity in Susan's room that was, for some reason, taking longer than normal to dissipate. Walking down the hall, Mike had sensed that leaving Susan's room had eased David's level of anxiety a fair amount; but now, looking at David's face, he wondered why David continued to look so serious. Of course, Mike considered, it could be just the wild card, mood, at play. Mood, which in all fairness, affects everyone from time to time; but, in David's case, when memory failed, mood would often take its place, and mood was a more significant throw-of-the-dice than was memory. But then again, perhaps mood is sometimes an echo of a memory.

Mike hoped that perhaps a little, light chit-chat would soothe David. Mike patted David on the leg, in an attempt to draw David's attention away from the nurses' station, and said, "So, Dad, Susan's had a little boy."

David nodded slightly but kept his attention on the nurses' station. Mike tried again, again tapping David on the leg, "Pops, Pops . . . look at me." David turned his head and looked at Mike. Mike mustered up the best smile that he could. It wasn't hard because Mike had every reason to be happy that day. He continued, "Susan, your granddaughter, has just had a little baby boy. That's pretty great, don't you think?"

It was easy to tell that David had no idea what Mike was talking about. Mike continued nevertheless, "That makes you a great-grandfather."

"Oh, I see," David replied with no great enthusiasm.

Mike, realizing this tack was going nowhere because David, particularly under stress, did not do well with conversations involving short term memory and associations, shifted to something that involved long-term memory, hoping that David would do better with that.

Mike pointed to Joey and said, "Joey Franks here tells me that he used to be a newspaper reporter and knew you from back when you were in the FBI. I bet you guys have some great stories to tell."

David didn't take the bait, so Joey jumped in, "Yeah, those were quite the times." Still nothing from David, so Joey continued, "Yeah, quite the times. Of course, David kept everything pretty much buttoned down back then, but there was this other agent, a real character as I recall. Seemed like the two of you were partners in a lot of things, at least for a while anyway," Joey directed his voice to David. "Think his name was Bert, yeah, Bert Ashton."

"You're kidding!" Mike blurted. "Bert was my dad."

"No kidding," Joey said with more than a little amazement on his face. "So," he said, giving himself a moment to think, "So, you . . . you and the DeRieuxs go back a long way. So, you actually married the girl next door; how about that."

Mike replied, "Well, she wasn't exactly the girl next door, but we do go way back. We lived in different parts of town, but yeah, I've known the DeRieuxs ever since I can remember. David and Lillian are pretty much like second parents to me, always have been."

Mike, still trying to sooth David by getting him involved in a pleasant conversation, said to David, "You remember Bert, don't you, Dad?"

Usually, David responded with some happy tidbit when Bert's name was mentioned, even if it was just some good-natured nonsense. But some days David's recall and willingness to participate were better than others, and today, it was harder than usual to tell what was going on within David's mind. At the mention of Bert's name, David gave a slight smile, but it was impossible for Mike to know if the smile was provoked by the memory of Bert, or merely some sort of a reflex action that had been ingrained into David over time. Furthermore, David's slight smile had a hint of a grimace within it, making it difficult for Mike to decipher the conflict within David's mind, which was displayed on his face.

Filling the gap in the conversation, Joey said, "So, your last name is Ashton, Mike Ashton. You know, people don't use last names as much these days when making introductions as they used to, or I might have put that together sooner. It's funny, I remember the old-timers around here; they'd meet a boy or young man, and the first thing they'd say is, 'whose yaw daddy,' or, 'what's yaw daddy do?' They weren't trying to be blunt, or mean, or anything like that; that's just what the times were like. People, in a lot of ways, I guess, were much more direct back then, more matter-of-fact. It was kind of a shortcut. If they knew your daddy, and liked him, well then, it was like an instant old-home-week. If they didn't know your daddy, and you were a local, well then, they'd assume your daddy wasn't much or they'd know him, and you'd probably be treated a little cold—at least until you proved yourself to them. On the other hand, if your daddy had a bad reputation, well then, it was hard to keep that to yourself back then, and your road was most likely a hard one—usually better off leaving town for a fresh start. Different times. Not really fair, by today's standards anyway, but, fair or not, that's how it was."

Mike, still hoping to engage David, turned to him and said, "Pop, what did your father do?"

David replied in a neutral tone, "Oh, I'm not sure."

Mike, not giving up, said, "He and his brothers had some sort of a parking garage in Chicago, didn't they? Wasn't it near Rush Street, Pops, somewhere between Rush Street and the Drake Hotel?"

Mike and Joey gave David a few moments, hoping that he would pick up the ball and respond. When he didn't, Joey said, "You know, Mike, thinking about it, I'm remembering your father more now. He was a huge man, wasn't he? I don't mean fat, but he was really tall and, well . . . sturdy . . . really sturdy built I guess you could say. You're by no means a small fry, but, well, if I remember correctly, you don't really resemble your dad. I don't recall knowing or ever meeting your mom. Do you take more after her side of the family?"

"Well, I like to think that I take after them both in many ways, being raised by them and all, but I was adopted. I have no idea who my birth parents were. I imagine that I probably resemble them, physically, but I like to think that I have the soul of an Ashton. My parents were really good to me."

The three men paused and watched as a young man, looking to be in his mid-to-late twenties and carrying a small teddy bear, walked past the waiting room area, passing between them and the nurses' station, and then down the hall.

Joey observed, "Looks like a young, first-time father there with the teddy bear and all. Wonder if he got it in the gift shop here; I'll bet they sell a zillion of them. Might be a little soon for a teddy bear, but then again, at this point, it's as much for the dad as it is for the baby. He'll probably get his baby a ball and glove next week, if it's a boy."

Mike said, "I had a teddy bear when I was young. Had it for the longest time. Wonder whatever happened to it? That would have been something hard to throw away, but I guess you eventually outgrow everything. Kay says when she was little, she had a blanket for a long time—a small, soft, pink blanket; a 'security blanket' she called it."

Mike turned to David. "Hey Pops, did you ever have a teddy bear or security blanket when you were a kid?"

David replied in a low, deadpan, distracted voice, "I don't know."

Mike followed David's gaze. David was fixated on a man in a white lab coat and tie, who had just approached the nurses' station and was now slightly hunched over the end of the counter, apparently reading something on a clipboard. Mike couldn't understand the interest that David continued to show with the nurses' station, nor could he understand why he was having so much trouble drawing David into a conversation. How could such mundane activities be so captivating to David?

Mike looked at David, then back again at the station. What was he seeing that could possibly be so fascinating, so bothersome? Everything looked calm and normal. It wasn't as if there was a lot of activity or loud noises. People weren't moving quickly or erratically, or anything like that—things that sometimes disturbed David. All that Mike could see was a nurse and what looked like a doctor, quietly going about their tasks.

The nurse looked nice enough. Most of her body was hidden behind the station's counter and a pushcart, as she moved back and forth, portioning out drugs and loading them onto the cart in preparation for her rounds. She looked young, late twenties, early thirties perhaps, blond hair, cut to hang just above her shoulders, curved inwards to make two semi-circles framing the sides of her face. She gave a pleasant-enough impression, though she neither smiled overtly nor frowned, but was merely matter-of-factly going through the mechanics of a routine part of her job.

Mike returned his attention to the doctor. He couldn't quite put his finger on it, but there was just something about the doctor's demeanor that, Mike sensed, added an element of tension to the environment; perhaps added to the formality of the moment for the nurse. Then again, Mike thought, maybe not. *Maybe I'm just projecting my anxiety, David's anxiety, onto them?*

Mike continued to watch the doctor. He was still leaning over whatever paperwork it was that he had been reading. He was a lanky looking fellow with full, thick hair; cut short in a manner that accentuated his noticeably small ears. He picked up a large plastic bottle that, Mike assumed, was an institutional-sized bottle of some sort of pills, and stood up straight as he read the label, revealing that he was in fact an unusually tall man, especially when compared to the nurse nearby.

Mike looked back at David, then at Joey, who was also watching David, and then back again to David. Tapping David on the leg, hoping to break David's absorption away from what he was watching, and into a, hopefully, soothing conversation; Mike repeated his last question to David, "Hey Pops, did you ever have a teddy bear or security blanket when you were a kid?"

David, still, was not to be drawn away. Mike, not knowing what else to do, said to them both, "Pops here used to carry a book around all the time when he and Lill ran errands together. He almost always had a book handy to fill his spare time, if he had to sit and wait somewhere." Again tapping David's leg, "What was that book called, Pops? You always had it with you. 'The Practical Cogitator', that was it; wasn't it? Wasn't it supposed to be a collection of great writings, thought-provoking stuff? Wasn't it written, or more like put together into a collection, sometime after the war, with the idea that soldiers in the future could carry it with them so that they could have something to read and think about during the long, dull periods? That was kind of like a teddy bear for you, Pops, wasn't it? Kind of an adult's version of a teddy bear?"

David watched as the doctor motioned to the nurse to come over. The doctor said something to the nurse, holding the bottle in one hand and pointing to something on its label with the other. Then, the doctor handed the nurse the bottle, and she returned with it to her task, portioning out the medications.

David, as if whispering to himself, but just loud enough for Mike to hear, repeated Mike's last two words, "Teddy bear, teddy bear."

Then, David turned to Mike and looked straight into his eyes. Mike had the odd sensation that David was looking at someone else. David whispered in a low voice, but as grave a voice as Mike could ever recall hearing, "Mihail, he's here. VanZant's here. He's broken his promise; he's violated our agreement. There's no limit now as to what he might do next. Do you still have the gun that I gave you?"

"What?" Mike gasped, groping for some context in which what David had just said would make any sense.

David turned his head back towards the nurses' station and continued, "Look. He's pretending that he doesn't see us." David turned his attention back to Mike, put his hand on Mike's knee, leaned in, and said, "Mihail, we have to kill him, even if it exposes the things we've done. He's giving us no choice. We have to kill him."

Chapter 24

The Second Boy

Camp Forrest
July 1946

David, waiting for a voice to come back on the line, stood next to the desk in the guard shack holding the phone to his ear with one hand and holding a scrap of paper in the other. He looked at the number on the paper, then at the corporal sitting at the desk who was busy making entries into some sort of logbook.

"Hey, Corporal," David said, "do you recognize this number; do you know whose number it is?"

The Corporal looked at the number and replied, "Don't know that one, sir. It's a base number though," and then returned to his work on the logbook.

David looked out the doorway, wanting to keep his eye on Johnson. A truck was still blocking his view. David was uneasy with this disruption in his plan. So far, it was just a slight delay, but the little things were quickly mounting up. He didn't like being on hold; even a small amount of time seemed long. The man on the phone, identifying himself as Private Murphy, had put David on hold before David had a chance to get any other information about who or why he had been asked to call. Not many people knew he was there. David assumed it was Bert who had sent the message for him to call, but that number was not any that David had expected Bert to use.

David again interrupted the Corporal's work. "Corporal, do you know a Private Murphy?"

"Um," the Corporal said as a place holder while he accessed his memory. "Not here, not on this base. But that doesn't mean that there isn't one here somewhere."

The truck blocking David's view revved up a little as the driver pushed in the clutch, put the truck into gear, and finally moved out of David's way.

David's car was gone! Johnson was gone!

David dropped the phone receiver onto the desk and jumped into the doorway, first taking a long look down the road leading into the base, and then a quick glance in the opposite direction. Hurriedly, he walked around the circumference of the guard shack, checking all directions. Johnson and the car were gone. Sergeant Cooper was nowhere to be seen. David hurried back to the phone and picked it up. "Hello, hello," he said loudly into the mouthpiece. Silence—he was still on hold.

David hung up the phone and addressed the Corporal, "Where is Sergeant Cooper?"

The corporal shrugged his shoulders and said, "Who?"

"Cooper, Sergeant Cooper. He told me that he had just come on duty here. He's the one who came out to my car and said that there was a phone message for me."

"Oh, right. There was someone here just a few minutes ago, dropped that number on my desk, said you'd be here in a few minutes for it. He was a Sergeant, but I didn't catch his name. Is that the Sergeant that you're looking for?"

"Yeah, but you say that you don't know him?"

"No, sir."

"Did he look at all familiar to you? Ever work with him, or see him around the base, or around town?"

"No, sir."

"Damn it," David said to himself as he pulled the papers from his jacket pocket and dialed the number of the guesthouse where Bert and the family were supposed to be. The line was busy.

David hung up the phone. The Corporal had stopped fiddling with the log book and was looking at David. It was more than obvious that something was wrong.

"Soldier," David said, "I need a car. I need a car fast. Is there one here that I can use?"

"No, sir, I'm afraid not."

"Do your MPs have radios?"

"Yes, sir."

"Call them," David said, pushing the phone squarely in front of the Corporal. "Tell them to get here fast. Really fast, as fast as they can. No sirens though. Tell them no sirens."

The Corporal looked at the phone, then up at David. He was used to taking orders but not from anyone outside his normal chain of command. He picked up the phone and dialed. It didn't matter, whatever was going on, the Corporal wanted the MPs there; he'd turn it all over to them.

A man, early middle aged, in a pickup truck and straw hat, stopped at the doorway to check in with the guard. David stepped quickly through the door. "Excuse me," David said, as he nudged the guard away from the truck driver's window, flashed the driver his badge, and said, "I'm sorry sir, I'm going to need this truck. Please, leave it running and get out."

Before the driver could answer, David turned to the guard and ordered, "Keep this truck here for me."

David turned to go back to the desk. The Corporal had gotten up and had followed David to the doorway to see what was going on. David grabbed the Corporal by his shoulders, turned him around, and ushered him back to his desk. "Sit back down here," David said as he guided the Corporal down into his seat, still with his hands on the Corporal's shoulders. "I need you to do a few things for me."

There was some other paperwork on the desk. David grabbed whatever was closest, turned it over so that he had a clear page upon which to write. He copied the number that he had just been told to call, the number that had kept him on hold, Private Murphy's number. Below that, David wrote the number for the guesthouse.

He showed the two numbers to the Corporal and said, "Keep calling these two numbers until you get someone." David added Bert's name to the paper and continued, "Hopefully, you'll get ahold of Bert Ashton. He's the Special Agent that was here with me earlier. If you get him, or if he calls here, tell him I'm on my way to the guesthouse. Tell him something's wrong. Tell him Johnson was here, but he's not with me now."

The Corporal was clearly uncomfortable, "I, I don't know, sir," he hedged.

"By God," David bellowed, "Do as I say, soldier. When the MPs get here, send them to this address." David checked his papers and added the guesthouse address to the sheet that he was leaving with the Corporal. Find out where Agent Ashton is and radio his location to me."

"Sir," the guard at the doorway called. David looked up at him. The guard announced, "The MPs are about here."

David went to the doorway and looked down the road. He could see two jeeps coming fast.

"Good," David said out loud, apparently to everyone. Then, to the man still sitting in his truck, David said, "I'm sorry, sir. Sorry for keeping you. I won't be needing your truck after all. Please accept my apologies."

David went back over to the Corporal and said, "Look, the MPs are about here. Looks like there's two jeeps. They both have radios, don't they?"

"Yes, sir."

"I'm going to take one back to the guesthouse and leave the other one here. If you hear anything, call me on the MPs radio. Okay?"

"Yes, sir," the Corporal replied, then he hedged a bit, "That is, if the MPs go along with you on this. Then, I'll radio them if I hear anything."

"Thanks," David said, already heading out the door. Pausing in the doorway, he turned back to the Corporal and said, "Soldier, this is important."

By the time the MPs were slowing down to the guard shack, David was standing at the back, holding his badge up high in one hand and motioning them over to him with the other. Before they could ask, David directed, "I'm Special Agent David DeRieux of the FBI. We have a situation going on here that I need your help with, fast. One of you stay here at the guard shack; the Corporal inside will fill you in on what's going on. The other, you," David said, pointing to one of the MPs, "I need you to take me to this address, fast. It's a guesthouse. There's supposed to be another FBI Special Agent there, but something's wrong. I need to get there fast," David said as he climbed into the jeep.

To his relief, the MPs didn't argue. The one whose jeep David had climbed into said, "Okay, but we'll have to call this in first."

David said, "I understand; that's fine. Go ahead and do it—call it in, but radio it in on the fly. Let's go."

The MP staying at the guard shack said, "Okay, okay. You guys go. I'll call it in."

David held on as the jeep sped down the road. Over the radio, they could hear the other MP calling in their activity. The MP looked again at the address, then, over the sound of the radio chatter, said to David, "Okay, suppose you tell me what's going on here. What can we expect to find at this address?"

David needed the MP's help but didn't want to give out any more information than was absolutely necessary. He said, "We are using that guest house as a meeting place. We have a Special Agent there, his name is Bert Ashton, with a couple of . . . guests—a woman and a young boy. I was supposed to escort a man there that I met at the guard shack. We were about to leave when I got called back to the shack for a phone message. A truck blocked my view. When it moved, the car and the man I was supposed to escort were gone."

The MP asked, "Is this man—the man you were supposed to escort—is he dangerous in any way?"

David thought, then said, "We didn't think so. Let's be careful though. Keep alert. Special Agent Ashton is hopefully at the guesthouse. You can be confident in taking directions from him. Probably not anything going on there, but I couldn't get through on the phone, so I need to check this out. There's another guy though, a Sergeant Cooper; do you know him?"

"No, sir," the MP answered. "There's got to be a lot of 'Coopers' around though; it's a common-enough name. But I can't think, off hand, of any Sergeants around here named Cooper."

"Well," David continued, "I think he sidetracked me. Gave me a number to call and then disappeared with my contact. I didn't see a weapon on him, but he is an unknown. He could be dangerous."

As they neared the house, both David and the MP could see two adults and a child lying in the front yard. As they got closer, they could see that it was a man, a woman, and a child. The man was closest to them, lying face down, and moved his head to look up at the approaching jeep. The MP stopped on the street in front of the house. Before the jeep came to a complete stop, David pulled his gun and hopped out. From what he saw, he had a sick feeling that the woman and the boy were dead. The man started to get up.

"Stay put; stay down," David yelled. The man put his head back down on the ground and stretched his arms out on the ground in the hands up position.

"Bert!" David yelled. "Bert! You here?"

"David, David, I'm in here," Bert answered as he walked slowly out of the front door with his pistol in his hand but pointing down. "The house is clear."

Bert gave a quick glance at David and then at the MP who was crouched behind the hood of the jeep, gun drawn, but not sure if he should be pointing it towards the man in the doorway or the man lying in the yard. David, still with his gun drawn but also pointing down, moved forward and knelt, first by the child, and then by the woman, checking each of their necks for a pulse.

David shook his head. "They're gone."

Bert hollered to the MP, "Soldier, point that gun in a safe direction."

The MP looked to David. David nodded his head that it was okay.

The MP lowered his gun and walked out from behind the jeep and onto the edge of the front yard.

"Who's this?" David said to Bert, as he moved towards the man lying on the ground.

Bert, not moving from his position in the doorway, answered, "Don't know. I'm pretty sure he's just a Good Samaritan that stopped to help, before realizing what he was getting caught up in. I didn't see who did the shooting; didn't even know anyone was out here until I heard the shots. David . . . Johnson was here."

"What!" David exclaimed.

"Johnson was here, holding a soldier, a sergeant I think, at gunpoint. Anyway, I don't think Johnson did the shooting. Someone else was here—at least two others. One held me at gunpoint for a minute—while the gunshots were going off. Then, as quick as he came, he just left. I did get here, though, in time to see this guy drive up. Johnson ordered him to lie down on the ground. And then Johnson, still holding the sergeant at gunpoint, drove off in his truck."

David, now standing over the man on the ground, said to the man, "I'm FBI Special Agent David DeRieux. The man in the doorway is Special Agent Bert Ashton. Is what he just said about you true? Are you a Good Samaritan that just happened to stop by?"

"Yes, sir," the man cried out.

"Are you armed?" David asked.

"No, sir."

"Then you've got nothing to worry about, but since we don't know what's going on here yet, get up slowly, don't make any fast moves, keep your hands out where we can see them."

The man got up slowly. David said, "I'm sorry, but I'm going to have to frisk you. Please walk over to the jeep here and put your hands on the side of the jeep."

David followed the man over to the jeep. David was a little surprised that Bert remained in the doorway. As a rule, Bert would move closer, as a backup, when David had to frisk a suspect. There had to be some reason that Bert was keeping a post at the door. That worried David, but he didn't want to ask, at least not in front of the MP or the man that he was about to frisk.

As the Samaritan put his hands on the side of the jeep, David holstered his gun and frisked the man. He was clean.

David motioned the MP over and instructed the MP, "This gentleman is not armed, but please watch him. Keep an eye on him until we get this sorted out. Stay alert, but I think you can holster your weapon." David then addressed the gentleman, "I'm sorry, sir, for the inconvenience and all that you've been through here, but we're going to have to keep you here for a little while. We're going to have to get some information from you before you leave, a statement and some contact information."

The MP holstered his pistol and said to David, "I'm going to have to call this in. This is a military base, and this is a major crime scene. Our people are going to have to take this over."

David replied, "Well, normally you would be right, but even though you're here, technically, this base is on 'Inactive' status. Look, go ahead and call your people. We'll both make some calls, and we'll both hear from the higher-ups; but, for the record, this is not an active base. This is Federal property, I'm a Federal Agent, and I'll be in charge here until we hear otherwise."

Bert called from the doorway, "David, I need to speak to you for a moment."

David pulled the MP a little over to the side and spoke to him in a low, calm voice, "Listen, we need your help. Call your people, get some help over here; but for now, your main job, really your only job, is to keep an eye on this man and to keep everyone off this crime scene. It's important that nothing is disturbed until we have a chance to go over everything. I can't tell you enough how important that is. I think that gentleman, the Samaritan, is probably okay, but stay alert, keep a cautious eye on him, don't take anything for granted. Okay?"

"Okay," the MP agreed. "When my supervisor gets here, the two of you can sort it out."

David walked over towards Bert. As he got close to the doorway, the two locked eyes. David marshalled his calm and in a low voice asked, "What's going on here, Bert?"

Bert took a couple of steps back into the living room, bringing David along with him, and in a voice scarcely over a whisper, making doubly sure that the MP couldn't hear, replied, "You remember I told you over the phone that there was a surprise package here?"

"Yeah," David answered, drawing out the word.

"There's another boy here, inside, hiding in a bathtub," Bert said, pointing to the doorway that led to the kitchen and the bathroom beyond it.

"What?" David gasped, his eyes opened wide with amazement.

"There's another boy here. Johnson's wife, in addition to her son, brought a second boy with her. One of the men that helped smuggle her out of the Soviet Union, apparently at the last minute, insisted that she take along this other boy as well. I guess it was part of his price for him helping her get out. Anyway, that boy out front, that's not Johnson's boy; it's the extra boy. Johnson's boy is hiding inside, scared to death. He's hunkered down, hiding in the bathtub in the bathroom—just past the kitchen."

Stunned, David said, "This is unbelievable."

Bert continued, "Yeah, it's a real mess to say the least. I don't know what's happened here, but for right now, we need to move fast on one thing. Whoever did this, whoever is responsible for this, I'm thinking that they might not know that there were two boys and that Johnson's boy is still alive. I'm thinking we need to keep it that way. We need to get Johnson's boy out of here before a lot of people get here."

"Okay, you got a plan?"

"Yeah," Bert said. "But first, like I said, I don't have any idea of what's going on here, but I should tell you what I know, quickly, before people start showing up. Otherwise, it might be a while before we have a chance to talk alone. Here goes, here's the skinny: Someone called me on the phone, said you wanted to speak to me, had me on hold in the back bedroom. Johnson's boy was in the bathroom next-door, with diarrhea." Bert paused, "That wasn't you calling on the phone, was it? Did you have someone call me?"

"No," David answered. "I tried to call at one point, but the phone was busy. Anyway, go on."

Bert continued, "While I was on hold, a gun shot rang out, coming from the front living room. An average build man in a mask, plain street clothes, brown hair, stepped into the bedroom doorway, holding me at gun point. Two more gunshots came from the same direction as the first. The man told me to turn around and face the wall. I complied. He must have left right away; I turned my head after a short moment and he was already gone. By the time I got to the front door, the two out front had already been shot. Johnson was behind a man in uniform, a sergeant I think, holding him at gunpoint next to the side of the house. No one else was there, but I don't think Johnson shot the woman or the kid—not from the direction of the sound of the shots, and not by the way that they fell. It's hard to tell for certain, the direction of sounds can be tricky, but I'm pretty sure the gun shots came from inside this house, from the living room, probably just inside the doorway. I could smell gunpowder in the living room when I first got there. Out front, you heard what I said about the Good Samaritan driving up. I'd be surprised if he has anything to do with all this, but, Jesus Christ, who knows what's going on here. Anyway, I told the Samaritan to stay put on the ground. Then I went back inside to clear the house. That's when I found Johnson's boy hiding in the tub. He must have gotten scared when he heard the shots fired. Probably a good thing for him; probably saved his life. Then, you drove up; and now, well, here we are."

"Okay, Bert, so what's the plan?"

"There are two cars in the driveway at the side of the house, our Bureau car, and the car that the base loaned to us. Johnson shot the base's car, the one nearest the street, in the radiator. But the other car, our Bureau car, I think it's okay. Here are the keys. You get the boy, Johnson's son—or at least Johnson's son if these people are who they say they are. Anyway, the boy's too young to be a spy. For now, get the boy, and the two of you take off in the Bureau car. Hide him with someone, quick, and then get back to me as soon as you can. How about your sister, Edna? She's in Murfreesboro; isn't she? Would that work?"

David thought out loud, "Yeah, yeah. I think that might work. I think I could do that. I'll give it some more thought on the drive. If I get a better idea, or if she can't take him, then, worse case, I can hide him at my house for a while, if I have to."

"Okay," Bert said. "This place is going to be swarming with people any second now. Let's get you and the boy out of here, right now."

David followed Bert to the bathroom behind the kitchen. Bert was right; the little boy was terrified. Bert said to David, "Poor little guy's scared to death. He knows me a little, but you're a complete stranger. The little guy doesn't speak any English, none at all that I can tell."

Bert reached into the tub and gently lifted the little boy into his arms, holding him to his chest like he was burping a baby, gently stroked his back, and, in as soothing a voice as he could muster, said, "It's okay, little fellow. You're gonna be okay. You just need to go with Uncle Dave here. He's going to take good care of you, for now."

Bert said to David, "Sit on the side of the tub there, Dave." When David sat, Bert transferred the boy onto David's lap, saying again to the boy, "This is Uncle Dave, he's going to take good care of you."

The boy seemed to sense from the gentle tones and the gentle touch that he was in friendly hands, though he was still plenty scared.

Bert said to David, "I'll be right back." Bert moved quickly to the office-bedroom next to the bathroom and pulled the cover off the bed and returned to the bathroom. Wrapping the blanket over the boy, Bert said, "Okay, you two need to get going. Follow me."

David, holding the young boy snug to his shoulder, followed Bert back through the kitchen, into the living room, and to the backdoor off the living room that led to the backyard. Bert, holding the door open, pointed down the side of the house and said, "The car's at the end of the house there. From out front, I don't think the MP can see you getting into the car; but of course, he'll see you drive away, and he'll probably hear you close the car doors. Keep the boy down, hidden, even if you have to be a little firm. It won't be for more than a minute or two and you can make it up to him later, if you need to. Probably won't be a problem though; I think his natural inclination is to hide. Anyway, get going. I'll go out front and keep the MP from interfering. I'll keep him off the radio as long as I can, but, as soon as his people get here, he's gonna tell them everything. He'll for sure tell them that you left. He won't know that you've got a boy with you, but I'm sure they're not going to be happy that you left. Anyway, the MP knows that you weren't here when any of this went down. I'll tell them that you had an important lead that you had to attend to immediately. They may not like that, but there's nothing they can really do about it. Just get past the gate, out of the base, before they have time to stop you there. Who knows, they may decide to lock down the base for a while. Jesus Christ, this is a hell of a crime scene. I was here, and even I don't know what really happened. Anyway, good luck," Bert said, as he turned back into the house, heading for the front door to keep the MP busy as David and the boy made their escape.

Chapter 25

The Body in the Garage

Camp Forrest, TN
July 1946

The illuminated body, lying face down on the grease-stained concrete floor, was the image that captivated David as he entered the garage. Until recently, before all its equipment had been auctioned off and removed, the garage had served as a machine shop for the Army base.

By now, it was dark and there was no electric power service to the building. Through two adjacent garage-bay doors, which remained opened, two cars had been pulled into the empty expanse of the building and were angled so that each of their headlights shown straight onto the motionless body. The bright beams cast long shadows off both the living and the dead. All the dark shadows seemed to have been given a life of their own as they danced across the floor and ran up the back wall.

Bert and an Army MP squatted next to the body, not yet covered with a sheet—their backs to the lights and to David as he entered the building. Because of the fumes, the cars' engines had been turned off and the battery of one of the cars was beginning to weaken, its light starting to dim. As David passed in front of the headlights, his shadow passed over Bert and onto the back wall. Hearing David's footsteps and seeing his shadow, Bert stood up and watched the silhouette approach. Even before Bert could distinguish David's face from the glare of the headlights, Bert could tell that it was David. When David got close enough for the two to lock eyes, they acknowledged each other with a simple, silent, nod of the head. That was enough for Bert to know that the boy was safely hidden. Turning back to the body, standing shoulder to shoulder, Bert and David looked down at the corpse. After a moment, Bert turned his head to the nearby MP and said, "Would you mind giving us a minute alone here?"

"Sure, no problem. I could use a smoke," the MP replied as he wandered off to the front of the building on the dark side of the headlights.

Bert and David remained standing, examining the body in silence. After a few moments, Bert, still looking down, said, "You got back a lot quicker than I expected. That's good. Everything go okay?"

Without looking up, David replied, "Yeah. Really went as well as we could have hoped for. After I got off the base, as soon as I could, I stopped at a pay phone and got ahold of Edna at her home, at her in-law's farm outside Murfreesboro. I didn't tell her any more than I had to. I just told her that I had a young boy with me, a three-year-old, and asked if she could keep him for me for a couple of days, on the quiet. She said that would be fine. Her in-laws have a truck that she can use when they're not needing it. So, I told her I had the boy with me now. Told her that I was on the other side of Shelbyville and asked if she could meet me there. She said that she could leave almost right away, so that was great. She knew a spot that we could both find, so we met there. She had her husband, Hank, with her when she got there, but that's no problem since he was going to know about the boy soon enough anyway. Probably better that he was there; gives Edna a lot less to have to explain since, at this point, Edna doesn't know any more than he does. Anyway, I think it's going to be okay. They both seem to get it—that it's something I didn't want to talk about just then, and that we needed to keep this quiet. Another thing in our favor is that it's not really all that odd for a farmer to take in a youngster, especially a young boy. It threw them a little that the boy doesn't speak any English; but still, I think that works in our favor. Thinking about it, it does make it safer for us that the boy can't speak any English in that he can't tell his story or have to answer questions."

In silence, they both continued to look down at the body, trying to absorb what they were looking at, attempting to place it within some context in which it would fit, or better yet, make some sense of the bizarre chain of events that had taken place within the last few hours. The object of their study, a man dressed in an army sergeant's uniform, lay front down with his head turned to the side.

David, in a hushed tone, was the first to speak. "Look at his face."

Bert replied, "I know; it's a mess. It's all smashed in."

David asked, "You think this is the guy that Johnson drove off with? He was about the same size, same hair; had those sergeant's stripes on his sleeves."

Bert said, "Yeah, it's got to be him." Bert pointed to a dim corner within the building. "I'm pretty sure that's the truck Johnson took from the Samaritan and drove off in with the Sergeant."

"Then what's Johnson driving now? Surely he didn't leave here on foot." David thought for a moment and then added, "You know, Bert, when Johnson showed up at the front gate, I was looking down the road leading up to the base. I was expecting him to arrive from outside the gate. But that's not what happened. Johnson came up from behind me. He was already inside the base. I wondered about that at the time, but things were moving so fast I didn't get a chance to ask him about that. I wonder if he was holed up here, in this building, for a while. Since he abandoned that truck, maybe he had another vehicle here. You think this place is part of Johnson's escape plan?"

"Could be. Johnson had to get to the base somehow. Maybe he drove and left a car here. It's a little bit of a long way, but he could have walked to the front gate from here. As cautious as Johnson is, it fits in that he would have an escape plan; probably be more out of character for him not to have one. I'll bet you're right; I bet he had a car stashed here. For that matter, it could have been a truck or motorcycle, hell, maybe even a hot air balloon. That wouldn't be any crazier than anything else that's happened today."

"You know, Bert, something else has been bothering me. When that Sargent and Johnson drove from the gate to the guest house, how did they know where to go? How did either of them know which house or building we were using? At the time, I just assumed that the Sergeant had kidnapped Johnson. But you said, back at the house, when you got to the front door, after all the commotion, that Johnson was holding the Sergeant at gunpoint."

"Yeah, that's right," Bert confirmed. "But who shot the wife and kid? Those shots, I'm pretty sure they came from inside the house. And then there was the guy holding me at gunpoint in the back of the house while those shots were fired. Who the hell was he? He wasn't in uniform, so, this isn't him. Aside from Johnson and the Sergeant, I'm thinking that there had to be at least two other people there. Maybe the shooter in the living room was also in a Sergeant's uniform? Maybe there are two sergeants? But then the truck in the corner over there, that's got to be the one that Johnson drove off in. I'm betting this is the same Sergeant that met you at the gate. Unless, of course, this is some sort of a rendezvous point, in which case all bets are off. Any way you look at this, there is one thing for certain: a lot of people seem to know a lot about our business." Bert paused for a moment, then said aloud what they were both thinking, "Who are these people? Where are they getting their information?"

"Yeah, that's the question. There's an awful lot we don't know, and even what we think we know is based on assumptions that seem reasonable and likely. But you tweak even one of those assumptions and then, pow, everything takes on a different meaning."

Bert had no answer. David said, "What the hell is happening here, Bert? Can this dead guy tell us anything?"

With a slight wave of his finger, Bert pointed to the Sergeant's head. "Well, look at his face. I mean, to do that to someone, to smash their face in like that, well, you've really got to be mad. You really gotta hate the guy; I mean hate him bad."

David asked, "Have you turned him over any, looked in his pockets or found anything?"

"No, not yet. The MPs say they've got a camera that they're bringing over—should be here any minute. I thought I'd just wait until we got some photos and dusted for some prints before I touched or moved anything. No doubt there's going to be a lot of scrutiny on everything here. You just know that everything about today is going to be looked at under a microscope."

"There are a few things though," Bert continued and pointed to one of the sergeant's hands that was stretched out to his side. "Look at his fingers, David. Some of them have been smashed. And look at this," Bert said as he squatted down and circled in the air with his index finger the area around one of the sergeant's knees.

David squatted down for a closer look and observed, "It looks like it's a little wet there. Is that blood seeping through the material?"

"Pretty sure it is," Bert said as they both stood back up. Bert pointed to an area of the floor just outside of the glow of the headlights. "We found a tire iron on the floor just over there in the shadow. Dollars to donuts, that's the tool that was used on our friend here. Judging by the condition of his fingers and the blood coming from that knee, I'm thinking de Sergeant was worked over pretty good before he was killed."

"I think you're right. You said Johnson drove off with a Sergeant at gunpoint. It's got to be that same Sergeant who diverted me away from Johnson at the gate; has to be. You said you didn't see who shot Johnson's wife or the boy, but you think the shots came from inside the house. Looks, to me, like Johnson tortured this guy for answers. I'm betting he's just as confused about all this as we are—probably more."

Bert agreed, "I'm thinking the same thing. Wonder what the Sarge told him. Man-oh-man, look at that face, or what's left of it. It's pretty safe to say that Johnson left here mad—really, really mad—and understandably so. Just wonder who he's going to blame for all of this? That's a list you don't want to be on. Would be a miracle if we're not on it."

Chapter 26

The Chaplain

Camp Forrest
July 1946

Another shadow passed over David, Bert, and the dead sergeant. The two turned to see who was approaching, but again, the glare of the headlights prevented them from seeing clearly what was between them and the light. As the figure got closer, they could tell that it was a man in uniform, another warrior. It wasn't until the man was virtually upon them that he appeared as a man of God; the gold cross of an army chaplain was pinned to his collar. Other insignias of rank affixed to his uniform showed that he was also a lieutenant.

No formalities were exchanged other than a meeting of their eyes. Even a reflexive nod of the head from David or Bert was stilled by the palpable graveness that resided within the Chaplain. The Chaplain looked to be in his late fifties, but his age, like other aspects of his demeanor, seemed largely undefinable. He could easily be much younger—or less likely, older. In any event, the rank of lieutenant seemed incongruently low given the man's apparent age. Later, both David and Bert would use the same word, "deflated", to describe the Chaplain. It was as if, for a man of God, the spark that had once animated his spirit was now long gone. He was but a shell of a man. It was manifest in the dull hollowness of his eyes as well as in the slackness of his face and the negligence of his posture. Rebellion was now the only force that propelled the Chaplain. But it was not a vibrant, healthy rebellion. It was not the uplifting vigor of the righteous against evil, but the weak, dying spasms of the utterly defeated, whose downfall is only compounded by the realization, at the end, that their beliefs were all false. It had the feeling of a mutiny in which there was no choice but to overthrow the Captain, but no better leader was apparent, and all participants, nevertheless, would be punished in the end for their treachery.

After a brief, non-verbal assessment of one another, the Chaplain, with discernible reluctance, looked down on the body—the faceless corpse, shrouded in the uniform of a sergeant. Fingerprints and photos of the crime scene had yet to be gathered, so David and Bert were careful not to disturb the body. Even so, they had seen enough to get a good idea of what had transpired and now felt compelled to observe the Chaplain. Not wanting to be conspicuous about their scrutiny of the Chaplain, both David and Bert joined the Chaplain in tilting their heads down towards the body; but with their eyes bobbing upward and to the side, through veiled glances, David and Bert centered their attention on the Chaplain.

After a long minute, the Chaplain took in a slow, deep breath and, in a subdued voice, quoted the all too familiar verse, "A thousand shall fall at thy side, and ten thousand shall fall at thy right hand; but it shall not come nigh thee."

David and Bert glanced at each other, both thinking the same thing. Bert was dying to say, "What the hell, Chaplain; I'm pretty sure this one got a full blown dose of 'come nigh thee.'" But he held his tongue, curious as to what, unprompted, the Chaplain would say next.

They didn't have to wait long. The Chaplain, still looking at the body, asked, "Was this a righteous man? Was he good, or was he bad, or do we even know? Wait, wait. It doesn't matter. The sons of God roam the earth, and they are not constrained."

David raised his eyebrows and cleared his throat; the Chaplain looked up at David. David repeated back the Chaplain's words in the form of a question, "'The sons of God?' who are you talking about, Chaplain?"

"Satan," was the Chaplain's simple reply. "In the Bible, Satan, Satan and other fallen angels and demons, are often referred to as 'sons of God.' Surprising, disturbing, isn't it."

David let that sit for a minute, then, taking another tack, asked, "What are you doing here, Chaplain? Do you know this man?"

"No. Like I said, I don't even know if he was a good man or a bad man."

David replied, "Well, you can know a man and still not really know if he is good or bad, or somewhere in between. Usually, though, when a Chaplain shows up, there's some sort of a personal link. Someone who knows the deceased calls his pastor or priest."

"Sorry, I don't know him. The Base, the MPs, they called me—standard operating procedure. Whenever there is death, destruction, suffering; I get a call."

Bert queried, "Chaplain, you look like something's bothering you, something more than just this crime scene. Surely, in your position, you've seen worse than this. Surely you've had to attend to dead bodies before."

The Chaplain nodded slowly a few times, as if internalizing the question, and then, in a defeated voice, said, "Thousands."

David nudged the Chaplain to continue with his thought. "Thousands you say?"

"Well, I don't know . . . hundreds at least, maybe a thousand. I lost count long ago. I've no idea exactly, or even roughly, how many; but yes, well over a thousand, easily over a thousand. Once the numbers grow, once the bloodshed goes beyond a certain point, there comes an inflection point—a point in which, overwhelmed by the carnage, reason and value become the casualties. It's overwhelming. But it always seems to play out the same. The difference between a thousand, and a thousand and one, becomes just a number on a piece of paper. The priceless value of an individual's life, an individual's soul, is replaced by heartless, thoughtless justifications and statistics. Individuals lose their distinctiveness, absorbed into a mob, a blob of flesh and suffering. An accurate account of each individual, surprisingly early on in the process, is considered to be impractical. Yes, I've seen it with my own eyes. 'The sons of God'—Satan and his demons—become exhilarated, dancing amongst the screaming carnage, while those with any sense of decency simply go numb. The decent go numb, or they go mad." The Chaplain, exuding deep remorse, shook his head and said, as if to himself, "I've played a part in this unholy drama, this travesty of sending innocent sheep to their slaughter."

David responded, "You were in some battles then?"

"Yes, yes I was. I was on the beaches at Omaha; I was in the forest in Ardennes; I was witness to many of the skirmishes in between." With a visible shudder that he was unable to control or conceal, he added, "I was at Dachau." Then, in a voice that was so low that David and Bert wondered if he was talking only to himself, "Sheep to the slaughter . . . sheep to the slaughter." Then in a slightly louder voice, "If the purpose of a shepherd is to protect his flock, it is only so that there is more to slaughter in the end." The pastor paused for a brief moment, then continued in a voice that was directed to David and Bert, and anyone else who cared to listen, "From what I've seen, the difference between men and animals, of which we supposedly have dominion over, is that animals are never assured the protection of a loving God—quite the opposite. In our Holy Bible, in the early Testaments, animals were frequently sacrificed to God as burnt offerings. Living creatures, killed and burnt; not for food, not for physical sustenance, not for any civil purpose; but only for the glory, the glory and the pleasure that God derives from the sacrifice, the killing. Yes, there can be no doubt; the shedding of blood holds great importance to God. Why else would there be so much of it? It goes all the way back to the very first generation. Cain and Abel each gave sacrifices to God. Cain was 'a tiller of the ground,' so his offering was of the crops that he had grown. Abel raised sheep, so he offered sheep. And what did God think about those two offerings? Well, the Bible tells us in no uncertain terms: 'And the Lord had respect unto Abel and to his offering: But unto Cain and to his offering he had not respect.' Smoldering flesh was what God craved. Smoldering flesh, wholly for the pleasure and the glory of God. But it wasn't just animals. Early on, there was human sacrifice aplenty. Parents sacrificing their children, butchering their own children to appease their God or gods. The Old Testament did eventually put some commands in place to stop the sacrificial killing of people; but before that, there is of course the story of Abraham. Righteous Abraham, obedient Abraham; willing to kill his own son Isaac, at the bequest of his God; stopped by his God at the very last moment. Stopped, only after Abraham had bound his son helpless and placed him on the altar; knife drawn, fully prepared, by his own hand, to slice the flesh of his own son and let his life-blood drain from his body. Only then was that pious drama stopped."

David couldn't help but notice how the Pastor spat out the word "pious."

With only a slight pause, the Pastor continued, "And then of course, there is the sacrifice to end all sacrifices, the ultimate sacrifice, the sacrifice that changed the world—God sacrificing his own son. And not just killing his own son, but killing him in as gruesome a manner as imaginable—nailing him to a cross and leaving him to linger. And why? What is the lesson to take from that, the lesson that has been instilled in us all since our earliest recollections? We are told that it was an act of compassion, of God's love for us. We are told—and from our youth we are trained to believe—that God allowed the torture of his most innocent son for our benefit, as appeasement for our sins. We are told that, because of this gruesome death, we are saved; we are redeemed. My god, where is the sense in that! We have dominion over animals, but if you had two dogs, and one was bad, and one was good; would it ever occur to you to torture the good dog to death, and to somehow think that that would make amends for the bad dog. Of course not. Of course not. There is nothing moral, nothing pious, about torture; especially in torturing the innocent. It doesn't make sense for dogs, and it makes even less sense for people. And then we are taught that we are born, that we are created as sinful creatures; that sinning is a part of our inherent nature, that we cannot help but to sin. We are taught that we have free will, and then we are taught that we cannot help but to sin. We are taught that, because of our sins, from which we cannot escape, we are damned. We are taught that the best that we can do, that to save our own skin, save our own souls from eternal torture and damnation, that we must embrace a morality that embraces the torture of the innocent for the sake of the guilty.

"Where does that leave us? I'll tell you; it's right in front of us. All our lives we are torn in two by our ancient faiths. All our lives it has been staring us in the face. Just look at the symbol of our faith, that symbol, that image that rests upon the altars at the front of our churches, that symbol that hangs above our doorways. It is the cross, a device of torture; and in some churches it has a dead, tortured body, hanging from it. It's everywhere. And when we look at it, when our children look at it, what do we see? It's like we've all been brainwashed. We see a symbol of love, peace, protection, comfort, redemption. We look at a torture device, and somehow, that is what we see. It's like we're torn in two and then brainwashed back together again into thinking that the insane is sane, that the violent is peaceful. It's a form of delusion, a form of madness. It makes sense only because we have been taught that particular delusion all of our lives. We were taught that from childhood, from our earliest recollections. We teach it to our young, when they are trusting, when they are too young to question, to think critically and reasonably about the validity of the ideas that are being impressed upon their young brains. And then, once those teachings have become indelibly impressed upon our minds, it never occurs to us to question them. In fact, questioning anything becomes a form of blasphemy.

"Well, I've been shaken; my mind has been shaken clean. I've seen enough tortured bodies. I've seen enough pain, suffering, fear, and despair to know that it is not something to accept without question. A torture device for the rally point of worship? It makes sense only to those who have been thoroughly brainwashed. It makes sense only to those who have not witnessed violent, prolonged death in numbers that are beyond obscenity, beyond the decent reasoning of man, or any decent deity. Yes, there is a great difference between the academic rationalization of the merits of suffering and the reality of suffering. No! There is no compassion in violent death. Thinking so is misguided in the extreme. Believing, accepting without question, that violent, senseless death is an act of compassion—that is the true sin. And to believe that there are two sets of morality—one for God and another for man—is to throw rationality to the wind and embrace a capricious morality based only on the whims of an all-powerful tyrant. That is no way for men to live; that is no way for men to base their lives. Without rational thinking, without a rational morality, we are no more than animals. We are sheep, docile sheep that rarely question or even recognize the moral absurdities that stare us in the face. In the church in which I grew up, on the wall, behind the altar, above the cross, were the words written in gold leaf letters: 'God is Love.' Sitting in the pews, Sunday after Sunday, those words were ever-present. They were fundamental to all our beliefs; they were accepted without question. We read those words; we felt God's presence. We took those words to mean that God loved us; that God would protect us. But I have left the sanctuary; I have seen the world as it is. I have seen the world as it has been throughout all of history. God doesn't love us; God loves to be worshiped. God loves it when we worship him no matter what he does to taunt us, especially when he taunts us. I have left the sanctuary; I have witnessed countless men, women, and children—righteous men, defenseless women, innocent children—subjected to unimaginable trauma. I used to believe with all of my heart and soul that, by and large, God would protect his flock. I no longer believe that; how could I?

How trusting, how naïve I was. But I've been through the hell of war, and I've learned a thing: Our most fervent beliefs are no better than childhood wishes, until they have been tested by fire, until they have proven themselves to be true in the harsh arena in which deviltry runs rampant. No, I've seen it with my own eyes, and no doubt can remain: The sons of God roam the earth, and they are not constrained."

The unflappable Bert, while listening to the Chaplain, had grown increasingly uncomfortable with what was being said and had, early on in the Chaplain's monologue, passed the point at which he was seriously concerned that his mere proximity to such a man, such unchecked blasphemy, was putting his own immortal soul in peril. Bert considered himself, without question, to be a religious man in good standing with his God. He knew himself to be a good man, a happy man; a man conscious of his predisposition to shun those who were inherently and without cause ruthless, mean, vulgar, or ill tempered. He had married a pleasant woman, a happy woman, a woman of faith; and he, along with his wife, went to church on most Sundays. So what if his mind did drift during pretty much all of the sermons. He knew by heart the basic axioms of his faith, the tenets of his church, and was comfortable in those beliefs. He was a Christian. He was not perfect, but he was forgiven. There were crosses in his church and in his home. He took communion on a regular basis, and he knew in which drawer their family Bible, which had been passed down one or two generations on his wife's side, was kept. Financially, he was at least adequate, if not overly generous, with his donations to the church and felt that he could leave it up to others as to how many angels could dance on the head of a pin.

But this outpouring from the Chaplain made Bert uncommonly nervous. The Chaplain had clearly crossed a line, crossed it by a lot. It was as if the Chaplain had crossed the line that separated God from darkness. It was as if, in the midst of the battle, The Chaplain had crossed the front; he had gone behind enemy lines. It was as if he had gone over a wall, a wall not on earth, but a wall within his own mind. The Chaplain had gone over that wall, and now he was back. He was back, a profoundly changed man, from a land that many, Bert above all, believed should never be explored. He was back, and he was telling others what he had seen.

Bert said, "You know, Chaplain, the ways of our Lord are mysterious. Maybe it isn't up to us to judge. After all, we weren't there when God created the earth; we can't know what His grand plan for us might be. We have to trust that, well, we just have to trust in Him."

David, surprised to hear Bert, of all people, offer a religious opinion, looked over at him.

The Chaplain was quick to respond to Bert's comment, saying, "Ah yes, yes. We weren't there when God created the earth. You quote from The Book of Job."

Bert looked to David; David gave a sight nod to the affirmative. Bert looked at the Chaplain and replied with a hesitant, yet oddly drawn out, "Yeeaah," that was as much a question in itself as an answer.

The Chaplain, receiving confirmation from Bert, replied, "I've thought about that story a lot this past year. I wish I had a nickel for every time, over the years, that I gave that same answer that you give, to some bewildered soul who had come to me, as a pastor, for answers, desperate to make sense out of senselessness. Something really bad happens to someone really good. A buddy or a family member comes to me, devastated, and asks, 'why, why?' So, we bow our heads; we say in a solemn voice that it is God's will. We say what you just said, that His ways are mysterious, that we can't know all that He knows, that we weren't there when He created the earth. We say that God loves us and that we must put our trust in Him. That worked for me for a long, long time; and then it didn't. I re-read that story, the Book of Job, and you know, I saw things in that story that I had never considered before, things that I had just glossed over before. In Sunday school, we are all taught that Job was a great man, a wealthy man, and above all, a devout man. We are taught that God decides to test Job's fidelity. God decides to test the extent of Job's faith by inflicting extreme hardships upon him. Job is extremely rich, maybe the richest in the land. So, God tests him by taking away all of his wealth. Job is deprived of his money, his children, his servants, and his livestock. He is made destitute. But despite the hardship, Job remains resolute, unwavering in his dedication and obedience to God's will. He says that we must take the good with the bad. Job says, 'the Lord gave, and the Lord hath taken away; blessed be the name of the Lord.'

"So far, so good. Job has remained faithful. So, he is tested further. In addition to being impoverished, Job's health is attacked, severely attacked. He is afflicted, from head to foot, with boils. Yet he remains true to his God. Job says, 'shall we receive good at the hand of God, and shall we not receive evil?'

"So, Job passes his tests, passes them with flying colors, and so, he is rewarded. He gets back his health and his wealth. He gets back more wealth than he had before. He gets back more livestock, servants, and children; and his daughters become the fairest in all the land.

"So, all's well that ends well, right? Isn't that what we all learned in Sunday school? Never doubt God; never doubt His judgment; above all, remain faithful, respectful, obedient.

"But there are things, aspects of this story, which are glossed over in Sunday school. For instance, we never talk or think about that first batch of servants and children, all those hapless people who get caught up in the middle of this test? If you read the story, as it is written, the servants are slain with the edge of the sword, and Job's children are killed by a great wind that comes from the wilderness and collapses the house in which they are all gathered for a meal. Well, what about them! How utterly dispensable they appear to be. Have they no value? As human beings, did they not have the same God as Job? Did God have no love, or even a passing consideration, for them? I don't know; maybe they were sinful and deserved death. But could they all have been that bad, bad enough to merit death? The story doesn't say they were killed because they were bad. No, they didn't appear to be any factor at all in the drama. They were merely collateral damage in the test.

All those people were killed, hacked up with swords . . . and we never give them a second thought. All those people are killed, and what value do we give them? None! They're just props, insignificant background in a story, a story that is supposed to teach us loyalty. But isn't loyalty a two-way street? Are we so insignificant that, unless we're the top guy, our lives are so casually dispensable? If God loves us, truly loves us, then don't we have value? And if we have value, how can God be so callous, so unconcerned with the demise of so many? The opposite of love is not hate; it is indifference. Those people, those props in his story, God did not treat them with love; God revealed his indifference to them. In the very story that is meant to teach us to retain our faith in the face of any adversity, any calamity; to never question the overriding wisdom of God's purpose; within that very story, God reveals his indifference to the common man, to the bulk of his creations. 'God is Love'? Those words ring hollow to me. Those words written in gold on the wall of my church, they should not have been written in gold. They should have been written in crayon, red crayon. They might as well have been written on the wall by a child—a child who thinks his parents will be proud of the markings that he has made upon the wall. A child who has been taught a version of the world that doesn't exist in reality."

There was a slight pause, but the Chaplain, not yet completed with his train of thought, his insights into God's dealings with Job, continued. "And another thing, why was Job tested in the first place? Testing a relationship, especially beyond reasonable bounds, does not strengthen the relationship; it destroys it. If God is omniscient, all knowing, then shouldn't God have known that Job would pass the test? What's the point of God putting a good man through such hardships when he knows beforehand that he will surely pass the test?

"Well, there's an answer for that. If you read the story, the test isn't wholly God's idea. In fact, God doesn't even conduct the test himself; Satan does. That's right. The story tells us that Satan, along with some of the other 'sons of God', go and visit with God.

God asks Satan about what he's been doing, and Satan tells God that he has been roaming about the earth. So, God brags to Satan about what a great man Job is. He asks Satan if he has seen Job. He brags to Satan that 'there is none like him in the earth, a perfect and an upright man, one that feareth God, and escheweth evil.'

"So, Satan taunts God by saying that Job is faithful only because God has blessed him and has protected him, and that if God took away what he had, that Job would, and I quote, 'curse thee to thy face.' So, God allows Satan to test Job. He tells Satan that, short of killing him, Satan can do whatever he pleases with Job. God knows that Job does not deserve to be left to the wilds of Satan, but in this story, God reveals to us that he cares more about winning a pissing contest with Satan than he does about his loyal servant Job.

"If someone, say a bully that you knew, came up to you and said that your wife only loved you because you protected her from bullies like him; what would you say? Would you tell the bully that he was wrong and walk away? Or would you puff out your chest to the bully and say, 'Okay, go ahead; go ahead and beat her up. I won't stop you. Just don't kill her. You go ahead and beat her up and you'll see; she'll still love me.' Of course you wouldn't say that, not in a million years. But that's what God said. That's what God said to Satan. He said, 'go ahead Satan, beat up Job; beat him up all you want. He'll still love me; you'll see.' It's insane. It's all so insane. Is God so small that he has to inflate himself before the likes of Satan?

"A good man loves his wife and his family. A good man is at least benevolent to his fellow man. It's not a competition, but shouldn't God have as much love for us, his children, as we are told to have for one another? I don't know what to think anymore. I know that it is folly to bite the hand that feeds us, but is it wise to kiss the hand that strikes us?

"Yes, there are things that happen, acts of God that are hard to accept, perhaps beyond our understanding. But then, there are things, too many things, which are so manifestly wrong, they simply cannot be accepted, not by rational men, anyhow. Men are not gods, nor should they act as ones. But men, people, are not without value. It is one thing to be humble, to worship God and to give him his rightful due. It is quite another thing for mankind to be merely a plaything for a thin-skinned despot."

David observed, "Well, that's quite a sermon you've just preached."

The Pastor responded, "I'm sorry; it wasn't meant to be. I've preached a lot of sermons in my time, but now, my preaching days are over. Yes, I was a pastor in a church, in Mississippi, when the war broke out. But back then, like I said, I viewed the world in a much different light than I do now. Back in those days, God was in Heaven, the devil, Satan, was in hell, and I was safe in my sanctuary. Back then, I believed that God was just; that God, by and large, would protect his flock from harm, from the evils of Satan.

"But then the war broke out, and I left my sanctuary. A lot of young men in my congregation, men whom I considered to be those of my flock, enlisted. They were so young, so brave, so eager—just at the start of their lives and destined to go far and high. We all got caught up in it, the war effort. I thought that it was proper that I go along with them. Of course, we didn't all stay together for long. Right off the bat we were scattered all over the world. But in spirit, at least, I thought that we would all be connected in some grand manner of brotherhood; connected in that we would all be in the same fight, on the same side, on God's side. I know now that I was wrong—naïve to the realities of this world. But at the time, I thought that I, I and the power of the word of God, could protect them; at least the righteous amongst them. How naïve I was. Now, the war is over, and it is time for me to return home. Now that the war is over, my wife writes to me that my congregation awaits my return; my wife writes to me that she is anxious for my return. Those who went away, many of those who were not killed, have trickled back. Most of those who were maimed have found their way back. A few, a few of the most grievously injured, some of those have not had the heart to return. A few have been so marred on the outside that they cannot bear being seen by those who once knew and loved them so well. They fear that the change is too great; that they are now so hideous, so unfamiliar, that reunion is no longer possible. How, they fear, can one reunite with that which is barely recognizable? And I, I share their fear; though my change, my scarring, is more of my mind than of my body. Of course, my body has changed somewhat. I know that my body has aged beyond the years that I have been gone, but it is still recognizable. No, it is my mind; it is the change within my mind that now alienates me from my home. And still, my congregation awaits my return. Those who never left, and those who have found their way back home; they await. They await a sermon that will make some sense of the forever-changed world in which we all now live. They seek answers, meaning, a sense of comfort that I am unable, powerless to deliver. So, I have stalled my return; I have taken the coward's way out. But it is only a temporary solution at best. The army has decommissioned this base, and in two days I will be decommissioned along with it, along with all the equipment of war that is no longer needed in the vast quantities that were so desperately needed so short a time ago. Yes, the battles are now over, for this war anyway. Many evil men have been killed; many virtuous men have been killed. But the evil at the root of it all remains untouched by our efforts."

David asked, "So, despite us winning the war, you now believe that the world is inherently an evil place?"

"No—I don't know. I don't know what to believe anymore. Nothing makes sense anymore. The more I see, the less I understand. Sheep, barnyard animals in the hands of meat packers, though sometimes treated roughly and without compassion, have a far less tormented death than most of the souls that I've ministered to. There is no context in which my last few years makes any sense. Sitting, praying in a quiet church, communing with God; well, what makes perfect sense in the quiet of a sanctuary, makes no sense in the vicious hell of a battlefield, or in the aftermath. Yes, the aftermath. After the explosions, after all the bleeding, panic, and screaming have stopped, there is the quiet of the aftermath, where all that remains are the burnt offerings. Burnt offerings lying motionless in the ash and smoke. It is an experience, a cognizance that can only be acquired by standing there, standing in the midst of all of the horrors. In truth, only one thing makes sense, and that one thing is too horrifying to accept. Yes, we may have some dominion over the animals; but who, or what, has dominion over us? As I said a moment ago, it has become abundantly clear to me that God is not who or what we traditionally think Him to be."

David noticed that the Chaplain had begun to tremble. "Are you okay?" David asked.

"No, no I am not. I fear that I am damned."

Bert, strangely solemn, asked, "Why? What have you done?"

"I've looked in the mirror. I've looked in the mirror and I've seen the face of a pastor from my youth. A pastor, from twenty-five years ago. A pastor who returned to my village after the first war, a veteran of The Somme. That terrible battle. I saw the face of a man who believed that he was damned. I see his face now. I see that his face, and my face, are one and the same."

Chapter 27

A Moonlit Night

Chattanooga, TN
August 1946

Mihail Nikolayevich Grigory, in the darkness of the early morning hours, lay flat on his back on the hard, dusty, plywood flooring of the loft storage area in the detached garage behind David's house. A well-oiled sniper rifle lay just to his side.

The loft was on the gabled end of the garage that faced David's house. The flat floor and sloped roofline formed a pup-tent-like triangle that ran across the entire twelve-foot expanse of the building's width, from the top of one sidewall to the other, and was about five-feet deep. Just above Mihail's head, facing David's house, was an oval window. No glass or screen, just wooden slats designed to keep the rain out while allowing the rising, hot summer air and gas fumes to vent from the building. Mihail knew he would have to deal with that window next, but first, having just climbed onto the ledge, he wanted to lie still, catch his breath, and listen for any sounds.

No one but God knows that I am here, he thought. *Is He watching me now? Does He ever watch? I do not care. This will not bring me peace, but perhaps it will appease, if only for a moment, the demons that goad me.*

The garage, the house, the block, the neighborhood—everything was quiet. The darkness of the night had helped to conceal Mihail's presence as he sneaked down the side roads and back alleys. But darkness also induces slumber; minds are lulled to rest and filled with dreams of devised places and alternate realities. Yes, darkness was his collaborator this night.

Mihail rolled over onto one knee, scooted up to the window, and examined the louvers that blocked his view. He ran his finger along the smooth, white paint on the rounded edge of one of the slats to gauge its thickness. *Yes,* he thought, as he brushed the dust off his fingertips, *I'll have to break at least two of these.* He braced himself against the wall with one hand and wrapped the fingers of his other around a middle row. He pulled lightly at first, pushing against the wall with one hand while pulling on the slat with the other, then, gradually, he increased the pressure. The slat flexed a little, then appeared to hold. Mihail relaxed the pressure, drew in a breath of air, held it, and gave a determined tug. In the quiet of the night, the cracking, popping sound of the wood splintering and then breaking free seemed louder to Mihail than it probably was. Even so, he was fairly certain that the sound, by the time it traveled across the backyard and through the open windows of David's house, would probably not be sufficient to awaken any sleepers. Nevertheless, for a few tense minutes, Mihail peered through his newly created peep hole, watching for lights to come on or for any other signs of life. All remained quiet, but Mihail could see that his initial estimate had been correct; one more row of slats would have to be broken for him to be able to complete his mission. The second row came out easier. Maybe it was because with one row missing, he had more room to grab ahold. Maybe it was because he had learned from the first row and now knew what to expect. Either way, the sound of the second slat breaking free was equally loud and equally unnerving. Again, Mihail watched with trepidation for any signs of waking. The dark remained dark, and after a few long but uneventful minutes, he felt satisfied that he had not been heard.

There was nothing more to do until daybreak but to wrestle with his thoughts. He turned and scooted away from the wall, giving himself just enough space to lie back down. With the back of his head flat against the dusty floor and just inches from the back wall, he stretched out his legs, allowing them to hang over the edge of the loft and dangle above David's parked car below.

Yes, he thought, *from this perch, once the sun comes up, I'll have a clear, bird's-eye view of everything: the backdoor, the yard, and the pathway leading to the garage.*

In the darkness, Mihail's mind began to drift. The wooden planks of the floor were hard against his back; it didn't take long for him to become restless. *This is really more of a ledge than a loft,* he thought, as he pulled his knees up, bringing his overhanging feet back flat onto the flooring. The sun was still well below the horizon but the glow of reflected light from a partial moon radiated sufficient light for him to see the shadowy objects around him. As the moon moved into a more favorable position, additional light flowed into the loft through the gap left by the newly removed slats. With his eyes adjusted to the dimness, Mihail could make out the faint outlines of the sloping roofline above and some dusty boxes to each side, along with what looked like a baby's crib, a stroller, and other outgrown household furnishings. *How much better even the smallest light than no light. How bright the sun must be,* he thought, *for a reflection of a reflection to reveal so much, sparing me in part from the lonesome isolation of total darkness.*

This past month he had gotten precious little sleep, but he dared not close his eyes, for when he did, it was always the same. First, there was the initial darkness, the light blocked by shut lids, the nothingness of closed eyes, solitude—the joyless peace that the troubled seek in oblivion. But the mind does not do well in isolation. His mind, deprived of images enhanced from without, would begin to fill the void and provide images from within, images largely of its own creation, a blend of the stored and the imagined. Horrible images. Images of the crumpled, deflated, outstretched body of his wife would invariably appear. His wife, alone, encapsulated in darkness. Then, the body of his son lying near to her would fade into his consciousness. Sometimes other details would appear, other particulars of that horrible moment—particulars of that front yard, the front doorway, Bert crouched behind the door frame, the sounds of gunshot still ringing in his ears. Then, a tightening of focus—the image of his wife's face would gradually grow larger, squeezing everything else out until it was all that existed in his universe. Her face, her beautiful face. Her eyes, those large, dark, brown eyes—soothing and familiar, opened wide and staring straight into his as if she were calling to him, pleading to him in desperation to save her from her peril. But there was a vacancy in her call; it was the visual equivalent of a fading echo as the original vanquishes into oblivion. As he looked into those eyes, the beauty dissipated as it became obvious that no life remained within. Her eyes had become cold; they were dead; they were nothing more than empty globes, haunting reminders of what once was overflowing but now was vacant. The sadness was too much to bear. One moment those eyes had been beaming with life; the next moment the warmth, the heat, the light of life had vanished; the spark was gone. It didn't seem possible that you could detect the absence just from the eyes, but you could. No, it wasn't just his imagination. But what was it; what was it that was missing? Why so great a difference? Surely something so intangible as life could not be seen in one's eyes? And yet, there was a distinct difference. Was it possible to actually see the spark within an eye? Was it possible to see the spark and identify it for what it was? It was difficult to say. No, it didn't seem plausible. The spark of life isn't something tangible, something of which you could take a photo and then point it out to others, circle it with a pencil and say, "See, there it is." But still, undeniably, there was a discernible difference. His mind searched for an answer. Then it came to him: maybe it was because the lifeless eyes were so still; maybe that was it. That had to be it. What other difference could there be? Even the slightest motion would animate them, give them the appearance of life. Maybe that's it; maybe that's all it takes. Maybe, when you boil it all down, life is simply motion, movement, change; awareness of the passage of time. He thought of those eyes; he thought of them when they were alive. No, there was more to it than that. There is more to life than just motion. There *is* a spark, a definite spark. He couldn't put his finger on it, but he knew it when he saw it. Yes, it was something that he could see, a warmth that he could feel deep within his bones, a tingle of energy electrifying his entire being, an element that he could know. It was a feeling that transcended time and space. But how was that possible? How was it that when she was alive, he could feel her warmth even when they had been separated by an ocean and a period of years? But now, now that he knew that she was dead, the sensation had changed. It was odd. Now, even though she was dead, when he thought of her in the abstract, when she was alive within his memory, there was still a warmth. But when he visualized her still body, the feeling of death was overwhelming, and that was something that he could not get past.

It was getting close to dawn; the sun's rays were beginning to creep over the horizon. The moon, when surrounded in darkness, had appeared bright and dominated the sky to the extent that it could easily fool the gullible into believing that it gave off a light of its own. But now that the sun was rising, the moon, although it remained above in the sky and retained some influence as it continued to tug at the tides as it tugged at his heart, had no other power but to fade away from sight. The shadowy objects surrounding Mihail became clearer. As the sun overcame the horizon, he was amazed how fast the room began to fill with light, although his humor stubbornly clung to the remnants of darkness.

It was now light enough for Mihail to read his watch. It had been about three hours, more or less, he calculated, since he had crawled up onto his hidden perch. Time had passed erratically in the darkness of the night, the hardness of the floor, and the isolation of his thoughts. But now that the sun was up, the DeRieux household would soon awaken. Soon, there would be movement against which to gauge intervals and boundaries; time would again reclaim a sense of normalcy in the hierarchy of the temporal world. Night would morph back into day and the endless cycle would repeat. The universe would once again appear as an enormous clock with all of its mechanisms out in the open as if simply awaiting to be discovered and understood; functioning in a rational manner, operating with a great deal of precision and predictability; until it didn't. There would be an interval of light, an interval before evening returned and the source of light would, like clockwork, dip below the horizon; the moon, watched over by the stars, would reclaim its dominance, and part of the world would once again cycle into the realm of shadows.

Yes, clockwork. Sunday mornings were like clockwork at the DeRieux's, and Mihail had studied this particular clock well. He knew that in four and a half hours, the DeRieuxs would leave for church, freshly bathed and sparkling clean. All dressed up in their Sunday best and full of breakfast, they would file out of their back door. The screen door would slap shut behind them with the crack of a starting gun as they traveled down the gravel path to their garage. Then, happily, off to church they would go. This morning, Mihail would rip the guts from that clock.

His stomach growled. He had not eaten any dinner that night, and now he had missed breakfast as well. Still, he wasn't hungry. He had not thought to drink any water and now a great thirst interrupted his numbness. Drained by emotion and blinded by a rage that for the past month had been relentless in its destruction, his body began to rebel. The great hollowness within grew larger. He looked up at the raw rafters and rough plywood of the ceiling above him, taking a particular interest in the irregularities in the wood. Since its purpose was structural rather than aesthetical, a courser grade had been chosen. There were knots upon knots interrupting the grain. In some places, the knots had fallen out, leaving holes, leaving weaker spots in the wood. But at that moment, the knots and irregularities were the things that gave the structure interest and character. A flawless piece of wood—the straight, tight, uninterrupted grain—is impressive in its strength and purity; but a length of wood, from which no limb has ever grown, is boring. Staring at uninterrupted perfection is a difficult way to pass long periods of time. Would an eternity of perfection be bearable?

Lying on his back and staring at the rough rafters above took Mihail back to his recent week spent in his makeshift hideout—a rustic shack in the middle of the woods, in the middle of nowhere, in an abandoned hunting cabin roughly eight miles from Camp Forrest; eight miles and the blink of an eye from the place where his wife and son had been so brutally killed. Then, as now, he had been consumed by one thought, one drive, one hunger: Vengeance! Vengeance filled his entire world. It was the force that now propelled his universe. Lying on his back on the floor of that cabin in the woods, the ceiling had been further from him, much higher above than the one now. Now, lying on the ledge in David's garage, it was more like lying on the floor of a cramped attic. Now, the ceiling was within arm's reach. If he sat up, he could touch it with his hand. If he tried to stand erect, he would bump his head against it. It was different in the cabin. Back in the cabin, with the rafters more distant and the slope of the roof steeply peaking high above, it reminded him of the rafters of a cathedral. Even so, he hadn't prayed; that had never been his way. And with the great injustice so freshly endured, the great violence wrought upon his family, beating his soul into numbness as he lay still on that floor—all of that trauma, most emphatically, did not bring Mihail closer to God. But looking upwards at the ceiling in the fanciful cathedral in the woods, it was natural for him, if only in passing, to think in grandiose terms, to consider the longer view, to question if there was purpose or justice in the universe. But such contemplations were only a brief diversion. His emotions quickly returned him to his immediate obsession: justice. Justice or vengeance, he didn't care how it was labeled; either would be served. If the universe wasn't, by nature, just, he would make it so—his part of it anyway. There was no point in dwelling on justice, or God for that matter. Vengeance was all that mattered. The guilty would pay; he would make certain of that even if it cost him his very soul.

But who were the real villains; who were the guilty; who would pay so that the scales could be balanced? As far as he could see, there were only two armies on the field. It had to be either David's people or his people—the Americans or the Soviets. He had grappled long and hard over that in the hours that he had spent staring at the cathedral ceiling in the woods. Without question, his people wouldn't think twice about killing someone, anyone. They wouldn't think twice about killing him, his wife, his son. No, they wouldn't lose a minute of sleep over something as mundane as murder. But generally, they needed a reason for doing even the routine, even if it wasn't a very good reason. They wouldn't bother to take out the trash if the can wasn't full. No, it wasn't his people. If they wanted to get to him, if they knew he was about to defect, if they so much as had an inkling that he was in cahoots with the Americans, they would have played it differently. They wouldn't have killed his wife and son, at least not there, not like that, not out in the open. If this had been their doings, their operation, they would have kidnapped him and his family outright. They would have tied him to a chair and beaten him. They would have used the threat of harm to his family as leverage to get him to talk, to tell all that he knew in a panicked attempt to spare his family. Then, when they were satisfied, they would have shot him in an unceremonious manner. His family, his wife and son? If they had all been in Russia, if his family had survived the interrogation, they may have been let go—freed, if you can call it that. Freed, but banished to the remote frozen wastelands within the Soviet Union. Exiled, yet still within the boundaries of their master's kingdom. Killing them, in Russia, would be redundant. Some would say that killing them would be a lesser punishment, punishment for the crime of wanting to be free. Mihail, having been sent to America to spy, had tasted freedom. He had taken a little bite, and now he wanted to share his great discovery with his family. But they were not in Russia; they were in the United States, and in the United States things were more complicated. Among other things, his handlers had to be mindful of the trail that they left. No, if it had been his people, he would have been kidnapped, questioned, and then he and his family would have been killed, their bodies never to be found. No, this was not the work of his people. This atrocity had to be the work of David's people.

So that was that, and David DeRieux was at the center of it all. All that mattered to Mihail was that David would suffer as he suffered. David would experience what he had experienced. In the cathedral in the woods, Mihail had devoted himself to killing David's son and wife in front of David. *And after that, what would David do,* Mihail wondered? It was all that he could think about. What would David do after the shots rang out and his wife and son fell to the ground? Would David spend the fleeting moments trying to revive and comfort them, try with his hands to hold the blood in, try to forestall the inevitable? If so, which would he go to first—it was an impossible choice. Or would he take other actions? Would he run into the house to phone for help, or would he charge the garage, the source of gunfire? *If he charges the garage,* Mihail wondered, *what will I do? Will I kill David from here, from the upper window, as David charges the garage; or would I want to face David, look him in the eye before taking that last shot?* He hoped not; he hoped that David would not charge the garage. He didn't want David's pain to end so quickly. As much as he wanted to look into David's face at the moment of his greatest despair, he hoped that David would stay by his wife or run to the phone inside to call for help. That would give Mihail time to slip away. He wouldn't have to look David in the eye for David to know who had pulled the trigger. David would know. David's world would be shattered; and for now, that was the most for which Mihail could hope. David's world would be shattered as his had been shattered. He would leave a scar upon David that would forever cloud David's thoughts. After today, David's world would never be the same. The sun would set on David's gilded life, never to rise again. Mihail thought of his life in comparison to David's. David was born in fortune. But, for whatever reason, he had succumbed to evil, and for that, the scales must be balanced, the great fortune must be forfeited. Mihail would see to that.

Mihail was suddenly aware of chatter—happy voices coming from the kitchen window and opened door of David's house. They must be at the breakfast table. He listened to the high-pitched squeals and laughter of children at play. He realized that he had been lost in thought, his mind back in the cabin in the woods, dwelling on revenge. But now that the sun was up, now that he could hear the voices of children and feel their innocence, his plan seemed less rational; his resolve weakened. But not by much, not by enough. The demons would not turn loose; they tore at his soul. A shudder rippled through Mihail's body. Maybe, he thought, it would be enough to just kill David, shoot him as he came out the backdoor and be done with it. Later, others would pay. But for today, for the DeRieux's household, maybe the life of David would be enough.

A burst of high-pitched squeals and laughter from the children seemed to confirm Mihail's leanings, but then he heard David's laughter, and it sounded to Mihail as the laughter of the demons mocking him. No, Mihail thought. God may have spared Abraham from participating in the death of his child, but I will not spare David. God had his chance to show me mercy, and he showed me none. This boy will die, and for David, it will be as though David himself drew the knife.

Mihail heard the springs on the screen door creak open and then slam shut. He quickly looked at his watch; they were leaving a little earlier than he had expected. Grabbing the rifle in his right hand, he sat up and swiveled around onto his left knee and peered through the gap that he had created in the window louvers. There he was, David's son. The boy walked over and sat on a small bench near the backdoor. Something seemed different about the boy; he seemed somehow quieter, less fidgety than Mihail had previously observed him to be. His countenance did not match the energy of the squeals and laughter that had moments ago crossed the yard. Also, there was something odd in the way the boy was sitting, something odd about the positioning of his legs and feet, and his hands covered a small toy or something resting on his lap. Although the distance was not great, Mihail raised the rifle so that he could see the boy through the magnification of the gun's scope, and his attention was immediately drawn to the boy's feet. His feet were stacked one upon the other, but in an odd manner. Mihail had seen that unique configuration only once before. The ankle of the boy's left foot, his bottom foot, was bent to the extent that the outside edge of his foot rested upon the ground, with the bottom of that foot almost perpendicular to the ground. His other foot, the top foot, rested on the upward facing side of the bottom foot. Mikahil recalled, as a youth, seeing his grandmother, on occasion, sit in that fashion—one foot stacked upon the other in the shape of a T. He couldn't recall ever seeing anyone else sit with their feet positioned just so. How odd.

Mihail heard the creak of the spring on the screen door being stretched open again. He moved his head away from the scope so that he could see who was coming through the door. It was David, pushing the screen door open with one hand while putting on his hat with the other. There he was. There was David—all clean, fresh, and nice in his Sunday suit. He didn't allow the screen door to smack shut behind him but closed it gently, pausing for a moment as he looked over at his son sitting on the bench. Mihail was a little surprised. For some reason, the boy didn't seem to take notice of his father but sat quietly, looking down at his lap, remaining—what Mihail considered to be—overly quiet and solemn for a youngster. What was wrong? David walked over to the bench and sat next to the boy. David rested his arm along the top of the bench, as if to cradle his son, and leaned in, speaking quietly to the boy.

Perfect, Mihail thought as he moved his head back behind the scope to target the boy. Mihail was so close to his target that the boy's head almost completely filled the scope. The boy was still looking down; Mihail centered the cross hairs on the middle of the top of the boy's head and moved his finger onto the trigger. The screen door creaked, the boy stood, and as he rose up, the object in his lap centered itself in the scope's cross hairs—it was a teddy bear.

Mihail's head jerked up. It was identical to the bear that he had bought over a year ago in a department store in Knoxville. Was that The bear, or had David bought a similar one for his son? Another little boy and young girl came through the door, followed by David's wife. Obviously, the little girl was David's daughter, Kay . . . but who was that second boy? The two children ran over to the bench while Lill dug around in her purse for her keys. Mihail looked through the scope at the face of the boy with the teddy bear and saw the features of his grandmother.

My son . . . my son! Is this my son? How can this be? It is! My son is alive! But who was it that was killed at the cottage? Who was that little boy that was killed alongside of my wife?

The phone in the kitchen rang. Lill had just started away from the house but stopped and looked at David as if to say, "Should I get that?"

David nodded his head and said, "Better get that, Honey. It might be the office calling."

Lill moved quickly, leaving her keychain hanging from the back door's lock. The sound of her voice, but not the content, could be heard all the way to the garage window. A moment later, she stood in the doorway with the phone pressed against her chest and called to David, "It's Bert. He wants to know if we want to meet them for lunch after church at Bethea's?"

Kay was standing next to her dad, looking up at him and nodding yes. David said, "Sounds good to me if it's good with you. Tell him we'll see them there around 12:30."

Lill went back into the house to settle the plans with Bert. Mihail put his rifle down and, as quietly as he could, lay snug against the back wall with his feet pulled up tight so as not to be seen as the DeRieuxs piled into their car and left for church.

Chapter 28

Lill's Ace in the Hole

Chattanooga, TN
April 2001

"We have to kill him, even if it exposes the things we've done."

Joey sat with his mouth hanging open. He had seen dim-witted people walking around with their mouths hanging half-open, and he had seen smart people, people surprised or shocked beyond their normal range of comprehension, slack-jawed by what appeared to be the temporary disconnection between their brain and their face. But the number of times that he had been surprised, dumbfounded to the point of catching himself with his own mouth hanging wide open, well, he could count that on one hand.

What the hell did David just say? Joey asked himself as he thought to close his mouth. Joey looked over at Mike and asked, "Did I hear that right?"

Mike, looking more concerned than surprised, replied, "Uh, yeah, yeah. I think you did."

Mike and Joey looked at David, who again appeared to be captivated by the activity at the nurse's station. They followed

David's stare and watched as the doctor left in one direction and the nurse, with her cart now fully loaded, started her rounds down the hallway leading to Susan's room.

The three sat in silence for a long minute or two. David's eyes remained focused on the doorway through which the nurse, with her pushcart, had left.

"We have to kill him, even if it exposes the things we've done." David's words repeated themselves over and over again in Joey's mind.

Who is David talking about? Joey wondered as he stared down at the floor, his mind completely absorbed by what had just happened. *Who does David think he has to kill? VanZant? Is he talking about VanZant?* Joey thought hard, *Yes, he did mention VanZant; he did say his name. He said some other things too; what was it that he just said? He said VanZant's name, and then he said, "he's here; VanZant's here,"* . . . *and then something about a broken promise or agreement, or something? And then he asked Mike if he still had the gun that he had given him, but, but; he didn't call Mike "Mike". He called him "Mihail". Why would he do that?*

What could have happened that would make David want to kill VanZant? Does David think VanZant poses some sort of a threat? Joey thought of Megan's phone call to VanZant in her attempt to get information. *What was it that Dorothy said . . . oh yeah, she said that Megan asked VanZant what his relationship was with David and what they had to do with plutonium. Great! Just friggin' great! What if there is something dicey going on between the two of them, something that's best not stirred up? With David's history, who knows what's buried under some of those old, cold-war rocks. God damn it! Why did that nitwit Megan have to call him?*

"You can go back in now," Joey heard a voice say.

Lost in his thoughts, the voice was like a switch turning his eyes back on. Still looking down at the floor, a pair of bright white nurse's shoes came into focus. His eyes followed the legs up, and Joey saw a nurse standing in front of him. She was the one who had earlier shooed them out of Susan's room in preparation for the doctor making his rounds.

"I'm sorry, what did you say?" Joey asked.

The nurse repeated, "The doctor's through. You are all welcome to return to Susan's room, if you like."

"Thanks," Mike replied for the three of them. The nurse smiled in return and went on her way.

Joey and Mike turned to David. He seemed a little better, but it was hard to tell. Joey said, nodding towards David, "He seems a little better."

Mike replied, "Yeah, yeah. Well, I hope so. I'm thinking maybe we should be getting him home. I'm afraid this whole thing here at the hospital is just a little too much, uh, activity going on."

Mike stood and was about to help David up, when Joey stepped forward a little, placed his hand on Mike's shoulder, and gently turned him away from David while saying quietly, "Mind if I have a quick word with you?"

Mike turned his head and glanced down at David. David seemed okay. Mike looked back at Joey and replied, "Of course."

Joey wasn't quite sure what to say or where to start. He paused, then said, "Well, um, I was just thinking . . . that was quite something, what David just said."

"Yeah, yeah. I'll give you that," Mike answered.

Joey was hoping for more, but that appeared to be all that Mike was going to venture. Joey continued, "You know, Mike, this really isn't any of my business, and I certainly don't want to intrude into your family's affairs, particularly now, with Susan, and, and, well, with Susan just having given birth to her child, your granddaughter. But, well, I was just wondering if this is something that you, or . . . or perhaps we, should mention to Lill. I mean, it's probably nothing but a little confusion on David's part, but . . . I don't know. And again, I don't want to intrude, but I did hear David, when he was talking to you just now, mention the name VanZant. Well, I've heard that name before. Anyway, I was just thinking that this might be something that should be mentioned to Lill, and, if you would allow, I'd like to help, if I can."

Mike said, "Yeah, who is this VanZant fellow? That's a new one for me."

"Well, I'm not entirely sure, not yet anyway. But I did hear David mention his name yesterday when David, Lill, and I were walking down the hall here at the hospital on our way up to Susan's room. He seemed kind of spooked about something, not sure what; but anyway, it made me curious enough to do a little digging."

"So, what did you find?"

"Not a lot, yet. His photo, VanZant's, appeared every so often, decades ago, in some of the Washington, D.C. papers. But, so far, none of the articles tell much about him—just photos of him at general society-type events."

Joey could tell that Mike was looking at him with quite a bit of apprehension. Joey said, "Please, don't get the wrong impression here. I'm generally not that nosey. Well, let me take that back. Truth is, I am nosey, by nature. I'm a retired newspaperman with, perhaps, too much idle time on my hands, but, even so, I generally don't make it a habit to go around looking up things on everyone I meet. It's just that, well, yesterday, something was truly disturbing David. Just like a few minutes ago, he was obviously very disturbed about something here, to say the least. And yesterday, here in the hospital, he said something about VanZant being here. He also mentioned the name Edna and something about plutonium."

Mike replied slowly, trying to be polite, "Well, Joey. I appreciate all you've done for us, but, well, I think—"

Joey interrupted, "Look, Mike. I understand your hesitation. I'm not trying to write a story here, or anything like that. It's just that, well, yesterday, at one point, I got the distinct feeling that David was trying to tell me something. We were walking down the hall on our way up to Susan's floor, when we passed an x-ray room. David stopped cold in his tracks, nodded to the radiation warning sign posted on the door, and then nodded pointedly at me as if he was saying something to me that he thought that I would understand. Please, I like David, always have. I like your entire family. I'd just like to help, and, really, someone should tell Lill about what seems to be going on with David. Maybe she knows something that will clear all of this up. Maybe, if we can figure out what is going on, we can do something to alleviate some of the anxiety that this is obviously causing David. But maybe, just maybe, this might be something new going on with him that she really needs to know about."

Mike said, "You know, I think we're getting a little ahead of ourselves. I think David is just having a bad day here. Places like this, places with lots of activity, strange people, things going on that he's unfamiliar with—he just doesn't do well these days in places like this. I think once we get him home, he'll be okay."

"Well, I hope you are right. But still, this seems to be beyond just being uncomfortable in a strange, busy place. This seems awfully specific. I mean, David did mention the name VanZant, twice. And then to say that we need to kill him; I don't know."

"Well, I'll certainly mention this to Lill, later. But first, I just think we need to get David home."

Mike started to turn back towards David, but Joey stopped him, saying, "Wait, wait. There's just one more thing."

Mike faced Joey with a look of increasing impatience. "Okay, what?"

Joey said, "I hate like the devil to admit this, but there is something else that I think you should know."

"Okay, what?"

"When I said that I did a little research on VanZant, actually, I farmed it out."

Joey paused. Mike prompted, "Okay, so?"

"So, as I said, I'm a retired newspaper guy. I still have contacts though, with people at the paper, and, well, I called an old colleague of mine, a woman who still works in the paper's research department, runs it actually, and asked her to see what she could find on this VanZant fellow."

"And?"

"And, so, she handed it off to her assistant, a summer intern, and she . . . she found him. The intern found VanZant, at least someone named VanZant, living in the Washington, D.C. area. But that's not the problem. The problem is, well, this intern, she kind of crossed a few lines. She took it upon herself to call him. She actually called and spoke with VanZant."

"So, what did Mr. VanZant have to say?"

"Well, that's the problem. VanZant—and I think it's Dr. VanZant—didn't say anything. But the intern, well, she wasn't very discreet. She asked Dr. VanZant what his relationship to David DeRieux and plutonium is. So, you see; I hope not, but it's possible that we've stirred up something here. When I first found out what the intern had done, I was pretty angry about it. But, at most, I thought it would just be an embarrassing faux pas on our part. But now, given what David just said about killing VanZant, and given David's cold-war background; well, like I said, I hope we haven't stirred up anything bad here."

Mike thought for a moment, then said, "Maybe this VanZant that your intern talked to is somebody different. Maybe he has no idea who David is or what your intern was talking about."

"Of course that's possible," Joey conceded, "and I hope that is the case, but, from what I understand, the VanZant that the intern spoke with never denied knowing who David DeReiux is. And, I think the intern, while it wasn't a long conversation, did speak to him for enough time that, if he didn't know who David is, he certainly had plenty of opportunity to say so. No, I think he's the guy. In my experience, if someone doesn't know who you're asking about, they say so pretty quickly."

Mike nodded in agreement. Joey was relieved to see that, to his surprise, Mike seemed less put out with him after his confession than before. Mike said, "This all does seem a little more real when you think that there might be a real live VanZant out there somewhere in the picture. Okay, let's see if we can get in a quick word with Lillian. But if David starts to get anxious again, then I think we just need to get him home as quick as we can, and we can talk with Lill later."

Mike looked down at David sitting in his chair. He seemed okay. He appeared to have settled down quite a bit, but it was hard to get a read on him. Mike reached his hand out to David to help him up while saying, "David, how about we go back to Susan's room for a few minutes, and then home?"

*   *   *   *   *

Joey waited in the hallway outside Susan's door. Mike tapped on the door, and then he and David went in. While Mike was getting David settled back into his chair, he turned his head and said to Lillian, "Lill, Joey and I were just talking, and he's come across a few things that might be of interest to you. He's about to leave, but was asking if you wouldn't mind stepping out in the hall for a minute to speak with him?"

"Certainly," Lill said, scooting off the bed. Kay gave Mike an odd glance as she helped her mother.

Mike gave a subtle nod towards David and said, "Someone got a little anxious in the waiting room. Got a little tense for a while. Joey just wanted a quick word with Lill, and then I think we should be getting David home, if that's okay with you all."

Mike escorted Lillian into the hallway where Joey stood waiting. Lill thought Joey looked a bit uneasy and turned to Mike as he shut the door behind them.

Mike, responding to the unspoken question on Lill's face, said, "Actually, Mom, both of us wanted to have a word with you."

Joey interjected, "Perhaps we could just sit down and chat for a minute in the waiting area," and he waived his arm towards the way to the nurse's station.

Joey walked slightly ahead, leading the way, while Lill held lightly onto her son-in-law's arm as the three made their way in silence back to the corner where Joey, David, and Mike had just been.

When they were settled in, Lill turned to Joey and said, "Mr. Franks, what is it that you wanted to say?"

Joey, as a retired newspaper reporter, had a knack for summing up a story. He relayed to Lill a brief but accurate description of how obsessed David was with the doctor and nurse working across the room at the nurse's station—obsessed to the point that David couldn't be drawn into a conversation. Joey concluded his recap, saying, "David's agitation grew to the point that he made a couple of rather startling statements."

Joey paused for a moment. Then, thinking that it might be better if Mike told the climax of the episode, Joey tossed the ball to him by saying, "Mike, what was it, exactly, that David said that startled us so?"

"Well, let's see," Mike said, trying to recreate accurately the words and content of what David had said. "He said something like, 'VanZant is here,' and then he said something about VanZant breaking a promise, or agreement, or something like that. He must have thought that the doctor at the nurse's station was VanZant because David kept staring at him and made some comment about that doctor, something about how that doctor was ignoring him. No, wait, he said the doctor was pretending that he didn't see us; that was it. And then David asked me if I still had the gun that he had given me. Of course, David's never given me any gun."

Mike paused, then said, "But the kicker was . . . the kicker was that David said that we had to kill him. I assume that he was still talking about that doctor."

"Yeah," Joey confirmed. "I heard it too. He said clear as a bell that we had to kill him, and then David added something like, 'even if it exposes the things we've done.' But there was one more thing that really jumped out at me. He called Mike, Mihail. Lill, what do you think is going on here? Do you know anyone called VanZant, Dr. VanZant . . . or Mihail?"

Lill rocked back and forth ever so slightly as she thought, then said, "No. No. I don't recall the name VanZant. Of course, Mihail is close to Mike's full name, Michael, but I don't think I've ever heard David call him that. But . . . but . . . there is something that David once said."

Joey and Mike watched Lill, waiting for what would come next. Lill continued her subtle rocking motion, staring off into the distance, remembering an odd, cryptic conversation that she had had with David many years ago.

"What was it, Lill? What did David say?" Mike asked.

Slowly, Lill turned her head towards Mike and said, "It was at Bert's funeral. Michael, it was at your dad's funeral. It was at the very end. Remember, after the service, we had all gone to the cemetery for the final graveside service. There was a man there, a man that I had never met before. I didn't see him at the church or at the visitation. He might have been there, but I don't think so. Bert had lots of friends. It was a cold, rainy, overcast day, but Bert had lots of friends. There were a lot of people at the service and at the cemetery. But I remember very clearly meeting him . . . because it was so unusual. His name was Mr. Johnson. During the graveside service, David and I were up-close, near the casket, near the family. But I remember seeing Mr. Johnson keeping to himself at the outskirts of the crowd. I hadn't met him yet, but I remember him because while most people were behind us, watching and listening to the pastor say the final words, Mr. Johnson was off to our side. I remember him because he seemed so all alone there. He just seemed so . . . all alone, so . . . all alone. Most of the people there were with someone or knew someone there. Most of the people there were friends, people who we, or Bert, had known for a long, long time. But while everyone else was watching the pastor, Mr. Johnson was watching us. It was rainy. Mr. Johnson, with his overcoat, hat, and umbrella, managed to stay on the outskirts, by himself, remote.

"When the service was over and we, David and I, were headed back to our car, when we got near our car, this strange but gentle man approaches us. David didn't seem at all surprised; it was almost as if he was expecting to see this man there. I can tell immediately that David liked this man, liked him a lot. I can always tell. David introduces us, tells me that his name is Michael Johnson. Then David said something that was a little out of character for him. David said something about how wild those days were. He was talking about his old FBI days. He was saying how wild those days were and how hard it was to know who to trust.

"Mr. Johnson asks Dave how Bert's family is holding up. They exchange a few pleasantries, and then, abruptly, David tells me that he would like to have a private word with Mr. Johnson and asks if I would mind waiting for him in the car.

"I say, 'Of course not,' and let myself into the car. We were only a few feet away at that point. Sitting there, in the front seat, I look over my shoulder and see David and Mr. Johnson step behind our car. I've never done this before, but I moved the rearview mirror so that I could see them. It didn't do me any good though. They both stood with their backs toward me, so I couldn't see their expressions or anything. I did, however, see Johnson hand an envelope to David, which he put in his coat pocket.

Lill paused. Joey could tell from her distant stare that, in her own mind, Lill was back in the front seat of that car. He gave her a moment, then gently asked, "Lill, do you remember what happened next?"

Lill nodded and said, "Yes, yes I do. I remember it like it was yesterday."

"What happened?" Joey prodded.

"The two only talked for a minute or two, maybe three. Then, Mr. Johnson walked off and David got back in the car. I tried to put the mirror back in place before David got back. I'm not sure if he saw me or not. Doesn't matter; he knew. When he sat down, he looked at the mirror, then glances over at me, then readjusts the mirror. He knew, but he wasn't mad, but he was quiet. That was unusual for the two of us. David just started the car, put it in drive, and drove slowly towards the cemetery exit, not saying a word.

"Then, as we're leaving the cemetery, David said, 'Lill, now that Bert is gone, I need to tell you something.' He doesn't tell me anything specific, but he tells me that in the two years before he retired from the FBI, some bad things happened. Of course I knew, at the time, that those last few years at the Bureau were more troubling for David than the earlier years. I don't think the criminals were more dangerous in the later years, but his job . . . he seemed troubled that last year. He wasn't earlier on, during the war. But that day, in the car, just after David had spoken with Mr. Johnson, David made a point of saying something bad had happened that last year with the FBI. He had never said anything like that before. He said that he didn't anticipate any problems or repercussions from events of that period, but there remained some very bad characters around, and he simply wanted to maintain a certain level of caution. He might have used the word 'defense'; I'm not sure. He said that while Bert was alive, they had each other's backs. David said he knew that I knew, without ever being told explicitly, that Bert could be trusted without question, and, that if something odd ever came up, and he wasn't there to deal with it, that he felt assured that I would know to call on Bert.

"I was puzzled. I asked David what he was talking about. I asked him if what he was talking about had anything to do with Mr. Johnson. It seemed obvious that the two were connected. That meeting Mr. Johnson, and David suddenly voicing those concerns . . . they had to be related. I asked David what he was talking about, but all that he would say was that now that Bert was gone, he just wanted me to know that if, sometime down the road . . . if he were gone, that he wanted me to know that Mr. Johnson, Michael Johnson, could be trusted. That if something odd or troubling ever came up, if anything beyond my understanding happened that caused me worry or concern, that I could call on Michael Johnson. David said that he didn't think that there would ever be any need, but if I ever wasn't sure, not to hesitate to call. David said that Bert had been our 'ace in the hole,' but now that Bert was gone, for me to think of Mr. Johnson as my new ace.

"I told David that I wasn't sure about that. I told David that I didn't feel entirely comfortable about that; that I had known Bert forever, but that I had just met Mr. Johnson, that I didn't even have his phone number, that I had no way of knowing how to contact him even if I thought that I needed to. David said that he couldn't tell me why, but just to know that Mr. Johnson would, without hesitation or reservation, do anything for our family or for Bert's. That he would be happy to. David patted his jacket pocket and said that Mr. Johnson had given him an envelope with contact information.

"We rode along for a few minutes in silence. It seemed like there was more to say, but I could tell that David didn't want me to ask any questions. Then David said, 'But, all things equal, it would be best if you didn't have to call upon Mr. Johnson; and, I'm pretty sure you never will have to . . . but, you'll know.'

"We ride for a few more minutes, then David says, 'One more thing. I'll put this contact information in a safe place for you, two safe places, just in case. If, or when, I die, give a copy of Michael Johnson's contact information to Bert's wife and tell her what I've told you today. Michael would do as much for her family as for ours . . . more really.'"

Lill looked over at Joey, then back to Mike. Mike said, "Well, that's quite a story."

"Lillian," Joey said. Lill turned her head to Joey. "Lillian. I think you should make the call. I think you should call Michael Johnson."

Chapter 29

Sunday Lunch at Bethea's

Chattanooga, TN
August 1946

"Four adults and three kids, please." The hostess pushed two tables in the middle of the dining room together. David sat at the head at one end and Bert at the other. Longwise along the table, the two wives sat on one side and the three children, David's two and the little Russian boy, sat along the other side. The little Russian boy sat at David's end of the table and had scooted his chair close to David.

The young waitress placed a glass of water in front of each after they sat down and then distributed straws to everyone from her apron pocket. From another pocket, she pulled out her order pad and a pen, and looked back and forth from David to Bert.

Bert said to the waitress, "Let's start off with a pitcher of sweet tea," then looked down the table to David and asked, "Shall we get the Sunday Special?"

The Sunday Special that week was Southern fried chicken, mashed potatoes and gravy, green beans, slaw, and, of course, biscuits; all served family style in large bowls set out on the table for everyone to help themselves. David glanced over to Lillian, who gave an approving nod. David replied to Bert and the waitress, "Sounds great, let's do it."

The after-church crowd was pouring in. The empty tables were quickly filling up and a line at the hostess station was beginning to back up as customers were now coming in faster than they could be seated. The smell of fried chicken was in the air. David looked over the table; life was good. The wives were happily chatting, their heads turned in together as they laughed about something. His son had a toy top that he spun on the table, bumping it around with his fingertips. He had created a perimeter by laying out his and his sister's silverware end-to-end, forming a little corral from which the spinning top could not escape. David's daughter was busy with a coloring book and a handful of colored pencils. She had finished coloring in the picture and was now working on her own original drawing in the empty space at the top corner of the page. The new boy, Mihail's boy, sat quietly with his hands in his lap as he watched with wide eyes the large steaming bowls of food being brought out of the kitchen and set upon one table after another, knowing that soon, one would be set on his table. David's smile widened as his attention was drawn to Bert as Bert shook out a large, red-checkered napkin, tucked a corner of it under the loosened top button of his shirt, and spread the cloth out wide to protect his shirt and tie from the forthcoming feast. Bert was putting the final touches on the exact placement of his napkin, brushing the cloth out smooth with both hands, when abruptly, his hands froze in place and his face turned grave.

David turned in his chair to follow the direction of Bert's gaze and in an instant, David's face likewise turned grim. The room, to David and Bert, despite all of the ambient chatter and clinking of glass and china, in a flash, seemed quiet as a tomb. They watched with stoic faces as Mihail, following the hostess, crossed the room, passing within a foot or two from their table. David noticed, as Mihail passed, that Bert had crouched somewhat in his chair, letting his right hand fall next to his right ankle. At that moment, David realized that his right arm had crept across his chest and his hand had slipped under his suit coat, just under his armpit. Without thinking, he too had moved his hand to his gun. The hostess led Mihail to a nearby table and set a menu down at a place setting that would have had Mihail's back to David's table. Mihail declined, pointing to another table located against the wall at the far end of the room. The hostess scooped the menu back up and led Mihail to the other table. Mihail chose the chair in which he could sit facing directly at David.

Mihail, having spoken a few quick words to his waitress, sat with his hands on the table, looking towards David, but David could tell that all of Mihail's attention was directed at the boy at David's side. David relaxed his right arm and rested it on the table. He noticed that Bert had straightened back up in his chair. David wasn't sure, but most likely Bert had transferred his snub-nose revolver from his ankle holster to his lap or trouser pocket.

Mihail shifted his eyes towards David and, with a slow, fluid motion, raised his hand just inches above the table, rotating his palm up, and with a slight wave of his fingertips, invited David over to his table. David glanced over to Bert. Bert gave a subtle nod of assent. David leaned towards his wife and lightly touched the back of her upper arm to get her attention.

"Excuse me for a minute, Honey. There's a man here that I need to speak to. I'll be right back."

Lill didn't give it a second thought. They hardly went anywhere where David didn't run into someone he knew. She automatically nodded her acknowledgement and returned to her conversation. David rose and walked over to Mihail's table. Mihail, with the sweep of his hand, invited David to sit across from him. The two sat in silence, both with their hands on the table, looking at each other, summing each other up; who would speak first?

Mihail spoke first. He asked, simply, matter-of-factly, "Is that my son?"

David, in the same simple manner replied, "You tell me."

Mihail's eyes widened. With an edge of urgency he asked, "What do you mean?"

David replied, "Well, that boy over there at our table, we believe that he is most likely the son of the woman that was killed. The problem, the reality is . . . I have no way of knowing if that woman was really your wife. I have nothing to go on other than what you have told us. You told us your wife and son would cross into Western Germany and show up at a certain town, around a certain time, and they did. But they had an extra person with them, another little boy. The woman, presumably your wife, told us that the extra boy was a last-minute addition. That getting him out to safety was part of the smuggler's price for getting your family over the border. Anyway, we picked them up and brought them all here. I'm guessing that you weren't expecting that extra boy. I'm guessing that you thought that it was your son who was killed, along with your wife."

Mihail said nothing but slowly nodded his head.

David continued, "My gut tells me that she was your wife. I'm sorry. My gut also tells me that you have been honest with me. But given all that has happened, faith in a gut feeling is precious little to go on. So far, we've had no real way to verify who they are or why they were sent here. As you well know, sometimes, just asking questions can be a dangerous game."

Mihail gave no immediate response. David shrugged his shoulders and said, "Things are not always what they appear to be. Things are not always what we hope them to be."

The two men again sat in silence. It was true, Mihail reflected; David had no way of knowing for certain who that boy was or, for that matter, who the dead woman was. But now, for Mihail, no doubts remained that his son was indeed alive. It was as if, after a long couple of weeks, his son had been resurrected from the dead. Speech escaped him as he sat, absorbing the confirmation of this morning's miraculous revelation.

The lack of sleep and sudden, erratic shifts of emotions now brought Mihail to the edge. He felt a brief wave of dizziness and his eyes blurred for a moment, but still, he was able to maintain his composure. David sat quietly, watching, wondering, trying to imagine what could possibly be going through Mihail's mind.

Mihail seemed to be fixated on the glass of ice water that was sitting on the bare tabletop, just off the edge of his paper placemat. The cool glass was beginning to sweat. The edge of the paper near the glass was getting soggy, and a little pool of water was beginning to form on the table. David watched what he took to be a look of acceptance, if not relief, gradually wash over Mihail's face.

Mihail, still staring at the glass as one might stare into a crystal ball while contemplating recent gains, recent losses, and what was yet to come, said, "Then, that is my son. I haven't seen him since he was an infant, so I don't really know him . . . by sight. But I know that the woman that was killed, the mother of that boy, she was my wife."

Mihail reached for his glass of water and closed his eyes as he took a long drink. Several large drops dripped from the glass onto Mihail's shirt as he drank. He set the glass back in its place, looked up at David, and continued, "My son, he looks well. How is he?"

David gave a sympathetic smile and in a gentle voice said, "He is well. He will be better when some time has passed, when he has had a chance to get more comfortable with his surroundings, some time to feel more secure. He is lucky that he did not see what happened at the guesthouse; though, of course, he heard the shots; he was aware of the commotion. We got him out quickly, quietly, to safety, but he's aware that something very bad happened that day. He wonders where his mother went. We've told him that she was in a bad accident and that we will take care of him; that he will be all right. Officially, Bert and I have kept him off the record. We haven't mentioned him to anyone. I mean anyone. The people responsible for getting your family from West Germany to Camp Forrest obviously know that he exists, but they shouldn't have any reason to follow up on him, we're hoping. Once they delivered them to us, their job was done. Their plane was there just long enough for them to refuel, and then they took right back off and went home. Later, they might have heard bits and pieces of what happened at Camp Forrest, but Camp

Forrest is a pretty big place. Unless they looked into it, there's no reason for them to connect that, uh, crime, with the people that they dropped off that day. Anyway, we haven't contacted them, and even if they connect the two events, they probably wouldn't think that it's strange that we didn't contact them. They would probably think that we had it all wrapped up and didn't need their assistance. As far as we, Bert and I, can tell; we, and now you, are the only ones who know that your son exists."

Mihail's head bobbled ever so slightly as he replied, "That is something good." Mihail took another pause, then asked, "My son, he is staying with you then?"

David answered, "Yes, for now anyway. He was staying with my sister until two days ago. Now he is at my house, but that can't be for very long. It's too dangerous. It is something that we should talk about."

Mihail's attention appeared to have returned to the glass of water. He had drunk most of the water from the glass; the contents remaining were mainly small cubes of ice. But on the outside of the cool glass, condensation was running its inevitable course; the pool of water had grown, and now, a little tabletop lake surrounded the glass. Mihail's eyes looked out of focus as they followed the object of his thoughts, which were now a million miles away.

David paused for a moment, trying to assess Mihail's condition, then, probing gently, asked, "Mihail, are you all right?"

David wasn't sure if Mihail heard him or not. Mihail reached out with his index finger and splashed the water surrounding the glass.

David asked again, "Mihail, are you all right?"

Mihail lifted his head and his eyes focused back onto David. "The sergeant who took your place in the car at the gate, the sergeant who held me at gunpoint as I watched my wife killed before my eyes, watched as my son, the boy I thought was my son . . . killed. When I had him, when I had that sergeant alone, he told me that it was you who had arranged all of this. That it was you that had my wife and child killed."

The two men held each other's eyes. David pictured the tortured body of the sergeant lying dead on the floor—the stillness, the headlights glaring from behind, the harsh shadows, the last remnants of warmth leaving that body as David, Bert, and the Chaplain stood over the remains of Mihail's handiwork.

Mihail, though his eyes were fixed on David, could hear the Sargent's shrieks of agony, the desperate pleas for him to stop, the frantic confession in order to stop the excruciation. There was no doubt; the sergeant had believed that it was David who was to blame.

David, with a quiet shake of his head, said, "No. It wasn't me. It wasn't Bert."

Mihail looked quietly at David. In a voice that sounded like an apology, confession, and accusation, all wrapped up in one, said, "I did not know what to think, so I thought the worst." Then, Mihail dropped his head and lowered his eyes, and in a low voice, a voice meant only for himself, said, "The Beast is gone."

David, barely able to hear Mihail's words, asked, "What do you mean?"

Mihail looked back up at David and said, "The Beast. I was speaking of the beast that was within me. The beast that had consumed me, from the inside out. When I saw my wife . . . and that boy . . . when I saw them killed, and I was helpless, powerless to do anything, powerless to bring them back . . . when that happened, a beast took over my soul, feasting upon me with ravenous energy. With every bite of my flesh, the beast grew stronger as my will to resist its influence grew weaker. Yes, the toxin, the rage that grew within me was a wild, ravenous, malignant beast that had to be turned loose upon someone or something, or it would devour me whole. The beast does not look rationally for a guiltless target; the beast seeks the easiest target; the beast seeks a familiar target."

David said, "So, where does that leave us?"

"The beast, the irrationality is gone. But still, a smoldering longing, tempered only by the need to protect my son, remains. A longing, an emptiness, a desire to learn the truth, to balance the books. The beast has been repelled, but his absence leaves a void. What will fill this emptiness . . . something must."

Neither man had an answer. Mihail said, "Tell me, David, who did this; why did they do this? Who gains from this?"

David thought for a moment, then replied, "I don't know. I don't know who is behind this . . . I just don't know. Our people, of course, are blaming it all on you, on the Russians. Whether they believe it or not, they have to. They have to blame you, otherwise, that leaves just us, the FBI, and other agencies. For a while, it looked like they were thinking of dumping it all on me, me and Bert that is. But I think they decided that they really couldn't. They couldn't make a case against me and Bert that would hold up. They couldn't dump it on us without a lot of it splashing back onto them. No, their only way out, the only way for the FBI to protect its reputation is to blame it all on you—blame the Russians."

"And, what do you think, David? In your heart of hearts, what do you think? Do you think that it was me? Do you think that it was 'the Russians?'"

"No. No I don't."

"Then who? Who does that leave?"

David said nothing.

Mihail shifted in his chair and then continued, "Did you tell anyone of my warning to you of VanZant?"

David tightened his lips in an odd, uncharacteristic expression, and admitted, "Yes, yes I did."

"Who did you tell?"

"Pretty much everyone."

"Everyone?"

"Yes, everyone. Everyone at The Bureau, that is. Everyone that was involved with the operation. Bert and I talked it over the morning after our Woolworth's meeting in Nashville, before I reported our conversation to the Bureau. We decided that I had to, that I had no choice."

"You had a choice . . . but I understand. I, perhaps, would have done the same. It was foolish of me to warn you of VanZant. I should have waited till later, if at all. I wasn't expecting to see him that day at the clinic. How different my world would be if he, or your sister Edna, had only picked a different day or different time to be at that clinic. An hour's difference might have changed everything. But it is done."

The two looked at each other for a moment in silence. Mihail asked, "What did they say? What did your superiors say when you spoke of VanZant?"

"I was surprised at their apparent lack of curiosity. As cautious and thorough as they were about everything else, we—Bert and I—were surprised how they seemed content to just gloss over the subject of VanZant. Bert and I even talked about that, specifically, at the time. We thought it plausible that they viewed VanZant as a red herring that you were throwing at us."

Mihail looked confused. David explained, "You know, 'a red herring.' It's an American idiom. It means something that is meant to distract us. It was plausible that Headquarters felt that we had bigger fish to fry, and they wanted to keep distractions to a minimum. That if VanZant was a factor, it would all come out in the wash. None of us, Bert and I included, could rule out the possibility that your defection might not be completely on the up and up, and that you might be trying to muddy the waters. But that didn't keep Bert and me from taking a peek at VanZant and the Clinic, even though we didn't have enough time to get very far into it."

Mihail asked, "So, you've talked with VanZant?"

"No. No, I haven't. I mean, not recently . . . not since I first met him a year or so ago, back at Oak Ridge. These last few weeks, the bulk of my time and attention, leading up to your defection, was focused on you. Of course, I couldn't ignore what you told me about the clinic, since it involved my sister, since there was a chance that she was in danger. So, when they sent me to Washington, to Headquarters, while I was out of town; Bert went to Nashville and interviewed Dr. Mallard at the clinic."

"David . . . when Bert spoke with Dr. Mallard, did they just talk about the clinic, or did Bert bring VanZant into the conversation?"

"Bert asked about both."

Mihail placed his elbow on the table, slouched forward a little, resting his chin on his thumb, and lightly rubbed the front of his lips with the side of his index finger as he looked off into the distance. "That's it then," he said.

"What do you mean, 'that's it'?"

Mihail straighten up, looked directly at David, and said, "It's VanZant; has to be."

With a very slight tilt of his head and squint of his eyes, David asked, "What makes you say that? How can you be so sure?"

Mihail replied, "Think about it, David. When you think about how all of this has played out, it all makes sense. The Sergeant, the Sergeant who told me that it was you who was responsible for the death of my wife and that boy. That is the key to all of this. Ask yourself why; why did he tell me that, if it was not true? Their plan wasn't to kill me; that would have been easy. Their plan was to turn me against you. That was their plan, his plan, VanZant's plan, all along. When Bert talked to Mallard, he might as well have been talking directly to VanZant. Mallard was probably on the phone with VanZant before Bert had even left the building. And back to that Sergeant . . . really, it was too easy. If they had sent someone better, more skilled, I might still have gotten away—but that Sergeant, he was too easy. They wanted me to question him; they wanted him to convince me of your betrayal, senseless as it was. VanZant knew emotions would be high; people would react rashly. He was counting on it."

David nodded. "That's possible; that's certainly possible. But it's pretty extreme; isn't it? For one thing, as bad as VanZant is looking to be, would he, could he, realistically be behind something so complex. I have a hard time thinking it's possible. Isn't it more realistic that someone—a plant, a mole, a double, a Russian agent or sympathizer; whatever you want to call it— knew that you were defecting, and knew that you would blow their cover, expose them, if your defection was successful? Someone like that, I would think, would be much more likely, and capable, of pulling off something like this. They would have a very strong motivation. Their very life might depend on stopping your defection, at any cost."

Mihail replied, "That's right, if that were the case. If there was a mole who knew of my defection, they would have quite simply wanted me dead. But that's not what they did. Whoever is behind this could have killed me at any time that day, but they didn't. Whatever the goal of that operation was, it wasn't to kill me. And if there was such a mole, he, or they, would have needed Russian help to pull off something that complex. No, if he had come to our people, that would mean that my defection was known. They would not have wanted such a show. They would have simply taken me in. It would have been easy for them. I had to keep all of my contacts and appointments until the very last. No, I'm certain. My people knew nothing of my defection or I wouldn't be sitting here now. Right now, they're trying to figure out where I've gone. They probably don't know much, if anything, about what happened at Camp Forrest. They'd have no reason to be looking there. They know that I'm missing, and by now, certainly, they know that I've defected; especially since, by now, they must know that my wife and son have, how do you say, 'flown the coop.' They probably think that I'm sitting in a basement somewhere talking to the Americans—trading my secrets for a new life."

David said nothing; he was still thinking it through. Mihail continued, "No, I'm certain none of my handlers knew of my plans, and really, I don't think either of us believes that it was anyone inside the FBI. Not directly, anyway. The FBI is a lot of things. You guys do a lot of really dirty tricks, but, if nothing else, it's pretty clear that, from the top down, the FBI hates communists. Communists and communism, the FBI hates them both. Me, I just hate communism. That is one thing that I have in common with the FBI. No, if it had been someone involved in espionage, either American or Russian, they would not have staged this farce. The Americans, they would have brought me in, tried to co-op me. The Russians, well, they would have killed me. No, it has to be VanZant. You're looking at him; he knows it, and he wants you to look somewhere else. If he can get me to kill you, well then, most of his problems go away. I'm telling you, it's VanZant. Nothing else makes sense."

"I don't know," David replied with some hesitation. "I just don't see how someone like VanZant could have arranged all of this. It just seems like this would be far, far beyond his scope. As bad as VanZant may be, or wants to be, he's not that large a figure. I mean, I don't see how he could have put something like this together. The contacts and resources that he would have to have . . . I don't know; it just seems like a stretch for someone in his position."

Mihail gave a grim smile and said, "You know, David, that's the problem with you Americans. You look at titles and job descriptions. You listen to what people want you to hear. You hear what you want to hear, see what you want to see, believe what you want to believe. Life is easy, and it stays easy that way."

David bristled a little and replied stiffly, "Well, I don't know about that."

Mihail said, "You should look to see who is richer than, perhaps, they should be. See how they are living. For good or bad, money is often a truth detector. VanZant is richer than you think. That is why it is so important to him that nobody takes a close look at him. He is richer than his job title would allow. He has no benefactor; he comes from meager lineage."

David said, "Still, if you're right—that it's VanZant behind all of this—well, he was sure risking a lot on a pretty complicated plan. I mean, there was so much that could have gone wrong. For one thing, the timing was pretty tight. They did a good job of sidetracking Bert and me with the phone calls and all, but if just one glitch, one unexpected thing had popped up, just one little hiccup, it could have changed everything and easily spoiled their plan. For instance, what if you hadn't been able to overcome that sergeant and drag him off to question him? According to your theory, everything hinged on that happening. I don't know. I'd like to be able to blame all of this on VanZant, but it just seems too complicated, too much of a risk for anyone to take."

Mihail said, "Well, maybe so, but the fact of the matter is, someone did do it. Yes, it's complicated, maybe a foolish risk; but still, it happened. Perhaps VanZant was betting that even if only parts of it worked out, that would be enough to put everything in turmoil. Any disruption that they can cause makes it look like treachery on your part. And, even if it all went wrong for them, even if you had captured that Sergeant, what did he know? What would he have told anyone? He thought you were behind all of this; that's what he would have eventually told anyone. That doesn't do VanZant any harm. For all we know, that Sergeant probably thought that he was working for the FBI; probably never even heard the name VanZant. Really, the more you think of it, the less complex their plan really is. If they just succeed in killing my wife and son, it doesn't have to be in front of me. Killing them is the thing that turns me against you, and how hard is that? All our plans were centered around keeping everything secret. Did your plans, your preparations, include a defense against an assassination attempt? I think not. It's not hard to kill someone who isn't expecting it. VanZant did this."

David had no immediate reply. Mihail said, "No, the only thing that spoils his plan is the one thing that has happened. The only thing that ruins it for VanZant is for you and me to talk, for the truth to come out. The truth is the one thing that spoils all of their deceptions. If it hadn't been for that extra boy, things would have gone much differently. VanZant didn't plan on an extra boy being there; how could he? If I hadn't discovered, at the last minute, that my son was still alive . . . well, VanZant was right; you would be dead, and no one would be thinking of VanZant."

David stiffened defensively. "What do you mean, 'the last minute'? Were you planning on killing me here, here in the restaurant?"

"No, no," Mihail said, realizing how bad what he had just said sounded. "I've not slept in a long time. Forgive my coarseness. I will tell you; I will confess. I was in your garage, up on the attic, the ledge, looking out that top window, looking at your back door. This morning, when you came out, when you were going to church . . . I had you in my gunsight. VanZant has played the game well. I was there to kill you. Then I saw my son . . . and everything changed."

A chill washed over David. He wasn't sure what to say or how he felt. All he could say to Mihail was, "You make it hard for me to want to help you."

Chapter 30

Into the Valley

Chattanooga, Tennessee
Fall 1946

"Ours is not to reason why, ours is but to do or die." Bert gave a single thump of his fist on the conference room table as if gaveling David and Bert's early morning office meeting to adjournment.

"Do and die," David corrected as he put one last item—a sheet of paper containing a carefully scrutinized list of names, birthdates, and cities of birth—into his briefcase and closed the lid.

"What?" Bert asked.

"It's not 'do or die,' it's 'do and die.' You say that all the time, but you always say it wrong."

"So, what's the difference? Pretty much the same thing, if you ask me."

"I don't know, Bert. If you think about it, there's a big difference. And, if you really want to be nit-picky about it, it's not

'Ours is not to reason why,' it's 'Theirs not to reason why, Theirs but to do and die.'"

"I'm not so sure about that, Dave. All my life, I've heard people say, 'Ours is not to reason why.' My mama used to say it all the time. Don't recall anyone ever saying 'theirs.'"

"Well, maybe not. People are certainly free to say and think whatever they want, but the original verse comes from a poem by Alfred Lord Tennyson called 'The Charge of the Light Brigade.' It goes:

> Someone had blundered.
> Theirs not to make reply,
> Theirs not to reason why,
> Theirs but to do and die.
> Into the valley of Death
> Rode the six hundred.

Bert didn't have an immediate response. After a pause, David added, "Not exactly the 23rd Psalm, is it?"

"What do you mean?" Bert asked.

"You know, 'Yea, though I walk through the valley of the shadow of death, I will fear no evil: for thou art with me.' Not exactly the verse that the Chaplain quoted to us either: 'A thousand shall fall at thy side, and ten thousand shall fall at thy right hand; but it shall not come nigh thee.'"

"Two different valleys; two different perspectives," Bert observed. "So, which is it, The Bible or Tennyson?"

"Wish I knew. I suppose it depends upon whether or not God allows blunders. Anyway, I just hope that today is the day that we can start to shine a little light on those bastards."

David slid his chair back and stood up, saying, "I better get going; my first interview is at twelve-thirty."

David reached for the handle of his briefcase, but before he could lift it from the table, Bert put his hand lightly on top of David's. David stopped and turned his head towards Bert. Bert stood, moving his hand to David's shoulder, and looked back at the door of the conference room as if to verify that it was still tightly closed, and then said to David, in a quiet voice, "So, David, do you think today's the day? Do you think we're gonna find that domino today that, when we tilt it, all the ones that hide behind will fall?"

"I don't know, Bert. I hope so. It's been a long couple of months, but we both know there's been no way around it. If HQ finds out that we're looking at VanZant's people, who knows what they'll do. They made it crystal clear that they're serious about this one and really tied our hands when they said that no one from the Chattanooga office was to, in any way, shape, or form, touch anything related to 'The Michael Johnson Affair,' as they've dubbed it. I know it's hard, but I think the best that we can do is what we're doing—slip in a file and an extra interview here and there, and hope that no one notices."

Bert bobbed his head in agreement. "Yeah, I know you're right. Just seems like an awfully slow way to skin this cat, but, for the life of me, I can't think of a better way. I know we've been over this a million times, but, what the hell. It's just bizarre the way this has all panned out. Why has HQ shut us down on this; what are they so afraid of? It's stupid, but I'm losing sleep over this. Life would sure be a lot easier if none of this had ever happened, or . . ." Bert looked down at the floor, shook his head, and finished his thought, saying, "if we could just let this go and move on."

David raised his arms with his hands open wide—the equivalent of a shrug—and said, "Yeah, I know, but we can't. Neither of us can let it go. We just have to be patient. We'll get them. Sooner or later, we'll get them. It's the same ole process we've been through a thousand times before; we look through tons of files and talk to lots of people, and, eventually, someone spills the beans, whether they mean to or not. Someone always does. We both know it. It's almost as if it was a law of nature. Most everyone has lapses, moments in which they're sloppy, arrogant, or some combination of the two. For those rare few who possess exceptional discipline, well, there is always someone within their sphere who knows them, or about them, who will blab or boast when given the chance. We've done this a thousand times and we'll do it again here; you'll see. It's just going to take a little longer this time since HQ has thrown some obstacles in our way, and then, of course, VanZant isn't exactly like the bulk of the people that we deal with, on a criminal basis. The movies have really glamorized a lot of those high-profile criminals, but we both know that, by far, most are just common thugs and grifters who tend to be on the stupid side. It's easy to forget how much harder it is when we come across someone like VanZant. Sure, he's a lot smarter and far more disciplined than most, but we'll get him. Sooner or later, he'll make a mistake, or someone around him will talk. They'll say something or do something that will give the whole shebang away, and then we'll have them. It always happens. Yep, sooner or later, we'll get him; you'll see."

"Yeah, yeah," Bert agreed. "I know you're right. I'm just getting a little impatient. I always do. I just hope that in the meantime no one gets onto us, especially Rogers. I hate lying to our boss. I'd hate to get him into trouble. If HQ finds out what we're doing, they'll throw him under the bus along with us in a New York second. Damn it anyway, what the hell are those paper-pushers sitting up there in Washington so afraid of?"

"I don't know, Bert, but it's something. It's definitely something. Like we've said before, those directives for us to stand down do seem to go well beyond the normal peccadillos of the Director. It's not exactly a secret that the FBI, that Hoover, does not suffer failures easily, especially spectacular ones, and that they'll go to great lengths to ensure that any failures, if they can't avoid being exposed, will quickly be pinned to someone, anyone, outside their inner sanctum. Everyone knows that. But sometimes, I can't help but wonder if we're being smart in what we're doing, what we're hoping to achieve."

"What do you mean?"

"Well, eventually, if we keep plugging away at it, sure, we'll find out what happened. It's just a matter of time. But then, when we do, what do we do with that information? I mean, two people, no, three people were killed. One tortured to death, a serious defection was blown, and a known spy was sent out into the wind. There are some seriously bad people out there, and, when we find out who they are and why they did what they did, what are we going to do with that information? If it all points to bad people outside the FBI, well, that's one thing. Maybe then, the Director will forgive us for violating their orders to desist. Maybe then, the Director might find it easier to just look the other way regarding our disobedience, rather than to create a stir that invites more attention. But what if it doesn't? What if HQ has shut us down because they know exactly where an investigation will lead, and they don't want us to get there? What do we do then? Chances are, we're going to find some stuff that we can't report and we can't walk away from. What do we do then? Like you said, you, me, Rogers; we'll all be thrown to the wolves if and when we expose truths that reflect poorly on the powers-that-be. Ridicule, especially public ridicule, is the one thing that the Director will do anything, and I mean anything, to avoid."

"I know," Bert agreed. "I've had the same thoughts. In the past, whenever things have gone wrong, and they couldn't have gone more wrong than with this Johnson business, they always come up with a scapegoat to take the fall—always—and right away too. Why not this time? Why no scapegoat this time? The only thing that makes sense of it all is, like you say, they already know what's happened, and they've decided that the best thing to do, for them, is to just shut everything down and try to walk away from it as quietly as possible. Don't you think?"

"Yeah, without a doubt. That's the million-dollar question all right. I mean, clearly, if we know nothing else about what happened at Camp Forrest, we know that some really dangerous people are still lurking around out there. There's no getting around that, and the guys in Washington have to know that too. You bet they know something; they have to. Otherwise, squashing a follow-up investigation so quickly and so decisively is a wildly imprudent thing to do. It's just too risky to remain blissfully ignorant of such obvious dangers, and it's certainly out of character for them to not go after the bad guys, to not even want to know. Yeah, they know something all right, and, whatever it is, they don't want to let us in on it."

"But, still," David continued, "we can't deny that shutting down the investigations does have some significant benefits for us also. It's a mixed blessing. Dropping any follow-up means that it's far less likely that our sins will be discovered; there's no getting around that. If the Bureau ever finds out about our relationship with Johnson, if they ever find out that you, Bert, adopted Johnson's son—oh my God, it would be devastating.

"Well," Bert said, "clearly they don't know anything about that. If they did . . . well, there's just no way they would gloss over something like that. It does show though, that they don't know everything."

"Yeah," David agreed, rubbing his lips with his index finger as he went deeper into thought. "They don't know everything. But what is it that they know, that we don't know? It's got to be VanZant. It just has to have something to do with VanZant." David shook his head. "Damn it, why did I have to bring him up in those meetings? At the time, he was only of tangential interest, but since I mentioned his name, since I brought him up at those meetings, he falls under the directives to stay clear of. And now, now Rogers won't even let us follow up on the Nashville Clinic. That order has to be coming directly from HQ."

"Well, Dave, that's on both of us. I mean, we talked it over beforehand, and we both agreed that you had no choice but to tell them about VanZant. Hindsight's twenty-twenty as they say, but, even so, if we had to do it again, given the circumstances, we would have done the same thing."

"Yeah, that's what I keep telling myself." David glanced at his watch. "Jeez, Bert, look at the time. I need to get going. It'll be late before I get back. We'll talk tomorrow."

*　*　*　*　*

David looked at the speedometer and then at his wristwatch. *Crap, I'm barely doing 20.*

It was about a two-hour drive from Chattanooga, up the valley to Oak Ridge, depending on traffic—depending on whatever manner of trucks, tractors, trailers, or other typically overflowing loads the locals might happen to plop down upon the winding, rural roads of East Tennessee.

The road straightened; David could see that it was clear to pass the trailer of livestock in front of him. *I'm glad I'm not going where they're going,* David said to himself. *At least they have no idea.* David glanced at his watch, *Good, with a little luck, I should get to Oak Ridge not much later than ten-thirty—time to pull and review a few files before my first appointment, if I eat at my desk.*

Once past the doomed cattle, David's mind began to wander as his car rolled down the road without any conscious effort or direction on David's part. *Is today the day—how did Bert put it— is today the day that the dominos might start to fall? It just might be. It just might be. I think we both had that same feeling, that feeling that something is about to give, something big. Hell, who knows; maybe today is the day. This list we've put together, this list of people that I'm going to look at today—it's pretty good; it's promising. True, on the surface, most are only peripherally associated with VanZant. But still, culled from such a long list of possibilities—yes, it's a good list, definitely worth the risk of sneaking them into today's schedule. No one's going to notice; no one's going to be the wiser. Yeah, I think Bert is right. Maybe today, the dominos will start to fall. Maybe today, the dam will bust loose.*

But life is like a seesaw, David reflected as the road led him deeper into the valley. *So often, especially these last few months, the good seems to have come counter-balanced with an overly generous portion of evil. What the devil? What the devil is sitting out there on the other end of this seesaw that I'm on? Bert's right though; they're afraid of something; that's for sure. But what? What the hell is HQ so afraid of? It's got to be VanZant. That has to be it. That has to be the reason why the Bureau wants the matter dropped. More and more, I'm thinking that Johnson is right—everything can be linked back to VanZant. Ever since Bethea's—hell, ever since Woolworth's—no, ever since that day in the lobby of the Vanderbilt Clinic, when VanZant so casually walked by, it's as if VanZant is the center of gravity for all of this mischief.*

So, where does this leave me? I'm covering for Johnson; is the Bureau covering for VanZant? Or, is it something else, something else entirely, something else that I just can't see?

That's certainly a possibility. After all, I can't know everything; I'm not God. But then, neither are they. But, from where they sit, they do see more than I can see. From where they sit, they must know more than I know; they must see a bigger picture. But, again, they don't know everything; they don't see everything. They don't know about Johnson. They don't see Johnson, and they don't know that his son is alive—and they don't know that Bert has adopted him. Those are some pretty significant things for them to not know. Yes, they may know more, all in all, but that doesn't mean that they know better—does it? At least I'm cognizant of the fact that I don't know what I don't know. Can the same be said for them, or does their hubris prevent them from admitting any such mortal limitations? Maybe it's not the quantity of what you know, maybe it's the quality. Maybe it's the way in which you use what knowledge and what power that you do have.

Power. They do hold the power though, and that's no small thing. Really, in a way, it's everything. For them, might makes right. Whether I like it or not, that's the way it's always been. Whether by force or by consent, that's pretty much the way it's always been. Whoever has the biggest gun, fastest sword, heaviest rod and staff, gets to say. Yes, the heaviest rod and staff—"Yea, though I walk through the valley of the shadow of death, I will fear no evil: for thou art with me; thy rod and thy staff they comfort me." We all sing from the same hymnbook. Morality, justice—sometimes even happiness—it's whatever the powers-that-be proclaim it to be. Yeah, like it or not, that's the way it's always been. For thousands of years, really, since the beginning of recorded time, gods, pharaohs, emperors, kings—all the despots—they've all claimed the high ground as their own. They've all been unyielding in their rigid demand for unquestioned obedience. I don't know; maybe back then, that's the way it had to be. Maybe back then, that's the only way that society, civilization, could work. Perhaps back then, anything else would have been even worse. After all, not everyone could be king; most had to toil in the fields, or the kingdoms would perish. For most of history, it was as simple as that. It took almost all the population to grow the food, and even then, it was often not enough. We pretend to know what life back then must have been like, but we're just kidding ourselves. How brutal it must have been, from one day to the next, not to know—not to know if you would have any food, or if you would be run through with a sword for lighting a fire with a piece of wood that the king declared belonged to him—that very same king upon whom you had no choice but to accept as your only real chance of even a semblance of security or civility in an otherwise barbarous world.

Though, I suppose only a few, if any, ever gave the mechanics of their existence much thought. After all, only the very few, the elite, were educated to any degree. Only the very few had the good fortune, the circumstances, or even the time, to be able to look beyond the blade of a plow or a sword. It mattered little if a peasant, farmer, or soldier thought the king good or bad; only obedience, not approval, was required.

Yes, perhaps back then, with human nature being what it is, the harsh realities of life, the harsh realities of mere survival, made no other system of governance possible. Someone had to rule, even if it was the fortune of most to toil— "to do or die," as Bert would say. Yes, perhaps, for most of history, there simply was no other choice. Perhaps, for most of history, it has been a valid argument that those, from the vantage point of their lofty perch—those, whose view, for whatever reason, was not confined to the length of a field within the shallows of a small valley—were better positioned to command, judge, and rule over those who were, by necessity, constrained to a more limited situation. As long as the interests of the king and the interests of his country aligned, I suppose there were merits to that argument, but how often did that actually happen? I wonder?

Well, there's no going back. It was what it was. Their times are not our times, that's for sure. But what about now? It's been a long, long road, but we seem to have come so far. We clearly have the power to make choices for ourselves that our peasant forefathers never had—choices which drastically alter the pathways that our lives take. I can't help but wonder . . . do we make the most of these extraordinary opportunities? Have we become too complacent, too fat and happy? Have we become too naïve and too trusting in the source of our comforts—whatever that might be.

Yes, I think we take too much for granted. We're no longer subjects, serfs, property of the king, "bound to the soil and subject to the will of his master" — at least we don't think of ourselves as such. There is no Grand Inquisitor. We don't have Stalin's henchmen or some self-righteous do-gooder committee member looking over our shoulders, watching and directing our every move. We choose; we elect our own leaders. They are accountable to us. Sure, there are always going to be bullies and busybodies. Even now, there are always going to be ruthlessly ambitious people, constrained only by what they can get away with—self-anointed egomaniacs who believe the rules apply to others but not to them. But we've got checks and balances to protect us from them. We've got rules; we've got established laws.

But, but . . . we've also got a lot of secrets. A terrible lot of secrets. Are they, these secrets, beginning to do us more harm than good? Are we getting to the point where the secrets that we allow our leaders to keep . . . are they starting to subjugate us? All these secrets—they clearly limit our view; they distort our reality; they garble our reasoning and thus the decisions that we make. How different our decisions, our choices, might be in the absence of all these secrets. And it's not just the things that we are told, it's also the vast amount of information that is kept from us—for our own good? How different the light in which we view our leaders would be, how different the nature of our paths would be if we were only bold enough to rip those needless blinders from our heads.

So, is that it? Is that the only purpose for all these secrets: to limit our view, to narrow, simplify, and convolute our thinking; all to enhance the lives of our leaders and protect them—from what, us? So often now, so many of these secrets, they just don't seem necessary; they just don't seem legitimate. More and more, it appears to me that all these secrets do nothing but make chumps of the trusting. Trust is clearly breaking down. This Johnson Affair, this business with the Vanderbilt Clinic—it's all proof positive of that, and those aren't the only things. The examples are endless. Like straws on a camel's back, they are piling up. Clearly, they don't trust us, and it's looking more and more like we can't trust them—not if we want to keep our sovereignty.

So, where does that leave us? If we continue to blindly put our trust in them, our leaders, as we are so often forced to do . . . where does that take us? If our goals and values are the same as theirs, then, that's fine. If our goals are the same, and our leaders are decent, honorable men, then that's fine. But what if they're not? What if these men are not all that honorable? What if their goals are not really what they claim them to be? What if, in fact, what's good for us conflicts with what they perceive to be their birthright? — No, the unfortunate reality is that human nature, unconstrained, does not end well for the majority. Blind trust is a recipe for disaster. Left unconstrained, a spoiler always rises up. That's something that is never going to change. There simply has to be a check; there simply has to be a balance, an oversight—the pathway forward has to be clear and visible to all; otherwise, we're all just stumbling in the dark; otherwise, we're all just once again no more than peasants. Peasants, docile peasants being herded down a road . . . sleepwalking peasants being led to where—certainly not to the utopia that is so often promised? No, if we allow ourselves to be relegated to the status of mere peasants, whose fortunes are entirely dependent upon the capricious whims and condescending, patronizing, self-serving charity of our self-anointed betters—well, that can't end well.

Something is going to have to stop this, this . . . placid decent. I wonder. I look around and, more and more, I've got to wonder at the type of people who rise to these various positions of power and affluence. More and more, it doesn't seem to me that they are the best, the brightest—certainly not the most admirable or compassionate—despite all of their pretenses. No, it seems to me that, plain and simple, positions of authority are, more and more, being filled by those who are obsessed with a desire to dominate and are shameless in their pursuit. Ambition is not necessarily a bad thing, if tempered by other qualities. But this . . . this is just pure, unadulterated, unconstrained ambition. All too often, that seems to be the primary, overriding qualification—yes, that, combined with the requisite soul of a carnival barker with a penchant for the swindle. And we, we just let it happen. We just chalk it all up—all of this self-aggrandizing behavior—as charisma, and then somehow, magically, these shysters are transformed and elevated into celebrities. How easy it appears to be that those driven by such passions to dominate— unconstrained by any sense of shame—so easily brush past those whose passions lie elsewhere. Why do we let this happen? How have we let—what most consider to be their heart-felt values and convictions—how have we let them be so easily corrupted by a little glitter sprinkled in our eyes?

How far can this go? How far will we let it go? Will these elites eventually overplay their hand and expose themselves for what they are? At some point, will reality overpower the deception? Will enough people be shocked into wakefulness, rub the sleep from their eyes, and retake control of their lives, their destinies? It does seem that, from time to time, just when we appear to need it most, someone extraordinary rises to the occasion. Will that happen now; will that happen soon? But then, even when that does happen, it seems our gains, at least in modern times, are always so . . . transitory. Has mankind simply grown so accustomed to submitting, not only to God, but to their self-

appointed "Betters", that we can't help but to follow the path of least resistance and slip back into that groove, that comfortable role of being sheep to the shepherds? The bulk of mankind has, in fact, spent the better part of its history in a state of subordination—has time and pressure baked acquiescing into our souls to the point where only those at the extremes can break free and rise?

In the Garden of Eden, God could not allow man a bite of the apple. God could not allow us to know what he knows, to see all that he sees—not if he wanted to continue to rule an unchallenged kingdom. And perhaps, for man's own good, if God is in charge, we are better off not eating from that apple.

I don't know. A great deal of trust and faith is required to be at peace with such a decision. But, I do know one thing—our mortal leaders are not our gods. If they are to restrict our view, our knowledge, it is not for our benefit; it is for theirs.

*   *   *   *   *

David shuddered, then became cognizant that he had slowed, stuck creeping along behind a large tractor with faded red paint and huge rear tires—for how long now? Probably not more than a minute or two, but, so lost in thought, he couldn't be sure. David was on a straightaway, but there was too much oncoming traffic to pass. He looked across the valley to his right. Beyond a field of grazing cattle, he could see the rising western edge of the bottom of the Appalachian Mountain range. Crossing the Hiwassee River reminded David of how extreme the fog could be at times in sections of the Tennessee River valley. Locals would say that when it was bad, you couldn't see past the noise on the front of your face, which some days seemed literally true. But, then again, David knew full well from experience that, from time to time, even on the mountaintops the fog could be quite severe. Happily, today, the visibility appeared to be unlimited, and the sky was a brilliant, cloudless, clear blue.

But still, there was this damn tractor in front of him, blocking his way. Already, the day was beginning to feel short even though the last few minutes felt long. This unavoidable delay seemed such a waste of precious time. The tractor slowed even more, almost to a stop; but then, to David's relief, it turned off onto a narrow dirt road that David didn't even see until the tractor turned onto it.

Finally, David was back up to speed. As he drew closer to Oak Ridge and the tasks ahead of him for that day, his thoughts turned to VanZant, and once again, the passage of time became detached from his awareness. David's thoughts of VanZant segued to Johnson, then to the senseless killing of Johnson's wife and the little boy, then to the bloodied body in the garage, and then to the Chaplain . . . *the Chaplain . . . the lamentations of the Chaplin— the hollow man. Whatever becomes of such a man?* David wondered. *Indeed, whatever happens to a man when the entirety of his soul has been spent—emptied out—consumed? Burned out in a flurry of empathy and then left cold—frozen in a futile, relentless attempt to comprehend the inexplicable?*

Yes, the Chaplain, in his crisis of faith, had certainly brought up some disturbing aspects of religion and morality. But it's not as if he was the first to do so, and certainly, he won't be the last— but, without a doubt, his was the most severe case that I've ever witnessed. His complaints, they weren't just the all-too-typical rants of some radical malcontent clamoring for attention. No, that chaplain—his experiences were real; the scars that they left, they were real. The suffering that surrounded and engulfed him— unimaginable. But then, all that suffering, all that imagery— that's what gave his story, his doubts, his misgivings and questions . . . what? . . . Gravity?

No, that Chaplain—he wasn't just some half-baked malcontent. But, I have to admit, it's troubling to me that I don't really have a better answer to any of his questions. It's not like I've never given it any thought; it's just that I've never come up with any good answers—answers that, if I have to be honest with myself, are really satisfying. That's what's troubling—that at some point, when the answers don't come, we all just give up, put it off for another day. Sometimes we pretend that we don't; we take the easy answers that are given to us—that it's beyond our understanding or pay grade, that it's all for the best, and we let it go at that. We let it go because, because . . . because the alternatives can be disturbing.

Disturbing—those experiences, the things that Chaplain must have gone through . . . I can't even imagine. No, that Chaplain was right about one thing: living through something, particularly something really bad, is very different from just thinking in the abstract about that very same thing—some detached, purely academic, hypothetical event. Yes, reality—a harsh reality—can have a nasty way of testing the mettle, the practicality, the durability of our beliefs, no matter how strong we may think them to be.

But what bothers me, David thought, *is that a common denominator in so many of these moral quandaries is that the wrong person gets punished—the innocent. So often, the innocent get punished—brutally punished—and the guilty, they waltz off with the rewards. It just seems so wrong. It just seems so simple—that there is no good reason for it to be like that. Why does God let that happen? Why does the Bible, the word of God, flaunt stories in which that happens, as if that's the model for morality?*

David's mind jumped to the story of King David and Bathsheba. That story, and the Sunday-School explanation for it—that even a great man can sin, but King David repented, and the Lord forgave him—had never rested well with David. *Why the hell did God kill that baby? That innocent baby. What did it do to deserve death? It didn't commit adultery—King David did. King David commits adultery with Bathsheba, and then King David has Bathsheba's husband Uriah killed. Sure, to his credit, King David repents, but what's his punishment? God punishes David by killing the baby?*

I know, I know; in God's universe, the scales of justice must always be balanced. For every sin, someone must pay—always. So, God kills an innocent baby. God kills the child who was the product of David and Bathsheba's adulterous affair. A newborn infant pays the price for King David. In the eyes of God, justice is served. And then, David goes on his merry way, marries Bathsheba, and they have more children, one of whom is Solomon, a man who becomes a great king, perhaps the greatest. A man—a king—who God blesses with the greatest wisdom of all time. David and Bathsheba's first child is killed; but their next child, by the grace of God, is raised to unimaginable heights.

David shook his head. *Where was the justice when the innocent paid for the crimes of the guilty? Did one set of principles apply to God, another to man? If the principles of morality are not absolute, then, what are they? Certainly, I don't presume to have anywhere near the equivalent wisdom as God. That's not the issue. It's simply that in so many instances, God's judgments, actions, and inactions seemed so counter to any rational explanation—something has to be wrong. It can't be that it is proper for us to simply disregard our rational thought and substitute, in its place, faith. Why must the two so often be in conflict? And, when they are, why must faith take precedence? If God created us, then amongst his greatest gifts to us is our capacity for rational thought—it truly separates us and elevates us above all his other creations. Why—why would we ever be asked to forfeit such a precious gift?*

Of course, there is something to be said for faith. Without a doubt, faith can be a powerful source of comfort during periods of turmoil and uncertainty. Perhaps our capacity for faith is also a gift that shouldn't be too readily discounted—but blind faith? Are there, or shouldn't there be, limits—limits, beyond which it is reasonable to expect some degree of reason and understanding to play a dominant role? How far can blind faith be stretched; how far can it be twisted before all the comfort is wrung out of it? Obviously, there is no fixed point, no absolute or universal line of demarcation. Like all things subjective, it would be fluid, ethereal—different for each person and each unique situation. But is there no rock—no absolute, immovable anchor to which rational thinking alone can be tethered. It's as if too often, when we need it the most, at the extremes, rational thinking breaks loose, leaving only blind faith as a guide—that or nothing.

Crap. I think that Chaplain has really gotten to me—more than I had thought. Why the hell must everything be such a mystery, especially the things of utmost importance? What is the purpose— God's purpose—in not allowing our choices to be made on the basis of a clear, rational, understanding of what is what? Why all the mystery? Why muddy the waters? Why should eternity depend upon blind faith while even the proponents of the faiths tell us that there are strong forces of evil, hell-bent on playing our emotions and playing upon our inherent weaknesses to make the wrong decisions? I don't know; maybe that's its strength. Maybe when all else fails, faith, if it remains strong enough, overcomes. Maybe it's there as a last resort to grab ahold of.

*   *   *   *   *

Suddenly, David realized he was approaching the main gate to the Oak Ridge facility. He had slowed and was about to come to a stop. He had been so lost in thought for the last many miles that his driving had been entirely automatic to the point that he marveled at how little recollection he had of the last hour of his drive.

Stopping at the gate, he held up his badge for the guard to inspect. The guard added David's name and destination to the list on his clipboard and waved him through. Pulling forward into the compound, David thought, *Yes, the desire for justice can be overwhelming. But I won't make the mistake of punishing the innocent for the crimes of the guilty. I'll play no part in that. That would be a sin. No, I'll seek the truth; I'll find the guilty. I'll see that it is the offenders who bear the consequences of their actions, and not some innocent scapegoat slaughtered merely to appease the arbiters of morality.*

Chapter 31

The Clinton Engineer Works

Oak Ridge, Tennessee
Fall 1946

"Special Agent DeRieux, it's good to see you," Gladys said with a sincerely genuine smile as David entered the Records and Filing section of the Personnel Department for the Clinton Engineer Works. David remembered doing Gladys' pre-employment security background screening, about three years ago now, just weeks after her youngest had graduated from high school. Gladys was a short, plump, middle-aged file clerk, with a husband who had worked since the early days as a machinist in another part of the complex. Gladys did her job well and simply radiated goodwill. Life seemed better when she was in the room.

"What can I do for you today?" she asked.

"Nice to see you too, Gladys," David said as he set his briefcase up on the counter, popped it open, and handed Gladys the sheet on top. "I'm going to need the files on these people, please."

"Wow, looks like a bunch. You're going to have a busy day today."

"Yes, it's a few more than usual, but that's how it goes some days. Also, I've got a few appointments coming in after lunch. Can you set me up in one of the conference rooms?"

"Sure. I don't think any of them are being used today. Take your pick."

"Thanks, Gladys. If you don't mind, bring me the first couple of files as soon as you can, and I'll get started. As you say, I've got a busy day ahead of me today. Thanks."

David went into the first conference room which was located just off the small common area that doubled as a waiting area. He had used all the rooms at one time or another over the years. This one had a good-size table in it, long enough to seat about four along each side. David sat down at the far end of the table, the idea being to use the more remote end as a work area to do his research, spread the files out a bit, sorting them into their particular groups as Gladys brought them in; and then, conduct the few interviews that he had scheduled at the other end of the table.

David pulled the chair at his left from around the corner of the table and scooted it perpendicular to his chair to use as a little, lower, side table for his briefcase. He opened the briefcase, looked at the small stack of folders within, and appeared to pause for a moment. To a casual observer, it would be impossible to say if David was stalling for some reason or was simply lost in thought for a moment.

David reached into the case, lifted the edges of the folders on top, and pulled the file hidden at the very bottom out, placing it on the table squarely in front of himself. In it were the notes that he and Bert had painstakingly assembled—their strategy as to the best way to inconspicuously, layer by layer, peel away at the cloaks under which Dr. VanZant hid.

David opened the folder. The top sheet was a list of twelve people, a copy of which David had given to Gladys. Half the people on the list were people who the FBI, for one reason or another, wanted David to check up on. The other half were people that David and Bert wanted to scrutinize; people who were, in one way or another, associated with Dr. VanZant. Likewise, there were two lists of people scheduled for interviews. One list, David's private list, had five people. The official list, the list that David would include in his report, only showed the three in which the FBI had interest. Hopefully, the FBI would never know about the six extra files pulled or the two extra people interviewed.

Reaching towards the file, David's hand stopped halfway out, hovering above the list. *This is odd,* David thought, staring at his hand as if it belonged to someone else. *I'm feeling a little nervous, a little jittery all over.* David pulled his hand back and rested it on his lap while he sorted out his thoughts.

Of all the things that I've done since joining the Bureau, of all the risky things that I've done over the years; I've never really hesitated, never felt this uneasy. Why, all of a sudden, do I feel so uneasy? This is odd. Bert and I have faced serious dangers, serious physical dangers, but I've never felt this skittish. Why? Why suddenly now? What's different? What's going on? I haven't felt this *way—since when? Since I was a boy. No, I haven't felt this way since I was in grade school and some older boys almost talked me into vandalizing an old, abandoned building with them. They said it would be fun to break out the windows, that no one would care. I so wanted to be a part of them, to be associated with the older boys, to be one of them, but, in the end, I knew that what they were doing wasn't right. I knew that it wasn't right and that if I got caught, I would be in trouble, maybe serious trouble. Trouble with my parents, trouble with the police, labeled at school as a delinquent. But why do I have that same sick feeling now? Am I doing something wrong here? . . . Could this be just like those old schoolboy days but with a twist?*

I don't know; everything is upside down. Are the "big boys" now the FBI? Maybe that's it. Maybe that's the twist. Yes, once again, the big boys are telling me to do something that I know is wrong—to disregard VanZant and the Johnson Affair. Yes, rebellion is unsettling, even when justified. This business of spying on VanZant, VanZant and his cronies—this business pits me squarely at odds with the FBI. It shouldn't, but it does. It's no small thing to defy an institution. But, knowing what I know, wouldn't the greater crime be to do nothing, to just go along, do what I am told?

David jumped in his skin, startled as Gladys tapped twice on the frame of the open door, barely slowing as she entered the conference room. "I've got the files of the first two on your list," she said with a smile as she plopped them on the table just within David's reach.

"Wow, thanks Gladys," David replied, hoping that Gladys hadn't noticed his flinch. "That was fast. You're a marvel."

On her way to retrieve the rest of the files, Gladys spotted a man just entering the common area. As she drew near, her natural smile increased as she thought to herself, *my-oh-my, what funny little ears he has.*

"Hi, I'm Gladys. May I help you?"

"Thank you, Gladys. I'm looking for Special Agent David DeRieux. I was told that he was here."

"Oh yes, certainly. He is in the conference room just through that door," Gladys said, pointing the way.

VanZant gave a quick nod of his head in lieu of a thank you and proceeded towards the conference room, stopping just outside the door.

"Knock knock," he said, announcing his presence.

David looked up from one of Gladys' folders that he had just begun to read, held his breath for a moment upon seeing VanZant, but said nothing.

VanZant pointed to the stack of files spread out in front of David on the table and asked, "Anyone I know buried in there?"

"Interesting choice of words," David answered stiffly. "Anything is possible, I suppose."

"Yes, they say truth is often stranger than fiction," VanZant replied with a smile whose origins David couldn't, for the life of him, fathom.

David, tipping his hand more than usual, said, "I wouldn't take it personally. Eventually, we take a look at everyone. Everyone, that is, who has access to this plant."

The two stared at each other for a moment. VanZant pointed to a chair midway down the length of the table and asked, "Mind if I sit down for a moment?"

"Please," David replied in a neutral voice.

VanZant sat down, leaned forward on the table, and said, "I'm told that you have scheduled interviews today with people who are," VanZant paused, "associated with me."

David held steady eye contact with VanZant but said nothing.

VanZant cleared his throat, then stated in an abrupt and inpatient voice, "Let's cut to the chase, Mr. DeRieux. I have neither the time nor the temperament to play useless games with you or your sidekick Bert Ashton. You know, and I know, full well, that you are investigating me, and I want it to stop."

"People in hell want ice water, Mr. VanZant."

"I've heard that. But, first, people in hell do not have the bargaining chips that I have."

"And second?" David asked.

"It's Dr. VanZant, not Mister. We both know full well that I'm a doctor. Your attempt at provocation is really quite pitiful, Mr. DeRieux."

David leaned forward, resting his elbow on the table and cradled his chin on his thumb with his index finger stretched upward along the side of his face. "Let's assume, for the moment, that I have any idea what you are talking about. Why would I possibly care about whatever chips you think that you may be carrying? I would imagine that would be, as one might say, a matter between you and the devil."

"Well, the devil has many faces, but that is neither here nor there. For now, I'm here to make a deal with you, Mr. DeRieux."

David said nothing, but simply looked at VanZant with his best expression of indifference, thinking that that would, above all else, perhaps provoke VanZant just enough to needle even a slight bit of imprudence from him in whatever it was that he was about to say.

David's show of indifference was not lost on VanZant. He did notice, and it was a bit annoying to his vanity; however, it changed nothing, other than to hurry the process along. VanZant was being completely candid when he told David that he did not like to play games.

Moving on, VanZant stated abruptly, "I know about the boy," then paused to note any reaction from David.

David did his best to maintain his stoic expression.

VanZant couldn't tell for certain whether or not he could detect a flicker of emotion within David, so he pressed on. "I know about the boy, the extra boy that you and Bert have managed to squirrel away. Keeping secrets from your bosses, aren't you, Mr. DeRieux. That boy, he's the defector Johnson's little boy; isn't he."

Still, David said nothing and somehow maintained a neutral expression despite the bombshell that had just gone off in his face.

VanZant had to admit to himself that he was impressed with David's restraint, but knowing that David would ultimately have no choice, continued as planned. "Come now, Mr. DeRieux. As unpleasant as this is for the both of us, I fear the time has come for the two of us to come to some sort of an arrangement. A détente, if you will. Let's not pretend that there is no second boy. I had a man across the street from your little guest house at Camp Forrest. He saw everything. He saw Bert, a young woman, and two young boys go in, but only one boy came out, and he ended up . . . dead. Only one boy, a dead one, was on your official report. From what I understand, The Director takes a pretty dim view of agents who falsify or omit information from their reports. That is, reports made to him, anyway."

Again, the two stared at each other for a moment. David broke the silence. "You have just implicated yourself in murder and kidnapping, and a whole host of other, very serious, Federal crimes."

VanZant simply shrugged his shoulders as if to say, *"So, David, what are you going to do about it?"*

David's demeanor suddenly grew very stern. With a harsh voice and penetrating stare that was so unambiguously authentic that it gave even VanZant a moment of pause, as VanZant's entire agenda was typically dependent upon the lack of strong convictions in others, David said, "What are you doing here? What do you want?"

"Well, well," VanZant said, forcing a smile. "I believe that I've finally struck a nerve, hit pay-dirt, as they say. Well, I don't want to press my luck. That's not why I'm here. Like I said, I simply think that it would be of benefit to both of us if we could come to some sort of an arrangement. Let's get everything out on the table so there is no misunderstanding between us, and we can put all of this unpleasantness behind us and both move on with our lives intact. The sooner, the better. As I said, I know about the extra boy, Johnson's boy, the son of the Soviet defector. I also know that it was Johnson, well, the man, the defector that you refer to as Johnson, Michael Johnson, who tortured and killed that poor Sergeant at Camp Forrest shortly after the tragic deaths of Johnson's wife, and whomever that other little boy was. So tragic, so very tragic; and needless, wouldn't you say? And yet, much of what we both know about that tragic day never seemed to find its way onto any of your official reports. How is that? Considering all of this, um, inconclusiveness about the events of that day, the only thing that is clear is that you, my friend, are far more afraid to report all that happened that day, than you are of getting caught falsifying reports and harboring criminals. But, as interesting as that may be, here's the real icing on the cake, for me anyway. I know that not only did the Johnson boy survive, I know that your buddy, Bert, has just recently adopted him. My-oh-my, that certainly happened fast. You two must know someone, someone with some pretty good connections for all that paperwork to go through so fast and so quietly. I hear that Bert's new little boy now goes by the name of Michael David Ashton. Touching. It must really be touching for you to have another little namesake, if only the middle name. And to give that boy the American version of his father's name. Wow, how nice for Mihail. And it's a bold move; I'll give you that. A little bolder than I would have thought prudent. But again, I understand. The two of you, you and Bert . . . and let's not forget Johnson in all of this. Yes, the three of you must have felt pretty confident that you were all in the clear, with the adoption anyway, to have done all of this so out in the open. Yes, right out there in the open, in front of God and everybody to see. It's amazing, isn't it, how easy it is to hide something when no one is looking for it? After all, if no one knows about the boy, there is no reason for anyone to go looking for him or to suspect, when a little boy is dropped in the lap of Bert, that he could be the child of a murderous Russian spy. Yes, right now, no one is looking for that little boy, and there is nothing that ties you or Bert to Johnson or his misdeeds. But how easily that could all change. And, I can't help but wonder what the Soviets would think about this new arrangement, that is, if someone, somehow, were to let them in on your little secret? For that matter, I wonder what your supervisors at Headquarters, and The Director in particular, would think if they were to find out that not only have you and Bert covered for the criminal actions of Johnson, you have both conspired with him to hide him and his son from our system of justice. And not just hide the boy, adopt the boy. Wow, the two of you would really have to do some clever tap dancing to explain all that away. Of course, if that were to happen, if all this official 'inconclusiveness' were to somehow suddenly be all cleared up, and the truth of all of this were to come out . . . how unfortunate for everyone: you, Bert, the boy, Johnson. I don't know about you, but I would love to be a fly on the wall to see how Hoover reacts when they tell him that not only have two of his agents withheld information and made false reports, they have also covered for a rogue Soviet agent, and that one of those naughty agents has actually adopted the spy's son. Talk about taking the enemy to your own bosom. Well, no doubt—the boy would be taken away instantly. But that would be the least of it. You and Bert would be destroyed, utterly destroyed; personally and professionally. And your family, think of what would happen to your precious family. They would be punished along with you. And Johnson? Johnson would be hunted down like a rabid dog by everyone."

"If that were to happen," David said, "things would not be so pleasant for you either."

"Exactly!" VanZant replied. "That's exactly what I've been trying to say. We would both be, well . . . undone, if this all were to come out. Fortunately, there's a way out, for all of us. Let's simply declare a truce. We can agree that we don't particularly like each other, but it's not to our benefit to destroy each other. We both drop this, go our own, separate, merry ways; and life goes on as before for the both of us. What's the harm? I make a little money; and you . . . you, Bert, and Johnson keep the safe, precious little lives that you have carved out for yourselves. Live and let live, as they say."

David, questioning both himself and VanZant, pondered out loud, "The money is one thing. It's despicable, but if it's just a matter of you getting away with cheating the system, well, that's something that I can live with. But it's not just the money. It's more, much more. Because of you, people have been killed, lives have been ruined. And going forward, the things that you do, the scams that you pull, they hurt a lot of people. For instance, those girls at the Vanderbilt Clinic. Those girls that are put in danger so that you can line your pockets. What happens to them? And how many more will suffer in the years to come if you are not stopped?"

"All good questions, Mr. DeRieux. All good questions. But you know the answer. There's no reason for us to sit here and waste time telling each other what we both already know. Either way you play this, going forward, you're going to have some baggage. That's the way life is. So, it's all up to you now. You can stop me, or not. I would suggest that the price that you would pay for stopping me would be, well, horrific for you and your family. And the benefit to the world? Well, yes. You have the power to stop me, but really, in the big picture, would you be making the world that much of a better place. Get rid of me, and instantly, there are ten more just like me waiting in the wings to take my place. So again, it's still all for you to decide. But let me throw this into the mix. If the truth comes out, you are going down hard. There is no chance of escape for you once these little bits of information are let out and those concerned are put on the right track. But for me? Well, all in all, it's no secret that I would much prefer to avoid all of this scrutiny. But if it comes . . . If it comes, it's not entirely certain that the ax will fall on my neck. After all, as you pointed out earlier, I've as much as admitted my role in all of this to you. But other than that, what real evidence do you have. If this comes out, it will be my word against yours, and consider how far, by then, your credibility will have fallen. The Director, he doesn't like a scandal, even small ones. And this one is huge. No, I think for him, the easiest, most expeditious, most likely turn of events, will be for the FBI to, as quickly and quietly as possible, throw you and Bert to the wolves and drive on. They're more like me than like you. They're more . . . practical . . . about these types of situations. They'll have every reason in the world to, as you would probably say, let me slither away. No, I would say that it's not your obligation to close down my little business. No, it's really beyond what should be expected for a man—such as yourself—to destroy himself, and his loved ones, for such a small, transient gain. Come now, David; we're both grownups. We're both men of the world with responsibilities and obligations. We both know that this world is not a perfect place. Do you really expect to make it all that much better by sacrificing yourself? But I suppose that's what martyrs do. I suppose it boils down to whether or not you want to make a martyr out of yourself.

"So, come now David . . . what's it going to be?"

Chapter 32

Lillian's Call

Chattanooga, TN
April 2001

Mihail Nikolayevich Grigory hung up the phone. It had been decades since he had associated himself with that name; but now, in the blink of an eye and the sound of a voice, Lillian's voice, he was once again Grigory, Mihail Grigory. *Funny*, he thought, *it's been decades since I've thought of myself as Grigory. I've been Michael for so long now that Grigory feels like someone from another life, a stranger—someone I knew long ago, someone from a distant dream. If someone were to holler the name Grigory in a crowd, would I even turn around? Of course, it is natural that Lillian would call me Mr. Johnson. That is how she knows me; that is how she was introduced to me, and that is who I've been these last many years.*

And for her, she is correct. Lillian knows nothing of Grigory, only Johnson. Yet, the substance of her call had everything to do with Mihail, and little to do with Michael. Michael Johnson. Yes, Michael Johnson. How easy it has been to be Michael Johnson for all these years . . . all those lonely years. How easy it was to slip on that cloak, as simple as folding a paper jacket over a book.

A piece of paper is all it takes to disguise the substance of that which is contained within the volume itself. And then, once covered, once unseen, how quickly the substance of that book fades away from memory. How quickly and completely Gregory becomes Johnson; Mihail becomes Michael. How quickly the book becomes what the jacket says it is, with the depth of two pages—the picture on the front and a simple blurb on the back. What lurks in the middle becomes left to the imagination, and the imagined becomes the reality.

Time goes by; years slip by, and then someone pulls that book from a shelf, blows off the dust, and opens it to an old chapter. That's all it takes. Someone opens the book by placing a call, by dialing a phone, and a character from that book comes back to life. The indelible ink which defines the characters bound within the pages is read, and the characters cannot help but come to life within a mind and play out their scripted parts. Thus, Mihail Nikolayevich Grigory is awakened, brought back from the realm of set-aside memories. Brought back from the life that I thought I had so successfully abandoned, that life of crushed hopes and mortal fears. To have fled those horrors, plunging into darkness that entire period of time, that realm of mindless, senseless demons. To what end? To be awakened, after all those years, only to be once again drawn back into that realm of darkness and shadows. But what will happen now? What will happen now that light has once again fallen upon those long-darkened pages? Will the light that illuminates a slumbering Grigory also illuminate his demons? I fear it will. I fear it is not possible to resurrect Grigory from that realm without also waking those lurking demons. To shed light on any part is to shed light on it all—that unholy all. Those demons. Those demons who destroyed the best of what I loved in the past, those demons have been stirred, shaken awake; and now—now they rise up, not mellowed by the years that have passed. No, now they awaken with the vigor of the well-rested. Now, they have returned to trouble, spoil, and confound the present. But I wonder. By fleeing that life and throwing a veil over that entire period, did I prevail, or did the demons win out? And now, now that we are both awake, will I once again be eternally dogged by their venomous presence?

No! This time it will be different. This time I will face those demons. This time I will silence them. For all of time, I will silence them. I will kill them in the light of day.

VanZant must die. I will kill him, and they will be silenced. With the death of VanZant, they will forever lose their hold on me.

Mihail Grigory picked up the phone and dialed an old number from memory. Would it still work? A voice answered. Mihail said he was calling to inquire about the status of an order that he had placed some time ago for a fur coat, a fox-fur coat. The voice asked if he had an order number. Mihail recited a number and waited. A long pause, then, a short series of oddly specific questions with untypical, yet plausible, answers given. Another long pause, then, "Mihail, it has been quite some time. We thought you were dead, or worse . . . What can we do for you?"

Mihail gave an inaudible sigh and said, "I need for you to arrange a meeting for me."

Chapter 33

VanZant Gets a Call

April 2001

The ringing phone annoyed VanZant. Everything annoyed VanZant, but it didn't help that he was hungry—hungry, and a little bit drunk. A little bit drunk, lonely, and sitting in the growing darkness of another countless day's end. The blinds, as usual, remained drawn across the windows of his library, muting what little light was left from the day. If he bothered to give it any thought, and for now he didn't, he could have recognized that he was hungry and a little drunk. As to his awareness of being in a dark, empty house, he had long passed the capacity for such sensibilities.

VanZant turned his head and glared at the black phone barking at him from the delicate, antique table that separated his soft, leather, high-back chair from a matching, empty chair on the other side of the table. Small, square, ice cubes tinkled against the grooves carved into the sides of his crystal glass as he set his aged scotch down on its coaster and reached up, twisting the switch of the table lamp on, giving minimal illumination to a corner of his large, comfortably appointed library nestled within his likewise large, comfortably appointed, yet empty house.

He snatched the phone from its cradle and snarled, "Hello."

"Dr. VanZant . . . is that you?"

"Of course it is. Who is this?" VanZant snapped.

"It's me, Mallory . . . Dr. Mallory . . . from the Vanderbilt Clinic."

"Good Lord, Mallory. It's been, what . . . fifty years since we've spoken. What could you possibly want?"

Mallory looked up from his seat to the man in a dark suit standing next to him. The man nodded for him to continue.

"Well," Mallory said with a great deal of hesitation in his voice.

"Christ, Mallory, what is it? You could never get to the point before, and you don't appear to have gotten any better over time. What is it?"

"Well, someone stopped by to see me. I think we need to talk."

"Talk? Talk about what?"

"Listen, I don't think this is something we should discuss over the phone. No, we really need to meet and talk in person. It's important. I think you'll think it's important. That's really all I can say over the phone."

"Mallory . . . Mallory . . . where are you calling from?"

"Well, I'm calling from home."

"Calling from home; where is that?"

"Well, I'm in an apartment, a home, an assisted-living home. I'm still in Nashville; I never left."

"An assisted-living home, you say. What's that, a nursing home?"

"Well, it's not quite like that; it's not bad. I just need a little . . . well . . . it just makes life a little easier for me; that's all. There is a nursing home affiliated with it, but, where I'm at, it's not that bad."

"I thought you had some kids, Mallory. What happened? Why'd they stick you in a nursing home? Don't they love you? Guess not, huh."

Mallory again looked up at the man in the suit for guidance. The man rotated his hand in a circular motion, indicating for Mallory to move on with the conversation.

Mallory nodded his head to the man and said into the phone, "Listen, Dr. VanZant. We really need to talk; we really need to meet."

VanZant replied, "Mallory, you said someone stopped by to see you. Who stopped by?"

"Listen, I can't say. Like I said, this is not a conversation that we should be having over the phone."

"Well, at least give me an idea of what this is all about. If it's something that I think is important, I'll let you stop by. But, I have to tell you, I'm going out of town for a couple of days. Leaving tomorrow. There's a pot that's about to boil over if I don't stop it. If we meet, it will have to be after I get back."

The man next to Mallory shook his head "No" and mouthed the word "Now".

Following his instructions, Mallory said, "No, no. It has to be now; it has to be soon."

"Mallory, what's this all about? You have to give me an idea of what this is all about, or there isn't going to be any meeting at all."

Mallory looked again to the man in the suit. The man nodded.

Mallory said, "It's about David DeRieux. That's all I can say. That's all I can say over the phone."

"Really," VanZant replied in an uncharacteristically pensive voice.

Mallory looked to the man in the suit who put his index finger to his lips, signaling for Mallory to remain quiet.

VanZant, giving it a moment's thought, said, "I tell you what, Mallard. I'm going to be in Chattanooga tomorrow. I can meet you there, tomorrow. That's the best that I can do. Do you drive, can you get yourself there?"

The man in the suit nodded yes. Mallard said, "Yes. Yes, I can get there."

VanZant said, "Okay, fine. Do you know where the Chickamauga Battlefield Park is, just outside of Chattanooga?"

The man in the suit nodded yes. Mallard said, "Yes."

VanZant said, "Good. There's a monument, a tower in that park—'Wilder Tower' it's called. We'll meet there at the base of that tower tomorrow, tomorrow evening; say . . . 5:30. Don't keep me waiting, Mallard. If you're not there, I'm not waiting around for you; I'm leaving. I'm too busy for this nonsense. You better be there, and on time."

With that, VanZant hung up his phone. The dial tone on Mallard's end buzzed. Mallard, with a question mark on his face, looked up at the man in the suit. The man took the phone from Mallard's hand, said, "You're not going to be there," and hung-up Mallard's phone.

Chapter 34

The Interrogation, Part II
Conclusion

Chattanooga, TN
April 2001

"**W**ho are you thinking of, Mr. Johnson?"

"I'm thinking of a flame, a flame that has given off a lot of comforting heat, but, these last few years, not a lot of light. Even here, even now, I can feel that heat, but only in my mind's eye can I see that flame."

"Mr. Johnson, who are you thinking of? Not VanZant."

"No, not VanZant," the old man replied softly, his chin dropping down as he stared at the cooling cup of hot tea resting on the table before him. He reached out with his hand, his palm just inches above the cup's rim, in an effort to sense the last remnants of heat as it dissipated up and out into the ether. Feeling none, he said quietly to himself, "It's over. All the steam is gone. How fast it all cools once the source is removed."

"Mr. Johnson," Agent Morgan said, "you've admitted to killing Dr. VanZant, but you still haven't told us why. Is there someone else involved in all of this that we should know about?"

The old man looked up and met Agent Morgan's eyes. "No . . . no. I'm sorry. I'm tired. My mind is just wandering a bit."

"Are you sure? It sounds like there is someone else here, someone else on your mind—someone that you were starting to tell us about."

"No, no. I'm sure. It's just that, well, sitting here, in this interrogation room, with you FBI agents . . . I suppose it just reminded me of an agent I once knew. Someone I hadn't thought about in a long time. For all I know, he's probably dead by now."

Agent Morgan wasn't buying the old man's denial. The two looked at each other. Breaking the silence, the old man shrugged his shoulders and said, "When you get to be my age, your mind tends to drift. One thing reminds you of another. You'll see. Someday, you'll see. Things that are important to you today, when you're old; well, with many of those things, you'll wonder why you ever gave them such importance."

Morgan decided to move on with the questions, "Mr. Johnson, you started to tell us something about when you first met Dr. VanZant." Morgan looked down at his notes. "You said that you first met Dr. VanZant at Oak Ridge, back in 1946. Go ahead and tell us about that."

"Yes . . . yes . . . that's true. He was there; I was there." The old man gave a slight rock of his head back and forth as he thought, then added, "But nothing from the past changes what happened today. There's really nothing to be gained, for any of us, by dredging up the past. What can I say? That Park Ranger, he caught me. He just happened to come by at the wrong time, for me. Just my bad fortune, I suppose. In my earlier years, that would have never happened—getting caught, that is. No, in my earlier years, things were different; I was different. But now, now time grows short, and I must take what opportunities come, as they come, when they come. Waiting is a luxury of the young."

"Well, Mr. Johnson, that may all be well and good, but it doesn't really tell us much as to why or what happened here today. Come on, Mr. Johnson. Come on, tell us. Tell us why you killed him?"

There was a tap on the door. Without waiting for an invitation, the young man who had brought in the coffee and tea earlier cracked the door open and said to Agent Morgan, "There's a call for you."

Morgan looked up at the young man and said, "What?"

The young man repeated, "There's a phone call for you. You really need to take it."

Morgan looked at the old man, who looked back with no emotion. Morgan said, "Excuse me for a moment," and left the room, shutting the door behind him.

The old man and Agent Szezoponski sat quietly looking at each other. About two, maybe three minutes later, Agent Morgan returned.

Morgan took his seat across the table from the old man, looked at him for a moment, then looked down at his notes, gathered the papers together between his hands, tapped the bottom edges straight on the tabletop, placed them neatly in their manila file folder, and closed the cover over them. He looked back up at the old man and said, without preamble, "You're free to go."

The old man, as if he were being dismissed from an every-day misunderstanding, simply nodded his head and began to scoot his chair back to get up.

Morgan cleared his throat, just loud enough to get the old man's attention. The old man stopped still in his chair and looked up at Agent Morgan.

Morgan said, "As I said, you're free to go. I've been told by . . . well, I've been told that you're free to go and that I'm not to delay you or ask you any more questions."

The two looked at each other in silence for a moment. The old man had a look of patience that could last an eternity. Morgan said, "I've been told not to ask you any more questions, but . . . none of this makes any sense. Like I said, you're free to go; but, if there's anything that you want to tell me, that you're willing to tell me; I'd love to hear it."

Looking into Morgan's eyes, the old man saw a glint of earnest desire for unembellished truth. It was an emotion that the old man could relate to. He leaned back and, relaxing in his chair, gave a calm, gentle-sweeping outward motion with his hand, and said, "I started to tell you about an old friend of mine. A very good friend, indeed—perhaps my only friend. He was . . . a fortunate man . . . when measured against the things that really matter. And he was an interesting man. An interesting man, not because he had all the answers. No, he was an interesting man because he, more often than not, knew what the right questions should be. Conversations with him were different than conversations with most other men. He once told me, that the biggest thing—the biggest 'trick', he called it—was to be able to identify, examine, and, when necessary, put aside deeply ingrained, lifelong assumptions; because, many of those assumptions act just like a prism. They bend all the light that passes through."

The old man paused. Morgan asked, "Why are you telling me about your old friend? . . . Does he have something to do with why they told me to let you go?"

The old man said nothing, but smiled.

"Okay, I get it," Morgan said coldly. "I'm probably still not asking the right questions."

The old man remained silent.

Immediately regretting the crossness of his remark, Morgan said, in a warmer, softer voice, "I just don't get it. It just doesn't make any sense to let you go, but I can't argue with the person who's given me those orders. This type of thing is not supposed to happen. Who the hell is running this show; that's what I'd like to know."

The old man replied, "The people who are running this show are the same people who have always been running things—since the time of the pyramids."

Morgan interjected, "I bet the guys who built the pyramids didn't let confessed murderers go free. You know, Mr.

Johnson . . . you know . . . you're one lucky man. You would not have done well at a trial, not with all the evidence that's piled up against you here."

"I know," said the old man, smiling. "It's almost as if, for one reason or another, they don't want a trial."

"What are you saying?" Morgan asked.

The old man thought for a moment, then said, "My friend once told me about an observation that he had made, about midway through his life. He lived on a mountaintop. There was a road that ran along the border of his backyard. One day, it occurred to him that even though he could see and hear cars go by, he couldn't actually see the road upon which they traveled. From the vantage point of his screened-in porch, he could only see the tops of the cars as they passed by. Of course, he knew the road was there. He knew it well; and, more importantly, he knew its destination."

The old man paused. Agent Morgan said, "I'm not following you."

The old man continued, "One evening, after a particularly puzzling day, it occurred to my friend how often we see the tops of cars go by without ever really seeing the roadway upon which they travel. Often times, it doesn't matter. When the car's direction is in accord with the road we know—whether it is a known road, or even an assumed road—there is harmony. But, how often, we see people traveling in one direction, while telling us that their destination is in the opposite."

Again, the old man paused. The two sat looking at each other in silence. Agent Morgan sat still, though he felt fidgety. He was certain that the old man could explain everything to him with only a few, direct sentences—if only he would. But Agent Morgan, for the life of him, couldn't construct a question that would release the answer. It occurred to Morgan that, quite likely, there was no question that would pry the answer from the old man.

The old man broke the silence by saying, "I was reading something interesting recently. It was about some scientists— physicists or astronomers—I can't remember which; doesn't really matter. They were talking about the universe—how it works, what it's made up of. They were talking about 'Dark Matter.' They were saying that it makes up a huge part of the universe—eighty, eighty-five percent, something like that. But the interesting thing about Dark Matter is that you can't see it. You can't see it; you can't touch it; you can't smell it. There's really no direct way to detect it or to interact with it. Think about that. The stuff that makes up the bulk of the universe, for most of history, we didn't even know that it even existed. So, how do they know it's there, you might ask. They said that they knew it was there by observing the effect that it has on other things. That without Dark Matter, the way the universe worked, the way in which the galaxies moved, would not make any sense. Without Dark Matter, the universe did not act in a rational manner."

It was easy for the old man to see that Morgan was no happier with that response than any of his others. He continued, nevertheless. "Often, the universe doesn't appear to be rational. My friend believed that it probably was, if only we knew how to look at it correctly. I'm not saying that he ever figured it all out—not completely—but I think he came close, got a glimpse of it, anyway."

Morgan shrugged his shoulders and said, "Well, that's all very interesting, but what does that really have to do with anything? How does that explain my being ordered to let you go?"

Johnson stood up, to say one final thing before leaving. He rested his fingertips on the tabletop to steady himself and said, "All I'm saying is that if things don't make sense to you, maybe it's your perspective. Turn your head, walk to the edge of your borders; look, listen. You won't be able to see the Dark Matter, but you can tell an awful lot about its nature by how it affects the things that you can see. No, you certainly won't be able to see and hear everything; but maybe, just maybe, if you open your mind to all the possibilities, set aside the things that people say, and watch instead what they do; then, you'll see. Yes, then you'll see enough to get you by, for now at least."

Acknowledgements

First and foremost is my wife, Linda, who provided tremendous encouragement from the beginning as well as great advice and feedback throughout the long process—and it was indeed a really long process, so let me add patience to her list of virtues. Her remarkable wisdom, strength, and kindness are the source of great joy and inspiration to me as well as to all who know her.

Another remarkable person is my sister Jeannine. From my earliest memories, she has been a cherished and reassuring presence throughout my life. In each step of writing and producing this novel, she cheerfully provided valuable feedback, advice and encouragement.

Regarding my parents: There are many truly great parents in the world. It is my fortune to have such parents. They are the foundation upon which my life is built. Even though they have been deceased for quite some time, happily, they are with me each and every day.

And then there is Hobby. Thomas Hobson Jones, Jr. (Hobby to his friends and "The World's Most Fascinating Hobby" according to the bumper sticker on his car) has been my constant friend since before preschool. He is like a brother to me. Hobby was a great source of candid feedback for all aspects of this novel, but most importantly, he did an extraordinary job of proofreading—catching an amazing number of grammatical errors and pointing out awkward sentences that could benefit from a revision.

Cecelia A. Duchene is another friend who provided an extraordinary amount of help. Proofreading an early draft, she caught an embarrassingly large number of goofs and, throughout the process, gave valuable critique and feedback.

Similarly, deep gratitude goes to Joy Nolan, Lucius L. Hilley III, Jerry Harwood, JimmyLee Smith, Kelle Z. Riley, and Katy Reynolds for their remarkable contributions. Their wise editing advice and council certainly made this novel better.

Also, special thanks to Lyndie Ferguson, Isaac Oxentenko, Calvin Beam, Gary Sedlacek, Charlie Pfitzer, and Richard MacLean. Each of your many contributions are greatly appreciated.

I fear that shortly after this book is sent to press, I will remember others that I have neglected to mention here. To those, I apologize. My hope is that you know who you are, despite my omission, and know that I am grateful to you.

As many authors say in their acknowledgements, despite the great abilities and skillful work of the above individuals, combined with my tendency to not always take the advice given, any and all errors belong to me. Having said that, I am reminded of the words of my friend and fellow writer, mentioned above, Calvin Beam. When asked how many editors and proofreaders one needs, he answers, "One more than however many you had." No doubt, at some point I'll be telling myself that I really could have used at least one more editor. But still, my most heartfelt gratitude goes to all who have helped. Thanks!

About The Author

Jack Huguelet was born in Chattanooga, Tennessee. Except for the four years spent at Northwestern University, where he received a BA in Economics, Jack has lived his entire life in the Chattanooga area and surrounding mountains. Jack also has an MBA from The University of Tennessee at Chattanooga with a concentration in both Marketing and Finance.

Jack's father was an attorney and an FBI Agent during WWII and the Cold War years that followed. Late in life, retired Special Agent Huguelet developed Alzheimer's. Although he never revealed any secrets from his FBI days and work in counter-espionage, he was the inspiration for this novel.

While Jack has traveled many parts of the world—North America, Europe, and Asia—there is no place that he would rather be than in the gentle mountains and forests of East Tennessee, where he currently lives with his wife, a pair of Golden Retrievers, and a cat.

Jack invites you to visit him at www.HugueletPress.com.